A Song of Air Copy

Aleera Anaya Ceres

Paperback Cover design and typography image by: Storywrappers

Paperback formatting by: A.L. Kessler

Hardcover design and typography image by: Moonpress.co

Edited by: Lisa Nieves-Taylor

Map design done in: Wonderdraft

Dedication

To everyone with too much anger and nothing to do with it.
And to those existing within shades of gray.

Fae Elementals Glossary and Pronunciation Guide

Kingdoms, Cities, and Landmarks

Illyk: *Eel-ick*
Tuath: *Two-ahh-th*
Dana: *Day-nuh*
Vellm: *Vey-mm*
Ielwyn: *Eel-win*
Teg: *Teh-gg*
Orknie: *Orc-knee*
Lake Degara: Lake *Dig-are-uh*
The Arcana: *Arc-ay-nuh*
Lywyth River: *Lee-with*
Tir Na Faie (also known as the Feylands): *Tier Nuh Fey*
Ley Line: *Lay Line*
Castle Aileach: *Castle I-lick*
Terrlyn: *Tear-lynn*
Porir: *Pour-rear*
Herria Mountains: *Hair-ree-uh*
Verdt: *Veer-dt*
Ojor: *O-joar*
Wyrshl: *War-shell*
Seirz: *Seer-tz*
Covenglen: *Coven-glenn*

People

Shula Azzarh: *Shoe-luh Uh-zarrh*
Piriguini: *Peer-ee-gween-ee*
Ryker Valda: *Rye-curr Vahl-duh*
Clay Valentino: *Clay Valen-tee-no*
Julius Darah: *Jewel-ee-us Dare-uhh*
Valerio Ashera: *Vahl-eer-rio Ah-sheer-uh*
Weylyn Xanth: *Way-lynn Zanth*

Uric Adriel Nova: *You-ric Ay-dree-el No-vuh*
Orna: *Or-nuh*
King Amos Ashera: *Ay-mose Ah-sheer-uh*
Emperor Robert Laurel: *Robert Lore-rel*
Mairin Valda: *May-rin*
Iona Wylde: *I-oh-nuh Wild*
George Apidae: *George Eh-pihh-day*
Temair Beston: *Tim-mare Best-uhn*
The Kurreen: *The Core-Reen*
Malika: *Muh-lee-kuh*
Veles Riel: *Veh-less Real*
Corvina Rhian: *Core-vee-nuh Ryan*
Bryson Varik: *Brye-son Vaahr-ick*
Cassimir: *Cass-ee-mirror*
Rainer: *Rain-err*
Owyn: *Owen*
Gwyn: *Gwen*
Glyn: *Glen*
Queen Ineciu Morgayne: *In-ay-see-you Mor-gay-nn*
Cossima: *Cos-ih-muh*

Terms

Esses: (Pronounced like S. S.) A derogatory term for the Fae. Originally Seelie Scum, later shortened to S.S., then 'Esses'.

Mana: (Pronounced Mah-nuh) The word to describe the Fae entity/deity/god. It is magic, nature, and the elements, as these are holy amongst their race.

The Lagnh Sea
Gyshapur
Kaym
Vellm
Bazra
Kayron
Barrenhorn
Valley of the Dead
Telshaw
The Arcana
Myrim
Ielwyn
Badfa
Ojor
Wintshore
Castle Aileach
Loren
Crystal Forest
Tuath
Minn
Bridgertown
Hiel Lake
Lywyth River
Seirz
Arcancliffe
Covenglen
Vallart
Solle
Dana
Port Bay
Zaen
Teg
Lake Degara
The Arcana
Clyhr
Port Lays
Orknie
Eul
Porir
Terrylyn
Verdt
Wyrshl
Ley Line
Crimson Court
The Iron Mountains
Western Waters
Gold Court
Tir na Faie
The Feylands
Jade Court
Sombhra Mountains
The Seelie Court
The Pool
Elin Ocean
Obsidian Court
Naches Forest
Sapphire Court
Nymph Island
N
W
E

Trigger & Content Warnings

Trigger & Content Warnings

A Song of Air contains dark and graphic themes and tropes that could be triggering to some readers. If any of the following are harmful to your mental health, I urge you to proceed with caution as the book and series contains: the genocide of the Fae people in a fantasy setting, racism of Fae within a fantasy setting, post traumatic stress and trauma, bombing resulting in death, scars, and eyesight damage, mentions of forced migration, sexual themes, alcohol consumption, nonconsensual alcohol and drug consumption, brief mention of drug addiction in a character's past, descriptive violence, gore, death and loss of loved ones, grief, PTSD, enslavement, burning, decapitation, cheating, dubious consent, nonconsensual voyeurism, ableist language, and animal death.

If such material offends you, please do not pick up this book and/or proceed with caution. Your mental health and well-being always comes first.

A Song of Air is part of a six book series and ends in a mild cliffhanger. It is in 3rd person point of view and while each book will follow the story of a different Elemental, there will be scenes with several POV's throughout, including villains'.

Trails of Blood

The human lands smelled like iron and were shrouded in smog. Just north of the Ley Line, color didn't bathe the landscape. There were no trees that dripped golden, glittering sap from between the cracks of blue bark. There were no rivers that ran as dazzlingly as starlight streaking across a night sky. There was nothing but gray sky, the leftover taste of ashwood still lingering in the air, and humans that led Fae into their designated tents with smiles that were far more malicious than welcoming.

The bag on Bryson Varik's back threatened to haul her to the ground with its weight. A similar weight had taken up residence within her chest since the start of the war; when she watched her mother walk away with other Seelie soldiers, clad in Sapphire Court armor, only to never return. One that had become even more prominent over the last few days as she, her father, and sister migrated miles on foot to cross the Ley Line.

The war was over now, and the Fae had lost.

Even so, the humans offered them all a tentative peace in the form of asylum; a necessary outreach of their hands as the Feylands had become overrun both with iron and soldiers.

Everything Bryson once loved had been decimated.

"Strength, little ones." Her father's voice rumbled through her fear, and he swallowed the violent tremors of her hand beneath his massive paw, lending her bravery.

She desperately needed it.

Bryson's brown gaze swept over the new place she would now call home. Magic swelled inside her body as she took everything in. How easy it would be to create a gust of wind that could have swept the entire place away. It would have been so easy to give into her rage. To let it consume her and unleash her magic in a force so untamed that they needn't stay here at all.

As a storm of wind began forming at her feet, her father squeezed her hand in warning, forcing her to slam the door closed on all her angry thoughts and wishes, but the dreary sky reflected her mood for the rest of the week. And happiness was nowhere to be found.

She spent her days wandering through their makeshift camp, trying to avoid the keen gazes of the humans, who were starting to feel more like jailors instead of allies. She'd brought it up in the quiet night of their tent, but her father couldn't see that. If he did, he ignored it.

"Your mother died for peace and now that they're offering it, you question it?"

She didn't *want* to mistrust it. In fact, she wanted peace as much as everyone else did. But Bryson had a bad feeling. Like something was going to go very, *very* wrong.

She had no proof, of course, but she wallowed in the sensation the next day. She sat away from the camp, rebelliously playing with her magic, releasing what she could out into the sky in secret. Around humans, it was better to keep the elemental magic she possessed a silent thing; she wasn't sure what they'd do to her if they knew. One moment she was scrunching her nose at the stench of sweat and burning wood, and the next, the breeze flittered a scent against her nose that had her back going rigid-straight and the hairs on her arms standing on end.

She didn't even have time to scream before the first explosion hit.

It landed on the ground, sending a geyser of earth and grass through the air. By the time the second bomb hit, Bryson was already on her feet only to be knocked back once again. Propelled through the air for mere seconds, she couldn't cry out. A moment later, she landed on her back, the very breath whooshing from her lungs.

As she fought to stand on shaking feet, chaos rained down on the camp. Soldiers clad in the emperor's armor marched in, wielding iron and ashwood and explosives.

The effects of the iron slammed against her bones. Her skin itched where smoke touched it. Her eyes burned and tears streamed down her face.

Her own mind filled with as much chaos as there was around her. Thoughts of her father and sister urged her to run. She raced across destruction, her voice entangled with emotion as she screamed out for her family.

Wind cleared the smoke for a fraction of a second, lending Bryson a view of her family from across the field. Their eyes connected, and then they were running towards one another.

"Bryson! Look out!"

Her feet stuttered at his warning, her mind trying to catch up with everything that was happening around her. Her father and sister picked up speed. She saw rather than felt his hands reach for her. He yanked with impressive force, and she fell backwards...

...just as another explosion set off near their feet.

Fragments of iron shot out like daggers of glass, piercing the skin on her face and eyes. The pain was blinding, agonizing, and the moment her head cracked against the ground, unconsciousness trapped her in its deadly grip and dragged her under.

She awoke sometime later to a heavy weight pressurizing her chest, tears streaming down her cheeks, and darkness. She blinked away liquid from her eyes only to cry out as the pain seemed to intensify. Had night already fallen? Had hours really passed? She asked herself those questions, and yet surely she would have made out figures in the darkness...

A groan escaped, and the moment she opened her mouth, she tasted the coppery tang of blood against her lips. She spit it out, but it streamed into her mouth like water from a canteen. Through the grogginess and the pain, she realized it kept coming, dripping down her cheeks in trails of blood.

Her heart pounded with fear and denial, afraid to reach for a truth that was staring her in the face. Bryson tried to move but the heavy weight above her pressed her against the ground. Her hands reached blindly to push it off. When her fingers slipped through coarse hair, it gave her pause.

She blinked again despite the pain, despite the grating it caused on her eyeballs, despite her loss of vision, and felt again. She couldn't see and yet she recognized what—rather, who—was above her.

"D-dad?" Her body ached as she tried to rise, fingers grappling against the burnt earth. The sounds of attack had died down to embers. To the faint whimpers and cries of those injured and those who'd survived. Her heart pounded with unease as she searched but all she could find was darkness and the lonely scent of death. Her palms touched skin, a nose, a mouth; the contours of which she recognized.

"No..." The word left her on a whimper. "No, no, no."

Her fingers felt, her nose inhaled the clinging remnants of the scents that made up her father and her sister—close, yet so far away—and her ears picked up the lack of a pulse.

The lack of life.

The presence of death.

And darkness.

And trails of blood.

An Arrow Flies

30 years later...

Bryson stood on the tips of her toes, balancing precariously—silently—on the branch of an old pine tree. The sharp needle-like leaves camouflaged her body from the light of day. Shrouded in cold shadows, she held her breath, ears perked up as she waited...

...and waited.

The noises of the forest stilled. It'd been alive only moments ago; alive with the breath of the wind flittering against plants like a caressing touch, branches crackling like dry, old bones. Birds sang, their wings fluttering like rapid heartbeats as they flew from one spot to another.

Bryson heard and smelled it all.

The soft footfalls of deer against the dewy grass, the soft chewing as they grazed. She smelled sap, animal droppings, dirt, and the sweet pollen of flowers.

And when it all stilled, when it felt like everything paused and held their breaths for what was coming down the dirt road, Bryson reached across her back and pulled out an arrow from her quiver, notching it onto her bow.

The rolling of wheels, the clomping hooves of horses, the lightning crack of a whip, cruel laughter that grated down her arms, and the sound of whimpers and cries that cleaved her heart in two.

A sudden rage swelled in her chest at the sounds, but she tamped it down, turning it into an eerie calm as she stepped just a little further on the branch, until she felt the sun kiss her bare arms and the skin around her eyes from beneath the carved, wooden mask she wore.

She was familiar with those whimpers. With the bitter smell of fear. She'd been in a similar situation once. The memory of that time invaded her thoughts as the wagon approached where she hid. A whistle tearing through the wind beckoned her towards the light of the sun. A hawk circling overhead screeched out a warning, causing Bryson to draw back the string. Her arm and hands tightened in a firm grip as she waited.

Magic swelled through her, and as she let out a slow breath, a gust of wind blew through the atmosphere. It swirled around the advancing wagon, roping in scents and whispering its secrets.

It was only when a second whistle sounded that Bryson let the arrow fly.

The wind guided it true as it soared and landed home, straight into the throat of an emperor's soldier.

The body let out a strangled gurgle before it toppled off the side of the seat. The horses, surprised at the suddenness of a dropping body, whinnied, jerking to a stop as they jumped and pawed through the air.

The wheels shrieked to a halt, the wagon creaking as it wobbled from side to side. A door burst open, the sound like thunder cracking against the sky.

The second arrow was already in her fingers in the time it took another human to jump out and investigate. And before the human could cry out, it flew and struck through the socket of his eye.

His body fell against dry grass.

There were shouts and cries of anger and fear. She focused on the angry sounds and blurry forms. It was instinct at this point to recognize the enemy without seeing them clearly. It was in their tone, the lilt of their words, and the hint of cruelty beneath them. Her body reacted. And the wind guided arrow after arrow as they struck their targets.

It was only when every single body fell that Bryson let her shoulders relax. That she let out a breath. That her fingers met the mask placed strategically across her face.

The mask had been crafted by the talented hands of a friend, its twisted design made of bone, wood, paint, and feathers. She'd memorized the contours of the thing, amazed that it felt like a *real* face, complete with a gnarled, angry, monstrous expression. One that twisted even more grotesquely across her blurry vision. Now, it was just another facet she wore to protect her identity from those who would wish her harm.

Considering those villains were now gone, she pulled it off, tucking it into the sack she wore slung over her shoulder. With a flick of her wrists, she tossed the hood from her head, baring her bright orange hair to the sunlight.

Another whistle sounded, another cry of a hawk, and Bryson stepped off a branch onto open air. Using her magic, she made sure the wind guided her safely down to the ground. As soon as her feet touched, she rushed toward the cart. Her comrades were already there, pulling open the wagon to reveal the scared humans and Fae within.

Criminals under the emperor's reign.

Scared allies who needed help.

The smell of fear clung to the air. They were a blur of shadows and colors, their bodies plastered to the wagon walls like it could protect them from the masked creatures that suddenly towered over them.

It brought her own past to the forefront of her mind; when she sat on a hard bench, wishing the darkness would just swallow her whole and not spit her back out. She knew their situation *all too well.* She'd lived something similar once upon a time, back when her eyes still bled and the blackness of the world was new. Back when the wounds of her dad and sister's deaths were as raw and aching as the ones in her eyes.

She'd *been* a similar creature. Just a broken fragment of a Fae who had once known happiness. Of a Fae who had once known the love of a mother, a father, a sister.

Now she had nothing left except her magic, her pride, blurry vision, and a thirst for justice and revenge in equal measure.

But she'd been saved, and she believed it was her duty to save as well. Her mother would have wanted it. Because if she didn't give everything she had for the Fae who needed it the most, then she may as well have spat on the memories of her family.

While the prisoners were taken from the wagon, she let herself reminisce in her own memories; of what it had been like to be helped down from a wagon much like that one, to touch her bare feet against the grass and feel a sliver of sunlight against her face like a promise of the good things that would come.

She shoved that away, though. This was not a time for remembrance. It was a time for freedom. And cleaning up scum from the ground.

Her feet carried her towards the spot where the bodies had fallen. They were nothing but mere lumps of cloudy, gray metal. The closer she got to them, the clearer they became. Details eluded her. Unless she was standing directly in front of someone, face mere inches away, she could scarcely make much out.

She supposed she didn't need to see them at all to know they were dead.

Taking a life as quickly as she had was instinct. She never mourned them when her fingers released strings of arrows, or when the scent of copper filled her nostrils. Even when she could no longer hear the beating of their hearts, she did not weep.

She wondered if that made her a monster.

She bent, squinting and feeling around the still-warm corpse for her arrow. When her fingers met the smooth, wooden edge, she yanked it, the sick sound of wet flesh squelching as she did.

A low whistle sounded far from her side. Bryson didn't need perfect sight to know who it was when she had the pace of footsteps and the outline of a dark silhouette memorized like the prints of a hand on parchment.

"Right in the eye."

Bryson stood and turned to face the woman with a smile tilting her mouth. She probably should have felt ashamed for jesting about death, but if there was one thing she learned in life, it was that death was a cruel jokester and always got in the last laugh.

"*And* in the forehead. Damn, Bryce, I'm impressed." A hand clapped her back, but she'd braced for that bit of contact and didn't falter.

Her friend was very affectionate and showed her love through touch. It was always heavy-handed and brought with it comfort that Bryson found she needed more often than not.

"Are you, really?" Bryson wiped the bloody arrow on the grass before shoving it into the quiver at her back. "Or are you flattering me because you want something from me, Malika?"

Malika laughed. Bryson could make out the rich brown tone of her skin, the curvature of her cheeks when she smiled, and the length of her curls. The details were swallowed by the fog of her own shitty vision, but she imagined that Malika's whole face lit up with the action.

"Ladies, we could use some help over here!" Ev called out from beside the wagon. The rattling of the chains followed his words, reminding them that there were more important things to be done. Like saving captives from the chains of the emperor's tyranny.

Her lips twitched at the poetic turn of her thoughts.

"Ev is so hopeless without us."

"I heard that, Malika Wylde!"

"You were supposed to!" Malika called back. "You got this, Bryce?"

"Of course." Bryson flashed a toothy smile in her friend's general direction, though it disappeared the moment she walked away to help the others.

Do not weep for the wicked, a voice in her mind whispered. There was the screech of a hawk overhead, the stirring of the wind, and a moment later she felt the flap of wings just as claws descended and touched her shoulders. *It is unbecoming.*

Is it? she asked back in her mind.

Her familiar chirped on her shoulder and ruffled her wings. *A predator does not mourn its prey.*

Bryson sighed and reached up to run her fingers against her familiar's sleek brown and black plumage. "You're right," she said aloud. "They're monsters."

Even monsters have feelings.

If that was true, then a part of Bryson hoped that they'd died afraid. Like so many Fae had lived and died with fear consuming their souls. She wanted to berate herself for those thoughts, but couldn't. Would her mother be ashamed of her for thinking that? After all, she'd gone to fight for peace. She had preached the concept to Bryson and her sister for years before the war tore her away.

Even her father, Mana bless his soul, had tried to instill the concept into her as they'd trekked through the broken trail of Tir na Faie towards the human lands.

That had ended well, hadn't it?

The bitter sarcasm of her own thoughts threatened to rock her back on her heels. It was startling, the rare occasion her mind took that turn, that she jolted when a strong arm wrapped around her shoulders. It pulled her out of her past, and she relaxed a fraction as the familiar scent of cedar and lemongrass filled her nostrils.

"You did good, Bryce." Ev's lips pressed against the corner of her mouth. His arms brought stability, grounding her back into the moment. "And we got a good number. I think tonight warrants celebration!"

Her familiar shifted on her shoulder, crooning in Bryson's mind. *Killing others is such a strange human mating ritual.*

With a huff, Bryson shooed the hawk from her shoulder. She didn't want to hear her sardonic input, particularly when the others couldn't hear it to join in on the laugh. With a disgruntled shriek, her familiar took off to the skies.

"Do you really think Arlo will go for that?" Bryson asked, turning her face toward Ev's. She felt his smile press against her lips. Saw him with a brief flash of clarity before he pulled away and became blurry once again. It was a rhetorical question, of course. She knew what the answer would be.

"Of course. We did a good thing here today and everyone needs to decompress."

Footsteps gave away Malika's arrival once again. "He's right, Bryce. I could go for a relaxing night."

"Yeah, live a little, Bryce."

She sighed and smiled, though her mouth felt tight on the corners. Already, a headache was forming at her temples. The light of the sun was too bright and was beginning to hurt her eyes. "Fine," she agreed. "Let's celebrate."

She'd drink to the dead humans, at least.

"Let's go!" Ev tugged her into his arms, possessively guiding her away.

And then she'd spend the rest of the night wishing things were different than what they were and mulling over her familiar's words until sleep claimed her.

A predator does not mourn its prey.

The only problem was, Bryson didn't know where she fit on the scale that her familiar had so carefully balanced them upon.

Was Bryson a predator, waiting for the right moment to attack?

Or was she prey, hiding in the shadows, hoping not to be found?

Like always, the answer came to her with the flying, deadly precision of one of her arrows.

Bryson was both.

Arlo Blackwood

There was comfort in the steady sound of routine, yet the thrumming pulse of it made her restless at the same time. It was like a heartbeat echoing the same tempo over and over. Camp was like that, and the things they did to survive had become an integral part of day-to-day life. Nothing was new except for the voices that belonged to the latest hazy faces, and even those faded into the background over time.

But never their stories. Never their fear. Never their need for vengeance.

Or their need for a good party.

She knew from the blur of running bodies, the drumming beat of footsteps on the ground, the raucous cries of voices, and the slightest hint of magical Fae wine bubbling through the air that they were preparing for a celebration. She knew the sight of it would surprise the captives they'd saved from the wagon, because they hadn't contemplated their freedom before this moment. They were being greeted with it now, though.

Arlo said it helped them forget.

Bryson remembered her own experience from so long ago. She always bit her tongue when Arlo spoke about how the celebrations helped captives feel more *alive*. Back then, she hadn't felt what he was describing.

She still didn't.

Because the upbeat rhythm of the lute and pounding feet on the ground only served to bring with it flashbacks.

She'd clung to the remnants of her past long after her family's bodies had gone cold, too afraid to stand up and face the darkness that plagued her vision. Blood streamed into her mouth, and she choked on it as easily as if it were tears.

Then there were shouts of rage, and humans dug through the rubble. Strong arms yanked at her fragile, aching body and she swung on instinct, too shocked to muster her magic so she lashed out with her fists instead. She screamed, flinging herself back down where their bodies lay.

She didn't want to leave them. It was the cruel, twisting hand of Mana that had taken them from her in the first place. She swore she could hear death laughing somewhere, even as she begged to join them. Or maybe that sound she heard wasn't death at all.

It was something far worse.

Her arms were nearly yanked out of socket as they jerked her backwards. She screamed as they manhandled her, swallowing a mouthful of blood in the process. They shoved her to the ground. Disoriented, her head jerked from side to side. She tried to sense them, but in her panic, she couldn't focus, hone in on her magic. The pain and blood in her eyes blinded her and the ashwood in her nostrils choked through her lungs.

Her eyelids blinked furiously, trying to expel the shards of iron stuck through. Even as she felt them slide out, the blood didn't stop flowing, and her vision didn't return.

"Looks like we caught an injured one." The unsettling voice slid down her spine as it approached. She scrambled away from it, but it was no use.

A collar went around her neck, snuffing out her magic completely. It didn't matter how hard she fought, how loud she screamed, or how desperately she prayed.

They took her away.

Within moments, her entire world had upended. An explosion and iron shards had taken away something vital and precious from her. Her family and her vision. And when she suddenly found herself without both of those things, she'd been lost in her own paralyzing fear. It was all she knew at first. Disorientation in a world that wasn't familiar, with sounds and scents that were cloying and almost impossible to weave through.

When they shoved her into the iron camps, it had been worse. It suffocated her completely and she wasn't only struggling to try and see, she was also struggling to pull oxygen into her lungs. Blood spurted from her throat with every hacking cough until she was sure she would die.

But she hadn't died then. Even when she thought infection and malnourishment would take her. When she was beaten by power-hungry guards and shoved into wagons for transport, she had not died.

She'd been saved, though she wasn't sure if it was by the grace of Mana or...

"Bryson!"

Arlo Blackwood.

He stomped loudly to get her attention, as though she couldn't see his blurry figure approaching. As if the wind didn't pull his essence towards her like the soft whisper of a warning. Sometimes, he still treated her like the young Fae with the broken sight he'd first pulled from that wagon. Not like the woman she was now. Healed, whole. Perhaps her vision would never be what it was before the accident, but at least she could *see*, at least she was alive, and that was more than she could say for others.

"Hey, Arlo." Ev pulled away from her to meet Arlo in the middle and clapped him on the back.

"Any problems?"

"None. Bryson is a good shot," Ev replied.

"The cargo?"

"Malika and the others are getting it organized as we speak."

"Good," Arlo muttered. "But tell me, why aren't *you* helping them?"

There was a brief moment of silence in which Bryson almost flinched. She didn't move, though. She kept very still. It was almost the norm that people treated her like she wasn't there when they spoke. But if there was one thing they didn't understand, it was that she wasn't *blind*.

Nor deaf.

She wasn't sure why they treated her like a piece of furniture.

"I—"

"No excuses, boy," Arlo interjected. His tone wasn't chastising, but nor was it kind. "Business first, celebration later."

"Yes, Arlo."

The subservience from Everette wasn't surprising. Though a human, Everette was Arlo's right hand and would one day take his place as leader of the camp. *If he lived that long*, a cynical and wretched part of her always thought but never voiced.

"Good. Now say goodbye to your girlfriend and see to your duties." His tone mellowed out into a humorous one that made Bryson relax her shoulders a fraction.

Ev laughed. Then he rushed towards her. He didn't say anything, though he didn't need to, before he pressed a kiss to her lips then turned and jogged away.

It wasn't until he was out of earshot that Arlo focused his attention on her. She always felt his stare like a heavy weight. What little she could see of it from a distance was piercing, calculating. Even through the blur, she could make out the black and gray of his hair and mustache, as well as the too-straight posture of his tall, wide body. A half-Fae, he had ears that were curved, but not quite as pointed as a full-blooded Fae's.

Malika had often described him as, "Rigid, like he has a stick up his ass."

Today, Bryson stared at the crooked nose that towered over the stern line of his mouth, with eyes bright like a hawk's as he took her in. His hair was pulled back with a strip of leather, and if there was a strand out of place, she couldn't quite make it out.

His clothes were clean. She always noticed he was *too* clean, and that was on account that her sense of smell was stronger than anyone else's. She smelled the soap on his clothes, and the careful precision with which he tucked flowers into his pockets. None of that drowned out his own natural scent, though. Like sap and dry leaves and a vegetable garden.

"How was the hunt?" He stepped towards her.

That's what he always called it.

The hunt.

Because they spent weeks plotting, tracking, and killing those humans. They would intercept them along roads as they transported Fae away to their camps and bring the bounty back to camp with them.

Arlo always looked at Fae like investments; his own commodities that he'd collected throughout the years since the war. Everything at the camp was based on give-and-take. Arlo rescued them, and so everyone had to give in return. That was probably a cold way of looking at it, but Bryson tried to be practical. Yes, while they were all a family, she didn't delude herself to believing that Arlo didn't benefit from them.

Especially her and Malika, as they were the only Fae there with gifted abilities.

"You heard Ev," Bryson replied. "It went well."

He was quiet, regarding her. "Will you help them find their place?"

Her shoulders lowered, and she hadn't even realized how tense she felt. "Of course." She always would. Perhaps she was not the best shoulder to lean on, but sometimes other Fae looked at her—at the scars around her eyes—and counted their own blessings.

She hated being treated like a simple attraction at a circus, but she was proud of who she was and her own survival. She wanted the others to be proud too, despite the scars or injuries they may have carried or garnered.

Bryson had her many uses, and this was only a drop in the cup, in Arlo's opinion.

"Good. Go help Malika."

Bryson didn't wait for further instruction. She walked in the direction of the medical tents, where Malika had set up near the herbal garden.

"And Bryson?"

She stopped.

"When you're finished, join the celebration. I know how hard days like this are for you."

Her chest tightened with his words, while simultaneously something warmed within her. Sometimes, Arlo was very harsh. Others like this, he was almost fatherly in his affections. He wouldn't show his feelings with a heavy-handed touch like Malika or gentle, clinging hugs and kisses like Everett. It was in other ways, like the softening of his voice to balance out his rough exterior.

"Thank you," she whispered.

She walked towards the medical tent, and he didn't call after her again. Not even to tell her that she hadn't promised she would attend the celebration.

He was right. Days like this were hard for her, and instead of dizzying herself with dance and drink, she preferred to decompress in a quiet place.

"Brood," Malika claimed. Perhaps that's what it was. Perhaps Bryson wallowed. But it didn't matter.

Because she had a job to do. And Bryson would do it.

Within the medical tent, the scent of herbs, oils, blood, and pain mingled.

And magic.

It bubbled through the enclosed space, sharp and biting and yet somehow soothing. Even the soft, suffering groans of the people clustered within brought with it a sort of comfort. Pain was good, Bryson thought. Pain meant they were alive. That they would heal.

Malika's feet were loud as they rushed around the tent, going from tables of herbs and medicines and back to the injured. There were the softer *tap-tap-tap* of several other footsteps as well, followed by the chittering squeak of the voices of the camp brownies.

Bryson was careful walking in, weaving her way around bleary, small bodies. Back when she still had her full sight, when she still lived in Tir na Faie, back when they had their family manor, she remembered the brownies that scampered through the halls on thin legs.

She remembered how they all looked like small trees, with textured skin like bark that ranged from colors of white, gray, green, and brown, and dripped sap, moss, and magic. Their limbs creaked as they walked, and their excited chatter as they cleaned made magic burst like works of fire through the sky.

Brownies expelled magic through cleaning, and they *loved* to clean. Bryson could already feel the charge of magic in the air, and it gave her a small boost of energy as she followed Malika's scent of lavender, ginger, and lemon over towards the table.

Bryson was careful not to touch anything, lest she knock something important over.

"What can I do?" Her voice was soft and cautious.

Even though she already had her purpose within the tents, Bryson still always deferred to Malika, as it was *her* domain.

Malika huffed a breath. Her tall frame towered over her worktable, muscular arms furiously whipping together her concoctions in her rush to heal the Fae. She used magic, of course, but because the price of using it meant her energy waned, she had to substitute with other methods as well, at least for the more minor injuries.

"Go ease some of the patients' anxiety," she ordered quietly. "The camps had them so screwed up that they think I'm going to be just like those 'doctors'." There was open disgust in her tone, and Bryson understood.

She herself had only been evaluated by a doctor once when she'd been at the camps. It had been to have her eyes looked over. They hadn't been aware that she had magic because they couldn't overlook her bleeding eyes and then lack of sight. Like because she had one fatal flaw, it meant she couldn't possibly possess talent. People couldn't see past what was right in front of them, and because of it, Bryson always felt like she was underestimated.

They'd taken one look at her and declared her defective, then tossed her into an iron cage. It'd been the reason she hadn't properly healed, why she now had to squint to see colors and shades and figures and details, but at least she could still *see.* She hadn't been so fortunate at the time.

Malika had had it worse at the camps.

Sometimes, Bryson could still hear the screams. Like the pain and suffering had followed her in her dreams.

"Okay."

Bryson walked over, stopping just shy of the people to avoid startling them. She could see them recoil away from her as she got down to her knees in front of them. They made soft, whimpering noises that tugged at the strings of her heart.

She'd been there.

She knew the fear of the unknown, had lived it as profoundly as they had. It was one thing she realized about life; that even if they didn't suffer the same experiences, they could still relate to the trauma.

Bryson didn't understand the extent of Malika's suffering at the hands of human doctors. But they'd endured camp together, gripping one another's hands tightly through the tears and echoing shrieks of others.

Together they'd been abused, together they'd been tossed into an iron-barred carriage and taken away, uncertain of their futures. And together, they'd been saved.

She recalled it now. The way it felt like she was being choked within the confined space. The way the horses screeched and jerked to a halt, causing the wagon to teeter on its wheels. The sound of a door bursting open. The sound of death.

And then Arlo Blackwood, with blood dripping from a sword and the scent of a vegetable garden and pine clinging to his skin.

So she said to them what Arlo had said to her. "You're safe now." The words rasped out of her throat.

"Are we?" someone in front of her snapped.

She didn't know with absolute certainty. Humans were everywhere, and it wouldn't be long before they caught on to what was happening there in Ielwyn. Before someone realized that the Fae they sent away were missing, the soldiers as well. Would they be safe then?

She wondered if those thoughts had gone through Arlo's mind as well when Malika asked that same question right before they were pulled out to the light.

"I don't know," Bryson confessed. "But you're safe *for now,* and unless you want that iron to embed itself so deep into your bodies that you end up—" She cut off what she was about to say, biting her tongue so hard she tasted blood. She hated that she was often invaded with cruel sentiments about herself, despite her self-confidence. She hated that she stooped herself so low.

But that was what Arlo wanted. He wanted her to lie, even if she didn't feel the words that were spewing from her mouth. He wanted her to degrade herself, to act like she was ashamed of her poor eyesight and the scars marring her eyes and cheeks. He wanted others to see it. To say, *"Poor, half-blind Fae. I don't want to end up like her."*

It was Arlo's favorite form of manipulation. Or rather, his way of convincing the Fae to stay in camp.

And because he'd gifted Bryson with her own freedom, she did what he bade.

There was silence as the Fae in front of her seemed to contemplate what she said—or rather, what she didn't say.

"Does it hurt?" they whispered.

Her smile found the one who asked. "Not anymore."

It hadn't for a long time, but that didn't mean that memories couldn't ache. And hers *burned.* More than the scars ever could.

"Will you hold my hand?" the voice asked again.

Bryson expelled a breath and held her hand out. "For however long you need."

It took minutes, though she didn't count them, until a rough, withered hand closed over her own. It was wet and clammy, with disjointed fingers and missing stubs. And yet relief invaded her body through every crevice as she closed her palm over theirs.

The motion felt like a big step, but there was still so much more they would need if they wanted to heal. And it didn't matter that Bryson's stomach churned, or that memories of the past invaded, or that sometimes she felt like this was harder than killing.

Bryson had a job to do.

And so she would do it.

Invasive Thoughts

Her face tilted up towards the open air, nose leaning to where she imagined the stars were. Her body was sprawled against a wooden surface, her hands patiently resting against her lower abdomen. Night had fallen, the temperature dropped low, and the cold clung to her bones.

The wind ruffled against her curls, pushing the strands against her freckled cheeks. She relaxed her body, sinking deep into the wood, and let her magic go astray against the night. It whipped and flew in varying degrees of harshness.

Beside her, her familiar ruffled her feathers.

You are acting petulant, she squawked. *Stop that.*

Bryson let out a breath and her magic eased back. Without the wind, she was forced to listen to the pounding silence of the night. She didn't like it because torturous thoughts threatened to invade. Her magic picked up again, the wind ruffling the feathers of her familiar in a teasing way.

The hawk screeched with indignation.

"Calm down, you oversized chicken."

The disrespect...

Bryson chuckled at their easy banter, but the sound died as easily as it had been born. She couldn't stop thinking about the day, about the humans they'd killed and the Fae they'd saved. Soon, they would rehabilitate in the camp and slowly heal from their ordeal. At least their bodies, if not their minds.

She figured healing the mind was a longer process, one she didn't even begin to understand. Though she herself had healed from the pain, there were some wounds that were invisible and hurt more than any cut upon flesh ever could.

She felt herself drowning in those wounds even now, in the chaos of her memories as they invaded her mind. How terrible was it that the last thing she would ever see with clear vision was the way her father and sister ran towards her right before the explosion? That the last thing she would clearly see was his terrified face?

If only she hadn't been wandering, he wouldn't have tried to save her. He wouldn't have reached for her. He wouldn't have used his body to shield her and her sister...

They would have died anyway. That was one thing she knew for certain. If it hadn't been the explosion, it would have been something else. The camps, maybe. The hands of the cruel human soldiers. Sometimes, Bryson marveled at the fact that she herself was still alive.

As the thoughts crept along her mind, she felt an itching begin to form just beneath her skin. It was a burning anger that she felt could never be sated. A thirst for violence so potent, she sometimes frightened herself with the force of it. It battled against who she was and who she thought she should be, against the reality of the present and the teachings of her past.

She should move on from the tragedy, but it was that very same tragedy that gave her the ability to fight back and want for more. But even as she thirsted for it, Arlo's voice commanded her mind like it always did.

"It's not wise to want for more. That's how revolutions are started."

He was content with the lives they led. Thieving from humans, picking up Fae when they could. Arlo Blackwood didn't aspire for more, and he expected the same from the rest of them.

She always felt like opting to follow him often meant she was spitting on the graves of her family and their beliefs. But *their* beliefs had never been *her* beliefs, just like Arlo's beliefs weren't her own either.

She didn't *know* what to believe in anymore. So she killed to survive and helped Fae when she could, and then she came here to the little house built atop a tree to stare at a sky she could barely see.

Brood, her familiar said, a hint of teasing in her mental voice.

Bryson scoffed, swallowing the sound when the wind brought the crunch of footsteps towards her ears. She paused, listening to the noise and recognizing the owner of them right away.

I am going to hunt. Her familiar spread and flapped her wings, pushing a gust of wind against Bryson before she took off to the sky with a cry.

There was a curse as Malika climbed the rickety steps nailed to the tree, struggling to get to the top. That indicated that she was probably tipsy off the Fae wine the goblins brewed.

When she finally reached the top, she all but sprawled out next to Bryson.

"You breathe too loudly," Bryson said, sitting up.

"You bitch," she heaved. "If you're going to be mean, I'll take this wine back."

Malika knew very well that Bryson didn't really partake in drink, at least not so much that she would lose her footing and fall out of the damn tree. If she didn't drink or dance, it was out of self-preservation. That, and she didn't want to look like a fool.

"Here, just one glass won't hurt." Malika shoved it into her hands, and Bryson had to grasp it with her fingers, though the liquid sloshed over the rim and stuck to her skin. "Lighten up." She clinked her glass against Bryson's and her voice softened. "We did good today."

There seemed to be centuries worth of sadness packed into those words. It was only because of that that Bryson brought the cup to her lips and took a sip.

Silence enveloped them. Bryson could say with certainty that Malika was her best friend in the world. They were open and honest with each other, yet there was still an air of mystery surrounding the other Fae that always made Bryson curious. She never asked, though, and Malika never offered the story of her past. It was like their lives had begun when they met in that camp. Anything that had happened before didn't exist.

Though Bryson didn't doubt that there was an incredibly sad story to be told. Malika had mentioned a sister once. A single time. It had been in passing, almost as if she'd forgotten their sacred understanding not to mention the past. Malika hadn't brought it up since then.

They sat in companionable silence, staring out into the dim night that contrasted against even darker shapes. Nighttime made it that much harder to see, but it was a peaceful moment between them regardless, both of them sipping their Fae wine. The fruity drink fizzled against Bryson's tongue, and she felt the effects immediately.

"Your boyfriend is looking for you, you know."

Bryson's brows kicked up in amusement. "I'm sure he is."

It wasn't like her hiding place was some big secret. If he was looking, he should know exactly where she would be. Just like she knew exactly where *he* would be; deep in cup after cup of Fae wine, heavy in celebration with the others.

At least until he finally found his footing enough to wander to where she lay to see if she was okay.

As if on cue, footsteps sounded in the distance, heading in their direction.

"Well..." Malika took a loud swallow of her wine. "Looks like he finally found you." There was a smile in her voice that Bryson didn't dare turn to meet.

From the ground, feet stepped up the little ladder until Everett finally reached the top. His heart was pounding, his every breath laced with exhaustion and the scent of wine. His dark hair was wind-kissed, his white smile wide.

"And I'm out." There was the clinking of glasses as Malika gathered her things. Meanwhile, Bryson could only squint in Ev's direction. "Have fun... You probably can't see this, Bryce, it being so dark and all, but I'm winking at you."

Bryson let out a laugh. If there was one thing she loved about Malika, it was *that* right there. The fact that she never put such a weight on her poor vision. Because it wasn't as big a deal as others made it to be. At the end of the day, it was something she would always have to live with, and it was irritating when others felt sorry for her.

Like Arlo and all the new Fae they saved.

As soon as Malika touched the ground, she jogged away, leaving Bryson and Ev alone together. Once they were, he took a seat at her side. She felt the warmth of his body seep into hers, and his scent enveloped her. Daffodils and wine. There were also touches of earth and smoke, hinting at his general activities of dancing near the fire.

His fingers moved, grazing the hand that held tightly to her goblet before he pulled it from her grasp. She heard him swallow the rest of the contents, knowing she wasn't going to finish it anyway, before he tossed the cup to the side. She heard it roll across the wood then stop just before it slid off the tree.

There was a beat of silence. "Are you okay, Bryce?" he asked, the concern in his voice genuine; it pressed to her chest.

She sighed, unsure of what to say or how to say it. Her friends knew how hard days like today were for her. She never had to explain why, and they didn't have to ask. Even if they did, she wasn't sure she could really give them a concrete answer. Her mind was a befuddled mess of emotions that were hard to sift through.

"I'm fine." The words didn't feel like the complete truth, though they didn't feel like a lie either. She was fine, even with the burning sensation in her chest harrying down on her. Sometimes, she felt like all she had left in the world was rage and absolutely nothing to do with it.

Everett sighed. "You know Arlo won't be leader forever."

She knew that. Just because he was half-Fae didn't mean he didn't age. He did. It was the more dominant, human part of him. Half-Fae lived longer than the average human, but less than a full-blooded Fae. So Arlo was training Ev for his eventual takeover. Even though Ev was human himself, he and Arlo were close. Close enough that Arlo would give up the reins of all that he'd built.

This war had done that; brought unlikely allies together to fight for a similar cause. Similar tragedies tethered the lot of them together.

"You won't have to humiliate yourself like that when I'm leader." Ev's arm wrapped around her, pulling her close. "You won't have to parade yourself around the new Fae, you won't have to show off your scarred eyes. Not if you don't want to..."

My scarred eyes.

The shrapnel from the iron hadn't only taken a good portion of her sight. The lesions caused once-brown pupils to discolor to a milky, white hue. It had also scarred the skin on her eyelids, thin spiderwebs that spread down to the tops of her cheekbones, cutting through freckles. They hadn't fully healed. How could they when she'd been thrown into an iron camp soon after? Her wounds had never been treated properly there, and they'd left their permanent mark on her body.

Malika said her scarred stare was frightening.

"Wouldn't want to scare the new ones," she jested, digging her elbow into his side.

"You don't frighten them."

Her silence was pointed.

"I'm serious. If anything, they're intimidated by the best parts of you."

"Oh, yeah? And what would those be?" she asked coyly, dropping her voice to a whisper.

Ev wasn't too attractive for a human. When they were close, she liked to look over his imperfect features, the nose that was just a bit too strong, lips that were too full. His dark hair swooped low against his shoulders, kissing tan skin, and yet there was comfort in the imperfect parts of *him*.

Bryson wasn't with Ev for his *looks,* after all.

"Let's see..." His fingers slid down the sleeve of her shirt, and she felt the warmth of him through the thin material. The slight touch made the wind around them churn a fraction and he released a chuckle that made her lips twitch. "There's your skin." His fingers stopped where the edge of her sleeve met her wrist. He encircled it, his touch light, seductive.

Her breath came out slowly. "What *about* my skin?"

He lifted her hand, bringing it to his mouth where he kissed the tips of her fingers one by one. They were calloused, but he didn't seem to mind. His lips traced over them, sliding down to the back of her hand. He shoved her sleeve up to her elbow, trailing kisses all the way up her arm.

"It's soft. Freckled."

"Hmm..."

"I could kiss your freckles all day." He kissed along her arm, stopping at the inside of her elbow and pulling away. For a moment, she lost his warmth until he grasped her by the hips and flipped her so she was straddling his lap.

She let out a breath of satisfaction when he pulled her down, grinding her center against the tightness of his own pants. Her hands clasped for his shoulders, tightening her grip as his hands traveled over her ass and the backs of her thighs.

His eyes flared and she was sure her own did too. She had to bite back her smile, the grip of satisfaction she got when he looked at her like that. Not like the others did. Not like something that had to be pitied. But like someone who was beautiful, even if she didn't always feel it.

"Your ass, for sure." He bent, his hair grazing hers as his lips clamped down on the side of her neck.

"Hmm..." A zing of pleasure swept through her body at the contact. "What else?"

He nipped her chin. "Your lips..."

"Oh, really—"

He interrupted her with a kiss. She lost herself in it, in him. His touch was a distraction from the chaos in her mind, if temporarily. But she would take it with the same fervor he gave. Their tongues tangled together in a fierce dance.

He was as quick in his undressing of her as he was with his seduction. It was always to the point and perfunctory, and her own hands grappled with his clothes just as quickly. A breeze sifted through the air, caressing Bryson's hair as he lifted her body by the hips, digging his blunt nails into her thighs.

Their warm bodies met, and he entered her in one, fluid movement. She gasped as they joined, pressing close together. There was silence as he began to move, then grunted against her neck, swiping kisses in the darkness as they moved together with the night sky and the stars above them. And the breeze flittering. And a hawk crying.

And Bryson's mind finally silencing.

Loyalists

Hope was such a delicate thing. It demanded to be seen, to be held within the roughened palms of a person who didn't know what it was like to care for something so fragile. It broke like glass, leaving behind the remnants of glittering flakes.

For a moment, Bryson felt that hope a few weeks later, sitting on the stumps of cut down trees in a circle with all her other comrades from camp. Arlo stood in the middle. His scent felt particularly aggressive that day, his presence a thing that demanded attention. From the distance, she couldn't quite make out the entirety of his features, but she pictured them as stern as his posture, his smell.

It wasn't until he began to speak that Bryson felt her heart speed up.

"Whispers have reached my ears," he said.

Ev stood beside him in a show of solidarity. This was normal behavior between the two. They presented a united front for the rest of the people at camp, both staring so stoically she could feel the weight of their eyes pressing down on her shoulders.

"I know we, as a group, have closed ourselves off from the outside for the most part, but I've still got ears on the ground," he continued. His footsteps thumped as he stepped down and walked a circle around them. He stopped in front of Bryson. "But I believe it is important to know what's going on outside." He paused, and Bryson felt her breath catch with impatience.

"Rumors have made their way to us," Ev continued, his voice booming across the small clearing.

This was normal too. While Ev deferred to Arlo, they took turns imparting news, usually about where their round of supplies would come from, or where the emperor's prisoners would be transported to, so they could intercept it.

Bryson sat at the edge of her seat.

"There's a group that calls themselves 'The Resistance'," Ev said, the disgust clear in his voice. "They're led by a group of Fae that have taken it upon themselves to fight and win a war against the kingdom of Dana."

Collective gasps broke through the wind. Even Bryson found herself rocking back on the stump, biting down hard on her bottom lip. She felt eyes on her and knew they were Malika's. She didn't turn to her friend.

"They're rumored to be led by the Seelie Prince and his guard." Arlo spat on the ground, and Bryson felt the hairs on her arms rise at the words and tone beneath them. She recognized it, as he'd used it before. Whenever he ranted about life outside of their camp, that tone overtook him and came out in biting words. "Our source says they're looking to conquer the human lands in retaliation for the lost war, and maybe gain back the Feylands in the process."

And just like that, the small, fragile thing called hope rose in Bryson's chest, swirling through her mind incessantly. Hope, because she had been so long without it. Even years ago, when Arlo pulled her from an iron cage and into the light, even as the sun kissed her cheeks, she felt nothing but hollow sadness.

For so long, she'd been drifting within that emptiness. Lost.

And now he was giving her something she didn't even know she'd craved.

Once upon a time, her mother had died for the Feylands, and they'd all lost their home. Now, there were those out there seeking revenge, trying to gain it back.

They'd already conquered Dana. *The Seelie Prince.* He'd done what Bryson's mother couldn't; what the soldiers of her court had failed to do: conquer a human kingdom.

"In their thirst for power, they've traveled far and wide, leaving chaos in their wake. Not even the West Isles was spared the wrath of fools who think they have a second chance at war." Arlo raised his voice, startling birds from a nearby branch.

Bryson tried not to flinch away from the harshness of his tone when he was still in front of her, and it felt like he was screaming in her general direction. Like he knew there was a small flame of hope inside, and he meant to tamp it down.

Arlo sighed. "I know I sound harsh, but where has a war ever gotten us? Fae in power will always command others to do their bidding. To fight and die and eventually to lose. We've seen it once, and we will see it again with the Seelie monarchy. They led us to war, and in turn, we all lost our homes and our lives. We have become a mere fraction of what we once were, and now they're on the rise, and I can bet you they would ask us to fight again. And *what* do we say to their war?"

"No!"

Voices shouted together. Voices of people Bryson considered friends and allies. All except her own and Malika's. Bryson's mind was moving too fast; it felt like the wind was blowing every single thought away.

When Arlo spoke again, there was smug satisfaction in his voice. "This so-called Resistance is no more different than the emperor and his ideals. They're fighting on opposite sides without realizing that they're both tyrants. And we at this camp do not follow any faction but our own. We take care of each other. We survive and we thrive. And we are loyal to no one but ourselves."

"Here, here!"

Shouts of agreement went out. Finally, Bryson heard Malika's voice join the fray. Then the pressure of Arlo's presence right in front of her became almost suffocating. He stared down at her, and she forced herself to look up at him. He was waiting... like a thunderstorm on the horizon ready to snuff out the fire that blazed inside her soul.

She tilted her head sideways and whispered quietly, almost angrily, "Here, here."

His lips curled into a smile as he stepped away from her. His throat cleared and for the moment, that was all he would say, as Ev took over the rest of the meeting.

"Now, onto far more important things... Our trackers have noticed that several faunas of the area have been going missing. We believe that despite the claims of the West Isles being blown up, the Kurreen are still at large. We'll be separated into groups to do a fell sweep of the area. Be careful and be vigilant, and if you see the Kurreen, do not hesitate to use deadly force. Because if they catch you, they'll do worse to you. Understood?"

There were calls of agreement.

"Malika, you'll stay behind to keep an eye on the newbies. The rest of you, here's how you'll be paired up..."

Life was hard. It knocked you down, fucked you up, and when you thought you were safe, it did it all over again.

At least, that was Bryson's experience.

After the meeting, she'd wandered on what felt like dead legs, lost in her mind, trapped in the spaces of Arlo's words. Like always, she was stuck with nothing more than thoughts and anger, and absolutely nothing to do with it.

Nothing except *brood,* apparently.

She huffed, and a gust of her magic pushed out to the skies. She wanted to stop in the middle of the forest and scream, to put that anger to use like her father always told her to do the moment her mother didn't come back from the war. Ever since then, she'd been riddled with emotions she didn't understand.

And ever since she lost her father and sister, she'd been living on a precipice, waiting for something to give.

If the Fae were taking down entire human kingdoms, then it was possible that they could rise again. That her mother hadn't died for nothing. That all this suffering could have been worth it, if only it meant freedom.

An ache spread down her spine, pressing against the scars on her back like a warning; scars that had been there since before she ever stepped foot in the human lands. The ominous feeling against that part of her had Bryson remembering the night it happened.

How she was walking beside her sister one moment and the next her legs buckled beneath her. Agony had spread like fire through her spine, in her veins, to her bones, down to her soul. She'd tasted dirt as she fell, screaming until her throat was hoarse with the action. She was sure she'd blacked out at one point, and when her eyes opened, she watched her sister run to get their father.

And she blinked, and there he was, lifting her. But the action pulled at the muscles on her back. It felt like she'd been carved open from the inside out, and warmth soaked through her clothes, and the wind drifted the coppery scent of blood into her nose, making her nauseas.

"What's happening to me?" Her lips trembled, and it was a struggle to release every word.

She wasn't sure she heard the answer, if he even gave one. All she remembered was that they'd hauled her up as carefully as they could manage, though the agony was jerking through every nerve-ending. It wasn't until they'd cut off her shirt and cleansed the blood from her back that her father gasped and stepped away, staring at her backside with grave sadness.

"What?" she'd demanded, pushing herself up on her palms.

When no one answered her, she'd stumbled from the table. Every move was full of anguish, and yet she somehow made it over to a mirror. She twisted, crying as her body screamed in pain. But when she caught a glimpse of her own reflection, tears streamed down her cheeks at what she saw.

Wounds were embedded in her flesh, like they'd been carved there with a knife, a searing hot knife. Three circles starting at the base of her neck down her spine; stamped within each one were intricate images of whorls and curves like clouds.

There was something artistic about the scars down her back. So much so, in fact, that it made her want to weep. She did. With her eyes full of tears, she turned to her father.

"What is this?" she asked, her voice breaking.

He didn't answer her right away. He regarded her with sad eyes, his own brown ones wide and glossy. "It means," he whispered, "you are the last."

Bryson didn't understand the words at first. They didn't register in her mind. "The last *what*?"

"The last of your kind. The last air Elemental."

Hearing the words was a blow. It felt like she was being told that someone close to her had died. That, of course, was ridiculous. She didn't know any other Elementals. They were a rare species. Having magic was rare in and of itself, but being an Elemental?

Her parents had often told her how special she was. That being an Elemental was a gift from Mana itself, and that she was meant to do great things with that power. That only a few were ever gifted with such abilities.

A few had dwindled down to one.

The proof lived in the scars on her back.

And they had ever since.

She knew she was just another Fae, but if there was intricate truth she was told that she believed with her whole heart, it was that she *was* meant for great things. Greater things than this...

As soon as those thoughts formed, she felt guilty. Wasn't what she was doing here good enough? Arlo would have said it was great work, that they didn't need anything else. Community. A sense of purpose.

Her mother would have scoffed in his face.

But her mother was dead. It wasn't her who had saved Bryson from that carriage. It had been Arlo. She owed him her life, and if this was what he wanted her to do with it well, she didn't have any other choice but to be loyal to him and his cause.

The only problem was, she wasn't sure she agreed with it at all.

Flower or Storm

Bryson's feet carried her through the woods. Overhead, her familiar circled, either hunting or keeping a close watch on Bryson after receiving all that information, she wasn't sure. Things in her mind were reeling, and her familiar knew not to add on to her already stressed state.

She'd been paired up with Ev for patrolling, something she was sure he had everything to do with. He tried to keep her close during moments like this, though she wasn't sure if it was so they could spend more time together, or if it was out of jealousy and he didn't want her to be with others...

"Bryson, slow down," Ev called out. He rushed to keep up with her fast stride. When he caught up to her, he tossed his arm around her shoulders, pulling her close.

Her skin itched at the contact.

Bryson noticed a pattern when it came to Ev. Every time after they were intimate, he pulled her closer, almost to the point of being *clingy*. He became her shadow and showered her with affection. She tried not to be annoyed with him, though, and never set up her own boundaries.

They were together, after all. Relationships were hard to form these days, especially for Bryson. When others thought of her as defective, Everett was different. He was kind to her, and she laughed when she was with him. The sex wasn't terrible, either. In fact, she enjoyed it.

The problem was, he enjoyed it *more*. Perhaps it was because she was Fae and he was human, creating a very obvious power imbalance. She couldn't use the full extent of her strength, and while he definitely gave her orgasms, there were times where she felt... unsatisfied afterwards. Like she had too much energy beneath her skin, and she didn't know how to blow it off.

Had Everett been Fae, their sessions likely would have lasted hours. For a moment, she entertained the idea of fucking a Fae. What would it be like? Would it leave her mind blown, her body sated, her thoughts quiet?

For an even crazier moment, she entertained the idea of fucking a mate. It was rumored that there was nothing better in the world. But Bryson had long ago swept those notions away and settled with what she had.

She was happy with Ev.

She didn't need anything else.

Bryson shrugged his hold off and kept walking, picking up speed. He had to rush to keep up with her, and she could already hear his heartbeat accelerating from the exertion.

She could almost feel his frown. "Bryce... What's wrong?"

"How long have you known?" she asked suddenly.

"Known what?"

"How long have you known about the Resistance? About Dana and the West Isles?"

That energy expanded through her body, and she expelled it with a gush of wind that ruffled the creaking branches of the trees.

His answer was slow and cautious. "For... weeks."

She stopped, whirling to face him. She heard his feet stumble on the ground. "And you didn't think to tell me?"

Beneath that rage, there was also hurt. Unlike with Malika, she and Ev shared secrets with one another. He knew about her past, about her parents and her sister. Her family had been loyal to the Seelie crown. He would have known what the news of the Resistance would have meant to her and the memory of her family.

And he'd kept it from her.

"Bryson," he chastised. "You know I can't discuss the workings of the camp with you. Arlo would—"

"Well, you aren't *fucking* Arlo, are you?" she snapped.

He gave pause at her crude tone. She could almost feel his shock like a tangible thing. He didn't choose his next words carefully, but matched her tone with annoyance of his own. "What does it matter if I tell you or not, Bryce? What difference would it make?"

She reeled back on her heels. "What do you mean what difference would it make?"

He scoffed. "It's not like you're a part of that damn Resistance. You're a part of *us*. Of our community. Aren't you?"

There was a note of accusation in his voice that made anxiety rise in her chest. Arlo had demanded her story when he'd pulled her from that wagon all those years ago. He'd pulled her aside and asked, said he needed to know. Over the years, his presence and fatherly affections made her feel like he was eclipsing the memories of her family. She'd fought like hell to keep them alive, and Arlo had noticed it seemed to tear her loyalties in different directions.

That blasted question made her feel that way. She owed Arlo. She owed this community. If she even whispered that she admired the Resistance, she would be shunned. Cast out.

"I am," she gritted out. "But that's not the point."

"No?" He sounded amused. "Then what's the point, Bryson Varik?"

She gritted her teeth, hating when he used her full name. Like she was a petulant child that needed scolding. For fuck's sake, she was older than him.

"The point is trust. I tell you everything, and you don't tell me anything!"

In the distance, a bird chirped and flew away.

"Bryson..." He stepped closer, and she wanted to flinch away when his hands came down gently on her arms, but she kept very still. "If I don't tell you things, it's only because I know they'll hurt you. You can lie to everyone else, but I know that you're still worked up about your family. I know you still feel a sense of loyalty to them, and telling you about the Resistance sooner would have only confused you."

"I'm strong," she argued.

He patted her arms, his voice condescending as he replied, "Sure you are. But you would have gained nothing from knowing sooner. But you know *now,* so why are you so angry?"

Why *was* she so angry? She gave pause to mull the question over in her mind. Sure, even if he had told her the truth sooner, there would have been nothing she could have done about it, except *brood.* But like she said, it wasn't even about that.

It was about being lied to.

It was about how everyone was quick to push her into the fray to shoot at humans and use her magic to save others when they needed it, but the minute she stepped back into camp she was little more than a delicate flower.

She wasn't a fucking flower.

She was a fucking *storm.*

"Forget it," she grumbled, pulling away from him. It would do no good to stand in the middle of the forest and argue semantics. It wasn't as if she could get her feelings across anyway. Not when she herself didn't even know how to voice them, and he would refuse to listen even if she did. "We have to look out for Kurreen."

She started to walk away, trying to drown out her mess of emotions and focus instead on her surroundings.

"Bryson, come on. Now you're pissed at me. You know I'm only giving Arlo what he wants until I can take over. I need you to fucking trust me. I need you to let me protect you."

I don't need your protection.

The words caught in her throat, even though she wanted to scream them to the heavens. She wanted to move on from the subject. She wanted to go on patrol and hopefully find the Kurreen so she could shoot the bastards in their throats and then go off and brood somewhere else at the end of the day.

She didn't want Ev touching her. She didn't even want him speaking to her.

And she most certainly didn't want his *protection.*

"Bryson!"

She huffed a breath. "Watch out on your left, Ev." His feet stumbled as he veered away from the direction she said. He tripped and fell shy of the edge where she told him not to. "There's a mushroom circle right there."

Corvina Rhian

A sheen of sweat coated Corvina Rhian's skin. Her heart beat in time to the rhythm of her hips slamming down against Clay's. With every move of her hips, he thrust deep inside of her, sending jolts of pleasure to her clit.

Clay's blunt nails dug into her hips, his grip tight against her as he moved her up and down against his shaft.

A soft whimper escaped Corvina's throat when he pressed deep inside, hitting a spot that made stars dance behind her closed eyelids. She quickly opened them, not wanting to miss a single moment of staring at Clay's face as they moved in tandem.

His golden hair clung in strips against his forehead and cheeks, bright against his tanned skin. His strikingly green eyes were half-lidded, his teeth clamping down tightly against his bottom lip. With his expression contorted in pleasure, his dimples were much more prominent on his cheeks and chin, endearing in a way that had Corvina smiling.

The smile wiped off her face as his fingers went between her legs, finding the spot where they were joined. He touched her clit and the orgasm came as a surprise. She cried out and her entire body shuddered. Her hips moved against him, faster and faster so she could chase that sensation that once upon a time had been foreign to her.

She never knew orgasms could feel like this. She never thought she could have sex like this. Where she was in complete control. Where she was on top, taking and receiving pleasure as she desired, instead of someone else finding pleasure within her and leaving her hurting and in tears.

Her magic sprung out with the force of her ongoing orgasm. It lashed out like whips, water wrapping around Clay's wrists and bringing them slamming down against the top of the bed. She didn't care that she was wetting the sheets or that the cold water was in perfect contrast to their fevered bodies.

This was about control and her taking it back.

"Oh, fuck." Clay arched up as the tendrils of liquid cut around his wrists. Inside, she felt him grow bigger and he throbbed, every pulse building an ache.

She knew it was on account of his own magic. Blood magic that he used to rip fulfillment from them both.

Just as she started coming down from her high, he blinked and brought it up again. It was there in the beating of her heart, the rasping breaths as her blood heated and traveled lower and lower right to the center of her clit. He didn't even need to touch it because she felt the heat as if he were. It felt like there were phantom fingers against her body, throbbing with her gasps and heartbeats and cries.

"Clay..." Her voice pitched.

"Yes, mate," he hissed. His magic pushed her body to the edge, left her dangling over it. And the smirk on his lips let her know he meant to keep her there, to tease and wring the desire out slowly, drop after torturous drop.

Two could play at that game.

Her own magic crept out, a cold whip of water wrapping around the base of his cock. As he slammed up, the water against her clit made the both of them groan together.

"Mate..."

"Yes?" she asked innocently, even as she commanded her magic to encircle his engorged member and tug at the base of his balls. It pulled, wrapping around him as sensual as a hand. Turning, tugging, squeezing. She put different amounts of pressure against him, teasing him the same way he was teasing her, driving him close to his own release just before pulling away completely.

"You're..." He snapped his hips up. "...killing me..."

She smiled, feeling suddenly wanton. There was something freeing about being on top, about driving a man like Clay Valentino completely mad with want. She never knew it could be like this. That she could feel... powerful.

It'd been days since she'd accepted him as her mate. Days they'd spent exploring one another. Days in which she relearned her body and herself and what she liked when it came to moments like this. There were some things of course she felt she wasn't brave enough to try yet, if she could ever. Things that she knew would trigger her, like hands on her neck, like pressing her face down into the sheets... Maybe one day she would get over the trauma and wounds of her past. The ones that Tobias, her deceased bastard of a husband, had inflicted. But for now, she enjoyed this.

Riding Clay. Snapping her hips against his. Feeling him inside, pulsing and hot, and the overheated sensation just beneath her skin.

"It's time to come, mate."

That was the only warning Clay gave her before multiple orgasms crashed over her. One after the other, without even being touched. He consumed her whole, and she squeezed him with a cry, her own magic tightening until he pulsed inside her and cried his own release to the ceiling.

Once the sensation ebbed, she sprawled across his chest. Her curtain of golden-brown hair splayed across his body. Her magic swept away, seeping into the mattress beneath them. For a moment, Clay lay there breathless before his hands reached up and pushed her hair away, cupping her cheek with his palm.

The smile on his face was a radiant thing, like staring directly into the heat of the sun. It warmed her, threatened to blind her. It was always like that, his smile. It felt open and vulnerable, like an echo of what she felt in her own soul whenever she was with him.

Her mate.

Her mate.

For so long, Corvina had dreamt of meeting him. When she was a young girl, she'd craved it. But when reality came crashing down and the war progressed, she'd been forced to set aside those dreams as passing fancies. Her father, the High Lord of the Golden Court, had gifted her to the humans in exchange for her court's survival. She'd been married to Prince Tobias of Dana, and yet her court still fell.

That was the beginning of her nightmares.

All Corvina had known in the human lands was cruelty and abuse. Until the Resistance. Until the Elementals. Until Clay.

She'd learned what it meant to be strong. And even if her gnarled, twisted fingers could not properly hold a sword, she had other things at her disposal that could bring down kingdoms. Her magic.

And her love.

Raw emotion tugged at her heartstrings the more Clay looked into her eyes and said nothing. She was only just learning about pleasure and what an honest relationship really looked like. Clay was looking at her with that open sincerity, and she felt she could read everything on his expression.

"You're perfect," he whispered. "Perfect."

Her heart warmed. He'd been doing that for days. Like he meant to remind her every chance he got just what he thought of her. And she loved every second of it.

The most important reminder of course would always be of her own making. She needed to feel comfortable with herself and her own body, to value her own worth regardless of what anyone else said or how the ghosts of her past tried to haunt her. Sometimes, it was just nice to hear it said aloud.

"Much as I'd like to have you ride me forever, it's time we got up." He curled his stomach with a groan, lifting. Her legs splayed open at the action, her thighs encircling his waist. His arms wrapped tightly around her hips, and he looked up at her through bright lashes. "Although, this position feels too good to change."

The tip of his cock stirred against her entrance. Wetness pooled between her legs all over again. She let out a soft mewl of want.

"We can't." Clay lifted her slowly. "They're waiting for us, and the hour is already late."

Much as she loathed to get up, he was right. It was late in the day already and she needed to check on Basil and her maids—*friends*, she amended. They weren't her maids any longer, not since her husband and the entire Wes family had met its end. Not since the Resistance and enslaved Fae in Dana rose up in arms and destroyed the kingdom, letting the Seelie Prince take over.

They no longer had a duty to Corvina, and yet they still did her favors in watching Basil while she...

Corvina's face heated. A part of her wanted to be ashamed, for the fear to rise up and rear its ugly head. But the greatest threat to her safety was gone. Her husband was gone, and nothing could harm her or Basil again.

They began dressing in comfortable quiet. Corvina still shied away from his gaze as she dressed. Her body was not the perfect specimen for a Fae. She was covered in scars from years of abuse. Even her fingers were gnarled and twisted and shook as she tried to pull her ribbons through her dress.

"Let me," Clay offered. His hands covered her shaking digits. His palms were smoother than hers and for a second, she felt self-conscious because of it. She had been a princess only days ago. Princesses were not supposed to have calloused fingers. But there were many parts of her body that she found ugly. Parts of her that had been tortured with iron so badly, they'd never healed the same.

Like her ears. The tips of them weren't pointed like other Fae's. They'd been cut through with an iron knife until they'd bled and healed into twisted wreck of flesh. She wanted to hide them for a moment, to drop her hair over the tips so others could not see what all Tobias had done to her, even though they already knew and had witnessed the abuse for themselves.

Slowly, Clay's hands pulled her out of those dark thoughts. He yanked on her ribbons, tying them into place. When he finished, he turned her, pushing aside her hair behind her ears. Almost as if he knew in which direction her thoughts had strayed.

"Beautiful," he said. "Perfect."

Her face flushed with warmth. The words she wanted to say got stuck in her throat. They tended to do that when he was near. It was still hard to believe he was real. This was real. That she had her mate in front of her and he was... perfect.

"Shall we go?" she asked.

He smiled as though he knew what she already wanted to say before he took her hand in his. Her fingers ached with phantom pains, but once his palm swallowed hers, she forgot all about that.

He led her outside of the room. The halls in the castle were very familiar to her, and their feet led them to the throne room where the others were waiting.

Julius whistled. "About damn time, you two."

Julius was Clay's best friend. A mountain of a Fae, he was leaning a muscled shoulder against an ivory pillar, flashing white teeth through his ginger beard in their direction. His ruddy cheeks flushed red with laughter at his own clever joke and beside him, his mate snickered.

Clay flipped Julius the finger, causing Iona to cackle with laughter.

Iona was a beautiful, if intimidating, Fae who was nearly as tall as Julius. She was muscular and curvy, with an expanse of smooth ebony skin and white curls shorn to her scalp.

The room was actually filled with the rest of their companions. The Resistance, or at least the inner circle of it. A few key players were missing, like Weylyn and the Seelie King, but everyone was otherwise in one spot.

Shula and Ryker, the fire Elemental and the group's scarred healer. They sat in wait with Basil in Shula's lap like it would become his permanent home. Her old maids, Gale, Juniper, Wren, and Dawn, stood off to the side with bags piled on their backs.

Corvina knew they were carrying her things. She'd told them that they were no longer bound to serve her, as she was no longer princess and Tobias was dead. They were free, and in their freedom, they could choose to do whatever it was they wanted.

What they wanted was to stay with Corvina.

She was humbled when they'd all said the same thing. Humbled that they liked her enough to stick around, even when she had no means to free them of their chains in the past or help them through life in the kingdom. They'd known that she was as much a prisoner as they were, even if she wore finer silks and gowns and jewelry.

The fact that they didn't look at her and have the urge to flee the other direction meant a lot to her.

Though she would have to take them aside and remind them they didn't have to carry all of her belongings. She could do it herself. There was nobody alive who would reprimand her for doing it.

"So, when are we leaving?" Clay asked, drawing attention away from them and the activities they'd been doing.

Prince Valerio stood gloomily to the side next to his guard, Uric. They both seemed particularly put-off today, and it seemed like shadows had perpetually settled over their heads.

"As soon as Weylyn deigns to grace us with his presence," the prince said.

Julius snorted. "As soon as he finishes sucking off—" Iona's elbow to his ribs stopped him from finishing that sentence.

He didn't even need to.

They'd all known what he meant.

Since they'd brought Corvina into the fold, there was something she'd realized about the inner workings of the Resistance. It was by observing, listening, and looking at things from an outside perspective.

It was the way Valerio stared at Shula that spoke of extreme pain. It lived on the expression and the panes and lines of his severe face. Much the same way Uric looked when he stared at the prince.

Corvina knew that Julius and Iona were a pair made from Mana, and their passion burned as hot as the Danarish sun.

She knew that Shula and Ryker were tentative, quiet lovers.

And she knew that nobody, not a single one of the Fae present, trusted Weylyn Xanth.

Which was a shame, she thought, because she found the mysterious, golden Fae rather lovely.

Even when nobody else did.

Farewell, Dana

"Report to me as you've been doing." The voice was cold and arrogant and dismissive.

A stupid combination for a stupid man, Weylyn figured. Those words lived on the tip of his tongue, and he bit down, tasting blood so as to not speak them aloud.

He found himself doing a lot of that lately.

Things had been easier when they all thought the King of Seelie was dead.

He hadn't needed to hold his tongue then.

"Of course, Your Majesty." The words tasted like a vile concoction on his lips. It only made his hatred burn deeper, his anger rise faster. For years, he'd been repeating the same words over and over again until they'd become an instinct.

Yes, Your Majesty.

No, Your Majesty.

Go fuck yourself, Your Majesty.

He wished he could say the words. He wished he did not have to hold back or hide what lived deep within him. But he'd been at it so long, what he wanted no longer mattered. He was in the king's service for a fucking reason.

One that was beginning to bore him to near-death.

"Keep an eye out on my fool of a son," the king added.

He lounged against a throne in a royal Danarish room made up of ivory and gold, upon plush velvet pillows, wearing a diamond-encrusted crown that did not belong to him, and ruling a kingdom that he himself had not conquered.

Overzealous fool, Weylyn thought. He was acting as though he'd been the one to fight against the slavers of Dana. As if he deserved the right to lounge upon that throne like he'd done anything worthwhile to warrant the robes and jewels adorning his body.

"He's been too wayward lately," the king carried on, oblivious to Weylyn's thoughts.

Probably on account of Weylyn's expression. Perfectly bored. Perfectly blank so it did not reflect on the thoughts he buried deep inside.

It made the king think he had no thoughts of his own. A fair assumption, considering Weylyn was already overrun with the piercing thoughts of others, but that did not mean he was blank inside.

It just meant there were secrets he collected deep within his own pockets.

Secrets he kept close to his chest because they would be so fun to exploit.

"Fool of a child," the king continued. "I'd slit his throat myself if I could."

Weylyn blinked. The animosity between the king and prince was no secret. Though usually, the king tended to keep his murderous thoughts in his own mind. He was too afraid to speak such words aloud out of fear that someone would overhear.

But Weylyn heard *everything*.

"Alas, the Fae seem taken with him, so I cannot."

A shame, really. Because wouldn't all of Weylyn's problems be solved if he let them kill one another off?

If only...

"You had better send me regular updates. It takes far too long to hear back from you. Let me know if you find the next Elemental and how susceptible they will be to join our cause. These women they keep finding..." He scoffed. "Weak specimens. All of them. Especially this new one. Her only value is that she was a Danarish whore and got us this kingdom."

Weylyn saw red flash across his vision at the casual degradation of Corvina. The king spoke heavy words, considering he was the one having to beg the Elementals for their help for his own gain.

If it were up to Weylyn, he'd be content to watch the fucking world burn with everyone in it.

But the king liked to shit where he ate, that was something Weylyn had learned about him early on. When he'd been younger, he'd seen it too. It had only gotten more visceral as the years let on.

And if the king was not careful with his words, he was sure to meet an untimely demise.

When Weylyn and the Seelie King finally joined them in the throne room, it was to impart last minute instructions as well as to add additions to their party.

Corvina watched closely while the king gave Valerio quietly whispered instructions, occasionally gesturing in the general direction of the Fae that would be joining them. The man was half-Unseelie half-High Fae. He had purple skin with a shock of white hair pulled back into a knot at the base of his neck.

He stood apart from the others, standing elegantly as he cast furtive glances in Weylyn's direction.

Meanwhile, Weylyn stared at *her.* The heavy press of his gaze against her sent a shiver down her spine. Though she confessed she liked him, his stare was uncanny and mysterious. Still, she felt a kinship between them, as he too was from the Gold Court and was the first to acknowledge her as a High Lady as if they *were* in court.

He hadn't known that it had been the small push she'd needed in moments when she felt she'd disappear. When things had felt too heavy days ago. When she felt like everyone was doomed to die because of her. Because Tobias would have stopped at nothing to get her back.

She'd underestimated how resilient the Resistance could actually be. How far they'd go to protect one of their own. And she'd felt humbled; for the first time in a long time she had felt a sense of family with these people. Like she could actually count on them to go the distance for her. Like she would now go the distance for *them.*

"You ready to go?" Clay interrupted her thoughts, giving her hand a tight squeeze.

She smiled at her mate, though her heart pounded up to her throat. For the majority of her life, she'd lived in the Gold Court and after that, Dana. She knew nothing of the outside world. Had never even stepped foot out of the kingdom.

Now, she was leaving.

There was something cathartic about that, but also frightening.

"As ready as I'll ever be," she replied breathlessly. What she didn't ask was what awaited them out there. She had a feeling even Clay didn't know, but she was sure that together they would find out.

"Time to go!" Prince Valerio called out. He'd pulled away from his father and was standing beneath the marble archways of the room. Sunlight blazed through the open space, shining down in dark contrasts against the prince. Uric stood beside him, the two bathed in shadows and sunlight, a dark gloom against the brightness.

On a silent command from the Prince, Uric spread his palms wide and a portal was created. It shimmered like the surface of a lake and reflected their own images like a mirror, distorted and blurry.

The prince turned. "Julius," he commanded. "You first."

Julius sauntered over to the portal, unsheathing his blade as he went. He took a deep breath and walked through, disappearing within its depths. Next went Iona, following after her mate. The prince gestured at Dawn, Wren, Gale, and Juniper. The four shared weary glances with each other and then Corvina. Though her own fear threatened to dominate her, she tried to appear confident, giving her ladies a nod of approval. After deep breaths, they walked through, disappearing to the other side.

Their party slowly began filing through the portal. Corvina noticed that the longer it was opened, the more Uric's fingers began to tremble. His skin, which had once been tight and beautiful, wrinkled like crumpled paper. His hair grayed, his eyes drooped, but he held strong. It was the price of his magic, no doubt.

When it was their turn to walk through, Corvina went to pick up Basil. She held him tightly in her arms, more for her comfort than his. Her son did not look scared, but rather excited at the prospect of an adventure. On her other side, Clay wrapped his arm around her waist. She wondered if he could feel her nerves down the bond.

Even without a bite to officially mark them as mates, she could still feel their connection and knew that he could too. His presence was reassuring as he guided her towards the portal. She stared at her distorted reflection and dared a glance backwards at the palace she'd once called home and prison in equal measure.

This would be the last time, she vowed. This would be the last time she ever stepped foot in Dana again. This was a place of the past, a place where she came to be tortured, brutalized, and raped.

It was also the place where she found her son and found her mate.

With a deep breath, she looked forward again.

"Ready?" Clay asked.

"As I'll ever be," she replied.

And together they stepped through the portal.

A Weapon is a Weapon

The sun was shining on the other side of the portal, and it remained that way for days. Curiosity had Corvina's head whipping from side to side throughout the journey. Their small party had landed in the kingdom of Ielwyn. They traveled by horse and carriage at a slow pace, though they spent most of the day walking and nights camping.

Nights were hardest for Corvina. She feared that every crack of a twig or breaking of a branch were humans coming to get them. To kill them. She hugged Basil close and tried not to flinch at the sounds. It was only Clay's presence that brought even a smidge of comfort to her aching soul.

She wasn't used to this. The walking. Despite having spent hours in the healing baths of Dana before they left, she knew she was at a disadvantage compared to the other Elementals. It wasn't only that her magic was a touch weaker due to spending most of her life in chains, but also that the abuse she'd suffered had left her hands disfigured, which made holding a sword difficult.

It could be done, of course. She'd done it before in her final confrontation with Tobias. She'd wielded it like she knew how to use it. Clay had tried previously to teach her. She recalled the feel of his body pressed tightly against her backside, the way his warmth and fizzling cider scent enveloped her senses. How his hands felt pressed against hers. A sensual dream, one she didn't want to wake up from.

That had been in the privacy of the darkness, though.

And even if Corvina had confronted her problems and they'd come out victorious, it was still a difficult task for her to volunteer during the afternoons in which they trained.

Shula and Iona moved together, fighting with swords and magic. There was an artistry in watching the way they moved. Shula moved like she was dancing, being chased by flames. Her whole body moved like fire, and her eyes glowed like vicious embers that would burn down kingdoms.

Iona moved like a force. Corvina had never seen a snowstorm in her life, but she imagined they were brutal. Cold. Calculated. Iona was *fierce*. And she showed no mercy. Even during training.

Corvina took a breath one evening, watching them work in tandem. She glared down at her crooked fingers. They didn't necessarily need to be straight for her to be able to use her magic, but she needed them to hold a weapon. She wondered if there were any she could accommodate to her grip.

It wasn't as though she wanted to fight, exactly. But it was what she'd agreed to the moment she'd decided to join the Resistance. To help them. To fight for a better world for herself and for her son. And to do that, she needed to know how to wield weapons in those moments her magic might fail.

"My lady..."

She startled, jumping slightly in her seat as Weylyn appeared next to her seemingly from nothing. He was silent, though she should have scented him from smell alone. It was sharp, a mixture of something spicy and sweet and penetrating.

He was regarding her with those glittering, golden eyes of his. His ringed fingers toyed with the ends of his long, black braid almost absently.

"Yes, Weylyn?"

His eyes sparked at her use of his name. Before she could question it, he held his hand out, palm upwards. "Would you care to train with me?"

It felt as though the camp had suddenly gone still to listen in on them. She wondered if this was surprising behavior for him and concluded that it was. In all the days she'd watched everyone train—the prince, the Elementals, and even her own companions Gale, Wren, Juniper, and Dawn—she'd never once seen Weylyn pick up a sword to fight.

He was always watching from the sidelines. A silent spectator who studied everyone's movements from afar. She wondered if he was calculating, memorizing the manner in which everyone fought so that he knew when the time came—and she wondered if it would—how to defeat them all.

And if he was offering to train with her, what did that mean? Was there an ulterior motive? No, she didn't think there was. Corvina didn't trust easily, but she didn't know why she trusted Weylyn of all people. Maybe because he was an outcast. She saw how the others whispered about him when he strode by, and it reminded her of when she'd been in court. The way the ladies snickered behind their fans and pointed at her like she was a spectacle to be ridiculed.

It drew her to him like a moth to the flame of a candle.

Slowly, she set her crooked fingers into his hand. "Yes."

Something zapped between the two and she inhaled. It wasn't the same sensation as when she touched Clay. It was brief, a soft demand. Like a push from Mana itself.

A soft smile touched Weylyn's mouth and they stood. As he led her towards the clearing, she threw a glance towards where Clay was. Sweat clung to his body from his own training session with Julius. His green eyes flashed a brief second on the spot where her and Weylyn's hands were joined. A moment later, he sent her a soft smile.

She hadn't realized the tension in her own shoulders had eased. After years of dealing with Tobias' jealousy and having to be careful with every move she made, it was comforting to see how Clay was different. If anything, he'd looked... *confused* instead of angry.

That brought her comfort.

Weylyn stopped in the middle of the clearing, dropping her hand. He went to grab a weapon. She thought he'd reach for one of the swords lined up near the cart. Instead, he reached for something smaller. When he approached her again, it was to press the hilt of a knife into her palm.

She stared at it then back up at him.

"Everyone else is training with swords," she whispered, feeling heat climb to her cheeks. A second of humiliation tried to overtake her. Curse her gnarled fingers. She couldn't even train like the others. It made her feel like a hindrance rather than a help.

Weylyn nodded, but didn't say anything.

Her brows pulled together. "Why a knife?"

"You know why."

Because she couldn't carry a sword.

She wanted to look away. The burning behind her eyelids was almost too much.

"A weapon is a weapon," Weylyn said simply. "It doesn't matter how big it is." He said the words like he believed them with his whole heart. "You could easily best me with a knife or a sword. This is for your own comfort and advantage."

When he put it like that, she wanted to believe him. So she nodded.

"A small weapon can be easily hidden," he said. "Sheathed beneath your skirts."

Her face flushed.

"An opponent will take one look and underestimate you," he continued. His voice was low, and she found herself straining to hear him. The others did as well, she noticed from her peripheral. "Surprise them in hand-to-hand combat, my lady. Now, attack me."

She blinked. "What?"

"Attack me."

She didn't know how she was supposed to do that. Taking a breath, she swung her arm in his direction. With a sigh, he lifted his forearm, effectively blocking her pathetic blow.

"Hit me with feeling, my lady."

"I don't know if I can."

His eyes sparked. "Pretend I'm him," he ordered, his voice lowering. It sent shivers along her arms. "Pretend I'm your bastard of a husband, come back from the dead. Pretend I'm him and you want to return every blow he ever gave you—"

Corvina swung with a cry. Her fear overpowered her for a second. She imagined Tobias really was alive and he was in front of her. For a second, she no longer saw Weylyn, but the man who had tortured and kept her captive for years.

All the rage she ever felt, the rage she thought she'd buried the past few days, came surging back up in a rush, like a tsunami crashing against a shore.

She attacked, a growl ripping from her throat that she barely recognized. She swung blindly and Weylyn dodged, all the while giving instructions. And somehow, through her haze of anger, she followed every single one.

She moved like she never thought she could move before. It was painful. It had her joints screaming, her scars throbbing, and her fingers crying. And yet she gave it her all. Weylyn parried back. He didn't hit hard enough to hurt. She thought he was being cautious on purpose. Then he tackled her, and she went crashing to the ground. Her head bounded on the grass and the wind was knocked out of her.

From above, Weylyn was barely breathing heavily, as though this hadn't been a workout at all.

"Now," he said. "When you find yourself in this position, you take the knife from beneath your skirts, and you stab the bastard in the gut."

The blade in her fingers repositioned, touching him on the side. "Like that?" she asked with wide eyes.

He smiled. "Exactly like that, my lady."

Clay watched the scene unfold with narrowed eyes. Never before had he seen Weylyn train. He didn't seem to be putting much effort into it with his movements and yet he looked completely fierce. His golden eyes flashed a violent color, and when he tackled Corvina, Clay's hands tightened into fists. He flinched, barely resisting the urge to rush for his mate, to gnash his canines, to pummel all his violent instincts into the Fae's face.

This was a strange moment and he wanted to watch it unfold.

"Are you going to intervene?" Julius asked from his side.

Clay slowly shook his head. He knew he should have been worried because of who Weylyn was and what he did. He liked to mess with their minds, slip into their most private thoughts, and annex their darkest secrets, only to whisper the words aloud and frighten them.

Clay should have worried he would do the same to Corvina. Yet as he watched, there was no menace coming from the other male. There was no mischief shining in his eyes. There was nothing that indicated that he wanted her to hurt. There was nothing but a sign of protectiveness.

And it was only because of that that Clay didn't intervene.

At first, seeing the way their hands clasped together made a flash of jealousy burn in his gut. It quickly dissipated and turned into confusion before he smiled at his mate. Though he'd only known her for a short while, he knew what type of person she was. Their bond was strong. She wouldn't look at another male even when or if other males looked at her. His jealousy was his own problem, and he wouldn't burden her with it. He wouldn't be like her dead husband.

So he would not interfere. It was her right, after all, to learn what the rest of them were learning. It was her right to learn to defend herself. It was her right to train and learn to survive in any way she knew how. And if protecting her meant he had to watch another male drop on top of her to train her fighting instincts, then so be it.

Clay would watch.

Besides, even if Weylyn had nefarious intentions with everyone else, he didn't feel like he had them with Corvina. She was different. He treated her differently. Clay wondered if it was because they were from the same court. Because she was his lady and he revered her for it. Whatever it was, he knew deep in his gut and instinct given to him from Mana that Weylyn wouldn't do anything to hurt Corvina.

That he knew for certain.

Drowning Fear in Drink

"Why is the trek taking so long?" Valerio's words were punctuated with his fingers hitting the map. His eyes glossed over the roads and forests and mountain ranges.

Julius watched the prince's frustration with his arms crossed against his chest. It was his duty to plot their way through the kingdom and ensure safe passage to Ojor, a small town in the northernmost part of Ielwyn. Valerio had realized they were taking the longer roads, and the prince was not happy.

"We need to avoid being seen," Julius countered. "We have a large party with us."

He could tell his prince was getting irritated. Not so much with him, but with his father. The king had likely demanded they hurry to find the next Elemental so that his plans of war could continue. He had taken that frustration out on Valerio, and Valerio in turn would take it out on the rest of them.

Julius already knew this song and dance because he'd lived it before.

Valerio's glare clashed his way. Julius ignored it, though a knot began forming in his throat. "It's because we are such a large party that we must make haste," the prince said coolly. "We do not want to dally in one place too long and risk being detected. There are women and a child traveling with us, and Uric cannot portal such a big amount so often without dire consequences. We need to take better pathways that aren't so strenuous."

Julius felt Iona's gaze on him, and he avoided staring back at his mate. Instead, he bent over the map, gathering the parchment into his hands. "I'll look it over," he told Valerio. "Find a better passage, send scouts ahead." He rolled the map up and saluted Valerio with it before he turned and left.

As soon as he was a few feet away from the tent, he heard his mate's footsteps following at his heels. He didn't speak. At least, not immediately. Not until they found a more secluded area where they wouldn't be overheard.

When he turned to face Iona, her hands were on her hips, white brows raised.

Julius sighed.

"What was that about?" she demanded quietly.

"What?" He feigned innocence, his lips twisting up into a smirk.

It didn't deter her. She stepped closer, placing her palm against his chest, right over the spot where his heart was beating erratically. And that alone was his tell.

Her eyebrow crested higher like she knew it too.

With a sigh, Julius raked a hand through his long hair. "You're busting my balls, woman."

She smirked, obviously way too satisfied with that comment. "Because they're mine and mine alone to bust. Now, tell me what's wrong."

He sighed. The thing about his magic, his strength, was that he was used to being the most powerful, the fiercest, in the room. He was used to battling and strategizing and making sure everything was perfect in the war they found themselves in. Julius took failure personally. He felt it reflected on him as a soldier, every defeat and every success.

Seeing the warring going on within his mind, Iona reached up and pushed aside a lock of hair. "Look..." She sighed. "I know we joined fast." Her fingers stayed, lingering near his neck where the mark of their bond was. "But I'm not fucking stupid."

His eyes widened, and he wanted to reel back. He didn't. He should have been used to her bluntness by now, but he found his mate still had the ability to take him by surprise.

"You wear a mask, Julius. You wear the mask of the drunken, jovial, care-free Fae. And while those may be parts of you, we both know they aren't the full story. You have more layers. There's a reason you drink yourself into oblivion and always have to have the brightest smile in the room. These are just facets of yourself, but there's more. I feel it. You can't fool me."

It was like she'd reached down his throat and rearranged his insides with her truths. He took a steadying breath, though he felt anything but. "You're right," he confessed.

He did enjoy a good drink, Fae wine in particular. It wasn't just because of the taste that sparked magic on the tongue. It was because it made him drowsy and flooded his mind with happy memories. So he didn't have to live with the horrors of battle that threatened to consume him.

He prided himself on not letting the past drown him like it did to other Fae, and if he needed the help of wine to do so, then even better. It left him levelheaded. It left him with a sense of self that was hard to describe.

But he had to now. He almost bit his tongue in an attempt to hold back the words, but relaxed his jawline. If there was one person who would never judge him, it was his mate.

"When I drink, I'm happy, and when I'm happy, I don't have to think about the heavy burdens that rest on my shoulders. I can just... be. I can be... confident."

For someone who prided himself on his honesty, he found it difficult to get the words out.

Iona didn't pressure him to keep going. Her hands were there, though. Steady and warm, despite the Elemental magic of ice she wielded, and keeping him grounded. They cupped his cheeks, forcing him to stare into her dark eyes.

"When I drink, it hides the fact that I'm scared."

There it was. His most integral truth, and his greatest shame. He, the strongest of the group, a soldier with the most experience, the protector, the one who planned the battles and trained recruits, was fucking afraid.

Iona's eyes softened. "There is no shame in fear."

He knew that.

"I can't let it overrule me," he whispered. "If the fear wins, people will die."

"Is that why you've been lagging on the journey?"

His face flushed. Her hands cupped his embarrassment, but didn't shame him for it. "We have a vulnerable group of people. Dana was a win for us, but things can only get more difficult from here. We're at active war. I watched soldiers and weak Fae die on the streets of Dana, and for a moment I thought that could be us." His breath stuttered, but he pushed forward. "That could be *you.*"

"Julius..."

"I've always fought for a cause, Iona. Always. I've fought for my people. I've watched friends, comrades, and enemies die. It has always been a part of war and battle, and so I shoved it aside. But when I think that it could be you?" His voice broke and he dropped his forehead to hers, breathing her in. Her scent of ice and apples. He relished in it. They mingled with his own and he wanted to sink himself deep inside her and never leave. To bury himself inside her warmth and stay with her forever. "You make me weak, Iona. You make me fucking weak. With you, everything I've pushed away resurfaces, and I can't lose you. Do you hear me? I fucking can't."

He gripped her hips, pressing his erection against her center, grinding against her in his desperate, frantic energy. He needed her to know. Maybe his words weren't the most eloquent, but he could show her with his body instead. Let her use him. Let him become hers to manipulate, he didn't fucking care.

"You aren't going to lose me." She gripped him by the chin, forcing his gaze to her. Their breaths mingled, harsh and erratic. "And I'm not going to lose you. We aren't going to lose anyone in this group, do you hear?"

They couldn't know that, he wanted to say. But she read it from his expression.

"We are stronger together," she whispered. "And together we will rise."

"Iona." He pushed her away by the hips, letting her see the rawness in his gaze. "What if we aren't?"

Her eyes flared and he felt the prickling bite of ice against his flesh as her magic surfaced between them. "Listen to me, Julius Dara, and listen well. I know your heart. I know you, and if there's one thing I know, it's that you care. Even when your strength wanes, you are fucking determined. And I know with absolute certainty, that if there ever comes a time when you aren't strong enough, you'll fucking find a way to save us. To save *me.* And if you are the one who ever needs saving, you know I can carry that burden too. And I fucking will. Because you're my mate, and I love you, and together, we will fucking *rise.*"

And then Iona yanked him down and closed her mouth over his, silencing any protests he might have come up with. But they were far away, and all he could focus on was her and her taste as her tongue pillaged his. He was engulfed by her essence. By her words. By Iona as a whole. He groaned in the back of his throat, dropping the map to the ground and pulling her to him, lifting her by the hips. Her legs wrapped around his waist, and he whirled, pinning her to the nearest tree.

She moaned as he pressed his dick against her core. He wanted her with a fierce ache that he felt low in his belly. He wanted her like he'd never wanted anything else in the fucking world.

"You're right," he breathed against her soft, ebony skin. "I'll protect you," he vowed.

"I know." She clawed at his scalp.

"I'll protect us."

"I know you will."

He wasn't alone. He didn't always have to carry the burdens on his shoulder. His mate was more than capable of helping, and besides, she was right. If the time ever came and his strength ever faltered, he'd never let that get in the way of his purpose. His mission.

His duty.

Silent Threat

"Basil, do be careful!" Corvina called out. Her son was running ahead of the group, kicking up dust and leaves, his laughter echoing through the air.

Gale chased after him, yanking her skirt up to her calves to avoid tripping. She was followed quickly by Clay, who sent Corvina a wink as he went by. The sight of her mate following and protecting her son warmed her inside and eased an ache she wasn't aware had started to build.

"If anyone can protect the little lord, it is Clay." Beside her, Weylyn uttered the words with a confidence that surprised her. She rarely heard Weylyn speak, much less to praise others. Despite his animosity towards the others, she didn't doubt that he respected Clay.

She didn't know why that made her happy.

"I know." She smiled.

"It goes without saying," he continued, "that if the blood letter does not treat you well, I will rip his innards from his mouth."

She blinked at the violence of his statement, surprised at it, and if she was honest, slightly perturbed. She wondered though why the threat didn't make her nervous. Had he been Tobias, or his brother, or King Wes, a chill would have slid down her spine at the words that were all but a promise she knew he meant to keep.

But there was a confidence in her chest that hadn't lived there before, and she knew that Clay would never hurt her.

"I suppose I should thank you for the sentiment?" She tilted her head to the side. They'd been walking side-by-side in companionable silence for quite some time now.

"Thank me for nothing," he said quickly. "I've done nothing to warrant it."

Her palms smoothed out the front of her traveling dress. "On the contrary, you've been very kind to me."

He scoffed. "If there's one thing I am not, it is *kind*." He all but sneered the word.

"I did not mean to offend you."

"You did not."

She felt as though she had and cringed internally. She was not very good at socializing with the others. Years of being forced to keep her feelings and opinions to herself had damaged her, and she was unsure what words were appropriate to say to others.

But Weylyn was... different from the others. And she'd already vowed to herself that she would *try* to find herself, her voice.

"If you don't mind, may I ask a question?"

He nodded his assent.

"Where were you?" she asked. "When the courts fell?"

His golden eyes flashed, and for a second, she wanted to recoil away from the rising force of his rage. It was almost palpable, suffocating, like a darkness given form. She knew it had been a personal question, though she hadn't expected such a vehement reaction.

"Awaiting my moment," he replied darkly.

Before she could ask what moment he was referring to, his eyes flickered. His footsteps faltered. It was a brief second of immobility, the price of using his mind-reading magic. A moment later, it was gone.

"Excuse me, my lady," he said and pushed past her. He walked like a predator, slow and prowling. As he passed by the others, they recoiled from his presence like he was something venomous they should not touch. She wondered what it made her, willing to be in his presence for such a long period of time.

While others averted their gazes, as if that could stop him from reading their minds and exposing their secrets, Corvina watched him. And because she was watching so intently, she saw when he passed a tall, purple-skinned half-Unseelie Fae with white hair and shared what seemed like a conspiratorial glance.

It was gone as soon as it came.

And just as easily pushed from her mind like it hadn't really been there at all.

A bed of bones spread out across the landscape. The rotted corpses were hidden deep in the earth, ivory only occasionally peeking out from between foliage. But Valerio could smell it. The land was quiet, the sky darkening as though it would rain, or as if Mana was sending them an omen.

The further they traveled the more unease slid down the Seelie Prince's spine. He could not quite place what it was. The dead bodies casually buried through the ground, their stench wafting up his nose? Or could it have been because the familiars in their presence had become even more agitated the longer they walked?

Ryker's cat hissed from her perch on Weylyn's shoulder, the hairs on her body standing in menace. Iona's bear pawed at the ground, growling and whining as his eyes darted around. Looking for a threat? Sensing one close by?

When they reached a clearing near a collection of trees, yet still out in the open, Valerio lifted his hands, demanding everyone come to a stop. His eyes scanned the tree line, smelling, staring, though he found nothing. Still, it was as good a place as any to camp.

They'd need open space to keep an eye out for any intruders and the trees to hide in case soldiers came upon them.

"We will make camp here," Valerio said.

They stared at him in question, likely wondering why they were making camp if it was still daylight,but he avoided every gaze. Valerio wanted the danger to pass. They were already deep in the kingdom of Ielwyn and he needed to speak with Shula, Iona, and Corvina.

They were unpacking their things, setting up rolls of blankets. He gestured at them, and the three Elementals made their way towards him.

"Do you sense them?" he asked.

They shared a glance between them, and for a moment he envied that connection. Envied the fact that they could sense what he could not.

"I can," Shula said. "It's like..." She paused, as if searching for the right word.

"Lightning beneath the skin," Corvina supplied.

Iona nodded in agreement. "Our magic reacts when we're close to each other. Like it wants to force its way out of our bodies." She cracked her neck. "Makes me restless."

"Then we will wait here," Valerio decided. "And we will venture out to find them tomorrow."

Corvina's eyes strayed to the forest. "I feel them there," she whispered. "Somewhere. I can't pinpoint where exactly."

Valerio nodded at the blond woman. That was all he needed to know. She was somewhere inside the forest of Ojor, which meant they were closer to their goal.

His father's goal.

After he dismissed the three Elementals, he walked to the edge of the forest, staring within. Uric's presence appeared next to him, silent and protective as usual.

"What are you thinking?" his friend asked, though he didn't need to. He knew Valerio all too well.

"They're out there," he said.

Uric nodded, the edges of his white hair grazing his cheeks. "We are being watched."

"Keep your magic at the ready," Valerio replied, glaring into the forest, as if he could see the unseen enemy that was watching from a distance. "We may have need of it."

When those watching decided not to watch anymore. When those watching decided they were sick of lying in silence.

When those watching inevitably attacked.

Net of Ashwood & Iron

The night was restless and the forest too silent. The scent of death lingered in the air, and it put everybody on edge. Clay was sure nobody slept last night, waiting with bated breaths as the darkness made way to morning. Something was out there; far away, but out there.

Whether or not that thing was a threat remained to be seen.

He wondered if it was the Elemental. Corvina, Iona, and Shula said they'd sensed them somewhere in the trees. Far away, but still close enough to have their magic fritzing beneath their skin. He'd caught Corvina scraping her nails across her skin throughout the night. Even though he'd placed his hands over her anxious fingers, he didn't think he'd helped to ease her turmoil.

There were dark shadows beneath her lids that morning, and a wariness that the three Elementals shared. They were primed for... something.

"Mommy, I have to relieve myself."

Basil's soft voice cut through Clay's thoughts. Basil was pressing his thighs together, holding himself as he hopped from foot to foot.

Corvina sighed, though smiled at her son. "We can go over by the cart—"

"No!" he protested immediately. "Everyone will see." He lowered his voice to a whisper. "*Shula* will see."

Clay smothered his laugh with a cough. Basil had fallen in love with Shula. He wouldn't be the only one. Between Ryker and Valerio staring at her like no one else noticed... The Fire Dancer had magic in her veins that wasn't just the element she wielded.

"Basil, there's nowhere else to go."

Basil's eyes widened and filled with an influx of tears. Before he could start wailing, Clay stood from where he perched. "I'll take him."

Corvina stared at him gratefully, but it was followed by the worried biting of her bottom lip. He itched to smooth it out with his thumb and press a kiss to her mouth. He understood she would be worried, filled with apprehension. They were in the middle of nowhere, a place she didn't recognize, and the wounds of her past would be too hard to heal overnight.

His heart ached for his mate and all she'd endured. Always living in fear of those around her, her friends, her son, and her own life. He wanted to reassure her that things would be different now, but he held back. He knew he couldn't promise complete safety. Not with the lives they led. Not when they were in the middle of a war.

But he would protect Basil. He would never threaten to harm him, and she had to know that.

"I'll protect him with my life," Clay promised, bending so he pressed a gentle kiss over her forehead.

She sighed, melting into the touch before pulling away. "You'll be careful?"

He flashed her a smile. "Always."

She relaxed in her seat while Basil took Clay's hand. Sometimes he marveled at the ease with which Basil had taken to him. It would be a lie to say that Clay felt like a father-figure to him. He didn't feel that yet, but he cared for the boy as much as he cared for Corvina because he was a part of her. He didn't think Basil would ever forget his real father, though the child hadn't shed any tears over his passing. Clay wondered if he just hadn't been given time to mourn. And if he did, when would it be?

Before he took Basil into the privacy of the trees, he nodded in Valerio's direction, letting him know with a glance that he would be back in a few moments.

"Come on!" Basil urged. He pulled Clay deeper into the trees, and Clay kept a firm grasp on him, eyes alert to everything around him.

He found it odd how quiet it was, like the forest lacked all breath, and he briefly wondered if it was cursed. The thought flew away when Basil ripped his hand from his grip and *ran.*

Clay let out a curse. "Basil," he hissed. But the kid was jetting into the woods, laughter echoing behind him. "Fuck." Clay went in pursuit. He was fast for his age, but he caught up just as he stopped at the edge of a rushing stream. Almost immediately, he yanked his pants down and began to relieve himself in the water.

Clay approached when he finished, putting a hand on his shoulder.

"Don't run off like that on your own, Basil," he chided softly. Corvina would have had his neck if she'd witnessed it.

Basil turned his face up to him. Bright round eyes stared at him, a tousle of dark curls ruffling in the wind. There was no trace of his father in him. He looked like Corvina, with his petite, upturned nose and overall innocence.

"Sorry," he apologized.

Clay smiled. "That's alright. Now, wash your hands and let's get back." They didn't need to stay in the forest longer than necessary.

Once Basil was done, he gripped Clay's hand tightly and they started back to the camp. Unfortunately, they'd only made it a few feet before the forest came alive with noise again. He'd been listening, and yet it still came as a surprise when a net fell over both of them, making them trip and fall to the ground.

Basil cried out, his body automatically racking in sobs and pain. Clay coughed, struggling to breathe. Because the net? It was covered in ashwood and iron.

He wanted to cry out, but he bit his tongue and tasted the coppery tang of blood. A moment later, booted feet crept into his vision. He glared, following the length up legs clad in tattered, dirty pants, and to the face of a human man. Bearded and ugly, he spat on the ground in front of Clay.

"My, my, my," he said in a gravelly voice. "What have we here?"

And all Clay could think in that moment was, *Oh shit.*

Born in Shadow

Uric stared at the cluster of trees, squinting through the foliage as if he could see through the shadows. Years of training kept him focused. He wanted to slip into the darkness much like Weylyn had earlier. To go out into the woods and investigate. He'd been trained for that, after all. But that had been years ago when his only duty had been to garner secrets and threats for a court he despised.

His duty now was to protect Prince Valerio.

From the threat he knew was out there.

"There's something out there," he whispered to his friend.

It seemed even Valerio couldn't take his gaze off the silence of the wood either. Uric kept close to his prince in the likely event that he'd need to grab him and make haste within a portal. He'd done it once and been chagrined for it, but he would do it again if he had to.

Sometimes, the prince didn't know what was good for him and had no sense of self-preservation. It was up to Uric to protect him from others and, more importantly, from himself.

Whether he wanted that or not.

That was Uric's duty, just like it had always been.

"I know," Valerio replied.

Behind them, Iona's familiar was restless. He'd been growing more agitated by the hour, pawing at the ground and huffing. It didn't matter how much the ice Elemental tried soothing the creature, he continued to huff his agitation.

Goosebumps rose along Uric's flesh, and he let out a slow breath.

"We should leave," he suggested.

Prince Valerio grunted. "The Elemental is somewhere in there."

Uric wanted to growl in frustration. "It won't matter if we're dead."

Valerio cut a glare his way. It was disapproving, and his lip curled with disgust. It made a part of Uric want to recoil. They were friends. They had been for years. But things between them were constantly shifting, the lines always blurring, and not in ways Uric particularly cared for or understood.

His friend was growing more irritable with him as the days went by. The methods Uric took to protect him for years were suddenly not enough. They made Uric seem like a fucking *villain.* But if that's who he had to be, then so fucking be it.

"My prince—"

Iona's bear roared. The bushes exploded. Bodies emerged. Shouts ensued.

Uric reacted on instinct, pulling a black dagger into his hand—the only gift he had left from home—and brandishing it, shoving Valerio behind him as people jumped from the trees. They cried out like animals, their calls savage, and the masks adorning their faces even more so.

They were made of wood and clay and feathers, painted into twisted, grotesque forms. They were meant to be fearful, Uric was sure of it. But scum hiding in the shadows did not intimidate him.

He was Uric Adriel Nova, son of the High Lord of the Obsidian Court, and he did not fear what came from the shadows because he was born in their depths and had seen the nightmares they held tenfold.

And if he had to use the darkness to kill those that threatened his prince, well, he would not hesitate.

Air. Blood. Death.

Clay agonized as his body was tugged within the net. Ashwood and iron pressed against his skin, burning the surface. He was more worried for Basil. His tears were muffled against Clay's shirtfront, though being half-human, the ashwood didn't burn his skin as much as it did Clay's.

"Sh." Clay kept a hand pressed to his back, pulling him closer to his body, as though he could shield him from the poisonous webbing that seeped into their skin. "I've got you." He murmured the words low in Basil's ear, low enough that the human grunting as he dragged them across the ground couldn't hear.

They were being treated like animals, and the man cursed the whole way at their heavy, combined weight.

Weak ass bastard.

Clay tried to get in touch with his magic, but the ashwood choked through his throat the harder he breathed it in. He could get past it, he was sure, but he didn't want to do that while they were still trapped, or else they'd have a difficult time getting out. Sure, maybe the others would venture out to find them eventually, but he knew that if he didn't protect Basil himself, Corvina would lose faith in him and would never trust him again.

And then there was Basil. He looked at Clay like he was some sort of fucking hero—not to the same extent as he did Shula and Ryker—but it still hit him in the gut just the same. If he wasn't able to protect him from this...

They *would* get out of this.

Because Clay refused to let this boy go through anything else. He deserved better than tears staining his eyes and ashwood pressing against his skin.

Clay vowed he would make them all bleed.

Every last fucking one of them.

"Stay brave, Basil," Clay whispered, the words quieting the boy's distress. "I will protect you."

He wasn't sure how long they were dragged along the forest floor or how far away they went. The ashwood clouded his senses the more he breathed it into his lungs. He coughed and tasted the tinny flavor of blood on the back of his tongue.

Fuck.

How much had they laced the net with? Usually he could withstand it enough to tap into his magic, at least a bit, but the direct contact, the inhalation of it into his lungs? It rendered him weak.

After a while, they stopped. It was then that Clay sensed the presence of other people. His eyes darted around the floor, seeing past dirt, grass, and dry leaves to even more feet spread across a field.

"Leave the beast alone," a second voice spat. "Looks like Rupp brought us something far more exciting."

The legs closed in on them. Clay twisted his body to look up at the humans. They all smelled atrocious, reeking of sweat, piss, and sour wine. They were an unimpressive bunch, and he'd have them all dead within moments as soon he was free of his confines.

"What have you got there?" a gravelly voice asked.

"Found them by the stream," their captor said.

Another man closed in, bending so he was looking directly at Clay. His drooping eyes widened as much as they possibly could. "A Fae and his half-breed."

Clay's anger spiked, but he kept his voice calm. "Now, gentleman... let's be civil."

This only caused their raucous laughter. "You hear that?" the one in front of him cried. "A civil Fae! That's like saying an animal has manners and thoughts!"

He didn't like the direction this was going. He wondered if they'd be stupid enough to remove the net from their bodies. If they weren't, then he'd have no other choice but to end them, using as much magic as he could possibly muster. It would hurt, but he could do it.

Was it wrong of him to want to give them all a chance, though?

"Look, you guys really don't want to do this."

They ignored him, laughing at Basil's whimpers. "How much do you reckon they'll take them for?"

Clay's entire body tensed, and he tamped down the growl that rose in his throat.

These men were slavers. *Kurreen.*

He thought they'd blown up along with the whole fucking West Isles when Shula and Iona unleashed their magic upon them.

The man bending down was leering at Clay. "For a Fae, he's got a pretty face. They'll want him for the brothels in Vellm. As for the brat, he'll fetch a pretty penny for a slave..."

Oh, fuck no.

Clay was about to unleash the force of whatever magic he still garnered inside despite the net, but there was a whistling in the air. The sound of something striking flesh.

"What the f—"

Chaos ensued. Clay twisted as much as he could, covering his body over Basil's to protect him. Arrows flew from the trees, and he watched with wide eyes as a body dropped from above. A gust of wind blew through the field, knocking the human men on their asses.

Clay's breath caught.

Is that...?

He didn't finish his thought before the wind picked up. The scent of magic cackled through the air. Somewhere, a hawk screeched. Magic was potent, and the wind swirled and swirled, lifting a gust of dirt around him and Basil.

Bodies grunted and fought, and death became imminent.

He heard knees hit the ground. A voice crying, begging, "Please! Mercy!"

But there was no reply before the man choked on his own blood.

And then there was silence.

The wind died down immediately, the dust clearing. Clay blinked dirt from his lashes, staring at a set of boots that stomped over to where he and Basil lay. He tensed, keeping his waning magic at the ready.

"Are you two alright?"

He looked up, finally placing a face to the whispered voice, and what he saw had him jolting.

A Fae woman stood before him. She leaned back on her heels, wielding a bow and arrow. The woman's bright orange hair flittered with the wind, the curls pushing away from her scarred, freckled face and brown eyes, discolored with white as if she were scarred there as well. It made for an eerie stare. It was almost deliberate, the way the wind moved. Like it wasn't exactly a force of nature, but emanating from *her.*

The scent of mist and rain, of a crisp, warm summer breeze encompassed her, permeating, relaxing. Like a touch of coolness against fevered skin on a hot day.

"We're fine," he answered, staring at her curiously. "Wait. You're—"

"Vision impaired?" She tilted her head to the side, her lips turning up into a smile. The action made the jagged scars surrounding her eyes and the tops of her cheeks seem even more stark. "I know."

"No, that's not what I meant."

"Really? That's usually what everyone means. Then again, I guess you wouldn't know that since you don't know *me.* It's not very obvious."

She stepped closer, skipping around the dead bodies on the ground. Basil sniffled and her attention cut to him.

"My name is Bryson Varik," she offered with a smile. "Let's get this net off you, yeah?"

Her arrows shot out, cutting at the net that kept them captive. A moment later, a gust of wind pushed it away and she stepped back quickly. Clay tossed the net aside, feeling instant relief as he pulled himself and Basil to a stand, stepping away from the contraption.

His body itched everywhere, yet he avoided clawing his nails down his skin.

Basil sniffled and righted himself before looking up at the woman. "I'm Thorne Basil Rhian."

Clay put a hand on his shoulder, offering comfort. It seemed to relax Basil, as he leaned into him, wrapping his arms around his thigh.

"Nice to meet you," the woman—Bryson—replied, smiling at Basil. It was disarming, how pretty she was. Just like it was disarming to see the white linked through the brown in her eyes. "Are you hurt?"

"N-no."

"Good."

"My name is Clay Valentino."

Bryson smirked and the wind ruffled again, and it only confirmed what Clay had been thinking—feeling—this entire time.

She was the one they'd been looking for.

"You're an Elemental, aren't you?"

Bryson's body tilted in his direction, and her smile was wide as she replied, "I am."

Embers, ice, water, & air

The words echoed in Bryson's mind.

Elementals.

The Resistance.

Her heart beat a crazy tempo in her chest, pounding against her ribcage. She wiped her clammy hands along the sides of her pants, and her fingers trembled. Elementals. The Resistance. Elementals. The Resistance. The words echoed like a drum in her head.

There was a charge in the air electrifying her skin. Her magic responded, pushing to the surface, trying to reach out to them.

She let it.

A gust of wind enveloped the three females in front of her, and the magic was met with more. With the smell of embers, ice, and water. The elements clashed gently together, playing like long lost friends. Until it was potent in the air.

She reeled her magic back in, a gasp pressing against her lips.

"You..." She started forward, wanting to touch them, to feel them, to memorize their every feature. She wanted to memorize the contours of their body, if only to know what the other Elementals felt like, what they looked like. Never in all her life had she thought she'd meet one Elemental, let alone three.

But a strong hand on her arm yanked her back, away from the comfort of something familiar and unknown. "Bryson," Ev hissed. "Don't."

She wanted to shrug off his hold, but she caught herself at the last moment, the other words in her mind registering.

The Resistance.

And she knew how Ev felt about the Resistance.

Her steps stumbled. *The Resistance.*

They were fucking *here.*

Was the Seelie King among the haze of faces? She had questions, wanted answers, needed them like she needed to breathe. After so long of feeling like she was underwater, it was like she'd finally come up for a gasp of air. Like she'd been floating through life, unsure of everything. And a gust of wind had blown the water away and she could see clearly.

She yanked her arm back, but Ev didn't relent. His grip tightened, and if she'd been human, she was sure he would have left a bruise with his grip.

"I don't give a fuck who you think you are," Ev snapped at them. "We don't—"

His words were suddenly cut off, his grip slipping from hers. She jolted, feeling the whoosh of air and scented another presence drop from the sky and land on Ev's back.

Ev grunted, and she stepped away on instinct. They crashed to the ground, their bodies tangling together in the scuffle. Ev cried out, groaning. The blurry figure thrashed, and there was the sound of flesh hitting flesh, the smell of Ev's blood and a spat curse. And beneath that, a sharp scent that speared through her nostrils and pierced down to her soul.

She shivered, gasping.

Then a voice cut through the fight.

"Weylyn," it snapped. "Enough!"

Immediately, the fighting ceased. The person hopped up and stepped back a few paces. He was near-silent on his feet, casually placing himself in front of the line with the Resistance as if this new person hadn't just knocked Ev on his ass.

She should have helped Ev up, but he managed on his own, grunting and cursing. And she was too focused on that new, casual, imposing presence.

Weylyn, someone had called him.

Her blood suddenly pounded in her veins. Her magic reacted within her. And Mana, it felt like something came *alive* beneath her skin. Her body leaned towards the newcomer, enchanted by his scent. It was sharp and brutal, one she was sure would make others dizzy, but it was like a beacon to her. It wrapped around her, something sweet and spicy in equal measure. Like cacao and peppers. It was piercing. Demanding. *Violent.* And she found herself enraptured in it.

Her feet moved of their own accord, stepping closer to him. Talking seemed to cease around her. The man in front of her stood still. Only the long, black braid swayed over his shoulder like a force of its own. His skin was covered in glittering gold, the kind of gold that seemed to mirror the shining in his eyes, sparking against the sunlight.

She was amazed she could even make it out, when she was inattentive to every other detail.

There was a sudden flash in her mind. Like a vision planted within the seeds of her brain. It was so surprising, she almost staggered backwards.

The image was of her. And by Mana, it was like she could see *clearly* again. Not just through a blur. She could see herself, wind-rustled curls wild down her shoulders, discolored eyes wide, pert mouth dropped open in surprise.

Then the vision changed, and she saw something else. A flash of the people before her. Specifically, the one who smelled of cacao and peppers. It was a brief flash. Of golden-brown skin and long black hair, of a dark mustache and beard around a seductive, smiling mouth, and eyes rolled to the back of his head.

And, by Mana, it felt like he was inside of her. As though the cosmos were dancing behind her eyelids. A gust of energy filled her body as she stepped closer and closer still to the man. And when she came to the edge of him, her hand lifted.

She heard a voice call for her from behind, Ev's she was sure, but she didn't care. Not when she was completely hypnotized, her body pushing her to touch. To feel.

And when her palm met a hard, warm chest, energy shot through her arm, making her groan and shiver as something within her body *snapped.* It felt like a lock clicking into place. Like something that had been absent from her soul found its missing piece and suddenly, she was *whole.* She was *filled.*

And for a second, she had no idea what it was. No idea until a deep, seductive voice purred through her mind.

"Hello," it whispered. *"My mate."*

To Claim a Mate

The bond slammed through his soul like a heavy blanket crashing against his senses. It clicked into place, settling where it belonged. He did not stagger backwards. He did not feel shocked, but awed and pleased and curious as the bond invaded his senses.

She stood before him, and he used his magic to push images into her mind. Of herself. Of him. And when her hand collided against his body, he shivered, a primal possessive instinct rearing its head, demanding he take. Claim. *Fuck.*

Down their sudden link, he heard her confusion. This woman. Tall, with unruly curls ratted from the wind and freckles that dotted across her face like constellations in an Unseellie Court. He had the urge to lick every fucking one of them, to explore how far down they went into her body.

To take.

To take what was rightfully his. To kiss the scars that trailed along her eyes, forehead, and cheeks. They resembled the cracks in glass, and yet she didn't appear fragile or on the verge of breaking.

Behind her, the man he'd tackled to the ground called her name.

Bryson Varik.

Air Elemental.

His fucking *mate.*

But she ignored the human.

Good girl, he wanted to praise.

Instead, he dove into her mind with greedy fingers. She gasped, like she could feel him inside her. *Soon,* he wanted to promise. Soon he would be. He could feel her questioning mind working at a rapid pace. She had no idea what was happening.

He would make sure she did.

He would make sure she fucking *knew* who he was.

And Weylyn Xanth smiled a cruel smile. *"Hello,"* he whispered within the confines of her mind. *"My mate."*

A Life Debt

A throat cleared, breaking Bryson from the fog she found herself in. She realized what she was doing, touching a complete stranger, violating his personal space, all because her instincts told her to.

Mana, what the *fuck* was she doing?

She gasped, yanking her hand away from his smooth chest. From the man she'd envisioned within her mind: a tall, lithe Fae man with golden-brown skin, long black hair, and a smile that reminded her of malicious intent.

She jerked backwards, nearly tripping on her feet. The impact of the words whispering in her mind were a shock of ice-cold water dripping down her back. The voice had been real. Like when her familiar spoke to her, though with a slight echo.

"What's going on?" Ev demanded, yanking her by the hood of her cloak, forcing her back to reality. Though she still didn't feel grounded, even as Ev threw his arm around her shoulders, pulling her to his side. She could hear his heavy breathing, and the gesture itself was... odd.

Her mind was still reeling at all the information that had been dropped like the bomb that exploded against her eyes so many years ago.

And in her mind, she heard a malicious chuckle. *"Possessive, isn't he?"* the voice asked.

And she knew, *knew*, it was the man in front of her.

Ev's palm pressed to her shoulder, sliding down her arm. He huffed a breath of annoyance as he pulled her closer, like he meant to draw her within his body.

That chuckle resounded in her mind once again. *"He can touch you all he wants,"* it whispered in a low timbre. Seductive. Dangerous. *"While it lasts..."* There was a pause as a shiver slid down her spine. It felt like he was speaking directly into her ear, whispering and caressing hands down her body. Yet he stood immobile in front of her. There was something intimate about the interaction, about having someone in her head. *"In the end, it'll be my arms around you and my lips pressed between your thighs."*

It sounded like a promise.

A promise that made her knees shake and her voice tremble. "Who are you?" she demanded, unaware that she'd said the words aloud.

But the voice that answered echoed through her mind. *"The man you practically fondled in front of everyone."*

Her head whipped back at the audacious words. What the fuck? She forced her attention away from him, turning her head to the others instead. They'd witnessed the entire interaction, and she could feel their discomfort in the air.

Someone coughed. "Forgive us," the deep voice said. The one belonging to the man with the pale skin, dark black hair, and what she could only assume were severe features based on the thick pull of his brows. "We have gotten off on the wrong foot. I am Prince Valerio Ashera of Seelie, and this is my court."

"I'm Bryson Varik, and this—"

"*Prince*?" Ev mocked, interrupting and pulling her tighter against his body. "Yes, we've heard of you."

"Have you?" the prince said, a hint of amusement in his voice.

"That's not a good thing."

Silence ensued Ev's words. She held her breath, wondering how this would play out. Anxiety thrummed beneath her skin. Ev was being rude to the Seelie Prince and all she wanted to do was bow. But bowing before someone that Ev and Arlo perceived as an enemy would put her on the wrong side of their ire.

Ev made a noise of annoyance. "Kill them all," he ordered.

Bryson jolted in his hold. Swords and arrows were drawn, and Bryson yanked herself away from Ev's body, standing in between the two groups once again. "You can't!" she shouted.

"And why not?" Ev was speaking to her as a leader and not as her boyfriend. She hated when he did that. When he treated her like the rest. She knew he did it so no one would accuse him of playing favorites, but he never showed her any ease, and sometimes treated her like he would punish her, only to hours later seek solace between her thighs.

A chuckle sounded in her mind, sending a shiver down her back. She shook off the feeling.

"Because Clay Valentino saved my life," she lied.

He hadn't. She'd saved his, but Everette didn't need to know that. No one needed to know the truth.

"Oh, but I *know the truth..."*

"Get out of my fucking head," she growled in her mind.

She felt the phantom touch of fingers slide over her neck like a vow and a threat at once.

"Bryson—"

"I owe him a life debt," she pushed on, not giving Everett a chance to speak. It was the only way he would let them live; she was sure of it. He may have hated the Resistance, but she knew he and Arlo venerated life debts. And even if they were a part of something the community didn't believe in, he had to give them a chance to prove themselves to them.

And if there were Elementals in their midst, then Arlo would want to exploit their magic even more, and that assured they would live.

Perhaps it was selfish, lying to bring them into their fold, but it was the only way Bryson could think to protect them all.

She could sense Everett lost in thought. Finally, he begrudged, "*Fine.*" His voice was tight. "But we take them straight to Arlo. Let him decide."

Bryson felt her whole body relax, though it tensed all over again when Ev grabbed her wrist and yanked her towards him. The press of his lips against the shell of her ear made her tense, and the words he promised made a cold sweat break out over her body.

"Arlo will make you pay for this insolence, Bryson." He pulled away, though she could make out every harsh breath press against her chest. "And I won't be able to fucking protect you from it."

She frowned. "I didn't ask for your protection."

Ev made a scoffing sound of disgust. "Remember that when you ask me to confide in you next time."

Her face heated with a blush as he turned away from her. "Let's go. I'll take you to our camp."

"What was that all about?" Ev hissed under his breath.

They led the group towards their camp. They were close, but their steps had slowed. The Resistance kept pace behind them, giving them a bit of distance, or at least the illusion of privacy.

Throughout the whole trek, Ev had steamed quietly, giving Bryson the silent treatment. He'd only just spoken, cutting through the silence with blade-like words. They made Bryson turn her face in his direction, though he didn't stop. He didn't even look in her direction.

"What do you mean?" she asked.

"Don't play coy," he snapped.

She flinched at his harsh tone, guilt a painful twinge against her chest. He had every right to be irritated with her. She knew what he meant. She'd forgotten herself, had touched another man in front of him. It hadn't been in any way except instinct and curiosity, but she imagined what it had looked like from an outside perspective.

From her *boyfriend's* perspective.

"What was—whatever that was—with that *guy*." He sneered the word like it was some type of venereal disease. His jealousy bled through his words, so obvious, so open.

It made her heart skip a beat suddenly as the man's words blew through her mind. She'd tried to ignore them, but they pressed against her from every angle, penetrating her defenses like an all-consuming magic she couldn't shake.

As it was, his presence felt close. His scent choked her nostrils, something spicy and sweet clashing against her. She couldn't even see the man and she could picture him smiling at her backside. For a brief second, his image flashed against her mind again, like he'd placed it there himself.

And she knew somehow that he had. Probably with whatever magic he possessed that allowed him to speak within her mind.

She shook him off, or as much as she could, and took a steady breath.

"Ev..." Her throat tightened. She wasn't sure what she was going to say or how, but she knew she couldn't lie to him. "He's..."

My mate.

But those words sounded wrong. He wasn't her anything. He was just a man who Mana happened to place in front of her and bound them with magic. She didn't know him, and he didn't know her.

But his voice, his words, he'd been so sure of their conviction as he purred within her mind.

Enjoy it while it lasts. In the end, it'll be my arms around you and my lips pressed between your thighs.

A shiver slid down her spine at the dark pledge.

"He's..."

Ev scoffed. "Spit it *out*, Bryce."

"A mating bond snapped between us," she growled out.

Ev stopped then, his feet skidding against the dirt. She stopped beside him, but a moment later, he was gripping her arm, pulling her to the side. He pressed close to her, his breath fanning across her face and tasting like wine. His dark eyes flared in anger, his chest heaving.

"What?" he hissed. "A mating bond?"

His tone was accusatory, and it made her own defenses rise. "Ev, it's not my fault." She hadn't gone out actively *looking* for the man. It wasn't like she could control who Mana decided to place in front of her.

There was a beat of silence and Ev sucked in a breath. "You're right," he whispered, and for a second, she heard uncertainty in his tone. "I—I just—fuck!"

He let her go and took a step back. He ran a hand through his dark tresses of hair. She could feel him retreating and it made her heart hurt. She had the urge to reach for him but held herself back. "How can I compete with a fucking mating bond?"

Her body relaxed and she reached for him then, her hands extending. She gripped him by the shirt front, fingers brushing along the coarse, dark hair exposed at the collar.

The others were approaching behind him, and she knew she had to prove where her loyalty in their relationship was, so she hurried and yanked him to her chest.

"Ev," she began. "I'll confess, if I touched him, it was because the bond caught me off guard. But I promise that I don't care about him. I don't even know him, and I don't *want* to know him." She smoothed her palms over his chest and stood on the tips of her toes so their eyes met. She saw the uncertainty in his gaze and didn't like it. After everything they'd been through, after everything he made her feel, it wasn't fair that this doubt had been planted between them. "The bond is optional, so I can reject it." His hair tickled her cheeks as it fell forward, curtaining them both. "I'm with *you*, Ev. And that's exactly where I want to be."

Her words eased his mood. His body relaxed against hers. Then his hold on her tightened, his hand going to her waist where he gripped her hip, nails digging in. He pulled her close and his lips brushed down to take hers in a furious kiss.

It was everything it had never been before.

Possessive.

Angry.

Devout.

His tongue tangled with hers, devouring, consuming, and she moaned as desire stirred low in her belly.

But as quickly as it began, it ended, and it wasn't until he pulled away that the scent of sweet and spicy filled her nose and she knew, even without seeing, that the man had witnessed the kiss.

And she wondered if Everett had done so on purpose.

She leaned away from him, taking a shaking step back, her chest rising and falling rapidly. "We should keep going," she suggested, glad her voice didn't shake or match the trembling happening beneath her skin. Bryson avoided looking anywhere else, lest her gaze stray to the enticing, mysterious man.

"Yeah." Ev took her hand, clasping their fingers together in a strong hold that he refused to let go. He tugged her forward and she almost tripped to keep up with his strides.

She didn't turn around, but she could feel the hot pulse of a smirk boring against her back. Her muscles tensed with every step, waiting for that voice to invade her senses again.

But she was met with complete silence.

And for the life of her, Bryson wasn't sure if she was grateful...

...or disappointed.

Sisters Reunited

The scurrying feet of brownies and stomping, heavy footsteps of goblins filled her ears. There was the fizzling scent of magic and wine in the air, and it felt heavy on her tongue. The familiar routine should have brought her comfort, but it only brought her dread.

When Arlo approached along the outskirts of camp, her spine steeled. It was only then that Ev finally let go of her hand, leaving her to stand alone like she was going to be on trial.

In a way, she was.

Because she knew the Resistance would not be well received. As it was, she could feel Arlo's anger pulsing like it was tangible. She mustered up her courage despite the anxiety coursing through her veins. Facing his glare had her heart pounding. He looked down his aquiline nose at her, blinking furiously between her and the Resistance at her back. His nostrils flared as he took a whiff of them.

Dozens of scents clashing together, though none more prominent than embers, ice, water...

Sweet and spicy.

A knot formed in her throat, and she took in a breath. Ev separated from her to go stand beside Arlo. The leader of the community came to a stop mere feet away from her. His garden smell also released waves of disapproval, of vibrating anger.

He didn't show it, but she could hear in the slow drawl of his voice. "What is this?"

There was a beat of uncomfortable silence.

It was Prince Valerio who stepped forward and spoke first. "Forgive the intrusion on your camp. My name is Valerio Ashera, Prince of Seelie."

If he paused expecting for Arlo to bow before him, Bryson fought the urge to tell him he was wasting his time.

"Hmm..." Arlo replied.

Arlo's eyes flicked to her. Like he knew, somehow, he *knew* that they were here because of her. She wondered if the guilt was on her face. She tried to school her features and was sure she'd failed.

"Arlo..." She started forward. To say what, she wasn't sure, but he cleared his throat roughly, his meaning clear.

Be quiet.

She snapped her mouth shut, biting down hard on her bottom lip.

"They're the Resistance." Ev cut to the chase, his own disdain dripping from his voice. He'd become a different person in front of Arlo like he usually did.

When they were together in the privacy of their little tree, it was always soft touches and whispered promises. Of what things would be like when he finally ruled. When they were in public, he was equally stern as their leader.

She didn't particularly like that change in him.

"Hmm..." Arlo curled his lip, looking down the line of the new Fae with disgust. "What do you want?" His voice was cruel, demanding.

There was a beat of silence.

"That's quite a long story," the prince said cautiously.

"You will tell me, or I will order my men to kill you where you stand."

Bryson's heart bottomed out to her stomach. The murderous intent in Arlo's voice was very real. The energy around them changed within an instant.

Suddenly there was the sharp scent of something soft with the undertone of something sharp. Like powder and steel. It zipped by her in a gust and then there was a voice, soft, threatening.

"You are speaking to the Prince of the Seelie court, halfling," the man said. He was tall with a shock of white-silver hair and pale, almost translucent skin that was stark against the dark leathers he wore. "You will take care who you threaten, or those will be the last words you ever speak."

The threat of battle around them made Bryson's magic rise to the surface. She could sense that presence in front of Arlo. Her magic pushed out, shoving the white-haired Fae away with a single gust of wind. His feet stumbled and he straightened. She could feel his glare cut in her direction, just like she could see Arlo's pleased smile. The brief sign of aggression from Bryson would placate Arlo momentarily. At least, that's what she hoped. It would also hopefully avoid a brawl.

"Uric," the prince chastised. "Don't."

Uric huffed and walked back to his place beside the prince.

"Now, if your tantrum is over with," Arlo drawled. "Let me be clear with one thing. You may be prince of the Fae, but this is not a court. Here you are just another person, and you are no royalty to *us.* So, if there is a reason you came upon our camp, you will tell me now, or you can die, or you can leave." He smiled. "Whichever you prefer."

"Of course, we will tell you why," the prince said. "But if we could speak privately..."

"No," Arlo interrupted. "You will speak now, or you will not set foot in our camp."

The prince's jaw gritted tightly, like he was fighting back his own annoyance at Arlo's blatant disrespect. "We've traveled across Illyk in search of someone, or rather, several someones."

The hairs on Bryson's arms rose at the start of the prince's story.

"And who might that be?" Arlo's brows raised.

"The Fae Elementals."

Bryson's breath caught, but she did not speak.

Both Ev and Arlo's gaze cut to her, but she barely breathed, let alone reacted.

To think that the Resistance had traveled far for her. Why? Did that explain the presence of the other three Elementals in their party?

"If you've come to kill my girlfriend," Ev began, dangerously low, "you won't make it past this field."

"We have no nefarious plans, I swear you this," the prince reassured, lifting his hands in a small sign of submission.

"Then what is it you could possibly want with *my* Elemental?" Arlo demanded.

Those words had a threatening growl rumbling through the recesses of her mind, and she knew who it was immediately. She shook it off, staring straight ahead, avoiding throwing a glance over at the golden-brown Fae male with his dangerous magic. She knew what she'd find. Possession. Murderous intent.

Everyone around her treated her like property.

My Elemental.

Arlo's words reminded her that he saw her as *his* because he'd saved her life. A reminder to her that she owed him a debt. He was staking his claim before the Resistance, one she would be an idiot to refute.

"We have reason to believe the Emperor of Illyk is searching far and wide for those like her. For those like them. Elementals."

"Why?"

"To destroy the Fae."

And he began to weave a tale. It was short and clipped, but it painted a picture vividly within Bryson's mind. Of the emperor looking for Elementals. Of their struggle as they traveled to the Feylands, the confirmation that their home was no longer what it had been. That the emperor needed them all; fire, water, ice, air, earth, and spirit, to destroy the Fae in one fell swoop. That the prince of Seelie was searching for them as well because the Elementals alone could make or break the Fae. They'd traveled, searching for them.

And they'd come for Bryson.

Because they needed her.

And for a second, as he told his tale, her mother's words sprang to the forefront of her mind. Her father's words.

That she was an Elemental.

And she was made for great things.

Suddenly, pieces started to fall into place. Her reason for existing. The restlessness in her body, demanding she do something far more important than what she was doing now, urging her to fight.

But that crashed against Arlo's sudden laughter, cruel and contradictory.

And it was that laughter that reminded her who she was and where her allegiance was supposed to lie.

It pulled her right out of her thoughts of the past. Of what she thought her future could be.

She straightened, walking over to Arlo and Ev's side, standing beside them. Presenting a united front.

"And what proof of this do you have other than your word?" Arlo asked.

"I am a prince—"

"And it is the words and actions of royalty who created this world for us in the first place, so forgive me if I am not so inclined to blindly trust you like your... *followers* here."

She wondered how much of a fight the Resistance would put up and her body tightened, waiting, ready. She wasn't sure if she had it in her to fight them at all, but she prepared her magic regardless. Even if she loathed to do it. Even if everything within her screamed that she should not go up in arms against the Seelie Prince. Against other Elementals.

"You do not believe us." The prince sounded both annoyed and amused.

"That is what I just said," Arlo snapped.

"Fine. You do not have to believe us. Only she does."

All attention cut in her direction. It made the palms of her hands sweat, and she resisted the urge to wipe them against the legs of her pants.

They seemed to be awaiting her response. It took a while for her to answer, because her thoughts warred together, two differentiating ideals angrily clashing. More than that, it was Arlo's demands, her parents' teachings, and this new information dropped readily into her lap.

And just like her anger, she didn't know what to do with this either.

But she knew what to *say*, even if the words tasted foul leaving her mouth, like they didn't quite belong. But she had to say them, because she had loyalties, if nothing else.

"My place is here," she said tightly. "With my community."

Ev's hand wrapped against the ball of her shoulder, squeezing her, obviously content with her answer. She could even feel Arlo's pride, pressing against her.

"But," she added, "I owe Clay a life debt..." Arlo's glare on the side of her face was a force. "I owe them lodgings and food before we send them on their way." She turned her face in Arlo's direction. "Just for a little while. Don't you think?"

She was playing with fire. He'd have them killed if she didn't say anything, she was sure of it. He did not have loyalty to the Resistance or the Seelie crown. But he did believe in transactions. In life debts. And he would believe in Bryson's word.

Whether it was true or not.

He would respect it. He didn't have to like it, but he would respect it.

"Of course," Arlo said then. "If you saved my dearest Bryson's life, then I, as well as she, owe you a debt of gratitude. You may stay here for the time being. But there will be no talk of battles or emperors or wars. You will find nobody in this camp empathetic to your plight. So, stay if you must. Gain your strength." He paused. "Then *leave*."

He whirled and Bryson followed. Arlo's hand splayed across her back, and he leaned close. "We will speak later."

She bit her lip but nodded.

Despite what he believed, she knew that she would pay for what she'd done, and she was not looking forward to it at all.

"Come," Arlo ordered. "I will show you your lodgings and our humble camp."

They followed Arlo. The noises became louder as they stepped foot inside.

"*Welcome* to our camp," Arlo's voice boomed through the space.

His voice drew attention in their direction. From the far end of the camp at the healing tent, Malika pushed aside the flaps and stepped out, drawing her hazelwood, lemon and herb scent with every approaching step in their direction.

Seeing her friend brought Bryson new strength. For a moment, she wanted to pull her to the side. A chance to speak with Malika alone. To tell her everything. From the mating bond, to the Elementals, to maybe even breaking their unspoken rule and talk about her past. What she needed was clarity. A shoulder to lean on.

It couldn't be Ev, and Malika *would* listen. She would help her make sense of her own violent thoughts.

She started forward slowly, a smile on her face. "Malika!"

"What's going on?" Malika stopped in front of them. "What—" Her voice faltered, and a choked sound exited her throat as her eyes went over the group of new arrivals.

Bryson rocked back on her heels, surprised to see the sudden tears streaming down her friend's face. She started to reach for her, but Malika dropped to her knees, the impact of the action making Bryson gasp.

Distress emanated from her every pore.

Then there was the scent of ice and apples. The sight of the ice Elemental stepping forward in Malika's direction.

And when the Elemental spoke, her voice came out equally choked. Equally tortured. *"Malika?"*

Bryson's heart pounded a violent rhythm as she stared back and forth between her best friend and the Elemental. She could see neither of them as clearly as she would have liked and yet she knew there was a resemblance. She'd studied Malika enough to have her memorized. The sleek curvature of her ebony skin. The shape of her eyes and her lips. The timbre of her voice. It was all there. The truth. Yet Bryson could not help but ask, "Do... do you know each other?"

Malika began to cry, and in between choked sobs, she managed a few words that made Bryson's entire world spin. "My sister... Iona... my *sister.*"

Ghost of the Past

Iona had learned not to jump to conclusions when it came to the Elementals. As far as she knew it, they all came from different parts of life, had lived different things, and suffered different hardships. But if there was an intrinsic truth about the Elementals, it was that they were fucking fierce.

Bryson Varik was no exception.

Their magic had collided like an explosion of sensation and feelings and scents. Iona could feel her immediately just like she could feel the other Elementals. Bryson permeated her senses entirely. Together they only grew stronger, and even her own magic burst beneath her skin like it wanted to come forth and clash against the others' to create something beautiful or deadly, she wasn't sure.

She wasn't sure yet how this new Elemental would fit into their fold or if she even wanted to be a part of them. Bryson's group of friends didn't give Iona confidence. In fact, they seemed dead-set on hating the Resistance. Their glares and anger felt personal, though Iona couldn't be sure what it was the Resistance had done to them to warrant it.

She immediately mistrusted them, particularly Arlo Blackwood. The man was half-Fae, with cutting bright eyes and long hair that he wore in a tight ponytail behind his head. He was tall with wide wrists and hands that he kept crossed against his chest. There was something that seemed sacrilegious in his movements, and she was sure if she asked Shula, the fire dancer would say that the moves he made and the things he said mimicked the Priests of the Brotherhood.

Even so, they followed the group into their camp. Everyone stared to the point of making her uncomfortable. Her fingers itched to reach for her blade, but one look from Valerio stayed her hand.

The camp seemed to harbor an abundance of different types of creatures. Iona's eyes darted over every single one of them. There were human and Fae alike; there were half-Fae with a clashing mix of human and Seelie, and even Unseelie creatures skittering across the ground. From goblins to brownies to other things with brightly colored skin, wings, horns, and strange features.

Magic fizzled through the air, creating a dust of colors that drifted from the sky like recently fallen snow. There was something ethereal about this tiny corner on their part of the map. A dozen scents assaulted her at once. She pushed her way through their group to get a closer look.

And Bryson called out to someone, waving her hand over her head. "Malika!"

The name gave Iona pause.

It made her heart beat faster and climb its way up her throat. Her entire body tensed. She felt like it had been forever since she last heard that name or even spoken it herself. Her fingers began cramping, and it was then that she realized they were tapping a familiar pattern against the side of her thigh. Her mind and body drifted, and it seemed like the camp began to disappear before her eyes, taking her back to a sunny day. To a beach. To smog pushing away the blue skies and shrouding it in darkness.

Claw marks against the sand. Blood and bodies. Her name being called over and over, desperate for help. The humans dragging her sister away, and Iona slowly descending into darkness with a single name on her lips.

"Malika."

She snapped out of her memory and back into the present. For a second it felt like the past and future had collided and that she was staring at a memory, at a ghost from her past given corporeal form.

The face was like she remembered, though thinner. Gone were her long dark braids and the smooth curve of innocence around her features. Her dark eyes looked haunted in a way that felt like a mirror to Iona's own pain. Gone was the sweet, innocent Fae that used to pray to Mana by their bedside late at night, until Iona would toss a pillow and demand that she be quiet. In its place was a roughness. In its place were scars.

And in its place was someone different.

And yet Iona would recognize her anywhere.

"Malika."

She stepped forward and her voice came out in a strangled cry. She drew her sister's attention towards her, and it was like the heavens parted and shone down a single ray of light upon them both.

The moment their gazes collided was the moment everything shifted.

They fell to their knees in tandem only a few feet apart from each other. Emotion swelled up inside Iona and the words that had glared on a page that she found within an iron camp months ago echoed through her mind.

Malika Wylde.

Sentenced to death.

She'd mourned her sister in the tradition of their people. She'd taken a dagger to her hair—hair was sacred in their court—and shorn it down to her scalp as a sign of respect and sadness. She thought she'd never see her again and yet there she was. Alive. Whole. Scarred.

Alive.

The foundations of her belief in Mana had been tested time and time again, to the point where she had feared Mana had left her. Her prayers had been unanswered for the longest time, and yet this... this was *integral.* It was like Mana was giving her a *gift* and reminding her to keep the faith.

"My sister." She wasn't sure who said those words first, but they tore out like a tragedy and a prayer. They echoed across the camp like a song of mourning and happiness put together. Iona and Malika crawled towards one another, and every step was heavy. Her palms scraped against the dirt until they met in the middle.

They didn't touch. Iona feared that maybe this was just an illusion. That once she touched Malika, the vision would shatter. That this was just the result of the past coming into her waking thoughts. That her troubled mind had finally caved into the memories, the trauma of all she'd suffered.

Yet when their fingers tentatively met, Malika didn't disappear. Their eyes held. As if they were both wondering if the other would shatter first. When neither did, their sobbing rose in tandem, and Iona's voice cracked when she spoke. "Malika, is it really you?" She hated asking the question, but felt it was necessary, lest this all be a dream she couldn't wake up from.

But it wasn't a dream.

Malika reached for her, grasping her cheeks within her cupped hands. They were callused, like Iona remembered, with brand new scars. She remembered the texture of her sister, and marveled at how she was the same. The same, but different.

Her dark hair was no longer held back by a maze of braids, but loose with tangled curls that went down to her shoulders. It wasn't as long as it had been all those years ago, and Iona wondered if she'd mourned their family like Iona had mourned Malika. If she'd taken scissors to her scalp and let time pass until it grew back again.

There was a sadness shrouding her as well, and where her sister had once been a quiet, gentle creature, Iona saw a hardened edge about her. A part of her despaired, for she knew that the sister she'd known had long died. And someone new was standing in her place.

"I thought I'd lost you." Tears streamed down Iona's cheeks, only to freeze in flakes of snow.

Malika chuckled, using her thumbs to swipe away the cold. "I thought you'd died. Where have you been all this time?"

"I fought in the war to find you." For years, she'd brutalized her body, became stronger, all to fight the humans with the hope that her sister was still alive. Because Malika's death was one she'd refused to accept until months ago. "When we failed, I—" Water, crushing her ribcage, invading her lungs. Landing on the cold, black shores of Porir. "I was in Porir for a while."

"So close," Malika whispered. "And so far."

Iona's heart cracked. If only she'd known how many miles away her sister really had been... Things would have been different.

Her eyes must have given away her thoughts because her sister pulled her close finally and wrapped her arms around her. "It seems," she whispered in Iona's ear, "you have a story to tell. So do I." She pulled away, kissing either cheek. "We will tell them, and we will know each other again."

And for a second, those words had sounded an awful lot like a prayer. Like the kind she used to whisper in the darkness of their room, over and over again to Mana.

Hoping they would come true.

Lost, Now Found

Bryson felt an ache build in her chest as she heard Malika and Iona whisper to one another.

Sisters. Long lost, now found.

She'd known. Of course, she'd known that Malika had a story to tell and that it wasn't a happy one. She hadn't known the extent of it. For a second, she felt a bitterness creep through her. Not because Malika had found her sister; Bryson was happy that they'd found one another again.

She was bitter for several reasons. Because Malika had never confided in her. Because now Malika's attention would be drawn elsewhere. But most of all, because Malika had received a gift from Mana, one that would never be granted to Bryson.

Because her family really was dead.

She'd tasted their blood and smelt their burnt flesh, had felt the weight of their bodies pressing hers down against the charred earth, and there was no power in the world that could ever bring them back.

It made her angry and restless. She didn't want to listen to them anymore, so she turned and started away, separating herself from the group, ready to flee to the one place that would quiet her racing thoughts.

Before she could, Arlo stopped her with a hand to her shoulder. "Bryson," he whispered like a quiet command.

She took a breath, knowing that there would be no rest for her mind right then. She allowed him to pull her away from the fray. He took her towards his tent and pushed the flap open for her to go in.

They were alone with the silence and the heated press of his glare.

She sighed. "Arlo..."

"Don't," he snapped. She clamped her lips tightly closed. "I can't possibly think there's an excuse good enough for you to have allowed them into our fold."

"Clay saved my life."

"You expect me to believe that?"

"It's true."

"How?"

She sucked in a breath. "There were several Kurreen—"

"We both know you could destroy the Kurreen in your sleep."

The praise shouldn't have warmed her, that he thought her so capable. But it did. It felt fatherly, proud. Exactly what she needed to hear. But it didn't take away from the fact that he was here to reprimand her, and it caused anxiety in her chest to spread slowly.

"There were too many," she lied.

"Oh? Then I'll send the scouts out to count the bodies..."

"Arlo..."

"You undermined my authority to sate your own curiosity, Bryson."

"I didn't!"

"Stop lying. You think me foolish? You think I don't know that you hold hopes for the Resistance and whatever it is they stand for? You are your parents' daughter after all."

Betrayal slammed into her at the words. She was trying. She was trying so hard to become a part of their community. And she was. She deserved to be there as much as anyone else did. She killed the humans, saved those who needed saving. She contributed by letting herself be ridiculed for her scars. The one time her ideals didn't completely align with Arlo's and he was questioning her loyalty?

He didn't need to say those words for them to be true. She could hear them in the tone of his voice.

"You're questioning my loyalty."

"I am." There was no hesitation in his voice, and it hit her like a fucking blow.

"I have been loyal to this group for years, Arlo." She tried to keep the hurt from her voice, but it bled through regardless.

"Are you sure? When we spoke of the Resistance before, I noticed you hesitated..."

Just because she wasn't sure what she believed in anymore. Because things were changing in the world. Maybe there was a time when she'd needed to hide out with Arlo and the camp, but the Resistance taking over Dana, being here, wanting her to help save the Fae? It was different.

He had to know that.

But she knew he wouldn't concede. She knew him well enough by now to know that he followed no laws but his own. He looked out for no one except his own.

And if she told him any of that, she would be deemed a traitor.

"I did hesitate," she confessed. Because he already knew the truth, there was no reason to lie.

"You did. Remember what the Seelie did to your parents. Their war killed them."

Anger surged through her body. He wasn't wrong. The war *had* killed her parents, and yet she wasn't sure if she could entirely blame the Seelie or the humans or circumstances. She wanted to. Mana, she wanted someone to pay, and so she made them with arrows and violence until her thoughts warred and she couldn't quiet them.

She tilted her chin up. "I remember," she said through gritted teeth. "More than most, I remember."

"Good. Then remember whose side you're really on." He moved around his tent, straightening his belongings in a slow, calculated manner while she stood there. "Get out."

She did as he bade, moving slowly. Her mind swirled, those terrible thoughts that tended to invade becoming almost overwhelming. Her magic inside stirred, demanding she release her frustrations in any way she could.

She kept them in check.

The uncertainty of everything was making her head spin.

The fact of the matter was, she didn't know what she wanted. Or maybe she did, and she was cowardly for not taking it or voicing it. If she did so, it was out of respect for Arlo. Because she owed him, and he knew it. He held her in a chokehold and kept her there for years until she felt like she couldn't leave or breathe without his permission. The worst part of it all was that she knew exactly what kind of manipulations he used to keep her shackled to him, and still she allowed it to happen.

She released a frustrated sigh and a second later, stopped in her tracks. There'd been no noise to indicate anyone had come close to her, but the scent hit her like an arrow through the flesh. It was sudden and commanding, and it made her skid to a halt right in front of the Fae man who smelled like spice and sweetness. He'd suddenly appeared before her, dropping from the top of a tree like a cat.

He was only a beat away, quietly observing her. It should have unnerved her, but all it did was piss her off. She tilted her head up and glared in his general direction.

"What do you want?"

He smirked in response, and for a second, a flashing image tore through her mind. Of his form splayed on the ground, her own body atop his as they writhed together in a ruthless, sensual joining. The vision was so staggering, she almost tripped backwards.

He stood before her, tall and lithe, covered head to toe in black. The only adornment on him to be seen were golden rings he hid beneath his crossed arms.

The long braid was arranged purposefully over his shoulder, and his lips were twisted into a smile.

It was merely a flash. A mere few seconds of his own desires that lasted what felt like an eternity within her own head.

He took a silent step forward, and his presence suffocated her. It clouded her senses, made her mind dizzy. Her hand rose to her throat, as if that could block her body from taking in his scent. His proximity alone made something crawl beneath her skin. Little bursts of shock that demanded touch to be eased.

And she knew he knew it when he replied with a sensual, *"You."*

He pressed closer and she forced herself to step away to avoid being clogged by his scent.

"You shouldn't say things like that," she growled. She was met with silence. That infuriated her and caused a gust of wind to pulse between them. It pushed him back, but his steps didn't stumble. She braved a few feet closer towards him, tilting her chin up in a brave movement she felt down to her bones. "I don't know what it is you want from me," she hissed, "but I am in a relationship."

"For *now*," he purred. The words felt like a taunt.

She tried not to rock back on her heels. "For *always*."

He chuckled and the sound pierced past her barriers and curled around her like smoke. "How long does the human have to live?"

Her magic lashed out, the air whipping around the both of them. "That sounds like a threat."

He remained silent for so long that her anger started to abate. She finally gave a resigned sigh, shaking her head back and forth.

"Look," she whispered, cooling her magic. "Just... don't expect anything from me, okay? We don't even know each other."

"We will," he whispered the words like a promise. "That I can assure you."

"Hey, Bryce!" The scent of daffodils and earth enveloped her like a comforting drizzle of rain. It by no means pushed past the more cloying scent of the Fae man before her. If anything, his own smell got stronger. It heated her nerves and made a flush crawl up her face.

Ev didn't seem to notice though, or if he did, she couldn't tell as he threw an arm around her shoulder.

There was a tense moment of silence in which she knew the two were staring at one another. It made her uncomfortable and she wanted to leave as quickly as she possibly could. She started to pull away, but Ev held firm, keeping her in place.

"Hey," he said. "There a problem here?" He directed the question at the Fae man.

He didn't reply, only smirked. And it angered Ev so much that his hand tightened painfully against the ball of her shoulder.

"Well, we got shit to do."

The Fae still didn't reply.

She knew Ev wanted to mark some fictional territory, to let this man know that even if he and Bryson were mates, Bryson belonged to Ev. But this wasn't going according to his plan, as the Fae didn't even reply. He was eerily silent, but Bryson could still *feel* him around her, inside her.

Wanting. Waiting.

Remembering the sinister tone of his voice and the threat he'd not-so-vaguely gave, she finally yanked at Everett, pulling him away and walking in the opposite direction. But even as she walked away from him, her body screamed at her. A physical reaction to the bond that lay invisible in between them...

...begging for her to go back.

A Favor Claimed

It was almost surreal to hold her sister's hand in front of a fire. For a second, Iona's mind flashed back to before. Before the war had decimated their lives and taken everything from them. She recalled sitting like this, with different people. With her parents, her brother, and Malika. Of roasting meat and watching the juices drip into the flames. Those nights were filled with laughter as they watched the stars across the Jade Court sky, their bodies tired and weary from a long day of exporting fruits and making fruit flavored ice for tourists... Yet they'd been happy.

Iona was happy now, but there was also a melancholy around the situation as she listened to her sister tell her story.

"I was supposed to have been executed," she whispered. "We all were. Everyone they'd hauled into that cart and was being transported away..." There was a strength in her voice, one never would have known she'd suffered once upon a time. "Bryson was there too, and we were friends... We figured we wouldn't make it out alive."

"How did you?" Iona's hand squeezed hers, but she doubted her sister needed that strength when she seemed to draw enough of it on her own. Even Malika looked down at their joined hands as if they surprised her.

Iona knew what she felt.

"Arlo Blackwood," Malika replied.

The half-Fae man who looked as though he'd wanted to kill them all.

"He killed the humans transporting us and freed us from the cart."

Iona hadn't liked him on sight, but her sister's eyes lit up when she mentioned him, like he was some savior. She supposed he was. And maybe Iona could like him, if only for saving her sister. But there was something slimy and suspicious about the man that she couldn't seem to get past, regardless of whatever good he'd done.

"We've been here ever since. Training, helping others like Arlo helped us." Malika shrugged. "We're a community."

A community.

Iona didn't feel that way with the Resistance. They were more than a community. They could never be something so simple.

They were friends.

Family.

"So, how did you come to be a part of... the Resistance." She gestured with her free hand, indicating at the rest of the Fae gathered around the fire, each in their own conversations for the night. Except Julius. He was off to the side, trying hard to pretend like he wasn't eavesdropping on their conversation.

"It's a long story..." But it brought a smile to her lips and tears to her eyes.

"We have nothing but time," her sister said, leaning back. "Tell me everything."

Iona opened her mouth to do just that, but a shadow suddenly appeared on silent feet. She sighed, looking up at Weylyn as he loomed over the both of them. He glared down at Iona, and a shiver almost slid up her spine at the glare he sent her way.

She'd never seen him look so unhinged. When he wore a smile, he looked mischievous and deadly. The frown was worse somehow.

"Yes?" she snapped.

His eyes flicked between her and her sister, and the mouth hidden behind a well-groomed beard and mustache smiled a cruel expression. No, she thought, the smile was definitely worse. "I need to speak with you," he demanded. "Now."

Iona rolled her eyes. "I'm in the middle of a conversation, as you can see." She released her sister's hand, keeping her fist at the ready. She'd already punched him once for invading her mind and being a total asshole. She had no qualms about doing it again.

From the side, she saw Julius tense as he glared between them. She didn't doubt he wanted to punch Weylyn as well. She gave a subtle shake of her head in his direction, though the little smirk on Weylyn's lips let her know he knew what it meant.

"I don't care," Weylyn said, barely sparing her sister a glance.

Malika rolled her eyes. "I'm Malika, nice to meet you." Her voice dripped with sarcasm.

Weylyn gave her a once over, assessing, and cruel, as if deciding how he should feel about her. He just as quickly dismissed her, turning back to Iona.

"You will come with me."

Iona quirked a brow. "Or what?"

He flashed his teeth. "You will not like the consequences."

Rather than being threatened, Iona felt curious. What had caused him to resort to obvious threats? Usually, Weylyn slithered in the shadows like a serpent.

While she didn't doubt he was capable of going through with threats—there was just something in his eyes—she wanted to know what it was he wanted.

With a sigh, she stood. "I'll be back." The words were directed at Malika and Julius. Her mate didn't object. Not like he'd dare to when he knew she could take care of herself.

Weylyn walked forward, leaving dust behind him. Iona had to nearly run to keep up with his pace until they were hidden behind a cluster of trees where no one could overhear.

He whirled on her, his long braid flying with the sudden movement.

"I need your help." There was a crazed look in his eyes.

Her brows rose, she was definitely curious. "With what?"

He toyed with the rings adorning his fingers then smoothed down his braid. Iona wondered if it was his way of grounding himself.

"It's Bryson."

"The Elemental?" *Of course, Iona, what other Bryson was there?* She mentally berated herself. Then she frowned in Weylyn's direction. She knew of his proclivities for invading everyone's minds and wrenching out their darkest secrets. If he'd done the same to Bryson and wanted to tease her like he had Iona, she'd punch him straight in the dick. "If you want me to help you hurt her, so help me Mana, Weylyn, I will—"

"I am not going to hurt her." He looked disgusted at the very idea.

"Then what do you want? Moreover, why should I help you? Leave the woman alone. You bother everyone else enough already."

Weylyn glared. "Bryson is my mate."

Iona rocked back as if he'd punched her. She... hadn't been expecting *that.* Mana, was the whole group of men in their party destined to find mates within the Elementals? It was a running joke between them all, and they'd even placed bets on it before they'd left Dana. It had all been good fun, and no one had really taken it seriously.

And now...

Fuck.

Iona pitied Bryson immediately.

The poor woman was stuck with Weylyn as a *fucking mate.*

Did he even deserve one? She wondered, then shook her head.

"And what exactly do you want me to do about that information?"

"I need your help in conquering her heart."

Of all the things he could have asked... Iona threw her head back and cackled. Upon seeing his unamused glare, she took a breath and blinked at him. "You're fucking serious."

He gritted his teeth and she saw the hard work of his jaw. He looked away. "You are aware she has a..." He choked on the word.

"Boyfriend?" Yeah, everyone got that. The pretty human man with the long, dark hair and big ego.

"She is proving difficult to convince."

"Mana, Weylyn, you just met her two minutes ago. She's not going to fall into your arms right away."

"You fucked Julius within days."

Her face heated. "I did kick him in the dick first."

"Semantics."

"Look," she snapped. "Even if I did help you, which I won't—"

"You will."

Her hackles rose at the promise of a threat in his voice. The tips of her fingers frosted over, and she closed her hand into a fist, feeling the crack of the ice. "I won't."

He moved silently, quickly, in a way in which she couldn't sense him or expect it. He was in front of her, his face so close that she could taste the scent of his body on her tongue. His glare was a force, his golden eyes flashing in the darkness, pupils dilating, his canines grating together.

"This is not a *fucking* request."

Her blade was in her hand before she even blinked, pressed the edge just against the flesh of his neck, nicking the skin with the blade.

"Get. Away. From. Me."

He didn't. He didn't move. He just pressed his neck against her blade himself, bending down until she was close enough to see the crazy gleam in his eyes and feel *fear.*

"I asked you as a courtesy," he whispered. "But now you leave me no choice."

A pain crippled her arm. Burning. Searing. Like something was being carved into her skin. Iona screamed and her sword of ice disintegrated into snow between them. She jerked back, clutching her forearm, watching as her flesh began to burn. It heated, not as painful as the scars along her back had been. This was a different kind of pain. A different kind of mark. It appeared on her ebony skin like a tattoo of a stamped, golden leaf just below her wrist.

"What the *fuck*?!" Iona screamed.

"Sh, sh, sh," Weylyn chastised, holding up a finger. "Wouldn't want your mate to come running."

"What the fuck is this, you bastard?!" A stream of tears slid down her cheeks as the pain settled. It seemed permanent, pulsing hotly. It felt like magic, but a darker kind. A deadly kind.

"Let this serve as a lesson, Iona Wylde," Weylyn purred, looking cruel and unapologetic, "to be very careful when you make deals with the Fae."

"What deal, you asshole?" Her fingers scraped against the leaf, but the paint didn't smear or smudge. It seemed to hurt even more.

He *tsk*ed. "It is even worse that you do not remember, considering you all but begged me for my gift."

It hit her then and she remembered. Back in a camp, an old man with no tongue who'd recognized her, who knew Malika. They hadn't been able to communicate and so she begged Weylyn for his help. He'd been all too eager to give it.

"Do not think this is a gift freely given" he'd said afterwards. "It was a favor, and I expect you to give me one in return. As to when I plan to collect? It will be when you least expect it."

She remembered the wild gleam in his eye like he just won a prize. She hadn't realized then what she should have. She'd been too desperate to find her sister, to know any word of what had happened that she hadn't taken a moment to pause, look, and understand what she was doing or getting herself into.

Making a deal with the Fae, even a magical one, that was binding had been something long out of practice, and typically had only been done within the Unseelie Courts. But here they no longer had any court, and magic within the human lands was scarce.

And Weylyn had blindsided her.

"You asshole," she growled. "You did this on purpose. You knew what you were doing."

Weylyn snickered. "You will help me."

"Or what?" she challenged purposefully.

His eyes narrowed, and as they did, the pain on her arm flared. It felt like sticking her flesh into fire and she screamed, dropping to her knees.

"Stop," she ordered. "Stop it."

The pain eased and Weylyn stepped towards her. She looked up at him and didn't think she'd ever hated someone more.

He didn't comment on it though he just looked down at her with that malicious smirk that she despised. "Help me conquer Bryson's heart and the bargain will be fulfilled. Try and fuck me over?"

The pain roared again, and she didn't have time to scream before it died down.

He smiled, flashing his teeth. "You will not like the consequences."

To Conquer a Mate

Weylyn paced back and forth the next day, keeping his hands clasped tightly behind his back. He stopped, stared at the clearing, and when no one came, resumed his pacing.

If that ice cold Fae of a woman reneges our deal, I will make her suffer.

Draped along his shoulders was Ryker's familiar. He couldn't seem to rid himself of the beastly thing. Especially not now, when he wanted her around even less. Because he could feel her claws digging into his shoulders and her amused voice flitter through his mind.

You are very entitled.

Don't chastise me, feline. He had the urge to chuck her from his body and let the wild animals have their way with her.

She purred with amusement. *The Elemental does not belong to you.*

"She does," he said aloud. "She is *mine.*"

No. She is Everett's.

Weylyn sneered at the mention of the human's name. The fucking rat bastard... The way he draped his arm over Bryson as though he owned her. The way he kissed her like she was his, and relished in doing so in front of Weylyn.

The only reason he hadn't ripped his entrails out the asshole was because Bryson seemed taken with him, and he did not want her to despise him for such violence just yet.

"I'll not let some pathetic, sniveling human keep her from me." He resumed his pacing. It was the only tell of agitation he would show. "Besides," he continued, "I already know everything about her." He smiled, content with his magic and the ability to dig deep into his mate's mind and know her every dark secret before she even told him. "He is not enough to sate my mate."

The cat rolled her eyes, and Weylyn's feet stopped when he heard the sound of approaching footsteps. He whirled, his anger building as Iona emerged.

But she wasn't alone.

Trailing after her were Shula Azzarh and Corvina Rhian.

He cut a glare to the ice Elemental. "What is this?"

She looked at her companions then back at him unapologetically. She was pissed, and he could read her hatred from her body language without having to dive into her mind. He knew he had frightened her the night before, but he did not care.

She'd deserved it.

He had tried to ask her in an amicable way, but when she'd proved difficult, he'd been forced to call in on their deal. So, she would suffer the consequences, and he would feel no remorse if she failed.

"You never told me I had to keep it a secret."

His teeth gritted as he imagined her whispering the words to Julius. Their whole party would know by nightfall, if they didn't already.

"You also said you need my help to 'conquer' Bryson's heart. Well, I'll need reinforcements if we're going to make you seem even the tiniest bit likable." She sneered at him, and he fought back a chuckle at her obvious disgust.

"Be careful where you pass your judgment, Iona Wylde," he warned. "I have seen your mate. If there is anyone with questionable taste, it is you."

Iona snorted. "Fuck you. Now, let's get this over with so I can get this thing off my arm." She went and perched herself against the edge of a large boulder.

Shula followed, casting wary glances at Weylyn as she passed. He fought the urge to hiss and frighten her on purpose, to scare her just a little more. As Corvina passed, she paused, smiling tentatively at him.

He returned it with one of his own.

"Now." Iona clapped her hands together. "How do we get this heartless, creepy bastard to make Bryson fall in love with him?"

The wind fluttered.

The trees swayed.

The cat stretched.

Weylyn was met with silence.

"Well, you're doomed." Iona made a move to stand, and Weylyn narrowed his eyes. Immediately, the magic of the binding deal responded, burning against her arm and making her cry out.

"Ahem," Corvina interrupted. He reeled the magic back and turned towards her. Her golden curls coiled down her shoulders, and she nervously plucked at the ends. "Did you have a plan of your own?" she asked in her mousey voice. "You know, to win her over?"

Weylyn gave a single nod. "Yes."

"Can I ask what it is?"

He smiled. "I plan on killing her lover."

Simultaneously, the three women dropped their mouths open.

"That..." Shula began. "That's not a plan."

"You're fucking insane," Iona snapped. "What the fuck, Weylyn? You can't just kill him because you feel like it!"

He shrugged his shoulders, appearing careless and confused, though deep down he felt a burning anger. "I will not let a sniveling human who smells like fucking *weeds* take what's mine."

"She's *not* yours, though," Iona argued. "She can reject the bond whenever she wants."

His gaze snapped to hers. "Well, you're here to ensure that *doesn't* happen."

"I can't predict the future!" Iona threw her hands in the air. "What if she rejects you anyway?!"

"Then you are of no use to me."

Iona screamed, dropping to her knees as the pain began to consume her. Shula dropped beside her, but Corvina stood, waving her arms. "Stop," she pleaded. "Weylyn, stop."

The magic immediately settled. Iona heaved a breath and Shula helped her stand. When they faced him, he glared. "It is only because of my High Lady that I take leniency on you."

Corvina took a breath, and he avoided her gaze purposefully. He didn't want to see the way her opinion of him changed, the veil ripped from her eyes as she realized what a monster he truly was when she esteemed him so.

Shula, however, glared his way. The depths of her ember eyes sparking with hatred and fire. "You're such an asshole," she growled.

He didn't blink or contradict her. He knew very fucking well what he was and didn't need her to tell him.

"You will help me," he repeated.

Iona glared and snow swirled at her feet. His lip twisted up into a smirk that said, 'Try me.'

After releasing a breath, she let her magic go and gritted out, "Fine."

The women joined together again. There was a stretch of silence as they looked at him. It was Corvina who broke the silence first. "So, the plan..."

"If I cannot kill the pathetic human, then what do you suggest I do?"

Iona chortled. "Have you thought about getting to know her? You know, like a normal person?""

He hadn't considered that as an option.

Fool, the cat purred into his mind.

He tilted his chin up. "She is mine," he said firmly. "It's been declared. There is no need for anything else."

"If you think that then you're doomed to fail before you even begin," Iona snapped.

Before he could respond, Corvina cut in. "What if you offer her your help with a task?" she suggested softly. "Become friends with her in that way."

"Why would that be necessary? We are not friends. We are mates."

Her bent, scarred fingers played with the ends of her hair. "You don't know her story." Her voice became a touch sorrowful. "You don't know what kind of hurt she's been through. If you persist, you could do more damage than good."

She was surely thinking of her own terrors at the hands of that sniveling cowardly human. If he were alive, Weylyn would have cut his gut open and carved his insides, just to hear him fucking scream. He deserved that and more for the offense.

Clay had missed an opportunity when it came to him.

Anyone who put a hand on his mate would find themselves without their fucking hands. And then without their life.

He wondered though if what Corvina said held merit. Was that what his mate wanted? To get to know him before she accepted the bond?

He shook his head back and forth. Fucking stupid, foolish advice, he wanted to growl. Because he was a monster. One only had to look at him to realize the truth of that. And he wasn't sure he wanted to subject anyone, least of all his mate, to what darkness lived within his depths. Regardless, she belonged to him now.

And if she had hurts? He would take them away and ensure anyone who harmed her died a slow death. And he would fucking take her. Conquer her.

He would insert himself so deeply into her life that she'd be forced to accept the bond. It didn't matter how long it took, there was one thing for certain.

She would be his.

His gaze cut up to Iona's. She must have seen something in him to make her take a fearful step back. "Your advice is worthless to me." She screamed as the pain consumed her. She fell to her knees, cursing him. And Weylyn turned, leaving her there for a few steps before he released the magic of the deal.

Her whimpers died down as the golden leaf disappeared from her skin.

"You asshole!" she called out.

He didn't turn around, but he acknowledged the truth to her words.

He *was* an asshole, but he was also worse than that.

But he didn't need to explain that to them.

They'd know it soon enough.

Human vs. Fae

Bryson knew what Arlo was doing.

He was keeping her busy.

Him or Everett or both, she wasn't sure. One thing was certain, they were doing everything in their power to keep her away from the Resistance. He'd spent the next few days giving her task after task. From night watches, to patrolling the perimeter, to insignificant things that consumed most of her days.

She had no time to breathe, let alone speak to Malika or catch a glimpse of the Resistance. Spending so much time helping the community did nothing to quiet the tumultuous thoughts that plagued her. Her chest throbbed whenever she caught a whiff of Malika in passing, along with the scent of her sister. Malika never seemed to notice Bryson anymore. It made Bryson feel forgotten and small.

She knew Arlo was punishing her for bringing them to camp and lying. And Everett was probably backing him because he wanted to keep her away from Weylyn.

Maybe she did deserve a punishment for it, for potentially putting the camp in danger by inviting strangers in, but Arlo was letting his prejudice get the better of him. She was sure he didn't know what to do with the Resistance. He couldn't kill them because of Bryson's proclaimed life debt, and he didn't want to look hypocritical in front of his people.

He had barely spoken to Bryson since he'd berated her and had made Ev give her the tasks instead. Ev always did so with an angry gleam in his eye.

Things at the camp were shifting. Even the people inside. Her own people had grown hesitant, Malika had grown louder, Arlo had retreated beneath a dark and dangerous cloud, and Ev had become more demanding of her, and it felt like she couldn't breathe.

When she finally got a surprising moment of free time, she felt herself wander towards camp. Her people were in the midst of sparring while the Resistance looked on. She felt the tension through the air, a charge of competition. Their camp always trained hard, but she could hear in the heavy clang of their swords the way they trained even harder, longer, faster.

She winced when Ev's sword cracked against Oliver's in a reverberating clang of thunder. It sent Oliver flying; Bryson heard the expel of breath right after his back slammed against the ground.

Ev laughed, and Bryson gritted her teeth against the teasingly cruel quality of the sound. It was followed by him walking over to Oliver and hauling him up from the ground. His clap on the back could be heard from far away, as could the laughter.

Bryson knew why he was acting this way. Because Weylyn was watching. They all were. She wanted to sigh. It didn't seem to matter how many times she told Ev that he had nothing to worry about when it came to her supposed mate, he wasn't going to believe it, and he was going to keep at it as if he had something to prove. To Weylyn. To the Resistance. To Bryson.

Bryson didn't like that attitude. Instead of taking her word for it, of trusting in her loyalty, he became cruel and possessive. It wasn't that she didn't sometimes admire those qualities in a person, but they seemed very out of place for Everett, and it made Bryson very uncomfortable.

She tried to put herself in a place of understanding. He was competing with a mating bond gifted from Mana. He knew what that implied and the importance of it, so maybe he felt the need to challenge everything to demonstrate his own power to Weylyn.

An unnecessary pissing contest, if she did say so herself.

"An exceptional display," Clay called out from the side of the Resistance. It made everyone quiet. "You all have yourselves a fine set of skills in your camp." The glide of a blade sounded, the swish as it was twirled through the air, though he was nothing but a blur to Bryson. "Would anyone care to train with *us*?"

Bryson sucked in a breath and held it. The others would defer to Ev; they always did. And she knew without a doubt what his answer would be.

"Fine," he said through gritted teeth and a false air of confidence.

He would hate to appear weak in front of his competition.

She watched as he lifted his sword, and she didn't have to look to know where he was pointing it. "But I want to fight him first."

Though she couldn't see Clay's expression clearly, she could just make out the nervous confusion right before he turned towards where Weylyn sat perched against the stump of a tree. Leaning forward, watching, his black braid swaying.

Bryson had tried very hard not to look in his direction when she walked into the camp, but she couldn't deny that she was aware of his exact position, of his gaze sliding heatedly down her backside. She could feel the unspoken words between them, like they were a whispered caress in her mind that she had to fight away at every turn.

She didn't look at him then either. She couldn't take her eyes off Ev. Her eyes begged Ev to look at her so she could ask him what in the actual fuck he thought he was doing. Bryson was very aware of the skills her boyfriend possessed. He knew how to fight. He was an excellent strategist. But he was going up against not just any Fae but a Fae that had already threatened his death.

Not that Ev knew about that last part, and Bryson had no plans on telling him that. It would just spark more animosity than there already was, and it wasn't worth it.

Her hands began sweating and she rubbed them against her knees to push away the anxiety.

She watched as Weylyn's figure extended slowly. She couldn't see his expression, but she could feel his eyes on Everett. Every movement he made was unhurried and felt almost calculated. Purposeful. She didn't know the Fae at all, but even she could note the predatory, murderous intent in the set of his body.

Bryson's breaths grew labored. Her legs locked tightly against the ground, avoiding the urge to run and stand beside Ev, as if that could ward off the Fae's approach. She couldn't do that now. If she did, it would not only offend Ev but also make him look weak in front of everyone. She knew that, of course she did, and yet she wanted to do it anyway.

Weylyn prowled towards Ev, though when he passed Clay, the Fae put a hand on Weylyn's shoulder, stopping his trajectory. "Wait," Clay said. He sounded uncertain. "You can't—"

Weylyn shook Clay off and leveled him with a stare that Bryson couldn't quite make out. "The human wants to fight," he purred. "Let us fight."

Clay shuffled from one foot to another. She wondered if he could also read the potential danger and disaster that could come from this. Instead, he sighed and reluctantly lifted his sword in Weylyn's direction.

Weylyn shook his head. "I do not need a sword."

Bryson's neck heated and she knew Ev's was probably doing the same. Weylyn was openly and very obviously insulting him.

This was definitely going to be a disaster.

Clay moved aside and Ev and Weylyn were alone, facing one another in silence. There was a charge in the air. Weylyn stood preternaturally still, placing his hands behind his back, clasping them together. He appeared like he was unbothered, unworried.

Everette lifted his sword and pointed it in the Fae's direction. "Shall we begin? Or will you continue to stare at me?"

Weylyn didn't reply. It was as if he wasn't there at all.

Bryson squinted as if that could fix her vision and allow her to see their features any clearer. It didn't. It only made her temples pound with the beginning of a headache.

"Well?" Ev prompted.

Still, Weylyn didn't move.

Ev shifted forward. "Very well."

And then he struck.

Faster than an average human could move, Ev thrust his sword in Weylyn's direction. It wasn't a friendly blow. It wasn't even a sparring blow. It was deadly, precise. He aimed straight for Weylyn's chest and Bryson's mouth dropped open, ready to cry out a warning.

But like lightning, Weylyn moved, twisting his body to the side and causing Ev to stumble forward. Ev growled, righted himself, and whirled on Weylyn once again. The Fae stood eerily still, even as Ev lifted the sword and swung.

Weylyn bent his body backwards, his braid flicking down his back, swinging low to the ground as he balanced himself. The sword swished near his face, missing by a few inches only.

Ev righted himself and Weylyn stood to his full height. Bryson could almost feel the smile dominating the Fae's mouth. It felt like nobody in the camp was breathing, witnessing this display. Weylyn didn't attack at all. He merely dodged. Every missed blow had Ev's anger mounting. He didn't become sloppy, though he did tire quicker. Every time it seemed he found an opening Weylyn would suddenly move. One moment he'd be there and within the next blink, gone.

It was like watching a predator play with its prey.

It was then that Bryson remembered.

Weylyn had some kind of mind game magic. He'd easily slipped into her brain, pushing images and words. She wondered if he was doing the same thing to Ev. There was no way they were evenly matched. There was no possible way Ev could beat him.

Bryson gritted her teeth the longer she watched. It was cruel watching Weylyn torment him. He let him believe he could get a blow in only to dodge at the last second, right before the sword swung his way.

Suddenly, a flash through Bryson's mind had her reeling back. She gasped as thoughts that weren't her own invaded. She felt her eyes flick to the back of her head, like she was watching within her own brain something that wasn't there.

Kill. Kill. Kill.

A voice whispered, urged. And in her mind, she saw Weylyn's hand shoot out and rip straight through Ev's chest.

It felt too detailed to be a stray thought and she gasped, forcing it out of her own mind.

As quickly as it had invaded, it left.

Bryson's feet moved by their own volition, stomping across the space just as Ev jerked backwards. Weylyn took a step, lifted his arm, and she knew, somehow she knew that he was trying to make those thoughts he projected into her mind come true.

But Bryson wouldn't let them.

Wind propelled her forward faster as she put herself in between them. Her chest heaved with a fearful breath. The closer Weylyn got to her, the clearer his feral gaze became. He was inches away from the killing blow, and she saw him reel back at the sight of her in front him. Even so, her magic lashed out, her instincts screaming at her to protect Everette with all that she had.

The wind pushed Weylyn backwards, just as his hand closed around the front of her shirt and tightened. Her eyes widened as the force of the wind combined with his hold on her, sent them both flying backwards.

They fell to the ground, Bryson sprawled across his chest. Almost immediately, his arms wrapped around her waist, pulling her close, even as their chests pressed together with every breathless heave.

Up close, his details imprinted into her soul. His every pane, the slight curve on the ridge of his nose, the well-groomed way he kept his mustache and beard. That vicious smile. The curve of every lash. The golden eyes that suddenly flicked white...

The impact of another vision slammed into her. It consumed her down to every single particle. It reeled her in, drowning her within her own mind. So vivid, so real. It felt like she could almost touch it. Touch him. In the vision, they were in the same position they were now, with far less clothing.

His hands gripped her naked hips, digging his nails deep until it caused grooves in her skin. He pulled her down onto him, spearing her, splitting her with his cock. It felt so real. Too real, she could almost taste the desire on his body. She could almost feel his hard cock sliding inside her as if it were truly happening. She could almost feel his lips reach up to take her mouth in a searing kiss—

And she could almost swear the desire pulsing between her legs was actually happening.

Bryson tore herself out of the vision at the same time she pushed herself up and away from him with her palms. She leaned back, staring down at the smirking Fae, her every breath pulling out of her like a ragged thing. She was straddling his legs, trying very hard to ignore the hard press of his rising cock at her center.

"Stop it," she said through gritted teeth. "Stop putting visions into my head."

He puffed out a breath, his hands sliding up the tops of her thighs. She swatted them away and he pressed them against his chest. "Is that really what you want?" he taunted in a voice smooth and deep.

"Yes. It is."

"Hmm." His golden eyes flicked to where their lower halves pressed intimately together. "From the smell of your arousal, and the fact you're still on top of me, I'd say you're lying, little mate."

"Well, I'm not."

And yet her body remained immobile for a few moments more. Her face heated. With shame or desire, she couldn't be sure. It was then that she became increasingly aware of their position, of the wetness that had suddenly pooled from between her thighs.

No, she thought, this isn't supposed to happen. With a growl, she shoved from his body, pushing herself to a stand. As she stepped back, her thighs shifted together, coating her skin with arousal that made her body flush just a few shades hotter. She prayed the others couldn't scent the evidence of what he'd done to her.

He'd placed that vision in her head on purpose. To provoke her. To provoke Ev. And that vision had felt like she was living it, colliding with her reality, causing her insides to pulse with a desperation she never knew was possible. His scent only grew stronger, permeating through her very being. Something electrified between them, demanding she pull closer.

Was this the magic of the bond?

She couldn't help her body's reaction to him, no matter how unwanted the advance was. She supposed she could forgive him if he was acting this way. Bonds of Mana made Fae do wild things. But she wouldn't forgive how purposeful he was in trying to kill Ev.

Ev.

She gave Weylyn's form on the ground one last, lingering look before she whirled to face her boyfriend.

The shame came in a blast as she witnessed his anger. Even from a distance, even with a blurry form, she knew. And beside him stood Arlo, his arms crossed tightly against his chest.

Arlo inhaled loudly, and she wished she could slink away and hide her own scent. Everyone knew what he did to her, and it was humiliating. "If the two of you are quite finished with... whatever that was, we have a job to do, Bryson."

Bryson straightened, mustering whatever dignity she still had left. "What job?"

"A wagon is set to approach soon. It contains Fae escorted by soldiers."

Bryson let out a breath, and with it, a sliver of her magic. It grounded her, eased her nerves, even as it drifted Weylyn's scent straight in her direction. She ignored that part and opened her eyes again. Not only was Arlo giving her purpose, he was also pulling her back to his side, reminding her that she had a loyalty, and more importantly, to whom it was owed.

She stepped forward, walking back over to Ev's side, though he pointedly ignored her. It stung, though she supposed she shouldn't be surprised after what Weylyn had done. Still, her chest ached with the sting of his rejection.

"Everyone knows what to do," Arlo announced, his gaze flicking towards the others. "And as for the Resistance? Well, I guess now is the time to prove just how good you really are."

Whispering Winds

"Ev—"

"Not now, Bryson." His response was clipped, angry.

He had every right to be, Bryce told herself that, but it still didn't make swallowing that bitter anger any easier.

"Ev, we have to talk."

"I said not right now!" His shout startled birds from their trees. From above, Bryson's familiar let out a sound of indignation on her behalf, but she offered no commentary into Bryson's mind.

It was for the best. She was tired of everyone invading her thoughts for the moment. Just like she quickly grew tired of Ev's anger.

"Don't talk to me like that," she hissed.

They were both settled in a high tree, on a thick branch, as they awaited a familiar signal from Malika that would let them know when the wagon grew closer. Their masks were placed over their faces, hiding their identities.

His attention finally turned in her direction. He stood carefully on the branch, his body leaning slightly against the trunk of the tree to avoid falling off. His bow and arrow were at the ready in his hands, his fingers curling angrily around them.

"Like what?" he spat out. His eyes shone brightly from beneath the wooden mask.

"Ev." Bryson sighed, resisting the urge to reach for him, if only because she knew it wouldn't be well received. "We need to talk about what happened."

"Oh, about how you disrespected me in front of everyone?" He scoffed and leaned away. "Or about how you all but *fucked* that Fae in front of me?"

Bryson's cheeks heated. "That's not what happened!"

"It certainly looked like it."

"Ev, it's not. He was going to kill you and I had to get in between. He's the one who pulled me, and we fell—"

"You think me weak. You don't trust that I can protect myself, protect you. You're stronger and faster than me, but I'm not a child." He sounded angry. He always sounded angry. It lived, brittle inside him just like it did inside Bryson. "Besides, you stayed on his lap for far too long. And if you could've seen your face when you turned around—" He broke off, making a noise mixed with impatience and hurt.

"What?" she demanded, her own irritation growing.

He sighed again, his voice growing softer. "That's how you look when *we* sleep together. And it *hurt.* Can't you understand that?"

Her heart ached for what she'd done to him. She hadn't meant to. It hadn't been her fault, but he was right. It had been disrespectful on many levels. If Bryson was one thing, it was loyal. Faithful.

"I know the mating bond is drawing you to him," Ev continued.

"You know I don't want him. I don't want the bond," she defended, though her voice sounded weak, even to her own ears.

"Sure." He didn't sound convinced. "It didn't look like that."

"That was an accident, Ev."

He just turned away from her and her flimsy excuse. He didn't say another word again, and they stewed in the uncomfortable silence. She'd hurt his pride. Not only by intervening in the fight, but by getting lost in Weylyn's vision for far too long.

His pride has been wounded, her familiar said from above.

I know.

There was a beat of silence. Then, *If you want to fix things between the two of you, maybe you should show him that you need him.*

Bryson frowned, scrunching her nose and staring up at the sky, as if she could see her familiar past branches and leaves. *He should already know that I do. After everything we've been through.*

If her familiar had shoulders, she would have shrugged. *I have noticed that humans like reassurance, especially when competing against the mating bonds of Mana.*

Her familiar went quiet after that, and Bryson didn't even know how to respond anyway. She didn't bother because a familiar noise whistled through the air. Something similar to the screech of a hawk, though she knew it wasn't her familiar.

It was Malika, giving the signal.

It was time.

Bryson notched an arrow into her bow and waited with bated breath. Ev tensed beside her, both of them glancing down at the opening from in between the trees.

Everything stilled, and the familiar scents of fear, the familiar sounds of clattering wheels echoed through the woods. Her eyes squinted from beneath the wooden mask, making out shadows and clonking wooden and iron figures. Her scent picked up the slack of her poor eyesight, and she gauged positions. But just before she could let an arrow lose, Ev did so himself.

She jolted in surprise. Shooting the first arrow and immobilizing the driver was *her* job because she was the best shot among them. Those were the rules. Those had always been the rules.

Yet Ev's arrow fired. Bryson knew the shot wouldn't hit the target with as accurate precision as hers would have. And it didn't. It struck the human's shoulder. The man grunted and doubled over, startling the horses pulling the wagon.

Ev let out a hissed curse and slid from the tree, climbing quickly to the ground below.

"Ev!"

He ignored her.

He was ignoring their plan.

What the fuck is he doing? she thought angrily as she climbed down after him.

This wasn't how they did things. They hardly showed their masked faces to the humans. It was supposed to protect them. They always attacked from a distance. Never up close. And they were never supposed to miss a shot, either.

Was Everette doing this because he felt he had something to prove? Because she'd embarrassed him and now he was trying to gain some of his pride back? Was that what this was about?

She couldn't ask any of that, though, because Ev had already touched the ground and raced towards the wagon.

The horses pawed the air, frightened at the current disruption. The human shouted for backup, and several more burst from the wagon to meet Ev as her boyfriend pulled his sword from its sheath. He met the humans with a clang of blades just as Bryson's feet touched the ground.

"Everette!" The arrow flew before she could blink, hitting its target far too wide. It didn't stop the human from charging for Ev, but it slowed him down considerably. His sword lifted in an arc, ready to slash down against her parrying partner...

Someone appeared in a blur of metal and fabric, sword blocking the descent. The Seelie Prince. He was a swish of metal and dark hair as he shoved the human away, protecting Ev's side. They parried, and Bryson notched another arrow in her bow.

"Ev, look out!"

Her warning was shouted too late. Even as the arrow flew, the sword came down against Everette, slicing across his chest just before the arrow pierced the human in the eye. He crumbled at the same time Ev did. At the same time the Seelie Prince finished off the other humans.

Then there was a beat of silence.

Right before everything burst into chaos.

Bryson rushed towards Ev with a cry on her lips as everyone Resistance and rebels alike burst from their hiding places, rushing around to do several things at once.

Some went to the wagons immediately, beginning to pry apart the iron to free the people from the inside. Bryson dropped to the ground beside Ev, her fingers pressing against the blood blooming against his chest.

Bryson felt the tears prick at the back of her eyes but kept them at bay. Ev groaned, his own hand reaching up to pull the mask from his face. His features twisted into agony, and she dug her fingers tighter against the wound, trying to block the flow of blood.

"Stupid," she hissed, leaning over his body. Her hair slid from its knot, caressing his cheeks. "Why would you do something so stupid?"

Ev gasped, and it took Bryson a moment to realize he was laughing.

"What's so funny?"

Before he could answer, Malika was dropping to her knees at their side, gently prying Bryson's hands away from the wound. "I'll take it from here, Bryce," she whispered gently.

Bryson fell back on her haunches, trying to steady her breathing as she watched Malika cup her hands above the wound.

"Malika, what are you—"

Bryson barely spared a glance at Malika's sister, who had come to hover. Bryson bit her tongue, fighting the urge to snap at the Fae Elemental and tell her that Malika didn't like people hovering while she worked. She held it back. It wasn't her place to come between them, even if the more jealous and bitter part of her wanted to.

Malika shushed her sister and light emanated from her hands, swallowing Ev's wound.

"Malika! Don't!" The ice Elemental reached for her sister, gripping her shoulder and yanking her backwards.

It was too late. Her magic had already fallen over Ev's wound, knitting his flesh back together. Malika's healing magic took its price as soon as it worked. It consumed her own energy. So when Iona pulled her, Malika didn't have the energy to move her limbs or respond. She fell back, hitting her head against the ground and pulling deep breaths into her chest.

Bryson pushed to her feet, standing in between Malika and her sister. Her magic lashed out, shoving Iona away from her friend. "What the hell is your problem?" she demanded.

"It's fine, Bryson." Malika sat up, her movements slow and aching. "She didn't mean it."

"You shouldn't be healing anyone," Iona gritted out, ignoring Bryson completely and walking around her to help Malika to a stand. "You know how it takes a lot out of you."

Malika and Bryson scoffed simultaneously, and it earned Bryson a blurry glare from Iona. She pretended not to notice as she bent to grip Ev's outreached hand, pulling him to a stand. He avoided looking at her gaze just as much as she avoided looking at Iona's.

"All due respect, big sister, you can't tell me what I can or can't do with my own magic."

"I see you haven't changed at all. Still being irresponsible with your magic and your health."

Malika scoffed. "You're one to talk."

Their voices began to clatter in an argument that Bryson eventually tuned out. She turned to Ev, willing his gaze to fall on her.

"Are you okay?" she asked.

His nostrils flared, his eyes finally drawing in her direction, flashing briefly before settling on a spot over her shoulder. His anger became so much more perceptible when he looked back at her. "And you care?"

He didn't say anything else as he stormed away in the direction of the wagon, sheathing his blade as he went.

Bryson sighed with exasperation, turning to the spot Ev had been staring at only to find Weylyn standing there. Unmoving. She couldn't see his eyes clearly, but she knew he was staring at her.

And then, his voice resonated in her mind.

"What a weak, foolish human, to take his anger out on you for his own failures."

"Get out of my head." She squeezed her eyes shut against the mental assault.

In response, she felt phantom claws glide sensually down her back. *"I would never treat you in such a way."*

"Get out!" She slammed her hands against her ears, but his voice only persisted. Lowering. And she felt him inside her brain, his body circling hers like a predator sizing up his prey.

"I would cherish you." That voice whispered in her ear, closer than before. Almost like he was standing right behind her, his breath fanning across her skin.

"Stop it." Her voice had grown weak.

"I would worship you." His hands glided along her thighs, rising higher with gentle strokes to her hip.

She wanted to jerk away from the seduction, but something kept her firmly in place. Her own legs, the power of a bond she didn't want, or something else entirely. Bryson wasn't even sure.

And when Weylyn's palm cupped between her legs, she wanted to double over at the pleasure that zapped through every inch.

"I would fuck you good, so good *that you'd see the fucking stars of the Unseelie Court in your mind."*

Bryson yanked out of his vision, gasping for breath as her eyes focused once again on his body across from her.

Everything had happened within her own mind, yet it always felt as if it were real.

Out loud, she whispered, "You wish." Though she was unsure if he'd heard her at all. It wasn't until she turned to stomp away that his voice trailed after her, little more than a whisper in the wind.

"I do wish... little mate."

Mana's Gifts

"I just don't understand why you have to be the healer," Iona argued. "Why does it have to be *you*? Why does it have to be *your* magic?"

That wasn't the first time Iona had asked that question, it wouldn't be the last, and Malika's answer would remain the same.

"My magic is invaluable. I help people because I want to, because I can, because it is my duty."

"You know the price you pay for it."

"A small price and you know it."

Iona growled and flashed her canines in her sister's direction.

"Don't you growl at me," Malika snapped back. "You don't get to tell me what to do with my magic. You don't get to tell me who to help, how to help, or when to help."

"I'm looking out for you—"

"Stop it. Stop trying to disguise your own manipulative, controlling urges as you caring about me."

"Are you saying I don't care about you?"

"On the contrary, Iona. I know you care. You care too damn much. Answer me this, what if I asked you to stop using your Elemental magic?"

Malika was met with silence.

"Exactly."

"It's not the same."

"How?!"

"I don't lose energy when I use my magic. My magic is different. My magic is more—"

"Special?"

"I didn't say that."

"You didn't have to, Iona. You are not superior to me merely because you were blessed by Mana."

"I didn't say that! And you were blessed by Mana too!"

"Exactly. I am *blessed*. Which is why I have to do what I must in order to ensure our survival."

Julius' gaze volleyed back and forth between the sisters as they argued. He watched them face off, both of them so alike he wasn't even sure if they realized it. From the tone of their nearly similar voices to the stance in which they stood—feet slightly apart, backs straight, furrowed brows, and crossed arms.

He stood a bit apart from them, his own posture stiff and ready to interject between the two should the need arise.

He hated seeing Iona in distress. It made his mating instincts rise. It made his body demand he eliminate all threats to Iona, to protect, attack, do what he must. But he couldn't. This was Iona's sister. The sister she had mourned. The sister she had risked everything to find, only to be told she'd died.

And now they were arguing.

Julius fought the urge to sigh at the sky.

"Malika, you've always done this." Iona took a cautious step towards her sister, as if she didn't quite know if she should reach out to her or not. Touch her. Vulnerability whispered in between the spaces of the two, and Julius was sure neither knew how to approach it or what to do. "You've always placed everyone else's health above your own."

"It was one little wound. I have healed worse."

"Exactly! You need to be mindful of yourself."

"Would you say the same thing to your healer? To Ryker?"

Iona was silenced once again.

Julius bit the inside of his cheek. He knew she wouldn't say it to Ryker. She hadn't said it to Ryker. In fact, the entire Resistance had put Ryker's life—and magic—on the line again and again until Shula had banned him from using his magic at all.

He found it hypocritical that Iona would ask her sister to push aside her Mana-given gift but wouldn't do the same herself or ask the same of Ryker. He didn't say that, though, because she'd kick him in the dick, and he valued that particular part of his anatomy.

Malika sighed and finally broke the distance between Iona and herself. She grasped her sister's shoulders, looked deep into her eyes, almost begging her to understand.

"I have to do this. Mana gave me this gift for a reason."

Julius' eyes went to his mate, waiting for her reply. She was glaring angrily at her sister, and once again, Julius found himself marveling at how alike—and how different—both sisters were. The same rounded nose, the same lips, the same eye shape. But Malika's hair was dark and braided. Iona had cut hers short, and the curly wisps were as white as snow, like the very ice she wielded threaded through the coils of her hair.

"Do you even still believe in Mana?" Iona whispered harshly. "Do you even still pray?"

Malika's arms dropped. "What does that have to do with anything?"

"I remember how you used to pray. Every night, you would whisper your wishes to Mana. You had so much faith. Do you still have that?"

Malika gritted her teeth. "What do you want me to say, Iona?"

"I want the truth."

"Fine." She threw her hands up. "I haven't prayed since we lived at Court. I lost my faith. I lost the urge to pray when I thought I was alone. When I thought my entire family had died. I lost the urge when I was forced to endure torture in the iron camps. But I've *never* lost my belief in Mana."

Iona seemed to stagger back. Julius tamped down the growl that wanted to arise and resisted the urge to go to her. They needed to hash this out one way or another, though he knew what kind of betrayal Iona might have been feeling. She'd told him of their past, that she'd adopted praying because it's what her sister would have done.

What must she have felt like to know that the sister she'd prayed for had given up her own prayers?

"Does the truth make you feel better?" Malika asked quietly.

Iona shook her head. "No. But I stand by what I said. *Stop* healing people. Especially people who don't deserve it."

"And how do you decide who deserves my help or not?"

Iona scoffed. "That human Everette definitely doesn't."

"And what makes you say that?"

"He hates us. Refuses to help us."

"So I should only help those who worship the ground the Resistance walks on? Is that what you're saying?"

"No, but at least if you're going to hurt yourself to save somebody, save somebody not so insufferable."

Malika's own canines snapped. Her temper finally flared, and her voice rose to a shout. "For the last time, you cannot tell me what to do. I know how to use my magic. I know my own limits way more than you ever could. I don't need your help. I don't even need you to care, because at the end of the day, I've lived most of my life without you. I don't need you."

Iona staggered backwards as the force of her sister's words landed. Like a blow to the chest, Iona gripped her shirt front and sucked in a ragged breath. She stared at her sister, betrayal crossing over her features.

Julius could physically see the heartbreak through the window of her dark eyes. The hope she'd harbored shattered right before him, breaking into thousands of pieces, and he could do nothing but watch it crumble, unable to put them back together again.

He started forward, but Iona was already moving, whirling away from her sister and stalking away into the darkening night, disappearing into the trees.

Julius needed to go after her. He had to.

He marched forward, stopping only a few feet away from Malika. When he turned, it was to pierce her with a glare that could crumble down buildings.

Malika was staring at the spot where Iona disappeared from. It took a single moment for the anger to diminish, as the impact of the words she'd said finally registered. Malika's palms went to her lips, smothering the gasp of surprise at the words she'd spat angrily. Slowly, her eyes flicked to Julius.

"I didn't mean it," she said, tears slipping from her eyes. "She has to know I didn't mean it."

"It doesn't matter now," Julius growled. A part of him wished he could reach over and shake her, but he wouldn't put his hands on Malika. No matter what she'd said to his mate, Iona would never forgive the transgression. "You said it anyway, and she will believe it to be true."

"She has to know—"

"She doesn't know shit," Julius interrupted. He could feel his anger rising, the kind that had nothing to do with the price of his own magic. "She doesn't know you. Not anymore." When Malika's tears kept falling, Julius willed his anger to be leashed. "Look," he said. "I understand. You are sisters, but you're strangers. I need you to know that Iona risked everything she had to try and find you. When she thought you were dead—" He broke off, remembering the moment so vividly. Remembering the agonized cries as she took the dagger to her coils, sawing through them in uneven, shaking strokes until there was hardly anything left.

He'd never heard such harrowing sounds before.

He pierced Malika with another glare. "You have been given a gift," he said softly. "A gift that Mana does not grant to many. You've already lost so many years; don't waste any more time arguing over something trivial."

He turned away from her then and took a step before he threw a glance over his shoulder.

"And if you ever say anything to disrespect or make my mate cry again, I will ensure you live to fucking regret it."

Iona pressed her forehead against the tree, digging her skin into the rough bark until she felt she would bleed. The tears froze on her cheeks as soon as she shed them, creating an icy trail that was as cold and as desolate as the feeling in her chest.

I don't need you.

Those words echoed over and over, like arrows piercing through her heart, one after another. She didn't want to believe them, but she did. She didn't want to accept it, but what other choice did she have? Her sister was a stranger to her now.

Yes, there was still a remnant of the Fae she'd known and loved, deep down somewhere. But the truth was, it didn't matter. Because life had happened. The war had happened. Neither one of them was the same person they'd been years ago.

She knew that.

Yet Iona felt like she was burying her sister all over again. She really had died that day, and someone new had been born.

It was a truth that was difficult to contend with.

Iona pushed away from the tree and curled her fingers into her palm. Her digits hardened to ice, cutting into her skin. Her muscles tensed, and with a fierce cry, she threw her icy fist out at the tree before her. Bark chipped away, creating an indent in the trunk.

Her guilt over the destruction was immediate, so she pulled away, turning as footsteps sounded behind her.

Julius emerged from the shadows, his ginger brows creased with concern as he approached.

"I'm fine." Iona turned away from him, even as the lie tasted bitter on her lips.

Julius didn't speak. At least, not until she felt the warmth of his mountainous body at her back. His arms came around her, caging her against the tree.

"You don't have to lie to me," he whispered.

Iona sniffled. "I'm fine." The tears sprang to her eyes once again.

"Iona—"

"I shouldn't expect her to be the exact same person. I mean, at least her complete disregard for her own well-being is still on par with who she used to be. That much hasn't changed."

"Iona—"

"It would be even stranger if she didn't help others. It would be so unlike her that—"

"Iona—"

"I just worry that her energy will wane. What if she gets hurt? What if she—"

"Iona!" His voice came out firm, rumbling against her backside. She jolted as his hands crashed against her, whipping her around in his arms. He held her close, his arms encircling her waist, pressing his palms against her lower back to bring her closer still.

She looked up into his eyes, and the sympathy she found deep within his green depths had her throat constricting. The tears immediately jumped to her eyes, and she tried as hard as she could to hold them back. But Julius, as always, saw right through her.

"Let it out, love. It's okay."

The first sob came out and she couldn't stop the rest that followed. Iona buried her face in his shirtfront, inhaling his pine scent, of forest and earth. Her tears soaked his front, and her mate only pulled her closer.

"You are allowed to mourn the sister you knew. You are allowed to mourn who she is now. Let your tears flow, love. Mourn the death of the life you knew; I know that's why you're really weeping."

Was it? Was that why the tears were flowing? Because of what this world had done not only to her sister but to her as well? It had hardened the both of them. It had changed them, made them into something Iona never thought they'd be.

"Weep, love," Julius encouraged, rubbing his palm against her back. "And then you'll go back out there and face your sister and apologize."

Iona made a noise of disbelief in the back of her throat but didn't argue, because Julius kept her pressed tightly to him, not giving her a chance to reel back and glare at him.

"You will apologize, and so will she. And you will move on from this. Because she is your sister. Your family. And Mana has given you a gift, one that not everyone has the privilege of getting."

Iona sobbed harder. "You're right."

"I know." He kissed the top of her head. "And now that the truth is out, now that you've mourned, you'll only grow stronger. With Malika at your side. Do you understand?"

She choked on an oncoming sob. "I understand."

"Good. Because life is too short for grudges and anger. So let it out, and let it go."

Her hands gripped him tight, and she took his advice, letting her tears fall until she had nothing left to cry anymore.

Julius was right. Seeing her sister in this new environment, knowing what had happened to her, how much she'd suffered, hadn't been the life Iona wanted for her. Despite all that, she was alive. Her sister was alive.

And that was a gift from Mana.
One she hadn't been expecting, but one she appreciated just the same.

A Violent Release

The night was lonely. Even as noises of nature consumed her surroundings, Bryson felt an aching, bone-deep sensation of abandonment curdling through her. Even her familiar had flown off with a ruffle of her brown and black feathers, unable to stand Bryson's somber mood. Malika was off somewhere arguing with her sister and Ev was with Arlo, strategizing and cursing the Resistance, she assumed.

She never realized how alone she actually was until these past few days.

It felt like her entire world had imploded around her. Everything had tilted on an uneven axis, and she was trying to balance herself and avoid the dangerous fall. But she was failing.

The pressure on her chest increased, and the sensation of tears pricked behind her eyelids. She refused to cry. She hadn't done so in years; she wouldn't do so now. She furiously rubbed against her eyelids, palms scraping against the scars spread across her skin.

The sudden urge to curse at the sky gripped her, but she stewed in silence instead, letting the wind ruffle her curls. Her own magic bubbled up inside her, looking for release. If she set it free now, she was sure to tear the tree house from its perch and tumble to the ground.

She'd meant to sit up there to find peace, but the night brought anything but.

Bryson looked up at the canopy of leaves, squinting into the night. Her temples began pounding, a dull throb that spread across her forehead and to the backs of her eyeballs.

"It's just stress," she whispered to herself, though she knew that wasn't true. Her eyesight was worsening. She felt it every year, how it was increasingly harder to see. At first it had been at a distance, gradually becoming blurrier up close as well. She lived through a haze of fog, and when the headaches began, she knew it could only ever get worse before it got better.

There was no fixing her sight. There was no healing the ache.

She sighed again just as footsteps sounded from down below. Bryson closed her eyes, listening to the pattern of them against the ground. Her whole body tensed as if primed for a fight. She recognized those footsteps as they approached her tree and began to climb. The scent of them only got stronger as they hauled themselves to the top.

She didn't move as he settled at her side. In fact, she made it very obvious she was ignoring him.

Everette sighed. "Bryce..." There was silence, almost as if he were waiting for her to fill it.

With what? What could she possibly have to say to him that she hadn't already? Anytime she spoke these days, she was met with his anger and disdain. Met with venomous words that just filled her with guilt, even when she'd done nothing wrong.

She'd contemplated it as she sat there hours previously. Everything that had happened with the Resistance, with Weylyn. She'd made mistakes, most of them internal. Entertaining Weylyn's mental conversations, letting him get into her head. But anything else had been out of her hands. Her body's reaction to Weylyn was primal, rooted from a bond she hadn't expected. It had caught her off guard, and her reactions to him had been knee-jerkingly quick.

But Bryson was loyal. She had been loyal. And if Ev refused to believe that, to see that, it was his problem. She would no longer beg him to understand. She would no longer lay herself bare only to be kicked emotionally over and over.

If there was one thing Weylyn had been right about, it was that. Ev was taking his anger out on her, and she was the last person in this camp that deserved it.

"Bryce, will you look at me?"

She didn't respond. Didn't open her eyes. If he had something he wanted to say, he could do so. And then leave.

She wanted to be alone.

Ev sighed again. "Bryson, I'm sorry, alright?" He made a frustrated sound. "I've been an asshole to you."

Bryson made a snorting noise of agreement.

"I have no excuse for my behavior. I was threatened by that Fae, and in my jealousy, I took it out on you. I can't apologize enough for that. You didn't deserve it, and I don't deserve you." There was silence, the rustle of his clothes. "Bryson, can you please look at me?"

Slowly, Bryson opened her eyes and found him staring down at her. This close, she could see the distress he wore like a second skin. It made his expression look severe. She wondered if his distress and regret should have made her happy.

It just made her feel hollow.

"I'm sorry," he repeated. "I'm insecure. I wanted to, I don't know, prove that I was just as strong, just as worthy as your mate."

"Stupid," Bryson replied. "I don't even know him. Who's to say if he's even worthy or not?"

"I know that now." His hand came down on her cheek, soft as his thumb stroked her skin. "Being human while you're Fae is not easy. I'm aware of the power imbalance between us. I feel like I have to work twice as hard to keep up with you. Then this Fae shows up and all those insecurities grew three times as big, and I felt like I had even more to prove."

Bryson let out a breath. "Stupid."

His eyes shone in the darkness; his hair fell over his cheeks. "Can you forgive me?"

Could she? Her answer came quickly. She could. Everette had so many faults, but this wasn't something he'd ever done before. To be honest, it wasn't something they'd ever had to navigate before. They'd both been way out of their element with this entire situation. Neither of them could've predicted any of it. They'd both been caught off guard.

She could forgive him for what he'd done. So long as he didn't do it again.

"Okay," she said softly.

Ev let out a breath of relief. He leaned down, hair tickling her skin as he pressed a slow, soft kiss to her mouth. "I hate fighting," he whispered.

"Me too."

"Why fight when we could spend our time doing much more enjoyable things?" His voice had dropped low, sultry, leaving no room to guess what it was he wanted.

That familiar dull ache spread behind her eyes.

"I miss us," Ev went on. He rolled over her, settling his weight comfortably above, holding himself up by his hands. "Before everything turned chaotic."

"Hmm."

What he meant to say was that he missed how things were before the Resistance showed up at their camp. She wouldn't agree because she wasn't sure she felt the same thing. If they hadn't, she wouldn't have discovered how important she—and her magic—was for the world. She wouldn't have met other Elementals. Malika never would have found her sister.

By the grace of Mana, this was meant to happen.

Ev just couldn't see it yet.

His palm cupped her cheek, and he gazed down at her with open adoration. For a moment, he breathed her in, closing the distance between them. "I love you, Bryson," he whispered.

Bryson closed her eyes against the onslaught of feelings his words caused. So many things warred inside of her at once. She couldn't reply. She couldn't say anything. Or maybe Ev just didn't give her a chance to, because between one moment and the next, his lips were tight against hers and he was devouring with an almost desperation that made her skin spark with desire.

She opened her mouth against his, letting their tongues tangle together. He blanketed his body with hers, pressing his hardness against her core. For a moment, she let herself feel. Let herself forget.

If only for a moment.

Bryson leaned into him, her fingers grasping against the hem of his shirt and sliding it up his muscular body. Her hands toyed with his skin, fingers scraping over the flesh at his back. She held back the urge to dig her nails in. Held herself back from being too rough. Too aggressive.

They broke apart to draw breath. Her neck angled to the side and Ev's teeth scraped against her skin. She gasped as his teeth nipped her. Her hips thrust up to meet his, and he grinded down hard.

They became a desperate tangle, pawing at each other's clothes, yet couldn't get them off fast enough. The distance placed between them these past few days had taken its toll, and now they were coming together again, clicking into place where they should've been, exactly how they were meant to be.

Ev's hands slid up her skin, shoving her shirt out of the way so he could bare her chest to the cool night air. The breeze made her nipples harden, and then his mouth was there to ease that ache. His lips clamped over her, tongue laving it up like a feast. One, then the other, Ev gave equal attention to both.

Bryson wriggled beneath him, needing friction, needing mindless thrusts. She wanted to feel the pain of the wood against her back. She wanted that pinch, the bite, to drown and choke on mindless pleasure for a little while.

"Fuck," Ev cursed against her skin. "Fuck, Bryson. Take me out."

Her hands were steady as they pulled at the strings against his pants before she slipped inside, grasping his cock at the base. Everette jerked against her tight hold, and she firmly stroked up and down, careful not to squeeze too hard, lest she hurt him in her grip.

Ev grunted in her ear, his own hands fumbling to shove her pants down. Once he managed, his calloused fingers slid over the folds of her lips, smearing her wetness against her clit, causing her to jolt at the small zing of pleasure.

"Put me inside you," Ev urged.

Bryson brought his tip against her entrance right before removing her hands. Ev surged inside in a single thrust, and her back slid against the wood. It wasn't the full grip of pain she desired, but it would ease the ache.

She thrust her hips up. "Move," she ordered.

Ev did. His hips snapped hard against hers while his mouth came crashing down on her neck. He nipped and sucked and clamped his teeth down on the most sensitive part of her neck. It was soft at first, but he slowly increased the pressure of his bite like he was trying to break the skin.

"Ev..." Bryson's hands grasped at his shoulders. "What are you—"

He'd never bitten her before. Not like that. A bite between couples, particularly if one was Fae, felt... sacred. And Ev knew that.

He pulled away, licking the spot he'd marked. She felt the sting of his abrasion, but he hadn't torn into her. "I want to mark you," he declared, thrusting harder. "I want to bite you. I want—fuck—Bryson!" His hips snapped harder, and he dropped his mouth to her neck once more. "*I* want to be your mate."

The words were so shocking, Bryson jolted against him, eyes widening. He didn't notice her shock. He was pounding against her, his breathing growing heavier and heavier. He didn't try to clamp down again. Almost as if he were waiting for her permission. Almost as if he were waiting for her to agree.

"Silly human."

Bryson gasped as that sultry voice drifted through her mind. For a second, her soul felt suspended as the breeze blew that spicy, warm, addictive scent in her direction. It consumed her more than the heat of any fire ever could. It wrapped around her in an embrace that she was too weak to fight.

Her eyes opened, and through the blur of darkness and leaves and branches, she caught a flash of gold.

Of him.

Then she was disappearing into her mind once more. There was nothing but darkness there. Darkness and the sensual threat of his presence. Phantom hands slid down her back, making Bryson shiver.

"Silly, foolish human. Trying to mark you while he ruts you."

Bryson's cheeks heated at the cruel, crude words Weylyn spat. There was an undercurrent of anger to them, and yet they remained dark and provocative.

She was well aware she'd drifted deep into the dark recesses of Weylyn's magic. She could no longer feel what was happening in her own body. Couldn't feel Everette fucking her, trying to bite her as if a bond between them could ever take place. She knew nothing of the reality.

She only knew this.

"Does he not know that you are mine?"

She felt a hand at her back, pushing her into that place where this dream and reality collided. So she could almost feel him.

"You are mine, little mate."

Suddenly, the vision faded. She was thrust back into reality. Back on that tree house. With the air caressing her fevered skin, teeth at her neck, and hips snapping rapidly against hers.

Bryson let out a breath of relief when she no longer saw a flash of gold, hiding and spying from the trees. Maybe he'd left. Maybe Weylyn had gone.

Everette pulled away, staring down at her...

Bryson bit her tongue to hold back a scream as Everette's face morphed, shifted, changed, and the features she'd come to know became someone else. Someone new.

Everette became Weylyn.

She gasped as he rose above her, his long braid swaying gently over his shoulder as he slowed his thrusts into sensual undulations. The sudden change of pace and pressure, even the change of the feel of that cock inside her, had Bryson gasping, reaching her hands out to grasp tightly at Weylyn's shoulders.

He smiled down at her, golden eyes flashing in the night. His canines extended and everything about him was filled with malice and carnal desires.

"You are mine to claim," he whispered. His sharp scent permeated through her senses, making her head spin and her mind dizzy. *"You are mine to* fuck.*"*

Bryson knew she should shove him away. She had to. This was a vision. This wasn't real. Reality was different. Not this crazy fantasy he'd summoned and forced on her. But it didn't matter how hard Bryson tried to fight her way out, she remained frozen.

And she feared it was by her own volition.

Weylyn's hands splayed over her body. His every touch was slow and deliberate, much like everything else he did. He touched her with purpose. It wasn't fast and eager. He moved like he had all the time in the world. Like this wasn't a vision. Like he wasn't invading a private moment. He commanded her body like he owned it.

His ministrations held her immobile for the briefest of moments. Her breathing grew labored, and she could only watch as he slowly divested her of her shirt completely. His gaze heated, golden eyes flashing black as he took in her nudity from the waist up. His gaze then dropped down to where they were joined. Where he'd stopped thrusting, only to observe the way his cock speared her pussy open. Where their juices mingled, creating a sharp smell of desire that consumed Bryson's senses.

"See how you are made for me, little mate? See how well you fit on my cock?"

He thrust against her. Slow. Hard. So hard she skidded against the wood and finally, finally, she felt that bite of pain she so desired. The roughness against the skin at her back. The pinch in between her thighs.

She needed to pull out of this vision now.

She needed to go back to Everette. She was with *him*. Not with Weylyn. This was *wrong*.

Her hand snapped up, circling Weylyn's neck. The Fae only arched it, giving her easier access to clamp her fingers tightly around him.

"Are you going to try and kill me?" he taunted.

"Yes." The reply was too breathless as it left her lips.

"You can try, little mate." His nails dug deep into her hips, and he angled her just right so he could thrust once more. *"But I am going to fuck you first."*

Bryson growled, gripping him tighter. She thrust up, meeting the snap of his hips. Her body curled and suddenly they were moving, whirling on the wood, so that she had him pinned beneath her. And somehow, through all that roughness, they still managed to stay joined at the waist.

His hands never once left her hips, and that smile never once diminished. *"You are my mate, Bryson Varik. Whether you want to be or not."*

Bryson shouted as he surged up inside her. She wanted to pull away. She should have pulled away. But in this position, she felt everything. Every pulsing beat of his cock stretching her from the inside. She was full, so full in the most delicious way possible, in ways she'd never been before.

She wanted to hop off him. Truly, she did. But she was weak. Too weak to resist when he was giving her everything she'd ever wanted. Pain and pleasure. The agony was drowned out by waves that crested and consumed. Every rough touch she ever desired, he granted, and she was too weak to say no. She was too far gone to even want to deny him what he would take either way.

So instead of fighting it, Bryson silenced the voice of reason in her head. She silenced the fears and the logic. She silenced everything that didn't serve her except her own pleasure, and she let herself *feel.* For once, the anger she had nothing to do with found its outlet, and Bryson began to move against Weylyn. Every jerk of her hips conveyed her rage, her frustration. All it did was cause the Fae to smile. Like he would be the receptor of whatever she unleashed, and he'd eat it with a smile on his face.

"Yesss," he hissed, his hands sliding up to cup her breasts. *"Fuck me like you despise me. Let me feel your hatred. I will turn it into love."*

She moved her hips, faster and faster, choking his throat until it constricted his airway. Until his words cut off. But the laughter persisted. Loud and wild, it echoed around them as his own hips lifted to meet hers with every jerk, every move. It created a friction between their bodies that pressed against her clit. Every stroke drove her higher and higher. Every touch was a claim, every word was a promise, and every surge of his cock inside her was a threat.

Her pleasure mounted dangerously high. She should pull away, Bryson thought. She had to, now before she fell over that edge. Before they went past that point of no return. Her more reasonable voice tried to rear its head, but before she could, Weylyn's fingers came down right where their bodies were joined, thumbing that sensitive nub, causing her palms to slap down against his chest.

Just like that, she lost all thoughts once again. Her nails dug hard into his flesh, drawing a thin line of blood. With him, she didn't have to worry about how hard or how rough she got. It was freeing. Her thighs clamped around him as she brutalized his chest, marking him with her nails in retaliation for every mischievous deed like this was a punishment. Her insides quaked, and as he thrust, her walls tightened around him...

Weylyn surged up. Like lightning, he was laying down one moment and then up the next, pressing their chests tightly together. He breathed her in, and she did the same with him. His smell of something spicy and sweet intermingled in her nose. It should have been too sharp for her senses, and yet she found herself inhaling it into her system, pulling it deep into her lungs and *moaning.*

"I will claim you, little mate," Weylyn whispered against her neck. His tongue darted against her pulse and the nip of his canines made her shudder. *"One way or another."*

Bryson shattered. Her orgasm slammed over her, and she opened her mouth to scream. Her eyes slammed shut against the onslaught of surprising rapture that coursed through her. She grinded against his body, chasing that violent release, looking to get lost in that void. He shuddered beneath her just as violently, and when their trembles ebbed, Bryson slowly peeled her eyes open.

"Wow," Ev whispered, his eyes wide with surprise, wonder, and blissful release.

Bryson let out a soft gasp and pulled away. Reality settled within seconds. The harsh truth of what she'd done. Every movement, every touch... It had been with Everette, and yet it felt like it hadn't been with him at all. Like it'd been with her—

With *Weylyn.*

"Wow," Ev whispered again. His dark hair was tousled wildly, and when she looked down, she saw the marks of her claws against his chest, the blood running against his skin.

"I—I'm s-sorry—" Bryson felt like she couldn't breathe.

"Oh, this? I liked it. You've never... you've never been so *wild* before. Fuck, that was..." He let out a breathy chuckle and leaned close to nuzzle her cheek with his chin.

Touching him felt like a betrayal. Being in his arms made her feel like a fraud. A chasm opened up in her chest and she could feel herself falling into it. The truth of what she'd done glared at her, and Ev... Ev was looking at her like she held up his world. If only he knew that she never would have done that to him had she known. She never would have marked him so violently. The only reason she'd done it was because she thought he'd been someone else.

And that felt like the greatest sense of treachery of all.

Bryson had always valued her loyalty. Everything she was crashed down within in an instant. At the single sign of anger and pleasure, she'd let herself go.

And had inadvertently hurt Everette in the process.

Bryson pulled away from him, grasping blindly at her clothes to cover herself. Her body still hummed with the aftereffects of her own release, but when Ev's softening cock slid out from inside her, she didn't feel a hollow ache. Didn't feel like she missed him inside her at all.

What have I done?

Her eyes stung with tears, and this time she couldn't stop them as they fell.

"Hey, Bryce." Ev reached for her, his touch gentle and reverent. She flinched away. Undeserving of his affection, of the love he so readily gave her. "What's wrong? Did I do something? Did I hurt you?"

She let out a laugh of disbelief.

If only he knew. If only he knew that the whole time they'd been joined together, she'd imagined someone else in his stead. She'd pictured someone else. She'd been fucking someone else. And the worst part about it was that she'd known. She'd known what she was doing, and a deep, dark part of her would do it again.

Weylyn had satisfied her in the confines of her own mind. He'd played her body like an instrument, wrought something she'd never felt before. He'd created more pleasure within her own thoughts than Everette ever could with his entire body. The guilt of those thoughts was immediate; she drowned in it.

That wasn't supposed to happen. She wasn't supposed to give in to him, no matter how much she liked it. And if Ev ever found out about what she'd done and she lost him forever?

She'd only ever have herself to blame.

Pretty Little Lies

Bryson wondered in the days that followed if she could shed her skin for a new one. Though logically she knew that Weylyn hadn't touched her, not really, she could still feel the phantom press of his palms sliding sensually against her skin. When she closed her eyes at night, she remembered everything with an ache between her thighs that burned. It could only be driven away by her fingers, gliding over her sensitive flesh until completion.

She hated how it made her feel afterwards.

Like she was hurting Ev all over again. Like she was somehow being disloyal by remembering the savage touch of Weylyn's hands and body and the dark promises he whispered in her ears.

She didn't want him to claim her. She didn't want to belong to the mysterious, golden Fae. But every time she remembered those words, something stirred inside her. Like Mana was awakening, demanding she give in.

She would listen to Mana on everything but this.

Bryson had managed to avoid Ev as much as she possibly could. She chose to busy herself, asking Arlo for task after task to keep her mind occupied on things other than Weylyn.

She had to tell Ev.

Bryson knew she had to tell him what had happened. But anytime she tried to form the words, they caught in her throat and she ran away. Especially when he looked at her so lovingly. Especially when he displayed her claw marks so proudly, with the buttons of his shirt open to reveal the evidence of what they'd done. Of what she'd done to him.

It only made her stomach churn.

When Bryson finished her chores for the day, cleaning and mucking out the horse stalls, she wandered through camp. Part of her avoidance of Weylyn had also extended to the Resistance. In fact, Bryson had barely spoken to them outside of their first meeting.

Even the Elementals, for all the curiosity Bryson possessed of the three Fae women, hadn't indulged in any type of conversation. Though by this point,

Bryson could recognize them by scent alone. By the way they walked, and by the sounds of their voices. If by nothing else, at least she knew them that way.

Shula Azzarh, the fire Fae, always smelled like a mix of confections and embers, with the subtle hints of medicinal herbs that clung to her skin and clothes, courtesy of her mate. He was a scarred Fae named Ryker, and whenever she saw flashes of his face, Bryson didn't feel so alone with her own scars.

Iona Wilde, Malika's sister, was the more... conspicuous... of the Fae Elementals. Her scent wasn't as sharp as Shula's, but her demeanor was more boisterous, as was her mate's, the giant ginger named Julius. They trained together almost every day, the sounds of their fighting and passion loud enough to echo through the trees.

Corvina, the water Elemental, was more subtle in everything she did. She didn't train with the others. She sat back with a group of humans and Fae that had come with their party, tending to her son and watching the others with quiet determination.

The Elementals all flocked to each other, too. And Malika trailed after her sister as well. It made a strange sense of loneliness spread through Bryson's chest.

Never before had she felt so alone.

Her own group of friends were sparring lightly near the Resistance. Bryson closed in to watch, if only because Everette wasn't there at all.

Weylyn was, though she forced herself to ignore him in favor of watching the swords clang together in percussive, fake violence.

"Basil, be careful!"

Bryson's attention turned to the water Fae. Her blonde locks were in disarray over her shoulders, the golden strands shielding her face. She'd spoken to her son, who was running around near where they were sparring.

"Mommy, look at me!" Basil jumped over a particularly high rock and as he landed on the other side of it, his feet skidded along the ground, causing him to trip. He let out a cry as he neared the area where they were fighting and fell in between the fray.

Bryson winced.

Basil pushed himself to a stand, and as he did, he was shoved back by a very adult forearm.

"Watch what you're doing, kid."

The force of the shove sent Basil sprawling to the ground once again. Only this time, instead of getting back up, the tears came, and he began to bawl.

Everything after that happened so fast.

Bryson's legs carried her in that direction, but Weylyn got there first, putting his lithe body in between Basil and Otis. Corvina arrived only seconds after Weylyn, pulling Basil to a stand.

Within moments, it appeared to be a battlefield. The Resistance on one side, the rebels on the other. And Bryson stood in the middle, between Otis and Weylyn. Her glare faced her friend.

"Why the fuck would you do that?" she demanded.

"He's in the way, and this is no place for children to be playing."

"You didn't have to shove him, Otis."

Weylyn stepped forward, his overwhelming scent crowding Bryson, though she didn't flinch away.

"This world is no place for the likes of you," Weylyn whispered, low and deadly. "Shall I eliminate you?" He started forward, his hand darting out—

Bryson grabbed it, and the touch of his skin against hers burned.

"You aren't killing anybody," Bryson hissed.

Weylyn's eyes flicked over her, the golden depths flaring alongside his nostrils. "Are you going to stop me?"

"If I must."

They stared at each other.

Up close, he appeared even more formidable than in the visions he liked to send out. It wasn't so much his stature, though he was rather tall. It was in the expression. The way she could tell there was something lurking beneath his eyes. Like a beast hidden within darker depths of waters, waiting for the right opportunity to strike.

"Fine." Weylyn pulled his arm gently away from Bryson's touch and he looked up at Otis. "Only because she asked so nicely. Otherwise you'd be dead."

"You owe the child an apology," Bryson told Otis. "Your actions were uncalled for."

Otis scoffed in disbelief. He glared at the Resistance, the same way Arlo did.

Arlo's reach touched more than half of the entire camp. It wasn't surprising. There was something very convincing about him, and he locked everyone else within the perimeters of his own views. Nobody thought fondly of the Resistance, and she doubted he'd apologize at all.

"Otis," she snapped, wind stirring at his feet.

Otis huffed a breath. "Fine."

Bryson stepped aside to allow him his chance to apologize.

"Basil?"

Bryson jerked her attention back to Corvina's distressed cry. Her head was flailing wildly from side to side, almost as if she were looking for someone.

"Basil?! Where is he? He was right here and now he's gone!" Corvina picked up the ends of her skirts, jerking her gaze around.

As if Basil would appear out of thin air.

Bryson gave a slow turn, squinting her eyes, wondering if she'd see the blurry sight of a small body.

"Basil!"

"Where is he?" Had he moved and they hadn't noticed?

"Children don't just disappear out of thin air!"

"We have to find him!"

"Basil!"

"No, Mana, please, no!"

So many voices rose at once, the panic evident in every single person. But Bryson didn't feel it. She felt a strange sort of calm wash over her. She raised her face to the air and pushed her magic out, letting swirls of wind waft all around her and fill every sense.

She caught the faint whiff of Basil's scent. Something similar to oranges. Her brows furrowed in confusion. His scent should have been much closer, unless he'd torn away in silence without anyone else realizing it. Her face slowly turned in the direction of the forest.

His scent was strong in that direction, though she wondered why nobody else had sensed it yet.

Steady, she walked over to a panicked Corvina and took the water Elemental's hands in her own. She gave them a strong squeeze.

"I will find him," she said. "We will all look. Please, try to stay calm."

The place where their hands touched seemed to create sparks of electricity beneath the skin. Like their magic was reacting to each other's proximity. A call of a wildness that lived inside them both. Corvina gasped and Bryson knew it must've been surging through her as well. Just the brief moment of contact was enough to make the magic inside Bryson swell. She'd never felt a power like this before. So grand that it seemed to want to explode.

What would have been like for all the Elementals to touch? What kind of havoc would they wreak?

Bryson's fingers smoothed over Corvina's gnarled ones. They were bent at crooked, imperfect angles. Corvina must have had a story to tell, and Bryson regretted the fact that Arlo constantly had her busy, unable to connect with these women, who she was sure were amazing in their own right. She wanted to know them. Wanted to know everything about them.

"Thank you," Corvina whispered.

Bryson pulled away and turned to dart into the forest. Her head tilted up and she scented the air. Nobody knew these woods like she did. Nobody knew the pathways and the scents better than her.

She followed Basil's fragrance. It was faint, like he'd run through here, feet barely touching anything. But soon, his scent was overpowered by another.

Shivers slid along her back as footsteps approached, and she tried to keep her anger in check as Weylyn approached her from behind.

The Fae didn't touch her. But he moved close enough to her side that she felt everything. A flash speared through her mind, memories of last night and the ecstasy she felt as she fell into his arms.

Bryson took in a breath and faced ahead, squinting as if that could make the images clearer. The action caused the scars on her face to itch something fierce, but she resisted the urge to swipe her hands over them.

"You will ignore your mate?" Weylyn said.

She wasn't prepared for the impact his voice had on her body. Whispers in her ear, through her mind. A claiming. The way his hips surged up to meet hers. The vicious way he clawed and demanded to be clawed in return.

She shoved all those memories aside and gritted her teeth. "You are no mate of mine."

"If you truly believe that, I would be writhing around in agony due to a rejected mating bond."

Bryson's nostrils flared and her temper spiked. "Leave me alone, Weylyn."

"You know I cannot do that."

I will claim you, one way or another.

His words from a few nights ago echoed through her. She let out a breath. This was the first time she had seen him after what had happened, and she needed to clear the air with him, because it was time she told Ev the truth.

"You invaded my mind. You spied on me and Everette."

There was a brief second of silence. "I will not apologize for watching you and your human fuck. Nor for giving you more pleasure than he ever could."

"That was wrong, and you know it."

"Was it?" He seemed to press closer to her, his body heat enveloping her like the rays of sunlight in the sky. "Was it so wrong to give you what you've been vying for this entire time?" His hands played with the ends of her curls, and she couldn't bring herself to pull away from him. "We are evenly matched, you and I. I can give you the aggression you seek. I would let you use me as you saw fit. I would fuck you like we were nothing but two wildlings in an Unseelie Court. Isn't that what you desire? What the human cannot give you?"

Bryson jerked away from his hold. "It doesn't matter what I want. You're missing the point entirely. I'm with Everette. I'm loyal to Everette. And I broke that loyalty to him because of your mind tricks."

Bryson knew it had also been her own fault for being so weak and succumbing to him. But he never should have invaded her mind in the first place. She'd told him to get out of her head several times. Why would she want a mate who didn't respect her most basic wishes?

Because you loved every bit of it.

She silenced the voice in her head. This time it wasn't Weylyn's. It was her own.

"I broke Ev's trust," she went on. "I cheated."

"What the human does not know will not harm him."

Bryson scoffed. "Are you saying you want to be the other man? My dirty little secret?" She found that very hard to believe.

"Oh, no, little mate. You misunderstand me completely. I want to absolutely destroy that human of yours. I want to tear him apart until there's nothing left but scraps. I want to obliterate him from this world because he is allowed the privilege of holding you at night, of fucking you until you scream. He is afforded everything I've ever wanted, and he doesn't even fucking deserve you."

Her feet skidded on the ground as she forced herself to a stop and whirled to face him, forcing him to stop as well.

"You don't get to decide who deserves me. You have no fucking idea what I deserve or not."

His eyes flashed and his smile kicked up. There was no offense in his gaze, but he looked at her like he relished in the challenge she presented. Like she was a delicate morsel that he wanted to swallow whole.

"You deserve someone who will fuck you until you cannot remember your own name. Not someone who will barely scratch your itch."

Bryson's eyes rolled. "Is that all you have to offer? Sex? I can get that anywhere. I don't need you."

Weylyn stepped forward then, so close that their chests brushed, and she could feel the steady beat of his infuriating heart. His braid swayed as he leaned down, slipping over her shoulder. "I could offer you the entire world, little mate. If only you'd let me."

And she believed him, too.

There was something in his eyes, a gleam, a promise of violence that let Bryson know he spoke the truth. He would cleave the world in two for her, if only she asked it of him. He would set it to flame, kill and murder and maim anybody who got in his way.

The idea thrilled as much as it frightened her.

She took a step out of his presence, trying to shake his scent from her nostrils and clear her head.

"Leave me alone," she said firmly. "I don't want the world, and I certainly don't want you."

"Little mate—"

"I said *no*!" Her magic lashed out, a vicious, choking force that swirled around him in a violent torrent. It choked around his neck like invisible ropes. And when he staggered, Bryson lifted her hand and pulled the breath from his lungs.

Weylyn clawed at his neck, choking and gasping for breath that wouldn't come. Bryson's rage fueled her magic, controlling the very air around them, preventing him from drawing a single breath. His face began to redden, and she let it, lifting him with the wind until his feet dangled beneath him.

And then she let him fall.

Weylyn dropped to the ground. He didn't cry out, but she could hear the soft gasps as he drew in breath after breath.

"Now you know what I'm capable of," she hissed, letting her magic swirl around his body. "Mate or not, I will kill you next time you cross my boundaries. I swear it on Mana."

Weylyn looked up then, his golden eyes flashing, his lips pressed into a thin line right before they curled into an unnatural smile.

"You think I fear you?" he whispered. "No, little mate. Your violence and willingness to murder me only makes me want you that much more."

Bryson fought back the urge to groan. He was crazy. There was no other explanation for it. He was absolutely insane.

Weylyn pushed himself to his feet, dusting his pants off with his palms. "I will respect your wishes, little mate."

The words rocked Bryson back on her heels, and she narrowed her gaze on him, the action making his form clearer. It felt like a trap, like a lie. She loathed to trust it.

"We have dallied long enough." He started forward. "Basil needs us. Lead the way, Bryson Varik. We have much ground to cover."

Lady of Gold

Bryson kept her head lifted, pulling wind from every direction her way. She filtered through the smells, finding Basil's distinct orange scent. Her feet picked up once she found it. Weylyn didn't question her as she followed it like a bloodhound. Her feet carried her near the river, where his essence was stronger, yet blended into the misty spray of the water.

She looked around, squinting. "Do you see him?" she asked Weylyn.

"No."

"He's here." She knew it. She didn't know how, but she did. She turned to Weylyn, about to ask them to disperse, but when she turned his way, he was incredibly, eerily still. His eyes flicked until nothing but the whites of them were visible.

A second later, Bryson felt her consciousness being yanked into his mind.

Not again, was all she could think before she was propelled into Weylyn's mind. But this time, there were no inappropriate visions. All around them was the forest they currently stood in, but everything was... different. Like they were standing through a phantom realm and not the human one. And over there, right near the river, crouched low, she could make out the outlined body of a small boy.

Weylyn walked towards him slowly. "Lord Basil?"

Lord? What? Bryson didn't ask the question out loud.

Basil's head snapped up in Weylyn's direction and then the child began to cry.

"My lord." Weylyn bent so he was level with the child. "What ails you?"

Basil sniffled. "I was there one moment and then the next I was gone, and nobody could find me, so I ran."

Bryson approached slowly. "Has that ever happened before?"

Weylyn slowly turned his head in her direction. "No."

"Is it... Mana's gift?"

"It must be." He turned back to Basil. "My lord, your gifts from Mana are manifesting."

His tears stopped flowing. "Gifts?"

"The way your mother controls water, the way Shula controls fire, the way Iona controls ice. Your own gifts are manifesting."

"I don't want it! Nobody can see me!"

"The price of your magic, little lord." Weylyn smiled at him, and it was so tender that for a moment, everything fell away. In that moment, Bryson didn't see him as a menace. Funny, how the single action changed his whole face.

He looked at the boy like he cared deeply for him.

"To become invisible, you are silenced completely. In sound, in essence."

"I don't want to disappear!"

Weylyn gripped Basil's shoulders and smoothed the tension in them. "Then you must learn to control it. Control your emotions, my lord. No more tears, no more anger, no more sadness. Control yourself. Relax. And you will become visible to us once again."

She watched, feeling rather useless as Weylyn coaxed the child into relaxing. And then slowly, the world around them began to fade until Bryson was thrust back into her mind, blinking awake like she'd been in some strange dream.

When her eyes followed the riverbank, Basil was there. Visible. Whole.

"Well done, my lord," Weylyn praised, that smile on his mouth so tender that Bryson had the urge to run her fingers across his lips. Everything he did was done with malicious intent, but when he spoke to Basil, it was different.

He was kinder.

More real.

She hated how it warmed her from the inside out.

"The child of an Elemental wielding magic."

It wasn't unheard of. Magical gifts from Mana were rare; only a small hint of the population had magic. Sometimes it ran through familial blood. More often than not, the magic-bearers were those that came from families without any at all.

But Basil's mother was an Elemental. And if he was manifesting his magic at such a young age, it was for a reason. Mana probably had bigger plans for the boy and set this specific gift into his veins for a reason.

Invisibility. And the price of it was that no one could sense him nearby. The invisibility dulled his scent, deafened others to his cries of help. Yet Weylyn's mind magic counteracted Basil's, and he was able to find his consciousness. And Bryson? Well, her senses were already sharper than others' due to her poor sight.

"You know you could have found him quicker than me from the very beginning," Bryson whispered accusingly, though there was no heat behind it.

Weylyn picked Basil into his arms and turned with long-legged strides. He threw that familiar malicious smile in her direction. "Oh, but you were having a very good time finding him on your own, little mate."

Bryson chuckled, and she found that even though he'd said those words, this time she didn't feel bothered by them at all.

"Basil, love, where were you?" Corvina cried out and pulled her son into her arms the moment they made it back to camp. She held him close, her tears soaking his hair, and he gripped her equally tight.

"My lady," Weylyn drew her attention his way.

Corvina looked at Weylyn with shining eyes.

Bryson could only be a spectator to the event. From what she'd gathered, everyone always gave Weylyn a wide berth, but she'd never seen the water Elemental stare at him like he was a pariah. In fact, she seemed to be one of the only ones who ever welcomed him. Even now she was looking at him with her eyes shining, admiration obviously glowing in them.

Something hot seared in Bryson's chest, and she rubbed it away with the palm of her hand, taking a deep breath to settle her nerves.

Even Weylyn looked at Corvina with equal admiration.

"His gifts from Mana have manifested," he said.

Corvina rocked back on her heels and Clay crowded behind her, staring wide eyed at Weylyn. "What do you mean?" he asked.

"Invisibility," was all Weylyn had to say. "The price is silence, the lack of essence."

Corvina closed her eyes. "As if being a mother isn't already hard enough."

Weylyn reached out to the woman, and Bryson held her breath, almost expecting Corvina's mate, Clay, to stop the trajectory of Weylyn's hand. To slam into him. To go feral. But he let it happen. Weylyn set a hand on Basil's head before he slid it down Corvina's arm.

The gesture was strangely intimate, though not in a sexual way. Not in the same way Weylyn crowded Bryson. This was... different.

"My lord will learn to control it. With the right teachings." Then Weylyn pulled away and Corvina smiled warmly at him.

"Thank you, Weylyn."

"Anything for you, my lady."

Corvina gave another sheepish smile before Clay led her back to where their group awaited them. They crowded around the couple, fussing over Basil in hushed, low voices.

Finally, Weylyn turned back to Bryson, but all tenderness had erased from his expression, and he was looking at her again with that mask of seduction. His lids lowered, eyes heating as they roved over Bryson's every inch.

She wouldn't be fazed this time. While her body did warm a fraction, she shoved it all down, giving way to curiosity instead. The way he'd been with Corvina and Basil... It made something in her chest burn, like the bond was igniting inside her.

Not jealousy, she told herself. It couldn't be that.

"Why do you call them 'my lord' and 'my lady'?"

He blinked, though showed no surprise at her question. She wondered if he even felt it at all. "Because they are the High Lord and Lady of the Gold Court."

Bryson reeled back at that information, her gaze jerking in Corvina's direction. She stared at the woman, at her son, and she was sure confusion clouded her every feature. The sunlight kissed her golden hair and made her skin almost shimmer, like she was shrouded in a halo of gold. Even with her hazy vision, Bryson could see how ethereal Corvina was.

"High Lady?" she echoed, turning back to Weylyn. "You're sure?"

His lips pressed into a line of amusement. "Her father was the High Lord, and with his passing, it is now Basil's title."

"I've never met a High Lord or Lady," she confessed. Then again, she hadn't met princes or kings either.

"There is another High Lord among us." Weylyn dropped his voice to a conspiratorial whisper, leaning into her, gold eyes flashing. "High Lord Clay Valentino of the Sapphire Court." He leaned back once again. "I suppose with Uric being the only known living heir to the High Lord of the Obsidian Court, he counts as well."

The image of the pale skinned, silver-haired demon flashed into her mind. She couldn't picture him as High Lord of anything, though the fact that he hailed from the Obsidian Court made sense. They were known for their silent brutality.

"I guess I should start calling Clay 'my lord' now?" she teased, finding the words easy to slip from her tongue.

"He is quite pompous and would enjoy it far too much."

Bryson pushed out a breath. "So, you're from the Gold Court..."

There was a beat of silence in which Weylyn didn't answer. His gaze was hot on her skin, caressing every inch before they flicked back up to her face. A slow smile curled his mouth. "In a manner of speaking, yes."

That explained his high regard when it came to them, though she'd also noticed, from what little she'd been able to observe, that he did not treat the Seelie Prince with that same respect. If anything, they all kept their distance.

She wanted to ask, but didn't voice it. Asking would mean an insight into his mind, and that wasn't something she wanted at all. If anything, she needed to get away from him. His proximity made her forget herself. It worried her how quickly he could crumble her resolve, how quickly she could fall into conversation with him. How quickly he could pull her in and make her forget.

That was a dangerous thing.

His eyes flickered, gold to white and back to gold again. His braid swayed as he stepped forward.

Bryson stepped back and away from him, putting necessary distance between them. Whatever friendship he thought they'd developed on this little outing was useless. Bryson didn't trust him. And looking at him just reminded her of her own betrayals and cleaved something in her chest in ways she didn't understand.

Weylyn froze when he saw Bryson stepping away from him. His jaw clenched a single moment before he relaxed it, assuming a careless, sarcastic air.

Bryson almost wondered if he'd crowd into her space, push his way inside her mind, force himself into everything she did. She wouldn't be so merciful if he did.

But Weylyn merely straightened. "Thank you, Bryson Varik," he whispered, "for your assistance in finding the little lord."

She took a steadying breath and tried to calm the rapid rhythm of her beating heart. "No thanks are needed," she said. "Goodbye."

"Hmm." He hummed and took a few more steps back, though he didn't take his gaze off her.

She couldn't stand it. The more he looked her way, the more she envisioned what had happened between them. Perhaps it hadn't been truly physical; they hadn't touched, but it still felt very real. She'd allowed it to persist, allowed him entrance to her body and thoughts.

Bryson wrenched her gaze away from him and whirled to storm away. Her feet nearly skidded on the ground as she caught sight of Everette up ahead.

She'd been so lost within the cloying scent of Weylyn that it had overpowered Ev's completely.

Tears burned behind her eyelids, and she shoved those away and marched on.

"Bryce—" Everette reached for her, but she shifted away before he could touch her.

She couldn't stand the thought of his skin against hers, and she hated the look of hurt she put on his face, and the look that would come after he found out the truth.

"Not now, Ev," she whispered, hoping he couldn't hear her voice crack. "I'll find you later, okay?" She didn't wait for his reply before she was running away, off to find something else to do that would keep her mind occupied and off what she'd done, the truth she'd have to face, and the feelings it provoked deep inside her chest.

Oh, Bryson, her familiar's voice drifted through her head, filled with sympathy, sorrow.

Not now, Bryson thought back. She didn't want to hear it. Didn't need to.

She already knew what her familiar would say. That she was a stupid, stupid fool.

And she was somehow breaking her own heart.

A Coming War

"We are not welcome here."

Valerio turned and regarded the merciless, marble-black eyes of his oldest friend. The words he'd whispered hung like a morose, steady-swinging noose between them. Any other time, at any other place, Valerio would have twisted the tight line of his mouth into a sardonic smile. Now, however, he felt the loom of threat in the very air they breathed and couldn't muster the energy to do so.

The hairs on the back of his neck had stood on end since arriving at this camp. A dreadful sense of foreboding clung to his gut and refused to loosen its hold. He liked to think he had enough experience now to know that something was going to go to absolute shit, and both his body and his friend were warning him of that fact.

Uric regarded Valerio with a familiar severity, the words he wanted to say echoing loud in the silence between them.

"I know." Valerio turned back to the camp. He had grown accustomed to humans and the disdain they wore so tightly on their souls, but it was an odd thing indeed when *Fae* were wary of him. He tried to understand their reasoning, but found it difficult to do so.

Finally, Uric gave voice to his thoughts with choking force, like they were forbidden Unseelie fruit plagued with rot and death. "We should leave this place."

Valerio closed his eyes, but that didn't drown out the sound of those words. They were a request, a plea, but they felt like a command. He avoided grinding his back teeth together in frustration. How easy it was for Uric to voice what he thought they should do, how easy he thought that Valerio should just succumb to those whims.

He could not.

His role was much more complicated than that now that his father, the king, was back to full health.

"I cannot help but wonder if every Elemental we find will bring us complications," Valerio mused quietly, though he felt no mirth in the words.

"My prince, please," Uric pleaded.

Valerio sighed. "Please *what*, Uric?" The glare he slashed Uric's way only made the Fae straighten, even more rigid than he'd been before.

"They'll not hesitate to put knives into our backs. We must *leave*."

Valerio's back tingled as if a phantom blade had lodged itself there to somehow put more emphasis on Uric's warning.

The weight of everything that was required of him was pressing down on his shoulders, and his entire soul was ready to crack into a thousand fragments of emotions he could not bring himself to face. He steeled himself against unwanted feelings and blew out a breath, scoffing at his own pathetic resolve.

"Look around you, Uric," he said quietly. "What do you see?"

His friend was silent a long moment, though Valerio felt his dark gaze heavy on the side of his face. "I see a camp."

"Want to know what *I* see?" He paused. "I see soldiers. People that can make a difference in our war."

A soft growl rumbled from the recesses of Uric's chest. "They want nothing to do with us."

"What if we convinced them?" He was sure his own doubts did not bleed into those words, even if the sinking feeling twisted somewhere deep inside him.

"We cannot."

"What if we *can*?"

There was no other choice, and Valerio refused to accept any other outcome. The fact was, they needed soldiers. Conquering Dana had been nothing more than luck, a small gift from Mana. But it was only the beginning. There was still so much more left to do. A single battle was all they'd won in years. They'd freed so many Fae from the confines of iron chains, yet they were not soldiers, fighters. They could be trained, yes, but the Fae lacked the numbers to wage war on the emperor. Something that was seeming more likely to occur.

The Emperor of Illyk would not stand idly by in silence as the Fae conquered his kingdoms. He would send soldiers by the horde.

And the Fae had to be prepared.

"Your task was to find the Elemental," Uric reminded him. "We have found her. We should take her with us."

He fought the urge to pinch the bridge of his nose between his thumb and forefinger. Instead, he stepped closer to his friend, leaning forward. His hair slipped from the confines of their knot, kissing his cheeks. Uric inhaled sharply at Valerio's proximity, his eyes widening, his throat bobbing as he swallowed.

Maybe it was due to the burning anger fierce in Valerio's gaze. Maybe it was the threat of his magic, pulsing a terrible beat around them. Or maybe it was simply because he could taste Valerio's breath on his lips.

It was a cruel thing to tease Uric with this nearness, knowing what lived within the Fae's heart. But in his anger, Valerio did not care how cruel he had to be or to whom.

"I know very well what orders the king has given me," he snarled, lip curling. "But I know my father. He wants us to find the Elementals quickly, because he's relying on them, but he would reprimand me for not procuring soldiers for his cause."

In any case, whatever he did was bound to be a sword with a double edge. If he merely took the Elemental and left, and the king discovered there was a whole camp of fighting Fae, he would rage against Valerio, punish him for his stupidity and not seizing an opportunity. If Valerio stayed and brought more Fae into their fold, the king would sneer down at him and lash out for not obeying orders.

There was no winning.

There was never any winning.

Sometimes Valerio felt things were much easier when he thought his father was dead. The guilt that swarmed his entire body as soon as he thought it was a consuming force. He should not think those treasonous things. Not when his father was the king of his people.

He'd not be bitter about how things turned out.

Instead, he would prove his own capability. He would prove he could do what his father thought him incapable of, even when he knew it would never be enough.

Uric's jaw twitched as his teeth clamped tightly closed. He heaved a harsh breath through the nostrils and then took a steady step backwards, away from Valerio and his anger.

He ignored that guilt, too.

"But you are right." Valerio straightened and smoothed his hands down his dark shirt. "The sooner we can convince them and leave, the better. I would not want the emperor's soldiers finding us here."

It seemed that no matter where they went, the soldiers discovered their whereabouts. At least, that had been the case before. Things were quiet, and the Seelie Prince did not trust they'd remain that way for long.

They needed to move. That much was for certain.

"I think it's high time we spoke with Arlo Blackwood," Valerio decided, staring at the largest tent in the center of the camp. The one that belonged to the half-Fae leader. He smiled then, feeling his magic whisper through the confines he kept it behind like a threat, a promise. "Let us hope, for his sake, he sees things our way."

"Is my hospitality not up to your standards?"

The impetuous voice that greeted them as they walked through the flaps of the tent grated down Uric's spine. An even greater irritation and offense was the absolute malice in those eyes paired with the curling, sarcastic smile as he stared upon the Seelie Prince.

Uric's fingers itched to reach for his blade and cut out the halfling's tongue for that disrespect. As it was, he was forced to control not only his temper, but his expressions as per his prince's command. It took everything within him not to sneer at this peasant.

"Your hospitality is adequate," Prince Valerio replied, his eyebrows raised and his smile in place.

Arlo let out a low chuckle. The man was looming over his thick, oak table, leaning against the map-covered surface with his knuckles. His posture was relaxed, the beating of his heart a steady thing. He didn't even tremble in the prince's presence like others would.

He was arrogant.

Uric hated him.

"If that is the case, then what is the reason you're in my tent?" His tone was suddenly laced with boredom.

"I wanted to speak with you once again regarding the war."

Arlo stared for a long moment, his gaze still and assessing. Finally, he sat himself down on his high-backed chair, leaning against the plush cushions while placing his elbow against the armrest. "By all means." He flicked his fingers. "Speak."

Uric kept his growl contained when he felt Valerio bristle at the command.

"A war has started," Valerio said calmly.

"From where I'm seated, the war has ended, and it was your family and all Fae who were caught on the losing end."

Uric heard the grinding of Valerio's teeth. "I'll not argue with you about what has passed. The present is what's important, and I promise you a war is coming."

"A war is coming for *you*," Arlo drawled. "Because of what you did in Dana and The West Isles. The emperor will retaliate, and you will fight a losing battle. Again."

"I see." Valerio leaned back on his heels. "You think because you hide in the trees, you are safe."

"I *know* I'm safe," Arlo argued, his eyes flashing. "We are safe because we do not involve ourselves in the affairs of others."

"Stealing prisoners from the emperor's wagons seems like you're pretty involved to me," Uric interrupted. He knew he shouldn't speak, but he couldn't bring himself to hold back the words.

This man, Arlo, was a hypocrite. Anyone with eyes could see it. He was involved. He was thieving directly from the emperor. That in and of itself was a challenge; it was courting trouble, yet he was using his dislike for the Resistance and the Seelie Prince to deny them what they wanted.

His reasons for hating them were still unclear.

Arlo's eyes flashed at Uric's words, mouth twisting a single fragment of a second before his expression cleared. Stoic, he leveled that stare at Uric. "I rescue those who have been enslaved." That glare slashed in Valerio's direction. "Because of the war *your* family started. The Fae I bring here are broken, traumatized. They are not fighters. Would you really be so selfish as to ask them to risk their lives again, when they've already given so much?"

There was a pregnant pause. By Mana, Uric wanted to curse. Arlo was manipulating Valerio. He knew just what to say to make the guilt consume the prince, to make him think twice. As if the prince did not suffer enough already.

"I would never force anyone to fight a war they did not want to," Valerio finally said, his voice quiet and reasonable. "But do not pretend you are far from the reach of soldiers, that you are immune to what is to come."

Arlo leaned back. "Immune? No, not immune. But we are far safer here than we would be among your ranks." He slapped his palm against the table before he pushed himself to his feet once more. "I think you've taken up too much of my time already. I have a great many things to do. Please, see yourselves out."

Uric's spine straightened, and a growl entered his words. "So that's it, then? You refuse to help us?"

Arlo's eyes flicked up. "Was I so unclear before that you need me to repeat myself?"

Valerio stepped closer to the halfling. "The Resistance—"

"Is no problem of ours," Arlo interrupted, his thick brows pulling together in irritation. "You have made your war once and brought it back again. The first time, you nearly eradicated us. This time, we will not help you wipe us from the face of the world. You created this problem, then by all means... you fucking fix it yourselves. Now get out of my tent."

Uric barely contained the snarl that wanted to rumble past his lips. He choked it down with such a force that it scraped through his throat. He looked to his prince, his palms itching, his body vibrating with the vicious need to pounce. All he needed was the order to do so. His fingers twitched near the handle of his obsidian blade, grazing the smoothness of it.

Valerio didn't give the order, though.

The prince let out a small, soft breath. "Forgive us," he said tightly. "For having wasted so much of your time."

Uric could tell he did not really mean the words, as they were said with much disdain.

They didn't wait for Arlo to say anything else. They merely turned and exited the tent. It wasn't until they were several feet away that Valerio finally spoke. "You are right, Uric."

Uric blinked and the prince turned to him, his mouth twisted with disapproval.

"It is unclear why Arlo hates us so much, and it only took an exchange of those few words to realize there is no convincing him. You saw it too, right?"

He nodded. "I did, my prince."

"We will find no help with these rebels." His dark gaze flashed across the camp. Across the many bodies that had treated them with outright hostility since they arrived. "It is time we made our proposition to the air Elemental and leave this place."

Finally, Uric wanted to exhale. Instead, he nodded once again.

"Come," Valerio ordered. "We must hurry. For a war is coming, and we still have two more Elementals to find."

A Mushroom Circle

"Bryson, come drink with us."

Bryson turned, staring at the blurry form of her best friend and Iona, as well as Shula and Corvina. They sat huddled together like they were the closest of friends, whispering conspiratorial secrets to one another.

That familiar surge of bitterness rose to choke through Bryson's throat. She had to fight back the glare she wanted to throw in Iona's direction, the hatefulness and spite that had been growing within her.

Here she was, suffering with too many thoughts and secrets shoved inside her own mind, with words she couldn't dare say to Ev or anyone else, the betrayal weighing heavily on her shoulders, and so much anger that she had no outlet for. She wanted, now more than ever, desperately for her friend.

Yet here her friend sat.

Sipping delicately at Fae wine from a goblet with her long-lost sister.

How easily replaceable Bryson was. How nice it must be to find your family alive and well after all this time.

The envy was as vicious as a tornado, sweeping destruction through her very system. She fought against the wind, but all she managed to do was to tangle herself in the chaos. She couldn't think. She could only feel.

She swallowed the rising lump in her throat and swiped her palms against her thighs. Among all her roiling emotions, there was a terrible longing and melancholy. She missed Malika. It felt like they hadn't spoken to one another in so long. All the words Bryson wanted to say rushed to her lips, which she pressed tightly closed as her gaze swept around the lot of Fae waiting for her to take a seat.

"Okay," she whispered and went to sit across from Malika.

It felt like inserting herself into a puzzle in which she didn't belong, like she was a random piece placed onto an entirely different board. There was a stilted moment of silence and she felt eyes on her. The Fae Elementals were assessing, likely wondering, just as she did, where she fit within their sphere.

"Where have you been, stranger?" Malika asked, pressing her palm against Bryson's knee. "I feel like we haven't spoken in forever."

Bryson swallowed the lump in her throat. "Arlo has been keeping me busy." Her words tasted angry and bitter, and they put a frown on Malika's face. But before she could ask, the Seelie Prince approached alongside his faithful, silver-haired guard.

Bryson resisted the urge to stand up and bow, aware that eyes were suddenly on her back, causing an itchy sensation to glide down her skin. She fought back a shiver as she stared at the prince, who in turn, looked right at her.

"We are leaving," he announced with no preamble, his voice a grave whisper. "Tonight."

The words sent a jolt of electricity down the line of everyone. Even Bryson found herself blinking with surprise. While the intimate details of his features were concealed from her, she could still make out every slashing angry line of his expression.

Something had happened.

Something grave.

"So soon?" Shula asked. Her confections and chocolate scent was oddly comforting, though it began to lace with the sharp smell of worry and fear.

"We have done what we came to do," the prince said. "It is time we move on."

"You're leaving?" Bryson found herself asking.

Her own worry settled tightly in the base of her gut and wouldn't dislodge from there. It twisted her insides, made her sick. They couldn't leave. They *couldn't*. She had waited what felt like years for them. She hadn't even gotten to know them the way she'd wanted to thanks to Arlo, and now they'd be disappearing.

Prince Valerio's gaze softened in her direction. "Come with us," he said.

Bryson's entire body jolted as though she'd been slapped with a bolt of magic.

Valerio turned to Malika. "*Both* of you."

Iona beamed at her sister, her eyes encouraging.

"What?" Malika looked to be as shocked as Bryson felt inside.

"We set out to find the fourth Elemental," Valerio said. "We found you, Bryson. We have told you what we need from you. We have told you what is coming. The decision now is yours. Come with us. Help us fight the war. Help us restore the glory to the Fae and take back what is ours. Help remake our world."

There was a quiet intensity to his words and a certain rightness about them that seemed to settle over her. Like they belonged within her very system. Like they were a wish, demanding to come true.

Help remake our world.

The world her mother had fought and died for. The world that had fallen and, in that aftermath, had taken her father and sister from her. The world she dreamt of before her own life had turned upside down. The world she thought she'd never have again.

He was offering her a chance to take it back.

Suddenly, a cacophony of things collided within Bryson's own mind. Voices, reasons, arguments, parrying back and forth within her head. Her mother's urgence, telling her to take the chance. To fight for the monarchy she'd lived and died for. To do the great things she was always meant to do. Her father's voice, whispering words of peace. Peace that they could have if only she went with them. Arlo's voice, his venomous hatred for the Resistance bleeding through the cracks of her mind, urging her to tell them to fuck off. Reminding her of the debt he was owed.

Then there was that darker voice.

The one steeped in violence and wanted revenge. It wanted blood. It wanted payment for all that she'd lost. That anger overflowed through the cracks, and she pressed shaking fingers to it, lest it seep out completely from her control.

"But Arlo—"

"Arlo Blackwood has refused to help us," Valerio interrupted Bryson. Anger seethed beneath his carefully constructed surface. "So we leave tonight. Come with us," he urged, stepping closer. "Help us fight. Please, Bryson. Help us."

Prince Valerio didn't seem the type to beg. He seemed the type to take what he wanted. He was an Seelie Prince for Mana's sake.

Bryson and Malika shared a look then. For a second, Bryson had her best friend back and she knew that Iona could not interpret the expression on Malika's face. But Bryson could. She knew, she understood on a level that the others couldn't.

Because *they* didn't have ties to Arlo, they couldn't understand the sudden reluctance that flowed through the both of them. The need to speak, alone, and discuss this sudden turn of events.

"We need to think about it," Malika answered for the both of them. She pulled away from the Resistance. From her sister. And, to ignore the look of hurt that Iona flashed her way, settled her gaze on Bryson instead.

"We do not have much time," Valerio said with barely concealed frustration. "Please decide quickly."

"We will," Malika assured, walking towards Bryson.

Bryson let her friend take her hand. She let herself be pulled away from the small group. She felt their eyes against their back, felt them straining to hear a word, yet neither Malika nor Bryson spoke. Not until they were well out of earshot.

"Shit," Malika cursed.

"Yeah," Bryson agreed. "Shit."

They stopped, facing one another. Malika ran a hand across her curls and looked to the sky. "Arlo is going to be so pissed."

"Yeah."

Malika dropped her gaze once again. She bit her lip, like she was chewing on her words before finally, "I am going to go with them."

Bryson wanted to pretend to be surprised, but she couldn't. She'd known. Of course she'd known that Malika would choose, not Bryson, not the Resistance, but her sister.

That burned.

Tears pricked behind Bryson's eyes, but she refused to let them fall. "I knew you would want to."

Unfortunately, Malika knew her well enough to interpret her tone. She reached forward, clasping Bryson's hands in her own. "Come with us," she urged. "I've known you for years, Bryson. I've known you've always wanted more than what Arlo has offered us. I've seen how it upsets you when he talks down about the Resistance. I might not know the full extent of your story, but I know you are not happy here and haven't been in a long time."

A lump formed deep in her throat. Had her best friend really known so much? Even if Bryson had never spoken the words, had everything she'd felt been laid bare for everyone to see? If so, then Malika had to know what kept her feet tethered to this camp.

"Arlo won't be happy."

Malika squeezed her hands. "I know he won't be."

"We owe him a debt."

At this, Malika frowned. "A debt we have paid over and over again. Look, I know he saved us, but we have done so much for him since then. We've helped him save others. We helped him build his camp. Our debt is settled, and now it's time to move on from this place, don't you think? Unless—" She broke off, tilting her head slightly to the side. "Is this about Ev? Of course it is, isn't it? You don't want to leave him. You love him."

Those words only seemed to burn Bryson's insides so much more. She closed her eyes against the onslaught of them as the memories invaded once again. Of Weylyn, of his touch and his taste, his sharp scent, and the promises he whispered darkly into her ears.

Of her betrayal.

"Malika," Bryson whispered. "There's so much you don't know."

"Then tell me."

Bryson opened her mouth and tried to form the words. She tried to tell her about how she'd betrayed Everette. Of the awful sin she'd committed. Of how she was going to break his heart.

Instead, she whispered, "Weylyn is my mate."

Malika jerked back, eyes widening with barely concealed surprise. "The tall, rude, weird Fae?"

A sob lodged itself in Bryson's chest at that description. So accurate and so painful. To think that her mate, the one Mana had chosen specifically for her, was hated and viewed that way by everyone he came into contact with.

"That's the one."

"Oh. *Oh.* I see."

But she didn't see. How could she when Bryson had kept it inside for days, fearing judgment, fearing everything.

"What does this mean for you and Ev?" Malika asked with great care.

What *did* it mean for them?

Bryson knew the answer before she even opened her mouth to speak. It was high time she finally made a fucking decision. It was high time she stopped hiding behind everyone else and owned up to what she'd done. It was time she brought herself back to reality and faced the consequences.

"I need to go speak with Ev."

She found Ev at camp. He looked surprised at her approach, though she didn't blame him for the expression that currently painted his face.

She'd been aloof for days. She'd avoided him ever since that night. Ever since she'd scrambled off his body in tears and left him in that little tree house alone. Confused, and alone. Now, she had to face him in the aftermath of that betrayal.

"Ev," she whispered, already feeling her insides break, shatter like glass into millions and millions of pieces. She had no right to feel what she was feeling. No right to those roiling emotions.

But when she looked at him, all she could see was someone else. Someone else clawing at her back, sinking canines into her neck. A flash of golden eyes, demanding her pleasure that she was all too eager to give and would do so again, because her treacherous body craved him like she craved air, even when she knew it was wrong.

"Bryson." Ev stood, dusting his hands against his pants. "What's wrong?"

That lump in her throat only hardened. "We need to talk."

He nodded at her grave expression.

They didn't go very far. Only a few feet...

...before everything went to shit.

Fuck, she wanted to curse as Weylyn blocked their path.

Bryson's face heated. She wanted to flip him the finger. Pull Everette away from Weylyn's special brand of danger and mischief. Fear, sudden and bursting, appeared inside her. What did he want? She'd avoided him too, but now that he saw her and Ev together, would he flaunt what they'd done in Ev's face before she got the chance to tell him herself?

Ev bristled next to her, that concerned look turning into an angry stare as he took Weylyn in. "What do you want?" he demanded.

Weylyn ignored Everette as though he were nothing more than a piece of furniture and stepped closer to Bryson. "You'll come with us, won't you?"

Her heart bottomed out to her stomach. Her throat closed up, pushing the words she'd wanted to say behind a tightly locked closed door with no escape. Her breathing grew into shallow pants and her already blurry vision tunneled. She saw nothing at the end of it except Weylyn. His intent gaze on her and maybe, that thing she felt down the unwanted bond that tethered them together? Hope. Desire. Lust.

It all coalesced into a maelstrom of sensations and she couldn't pick apart her own feelings from his. The voices in her head from his. It was all too much. Too overwhelming. Her magic pulsed in response to her distress, begging to be unleashed.

Above, her hawk cried out.

"What the fuck are you talking about?" Ev demanded. His hand slipped into hers, tight, possessive.

Bryson pulled away, ignoring the look of hurt he flashed her way.

Again, Weylyn ignored him. "You will, won't you?" He stepped closer. So close, she could taste the spicy sweet mix of his scent against her tongue. It made her throat open, her mouth water with sensations that she wasn't sure were his or hers.

"Bryson, what the fuck is he talking about?" Ev demanded, his voice rising.

She felt Ev draw in a crowd. Her cheeks flushed with embarrassment as several pairs of eyes trained on them. She'd known that the camp was tuned into the drama. Into the animosity between Weylyn, Ev, and Bryson. They hadn't all known why, but it was a palpable thing. Like looking onto a graying-black sky and waiting for the storm to hit.

"Ev..." She choked, eyes burning. "The Resistance asked me to leave with them. Tonight."

There was a single beat of silence. A single one before Ev was grasping her hands, holding them tightly enough that she would have bruised, had she been human.

"No," he said firmly. "No. Forget it. She's not fucking going with you people."

Bryson tried to pull away, but Ev's grip only tightened.

"That is not for you to decide, human," Weylyn spat, the word human like a curse on the tongue.

"She's not going with you. She's staying here with us. With me."

Bryson's heart thundered in her chest.

Her familiar squawked, tuned into her emotions and swooped low.

"Bryson, tell him you're staying with us," Everette urged, yanking her roughly towards him. His tone had taken on a desperate edge, one he couldn't hide. Up close, she could read the frantic gleam in his eyes, the way his nostrils flared. "Bryson, *tell him.*"

Bryson pulled her hands away from his, dropping them to her stomach. "Ev..."

When she didn't speak, when she could only look at him, Ev's expression immediately twisted into one of disgust. He took a step back, shaking his head.

"Bryson..."

"Ev, just... just give me a minute to think, okay?" She hated that her voice trembled. That everyone around them was witness to it. Even Arlo, who had come out of his tent to see what the sudden commotion was about.

She hated that he would be witness to a conversation that should have been private.

"No, Bryson. Either you're with us or not."

Weylyn chuckled, deep and low in his throat at those words. Ev slashed a daring glare his way before his eyes settled back on Bryson.

"It's not that simple, Ev," she whispered, voice weak.

"Like fuck it's not."

"Ev, my mother fought for the Seelie crown. She... she would want me to go. To do this."

And by Mana, Bryson couldn't stand the look of betrayal that carved into Ev's face right then. The anger followed quickly. It was expected, and still she flinched when he snarled at her.

"What does it matter who the fuck your mother fought for? The Seelie crown put everyone into this fucking mess. Look where it got your mother, your family. They're dead, Bryson. What does it fucking matter?"

The words were like a blow to her chest. She staggered back, away from Everette. He must have realized exactly what he said, because a brief flash of remorse fell over him before he masked his expression once again.

"Foolish, pathetic human male," Weylyn's voice whispered into her mind. *"Come with us, little mate."*

"I—I don't know if I can."

He *tsk*ed a sound of annoyance. *"You can. Do not refuse us this. Not for him. Not for Arlo. If you choose this, choose because it is what you want."*

"I don't know what I want."

"There are too many voices in your head, little mate."

"Then get the fuck out!"

She shook her head wildly from side to side, as if that could expel Weylyn from the recesses of her deepest, darkest thoughts, though she was afraid he'd already seen and analyzed everything. Every decision, every doubt, every bit of anger... He knew what lived inside her already.

"I can't believe you'd say that to me," she said aloud. "Everette, I..." She shook her head, feeling the turmoil through her entire body. But it was decided. She'd already decided what she'd wanted to say. If her own betrayal to him hadn't been the end, then those words were.

She'd betrayed him first, yes, but she'd also asked him to cease his anger, his disrespect. The insult he'd just hurled at her, at her mother, those words? They would live with her forever.

They would be what broke them.

"Everette, I can't do this anymore." She stepped further away from him. She was aware it was a cowardly thing to do, to pull away just so she couldn't see the details of the expression he would wear. Lest it break her heart all over again. "I can't. Not anymore."

He followed. "What do you mean?"

"I mean us, Everette. We... we can't be together anymore. We're done."

There was a bated breath of silence. Everyone was looking. Everyone was listening. Everyone was witness to what she'd wanted to keep hidden.

"No." Ev's voice cracked. "Bryson, *no.*"

"I'm sorry, Ev. This is how it has to be."

"Like hell."

He stormed over to where she was, but with every step he took towards her, she took larger ones away from him, her magic whirling around her, her senses sharp, stopping her just at the edge of a mushroom circle. He stopped in front of her, grabbing her arms roughly.

"This is because of him, isn't it?" he demanded, shaking her once and making her head rattle and her teeth clamp closed. "It's because that bastard is your mate, isn't it? You're leaving me for him, aren't you?"

Her face heated with shame, though her anger flared higher at the way he was manhandling her. She readied her magic between them, but pulled out of his hold, pressing her palms against his chest and shoving him back slightly.

"Ev," she warned. "Stop it."

His eyes and cheeks reddened. "No," he snarled. "Ever since he got here, you've changed! I thought you'd be brave enough to fucking be honest with me at least."

"Careful how you speak to my mate, human," Weylyn growled as he approached. "I'd take great joy in killing you if she hadn't already asked me not to. Though I find that is a promise I could easily break."

Ev rolled his eyes at Weylyn then glared at Bryson once again. "So you two have spoken about me in private? What else have you said? What else have you fucking done?" He stepped closer once again, his arms grabbing her shoulders, nails digging in. "Have you fucked him, Bryson?"

Her face reddened with shame.

"You have!"

"Everette—"

Her hawk screeched.

"You whore!" In his anger, Ev put enough force on her shoulders to shove her backwards. The action surprised Bryson, so much so that she was too late to stop it as she fell backwards and into the mushroom circle.

Distantly, she heard a growl. The screech of her familiar. She heard her name being cried.

And then, there was nothing but darkness as she fell through the void.

Into the Darkness

Weylyn's entire world tunneled into a singular moment clarity as he watched Bryson, as he watched his fucking mate, get shoved backwards and fall through the circle. A singular fucking moment. Between one blink and the next, she had disappeared completely.

And in the chaotic aftermath, there was little more than the screeching, distressed cries of his mate's familiar. That pathetic human scum calling her name desperately.

And Weylyn? His heart bottomed to his stomach, and he knew, he *knew* exactly what he had to do.

His body moved on instinct, rushing towards the same circle his mate had only just disappeared into. His name was shouted, but he did not give a single fuck about the orders of a prince. None of it mattered. None of them did.

Only Bryson. Only his mate.

And when Weylyn jumped into the circle to follow her into the darkness, he knew just where the magic would take him.

And he prayed to Mana he wouldn't be too late.

A Portal

Ev stared helplessly, hopelessly, at the spot where Bryson had disappeared. It had been a second. A single fucking second where she'd been there one moment and then she was falling, falling... And then nothing.

The seconds that followed were chaos. His head spun as his mind tried to grasp what had happened. Where she could possibly be. And when Bryson's familiar shrieked through the air, swooping low to dig her claws into him in retaliation, when that Fae bastard, Weylyn, rushed into the circle and disappeared himself, Ev knew what it was.

"What the actual fuck just happened?"

Ev dropped to his knees, the impact ricocheting up to his fucking skull. He could only stare numbly at the place they'd disappeared through. He blinked several times, almost as if hoping that when he next opened his eyes, Bryson would be standing back where she was instead of gone from his sight.

"I didn't mean to," he whispered weakly, though he wasn't sure anyone could hear the regret in his tone. The sorrow that funneled through his very soul.

"Where did they go?!" This voice was the Seelie prince's.

Ev felt his body being jostled. He felt himself being pulled to a stand, his body shaken while his brain rattled within his skull.

His vision cleared enough to find the Seelie Prince standing before him, his vicious glare a feral, frenzied thing as he shook Ev with his Fae strength, just enough to make Ev grit his teeth in pain.

"What the fuck did you do?" he challenged.

"I didn't mean to," Ev choked out. "I didn't... I wouldn't... oh, gods." He felt his legs give out from beneath him, but only the prince's hands kept him upright. All he really wanted to do was fall onto the ground and weep.

He hadn't meant to shove her. His anger had gotten the best of him. His rage had made him blind to what he was doing, to their surroundings. He hadn't—

"Release him," Arlo's cool voice interjected.

Ev suddenly found himself falling, dropping to the ground into a heap. And he couldn't bring himself to get back up again. His nails crawled into the ground, creating dentures in the earth, as if he could somehow create a crater big enough and find Bryson hiding beneath it.

But no.

Bryson was gone.

And she likely wasn't coming back.

"Where the fuck did they go?" Valerio demanded. He stared at thin air, like maybe they'd reappear again somehow.

Julius carefully circled around the mushroom circle, cautious and not getting too close, though his boots scuffed the dirt outside of it.

Above them, Bryson's familiar let out distressed cries of anguish.

And the three Elementals could only stare at the spot where Bryson and Weylyn no longer were.

Shula let out a breath. "Mushroom circles are portals," she finally said.

Everyone froze in their tracks. Iona's gaze snapped up to her mate's, and Julius' grim expression all but confirmed Shula's words.

"But... how?" Clay demanded.

Julius let out a sigh and stepped away from the treacherous circle and closer to the group. "Some places in the human lands are seeped with Unseelie magic. Places like this," he gestured at the circle, "are like Ley Lines of their own. They hold traces of portal magic from when Unseelie illegally jumped between realms."

"I didn't mean to! I swear I didn't!" The human man, Everette, was still sprawled across the ground, his nails digging into the earth as he wet the grass with his pathetic tears.

The Resistance stared at him with barely concealed disgust before dismissing him entirely.

"We need to try and find a mind link back to Weylyn, then," Valerio urged. "See where they are. Get Uric to open a portal to where they landed."

Julius shook his head. "I don't think it works like that. Who even knows if Weylyn landed in the same place as Bryson—"

"We have to try!" He turned to Shula, Iona, and Corvina. "Could you get a sense of where Bryson is?"

The three Elementals stared among themselves, worry etched over their every feature.

"I can't sense her anywhere near us," Corvina said softly, gently, like she was waiting to be reprimanded for an answer that did not appeal to anyone.

"What if you used the stones?" Clay asked, placing a reassuring hand on the ball of her shoulder.

"We can try," Iona agreed.

Shula nodded grimly as she reached into the pocket of her pants and pulled out a map and several stones. She knelt on the ground, splaying the map out before the other Elementals followed to their knees.

"Ready?" Shula asked, holding her palms and the stones face up over the map. The other Fae followed suit, cupping their hands beneath Shula's.

Valerio watched with bated breath as they channeled their magic. The energy around them seemed to crackle and buzz. Everyone was quiet as they watched.

Everyone except the sniveling human, chanting his apologies over and over again to the ground.

Suddenly, the three women dropped the stones and watched them land.

Three in Ielwyn, where they currently were.

One in the Valley of the Dead.

The fifth bounced along the map.

The final one...

It landed further south.

Right in the middle of the Unseelie Court.

"Fuck," Iona cursed, her eyes wide on that single rock all the way at the bottom of the map.

"Mana save her," Corvina whispered.

Shula closed her eyes then opened them once again. "Bryson is in the Unseelie Court."

The human whimpered and cried, louder now. "I didn't mean to! Bryson, I'm sorry. I'm so fucking sorry."

Beside Valerio, Uric sighed and looked at the human with a curled lip. "Pathetic," he whispered.

"The Unseelie Court," Valerio echoed. He shook his head back and forth, as though his brain were filled with cobwebs he was trying to dispel.

He tried to think past the panic. Past the looming doom of what would come if he failed to get both Bryson and Weylyn out safely. The things his father would say. The venom he'd spew Valerio's way. He could hear him now. He could feel the pain of the punishment down his back. A phantom agony both physical and mental.

He would make it hurt, and he would not cease to tell Valerio of how he'd failed. Again.

Yet above all that there was a more harrowing worry. For Bryson and though he hated the Fae, for Weylyn as well.

They'd crossed the Ley Line before. They knew what laid south of the human border.

Iron. Iron monsters.

And death.

And as he stared at the little rock placed carefully along that spot on the map, Valerio despaired and feared.

And he wondered if he'd find them alive… or if it would be too late.

Iron Gaze

It was like falling through a void. Falling through black emptiness, suspended in the air with nothing in sight while her insides rearranged themselves, twisting into knots as she fell... and fell... and fell...

An endless amount of darkness cradled her from all sides, the shadows like claws that reached for her body through the void. She was sure she screamed, but the sound itself was lost to her ears. It was emptiness. It was loneliness.

And when Bryson finally landed, it was face-first in the dirt. Her teeth scraped against the ground and she choked on grass and mud and the tinny taste of something that burned and scraped down her throat. Pushing herself up by her palms, Bryson coughed, hacking out the taste of whatever she'd swallowed, though it coated her tongue like a thick honey she couldn't dispel.

She blinked the grime from her eyes, every rapid rush of her eyelids a mirror of the pounding of her heart. Her eyes began to sting, and every blink felt like scraping rocks from her eyeballs. It was a sensation that was familiar to her, though one she had tried so hard to forget.

The burn came immediately, and Bryson cried out, swiping her muddy hands across her lids, rubbing them furiously despite the fact that they were dirty. But it didn't matter. The sting persisted. Like acid had been tossed straight into her eyes. She blinked and blinked and blinked. And every time an image of the strange forest surrounding her appeared, just like that, her vision faded slowly to blackness.

"No, no, no, no." The panic came quickly, and the words felt heavy on her leaden tongue. Bryson tried to move, her body squelching in the foul-smelling mud each time she lifted her limbs. Her nostrils stung and her next blink brought with it tears that touched her lips and tasted a lot like blood.

Bryson whimpered in fear.

Not again, she begged Mana. *Not again.*

But there was no denying what was happening. What this clearly was. She could taste it on her tongue, feel it in the air, and it settled heavy over her gaze, blinding her like it had so many years ago.

Iron coated all around her, and she was impervious to stop the effects from claiming her body.

Tears flowed freely as Bryson tried to grab her bearings. Her heart pounded and her chest began to heave. The entire world funneled through her vision, and she saw nothing but black spots dancing through her mind. She choked on her own breaths, a desperate edge of panic gripping her tightly and refusing to let go.

She was going to die. She was going to die. She was going to die.

Bryson tried to halt those thoughts, but they were persistent in her head, no matter how hard she attempted to banish them. She lifted her muddied hands to her hair, tugging tightly at the strands. Maybe the pain could help her focus, could pull her out of that dark place. Maybe when she next opened her eyes, she'd be able to see what was surrounding her. But she needed to calm down.

She needed to be smart.

It took several moments of deep breathing, of calming her erratic heart with gentle words echoing through her head. "You're okay," she told herself. "You will be okay."

She didn't even mind the fact that she was telling herself foul lies.

Once the words became a mantra, she felt them settle over her body. The tight rigidness eased from her muscles, and she relaxed into the earth.

And ever so slowly, Bryson dared to open her eyes once again.

Images seemed to flick in and out of focus at first. Gradually, that twisted vision began to clear a mere fraction. But still, all Bryson saw were shadows. There was no color. No images. Only blurry dark figures looming in the distance. She took a breath, held back her sob, and lifted her hand in front of her face, waving it from side to side.

Shadows. Nothing but a blur of shadows.

Her tears flowed once again, but she didn't let the panic take over.

"You're fine," she whispered to herself. "You've been through this before."

She had lost much more at the time. Her vision had completely gone then. At least this time she could see shadows. At least she could make out shapes now. All wasn't lost. Even if the iron grated her eyeballs and made tears of blood trail down her cheeks. Even if her insides burned and her throat felt like it was closing up.

Bryson took another deep breath and reached out with her other senses. What she lacked in sight, she would try to make up for with everything else. First, she scented the air. Past the foul mud that coated her entire body, past the tang of iron, she could make out nature, though it wasn't a nature she was familiar with.

At camp, things always had a distinctive scent. The magic flittering through the air in waves from the brownies as they cleaned, the shimmer of Fae wine bubbling against the tongue as it was brewed. Sap from the trees. Animal droppings. Bodies. It all mixed together to create something unique.

This was like nothing she'd ever scented before.

Mud, iron, and the raw touch of magic not her own. Not any she'd ever felt before.

She pushed out with the rest of her senses, listening intently. Near her side there was a riverbank, a rushing of cool water that lapped up to her feet. Bryson shivered against it and finally forced herself to her feet. She nearly stumbled as her boots squished into the mud and tore them from the sinking depths. Her entire body ached as she carefully stepped away from the edge of the river. Every movement was slow agony as she held her hands out in front of her, sliding her feet against the ground and kicking stray objects so she wouldn't trip.

Once she felt she was far enough away from the dangers of the water, she paused to assess her next move. Bryson had no idea where she was. All she knew was that she was in a forest surrounded by iron. Was she even still in Ielwyn? Her gut told her she wasn't. The fact she couldn't even hear or sense her familiar anywhere near solidified that fact. If she wasn't in Ielwyn, her friends wouldn't know where to find her or how. She could sit and wait to be rescued, but that brought its own complications.

She didn't know where she was. She didn't know what creatures roamed these woods. And without her sight, it would be infinitely more difficult to fight and navigate her way through an unknown place. Not to mention she could already feel her magic waning as it tried to battle against the iron.

She was useless.

No.

She halted those thoughts as soon as they formed. She was not useless, and she would not sit here waiting to be rescued; she wouldn't sit here waiting to die.

She had to move. She had to keep going. She had to try and survive.

"Come find me..."

Bryson jolted at the voice that echoed through the wind. She tilted her head up, straining her ears, wondering if the iron had gotten to her brain and she'd imagined the eerie echo.

"Come find me..."

There the voice was. Louder now. Closer. Like it drifted through the air to caress her ears alone. It sent a shiver down her spine. She should have felt wary, but all she could muster was a welcoming sensation. A burning curiosity.

"No, Bryson..." But even as she scolded herself, she couldn't stop her feet from moving in the direction the voice had come from. It whispered. It beckoned.

And Bryson was powerless to resist its call.

"Come find me..."

Her feet stumbled over rocks and sticks and fallen leaves. Brambles tore into her clothes from all sides, scraping against her cheeks and drawing blood. She held her arms out, feeling the air, feeling that desperate edge of panic start to rise all over again.

"Come find me..."

Her feet stumbled on the ground, and she burst past the foliage into what felt like open space. The soles of her feet curved and stomped against cracking rocks that nearly caused her to slip and fall. She lifted her iron-coated gaze to the air, breathing heavily, and suddenly there was a voice.

"Oh, dear, are you alright?"

Bryson jolted in surprise as a shadowy figure appeared before her. She could make nothing out save for a slumped, hunched body, and the trembling, creaking voice let her know it belonged to an old crone.

"You look like you have been through something awful," the crone went on. Her voice scraped like rusted iron, and Bryson could read the concern in her tone.

It made her shoulders relax a fraction. "There was a voice..." But it was long gone now. She hadn't heard it again, and it left Bryson wondering if maybe she'd just imagined the entire thing.

"Oh, dear." The crone stepped closer, and Bryson flinched as she placed her withered, leathery hands against her own. "You're shaking, child. And your skin is cold as ice. Come. Let me take you to my home. I will take very good care of you."

Again, Bryson found herself powerless to resist as she was led over hundreds, thousands, of crunching rocks that littered the ground. She nearly tripped, but the crone's grip was firm on her hands as she guided her up what felt like a slope.

"So wet and muddy," the crone *tsk*ed. "Let's get you clean, yes?" she offered. "No need to fear, dear. I am here now. And I am going to take very good care of you."

Rot and Decay

Bryson nearly tripped several times going up the slope towards the old crone's house. The ground was blanketed completely by crumbling rock or brick, and several protruding hard twigs. She rammed her shins into them several times, and it was only that hard, firm grip that kept her upright.

The crone didn't speak again for a few minutes Bryson took a moment to make sense of her surroundings. There was a looming shadow before her, what she assumed was the woman's house. Yet the closer they got to it, the more her senses sharpened, and so did the foul smell.

It's the mud, she told herself. *Just the mud.*

"We're here," the old crone said. There was a rattling as a wooden door was shoved open.

Then there was a rush of warm air against Bryson's body along with a horrid stench. She fought back the urge to gag as the crone ushered her within the door. Somehow, the rancid fetor inside was even more powerful. The air was hot and musty. It was like an extra layer of grime in the air that coated her body like a blanket, invading her nostrils in every which way.

She tried to hold her breath and only take slow sips of air in through her mouth.

"Come, come, sit, sit." The old crone guided her around the house. Bryson's body bumped into things, furniture she assumed, that caused what sounded like jars to rattle. She was shoved down hard into a creaky, wooden chair that trembled beneath her weight.

She looked around, blinking the iron flecks from her eyes. They watered, but her vision unfortunately didn't clear.

"You'll catch your death, child," the crone said. "Look at you, all skin and bones. That won't do, no. You must eat. Yes."

"I appreciate your hospitality," Bryson said numbly. Her fingers came up to rest against the surface of the table in front of her. She felt her way around it, but there was nothing but the gentle fabric of a tablecloth that reeked of mold.

"Think nothing of it." There was a rustling as the woman moved around. Bryson followed the noise with her ears and the shadowy figure with her eyes, hoping she would come into focus.

She didn't.

Finally, when the woman finished whatever she'd been doing, she came next to Bryson, slamming something down on the table in front of her.

"Soup," she declared. "Eat. It will warm your bones."

Bryson loomed over the soup, her body nearly seizing as she caught a whiff of it. It smelt strongly of herbs and something else that wasn't at all pleasant.

"Sheep stew," the crone supplied. "It will help you grow hearty and strong. Eat, eat."

Not wanting to appear rude, she felt around for a spoon. When her fingers came into contact with one, she wrapped them around it and carefully dipped the utensil into the soup. Stirring it only caused the weird odor to sharpen, so she bent low and pressed a spoonful onto her tongue.

Bryson nearly gagged.

It tasted raw of rot and decay. So foul, she nearly spit it out, but she could feel the crone's eyes on her, expectant, waiting. So, Bryson swallowed it down even as her stomach churned with nausea and bile rose to the back of her throat.

"Good, yes?" the crone asked.

"Hmm," was all Bryson could reply.

She couldn't bring herself to take another bite. As it was, the soup still felt thick on her tongue, the taste vile and gross.

There was a soft swishing sound, like the rumple of the hem of a skirt. A hiss.

Bryson blinked, but all she saw was the shadowy form of the woman.

Then, there were fingers slipping through her hair, caressing the strands with gentle care.

"Don't you worry, deary," the old crone whispered. The sudden change of her tone made a shiver glide down Bryson's back, though she couldn't be sure why. "I will take very good care of you."

A Ghoul's Graveyard of Bones

Falling through a void was not a new sensation for Weylyn, though it was one he thought he had permanently left behind. Those thoughts, of the past that was better left buried, flew from his mind as the darkness rose around him. The impact of landing on his feet jarred through his whole system. It rattled his brain and made him grit his teeth tightly.

Even worse was the sudden impact of iron in the air. It choked him in a punishing grip, deadly and dangerous, like it meant to suffocate the very life out of him with little remorse.

He choked it down and stared at his surroundings.

The circle had portaled him in the middle of a forest so unlike the one he'd just been in with the others. He swept his gaze around quickly, nostrils flaring as he inhaled. His booted feet throbbed, a sure indication that iron seemed to be eroded into the ground, pulsing like a living fucking thing.

To his side, there was a river that smelled foul and nearly masked the scent of his mate.

His mate.

His nostrils flared and his feet moved of their own volition, tearing through the brambles and foliage of the forest. He scented her against it, whiffs here and there that he followed like a bloodhound until he burst from the trees and nearly came crashing down to the ground.

Weylyn let out a low growl as he caught sight of what littered the earth. Of the foulest smell rippling through the air. Rot. Decay. Death. They were smells he was all too familiar with, and he knew then and there, seeing ivory and gray half buried in the dirt all around a small wooden cottage, what the creature inside was.

And inside with it?

His fucking mate.

Weylyn moved silently over the graveyard of bones that blanketed the ground. As quiet as he tried to be, they still crunched beneath his boots. Skulls smashed within their hollows, half-rotting corpses with putrid, torn green flesh lined up along the edge. The entire place was designed to keep predators away.

A ghoul's home was like the innermost center of a spider's web, filled with twitching corpses and husks without their souls. Nothing but skeletons and putrefaction.

Through a half-broken window, Weylyn saw a sight that made his heart pound in his chest, beating frantically like a beast to be unleashed.

His mate. Bryson. Sitting at a table in front of a fucking ghoul.

The ghoul took the appearance of an old crone right before it morphed into something far more terrifying. Something nightmares were made of. Its body melted, skin pooling down in clumps as it mutated itself into a tall, thin, *thing* with needle-like fingers that caressed Bryson's dirty hair.

"I'll take good care of you," the ghoul spoke, using the voice of an old, withered woman.

Bryson blinked up at the creature, brows furrowed. As if she couldn't see the monstrosity before her. As if she couldn't make out the gaping mouth and dozens of rows of teeth. As its head split, strings of saliva slid from tooth to fucking tooth.

Weylyn moved.

As soon as he did, the ghoul whirled, sensing a predator in its sanctuary, and screeched. It was a blood-curdling scream that nearly shattered his ears. He didn't care about anything except for Bryson's life.

The ghoul attacked him, slit pupils on either side of its head blinking red and black, claws extended like it meant to tear through Weylyn's chest and rip his still-beating heart from its cavity.

He dodged the claws, swooping low onto his knees. His own hands extended, a growl in his throat. The ghoul loomed over him, and he swept his hand up, tearing through hard flesh. He didn't stop. Couldn't stop. Not even when blood and guts rained down against him. Even as the creature let out a wild cry. Even when the ghoul fell and twitched, joining the bodies of all the people it had destroyed.

It wasn't until the thing stopped twitching that Weylyn finally turned to Bryson. She was wide-eyed, disheveled. Her hair was caked in putrid-smelling mud and there were tear marks and blood down her cheeks. Her eyes squinted, following his form as he approached. Before her, there was a bowl of raw, rotted meat and blood.

His eyes shot back to her, and he spoke, "It's alright, little mate," he assured. In his chest, where the bond she supposedly did not want lay, he felt a surge of warmth, relief. He tugged gently against it, like he could let her know that she was safe. And with him, she always would be. "I'm here now."

The Unseelie Court

Hearing Weylyn's voice speak in the low, slow drawl, saying words she once hated, was like a balm against Bryson's body. It soothed every ache and pain. It calmed her fears. And when she felt a connection, Mana's bond, spark between them, she grasped at it with firm fingers, eager for the safety he cast out to her. And she held on for dear life.

"I'm here now," he whispered.

She could only barely make out the outline of his form as he dropped to his knees in front of her. He smelt of blood, so overpowering she couldn't hold back the bile any longer. She turned and began to retch, vomit spewing all across the floor in wet, clumpy splatters. Her stomach twisted and she heaved, over and over again. Vomit burned up her throat and shot out her nostrils as she expelled whatever she'd swallowed. Her entire body rebelled against the swarm of sensations. Against pain, taste, and stench. When she finally felt like she couldn't get any more out, she weakly sat up, wiping the back of her hand across her lips.

"Weylyn..." A sob rose and she forced herself to choke it back down. To be strong. "Wh-what—?"

"It was a ghoul," he said. His voice was hard, angry. "They glamor themselves as something they are not and use hypnotic magic to lure unsuspecting people into their lairs to eat them."

Fear, cold and brittle, slid through her body. Her stomach twisted again, and she had to fight back the urge to heave.

"I've killed it," he stated.

She'd heard the wet sloshing, had seen the shadowy forms of figures moving. It had been frightening, as the stench of rot had overpowered everything else, and she hadn't made out Weylyn's scent when he'd come in. It wasn't until he'd spoken that she realized it was him.

"Weylyn, the iron in the air—I can't see." She hated how fearful her voice sounded. Hated to be perceived as weak, just like she'd always been perceived as weak because her sight wasn't what it once was. And now, with iron invading, it was worse.

Weylyn's hand cupped her cheek. She flinched before settling into the contact, sighing deeply. His thumb shoved away tears she hadn't realized she was shedding, and she found comfort in the gesture, even when she knew she shouldn't. It would only encourage him to believe there was something between them when there wasn't.

"You are safe now," he said firmly. "I am here."

Her breath stuttered from her throat. "What did that thing give me?" The urge to know was suddenly gripping. Her stomach twisted once again.

Weylyn sighed. "Little mate—"

"What did it give me?!"

He was quiet for a moment before he answered. "Blood. Rotten meat."

Bryson slammed her eyes closed and couldn't stop the next spew of vomit. She turned away from Weylyn, the knowledge of what that thing made her ingest making her nauseous all over again. Perhaps it would have been better if she hadn't asked. Or if he'd lied.

Weylyn's fingers caressed her hair, pulling the dirty strands back to her nape as she heaved until there was nothing left in her stomach. Until she felt hollow and gross at once.

When she finished, she all but slumped against his body and his hands were strong as he held her up so she didn't fall from the chair.

"Little mate." His tone took on a new urgency. "We must leave this place."

She was all too eager to do so. In fact, if she never stepped foot in this foul-smelling hovel ever again, she would be all too content.

In her eagerness to get away, she let Weylyn help her out of the rickety wooden chair and guide her away. She held her breath as they passed the smelly dead body of the ghoul. It didn't ease even when they made it outside. Even as he guided her over the lumpy ground. In fact, the stench seemed to follow them even as they left the place far behind.

Neither of them spoke to one another. At least, not until they were far, far away. Through it all, Bryson blinked furiously, but it was still difficult to make much out.

"Come," Weylyn urged.

The rushing sound of water reached her ears.

"Let us clean up, little mate."

She let him be her eyes, content, at least for a moment, as he led her to the edge of the riverbank. This one was not as smelly as the previous one. It smelt fresh and reminded Bryson of Corvina.

"Stay here."

Weylyn released her and she heard his footsteps slosh into the water, dipping and disturbing for a few moments. When he appeared at her side again, he no longer smelt of blood or death. Instead, of cocoa and spice, comforting, sharp, just like he was.

His grip on her was firm and gentle as he pulled her towards the water. It was a shock of cold at first, but she grew accustomed to it the deeper she waded, down to her waist. Surprisingly, Weylyn began gently sliding water against her, cleaning off the smell. And when he eased her back, she complied, floating on her back so he could slip his fingers into her hair, combing out the mud.

When he finished, Bryson dunked her head under, guzzling water and rinsing her mouth until she felt nearly clean once again.

"Come." He grabbed her elbow, pulling her back to dry land. "We must find a place to lay and rest." There was a beat of silence. "We are out in the open, and there are creatures far worse than the ghoul out here."

She followed at his side, his hand firm on her elbow. "Where *is* here?"

Another pause, and she wished desperately that she could look at his face up close and see the expression he wore. Finally, he said, "The Unseelie Court."

The shock of those words nearly sent her stumbling to the ground. It was only his hands that kept her upright.

The Unseelie Court.

The Unseelie Court.

"Fuck," she whispered aloud.

Weylyn snorted, almost as though he were echoing her sentiment.

Bryson had known that the mushroom circles were... dangerous, so to speak. Mushroom circles were seen as a bad omen, as portals that would push you into other worlds. They emitted a strange magic she'd avoided. She'd always been so careful, able to sense them before even coming into contact with them. What her eyes couldn't see clearly, her body had made up for.

But it hadn't mattered how careful she'd been. She ended up within one regardless.

And now she was in a court she knew nothing about, with iron permeating the air and pushing into her eyeballs.

It was like losing her sight all over again.

The rush of emotions made her face heat and she tried to keep them under control, but it was difficult. Rage, despair, it all came crashing down around her and she couldn't speak. Weylyn didn't seem to be inclined to do so either as he led her away. As he led her through a fucking court she didn't know, surrounded by iron, weak, helpless, having to rely on him.

She'd almost gotten herself fucking eaten, for Mana's sake.

She hated the feeling of helplessness. Hated having to rely on him of all Fae. Hated that relying on him did bring her dread and comfort in equal measure. She'd wanted nothing to do with him. In fact, she'd been planning on breaking things off with Everette and then telling Weylyn exactly where he could shove the mate bond.

Bryson let out a frustrated sigh and felt Weylyn's eyes sharpen on the side of her face. She ignored it, ignored him, trying to mask all she was feeling behind a stoic expression. Bryson became lost in her own thoughts for the rest of their walk.

"Here," Weylyn finally said. "There's a hollow in this tree we can take refuge in."

She nodded grimly and he guided her with a palm to her back, bending her so she could fit into the hole. It smelt damp and mossy, but it wasn't at all unpleasant. And it was warm within its confines, so she wouldn't worry about catching a chill.

Especially not when she felt Weylyn press close at her side.

She fought back a shiver.

"The Unseelie Court," she whispered, pulling her knees up to her chest and wrapping her arms around her legs. "Everette pushed me into the Unseelie Court."

Just remembering the way his hands shoved her shoulders, and then the way darkness immediately descended as she fell, made tears want to prick at her eyes. The sentiment was flooded with anger right after. She'd never seen Everette so angry. But it hadn't mattered how angry he was, that hadn't been an excuse to put his hands on her.

No matter what she'd done, how unfaithful she'd been.

Bryson let out a breath, knowing she couldn't dwell on that right then. It would do her, or Weylyn, no good.

"When we return, I will wring his worthless neck," he assured, like his words were supposed to placate her.

When we return.

"How *will* we return, Weylyn?"

He was quiet a long moment before his arm wrapped around her shoulder. She should have pushed him away. She wanted to push him away. Instead, little by little, exhaustion settled over her bones, and she found herself leaning into his comfort despite all her misgivings.

Just for the night, she told herself. *Just this once.*

"We will figure it out," came his reply.

Bryson's eyelids fluttered closed, sleep claiming her for its own. She swore she imagined Weylyn's warm lips against her skin, but she couldn't bring herself to open her eyes and look. Instead, she was content to let his voice follow her into her dreams.

"Sleep, little mate. I am here now, and I will keep you safe."

Kerrigan

"What have you done?" The whisper cut through the soft wind, then it rose higher as Iona's sister whirled her rage on Everette. "What have you *done*?!"

"I didn't mean to!" Tears and snot poured far too freely from the human. It was a sad sight to bear witness, and Uric found himself curling his lip in disgust at the entire display.

Iona's sister let out a ferocious sound and lunged for the human, fingers extended like claws she meant to bury in his throat.

It would be what he deserved, however Iona appeared at Malika's back, grasping her thrashing sister in her arms, her grip tight and reassuring.

Arlo paced back and forth along the campgrounds, suddenly stopping when Everette's anguished cry pierced the sky once more. He had been bawling for what felt like hours now, though logically they knew it had only been a few minutes.

With a growl, Arlo reached down and clamped his hand around the collar of his man's shirt.

"Get up," he snarled. "And shut up."

Everette's head shook wildly back and forth. "I didn't mean to!"

Arlo's lip curled with barely concealed disgust. "Control yourself, you fool. How do you expect to help her in this state?"

While he tried to pull himself together, Valerio flicked his gaze to Arlo, pointedly ignoring the pathetic weeping man. "How exactly do you propose we go about helping them?"

He waited for a response, knowing there would be none. None that this so-called leader could offer anyway.

And Arlo knew it too, based on the way his jaw ticked.

As easily as he dismissed Everette, Valerio dismissed Arlo as well.

It earned him a growl, which also went ignored.

"We need to get the Elemental back," he told Uric.

Uric's own jaw twitched, but he said nothing. He'd not defy his prince aloud, though his every nerve went on high alert.

"Weylyn, I could live without. But we need *her*. My father would be cross if we left Weylyn there. Can you open a portal?"

Before Uric could deign to answer, Arlo stepped closer and interrupted. "Let's go speak with Kerrigan."

Valerio's gaze strayed towards the man. There was an almost desperate edge to him, his eyes wide and manic.

"And why would we go speak to… *Kerrigan*?" Valerio inquired coolly, though everything about the question was mocking.

"He is our… collector, so to speak." At Valerio's raised brows, the man continued, "He has an arsenal of rare objects in his tent. Calls himself an artist. He makes the masks we wear to conceal our faces from humans. Kerrigan recently came into our camp a few months ago. I am sure he has something in his collection that could help us."

"All due respect that you are not owed, I think your people have done enough." Valerio's pointed stare went straight to Everette's red, crying face and back to Arlo.

Arlo's jaw grinded together. "This isn't a pissing competition," he spat.

"You certainly treated it as one," Valerio said. "And now look at what's happened."

The silence would shatter a blade.

"Please," Arlo gritted out. "We have to try."

Uric would not have blamed his prince if he chose to flip a vulgar gesture at the man and went about his own business. The entire camp had been less than welcoming since they had arrived. Their animosity had been obvious, cutting. Had they the chance, they would have stuck their blades into the Resistance's backs.

However, Uric knew, even before he saw his friend's posture change, just what Valerio would say.

"Alright," he agreed.

Uric bit back his growl of annoyance. Had it been up to him, he would have let his blade soar. Let it strike the halfling's worthless heart. But Valerio had a cunning, if not too sympathetic, mind and saw everything as an opportunity to gain an ally.

Uric would not fault him that, even if it was what he wanted desperately to do.

"Lead the way, Arlo Blackwood."

The tent of the so-called Kerrigan was a small thing that made Uric wonder how and what exactly he collected, as the thing appeared that it could hold nothing more than a simple cot.

Arlo stood on the outside of the closed tent flaps and called out, "Kerrigan?"

A low voice responded from inside. "Come in, Arlo. I've been expecting you and your guests."

Uric unsheathed the obsidian blade from his waist at those words, staring at his prince with an expression that urged caution. Though Arlo walked into the tent first, followed by Malika and the weeping, sniveling human, Julius and Iona followed soon after. Only then did Prince Valerio step inside, with Uric close at his back.

The tent smelt of smoke, though there was no fire burning inside, and what Uric had thought would be a tight fit in fact was not. The inside was far more spacious than the outside suggested, as if by a work of magic; magic that Uric could taste on his tongue.

Every crevice inside was filled with shelves of strange objects. Creatures in jars suspended in glittering liquid, weapons piled high atop one another, fabrics and ribbons and golden scissors that emitted a strange light...

There was a desk at the far end of the tent with a male slumped over it. His hand lifted, golden fingers flickering as he waved them all in.

"Come in, come in," he said. "I've been expecting you all."

Beside them, Iona scuffled her feet forward. "Wait..."

Then the hunched figure straightened and turned in his chair. As they were met with the face of the newcomer, Iona gasped beside them.

"Welcome," Kerrigan said. "It has been a long time, has it not?"

Iona stepped forward, her jaw dropped open wide. "George?" she exclaimed.

Kerrigan—George—smiled a grin with sharp, black teeth. "Hello," he said. "Iona Wylde."

Lost Forever

Iona had to blink twice. Then several more times, if only to make sure she was not as crazy as she felt. For a moment she thought her mind was playing tricks on her. Because there was absolutely no way she was staring at someone from her not-so-distant past.

But after gaping at him for what felt like several moments, she had no choice but to accept that *George was here.*

The last time she had seen him had been in Porir when she'd snuck through the streets of the city as it was being invaded by the emperor's soldiers. He'd given her fake documents for both her and her familiar so she could travel between kingdoms without being stopped by soldiers.

That had been so long ago now, but she hadn't forgotten his face. Not that she ever could. George Apidae was eccentric, always had been, and even though he'd so obviously changed his appearance, she could still recognize him in all his flower-crown glory.

Where he'd once had bronze skin, it now shimmered blue with smatterings of gold here and there. His entire body emitted a light glow like an ancient will-o-the-wisp. His long, dark locs were the same, tapering down his shoulders and waist. Though now, they moved against his shoulders as if they were living beings. He was still as graceful as she remembered, those long and shapely legs crossed, one over another, golden eyes shining like they held all the world's secrets.

He'd always been a mystery, and while Iona had trusted him to get her black-market deals back in Porir, she would never trust someone like him with her life.

"Iona Wylde." George leaned back in his chair, ever the king on his throne, surrounded by mountains of clutter and rare objects. The inside of the tent mirrored what the inside of his factory back in Porir looked like. Fae bones strung up with rope, fluttering pixie wings in glass jars, glimmering liquids that looked as vile as poison, and floating animal heads above his table... "Come to grace me with your presence." He smiled a feral gesture.

Those words and thick accent reminded her of the last time she'd seen him.

"George, what are you doing here?" She wasn't sure her shock would abate.

"I go by Kerrigan now," he corrected with a smile. "George was far too simple for a Fae of my caliber, don't you think?"

"Arrogant as ever, I see."

"What you call arrogance, I call confidence."

She could feel the gazes of those around them volleying back and forth between herself and George. Then she felt the press of her mate's hand against her lower back.

"How do you two know one another?" he asked slowly.

"George was my supplier in Porir," Iona said.

"Kerrigan," George corrected with a flash of a warning smile.

Iona rolled her eyes.

"You know this Fae?" Arlo asked.

Iona couldn't quite make out what was in the half-Fae's tone, but she knew she didn't like it at all. She fought back the glare she wanted to aim in his direction.

George sat forward, steepling his ringed fingers together. The gold shone against his bright blue skin, the copper, iron one standing out to Iona just like it always had. "Iona and I were almost-friends."

"Almost."

George smirked at her, like he was recalling fond memories of the two of them, though she didn't remember them fondly at all. She remembered his creepy lair, his ridiculous prices for the most basic of services, and the way he spoke in riddles and tried to swindle Fae into making deals with him.

"We need your help," Iona said.

George's smile kicked up even wider. "Ah." He leaned backwards. "You'll recall I do not come cheap."

Oh, she remembered far too well. He would take years' worth of wages for forged documents.

Beside them, Arlo let out a low warning sound. "You'll not charge us," he said haughtily. "You are in my camp, living off of my—"

George flicked his fingers disrespectfully in Arlo's direction. "Shut up," he said.

Arlo blinked.

Iona held back her laughter.

"You are no owner of mine, Arlo Blackwood. I may stay at this camp, but you do not lay claim to it, no more than the humans lay claim to the Fae or our lands."

Iona peeked over and saw Arlo's face go red with rage or embarrassment or both.

"How dare—"

George turned away from Arlo, dismissing him quite easily. "Prince of the Fae." His attention was directed at Valerio. "An honor to be in your presence, my liege."

Valerio's eyes shone with mirth and perhaps even the slightest bit of fondness. "I thank you, Kerrigan."

Iona snorted.

George's gaze cut to hers. "See? *He* is not disrespectful."

"Look, enough niceties. We need your help." Iona leveled her stare with his. "Bryson and Weylyn fell through a mushroom circle. We think they may be in the Unseelie Court. We want to know if you have anything that could help us bring them back."

George leaned back once again. His every movement was slow and deliberate. There was something calculated shining in his eyes, a clarity in there despite his blown pupils. He touched his fingers, twirling that iron ring round and round against his digit.

Finally, he let out a sigh. "I cannot help you," he said.

Iona blinked.

Malika let out a sound of disbelief. "What do you mean you can't help us?!"

George cut his gaze to Iona's sister, all the mirth melting from his whole body in an instant. "I mean I cannot help you, even if I wanted to."

"Why not?" Iona felt her voice growing smaller.

George looked at her again, and this time the affection in his gaze was obvious. "My sweet Iona Wylde..." He lifted his hand as if he wanted to reach out and caress her cheek. She swore she felt a tug on her being as he did so, but it was gone as soon as his hand dropped into his lap. "Besides having nothing to help you get them back, I would not help even if I could." He looked at all of them, both apologetic and almost gleeful. "The Unseelie Court is a wild and dangerous place. Even more dangerous, I dare say, than the humanlands themselves." He looked at Iona again, and this time she felt the truth of his words pierce her down to her core. "If the vicious and deadly monsters of the Unseelie do not get to your friends first, they will wish for death a thousand times over if the royals find them. I am sorry, but they are lost forever."

Bone and Rage

Bryson's eyes fluttered open to be met with shadows and light. Each blink came faster and harder than the last. Her brows furrowed, eyes squinting as she tried to make out whatever figures she could. Slowly, painfully, the world came to her in a clearer picture. Splotches of color contorted with the shadows, bright bursts of light and slashing, dark lines.

It wasn't what she'd had, but it was something.

Her eyeballs still burned from the iron that coated the air, and she felt compressions against her chest with every breath, like there was a heavy weight against it, making every drag of air burn.

But she was alive.

Comforting warmth slipped across the skin at her nape. Strong fingers pushing aside knotted red curls to play with her skin. Bryson found herself leaning into the touch and the strong, prevalent aroma of cocoa and spices. Weylyn's essence invaded her entire system, and she drew strength from it. From him.

She shouldn't have found comfort in the way his fingers slid a slow trail around to the front of her neck, pressing firmly against the unsteady jumping of her throat. Her breath hitched, nostrils tickling, senses clouding as Weylyn pressed closer.

Her eyes had closed against his proximity. She didn't want to look at him. Not when she could scarcely see and most certainly not when fear beat a compulsive rhythm in her body.

Bryson wanted to quit him. To be stronger than she was and push him away. But he was a force, a vortex she was twirling in, losing her head as her body lost control within him.

Maybe that was a reason they were in this mess in the first place, she thought as those strong fingers cupped the underside of her jaw, tilting her head up. His lack of a care for her personal boundaries were the reason they'd both ended up in the Unseelie Court.

His touch sent little currents dancing across her exposed skin. His thumb teased her bottom lip and her mouth dropped open on a gasp at the sensations he provoked inside her, all around her. Like little fireworks were being set off in her chest.

It was the bond. Bryson knew it was the bond, urging them closer, pushing them together.

But this was his fault. He invaded her mind. He made her lose all logic and reason. He forced his way inside her head. He'd fucked her, spiritually if not emotionally.

Weylyn's hand cupped her cheek, and she felt his long hair curtain around her face, tickle her skin.

Bryson was to blame as well, she thought. She'd let him get the best of her. She'd let him push past her walls. She'd enjoyed his touch, far too much, and in doing so, she'd betrayed Everette.

That palm met the side of her thigh, sliding to the underside to lift and hook it around his waist. Her limbs complied, wrapping tightly around his lithe body within the confined space. He pressed closer like he belonged between her legs and would make a home there for eternity.

Everette was at fault too, though, Bryson reasoned. He'd been treating her abhorrently for quite some time, his jealousy becoming a monster that changed him and the way he treated her. He'd shoved her. He'd pushed her inside a portal to the Unseelie.

Everyone was to blame, and if she went over it again and again in her head, she would find nothing but an everlasting circle, a wheel that turned and turned and turned and turned and turned and...

Weylyn's lips neared her own and she gasped, swallowing his next breath. She curved her body up into his, tilting her head up like she would to accept whatever he meant to give her. In this moment, she didn't care if it was weak. Sometimes it was okay to let your strength wane, she reasoned, so long as there was someone there to shoulder whatever evil came.

And Weylyn, she knew, would cleave apart the world to protect her.

"Open your eyes, little mate," he whispered near her mouth. "I want to see you."

They fluttered open. This close, she was met with few details. The outline of his sharp features, curtained by long strands of darkness. Like he'd undone his braid in the night and let the tresses hang free. His eyes were the brightest thing about him. They glittered and even through the haze of her vision she could make the burn of them clearly. Clearer than anything she'd ever seen. Brighter than they'd ever been. The thin line of his mouth curved up into a smile she had memorized.

"There you are," he whispered, like he'd somehow lost her within the void and had found her after years of searching.

And for someone who had lost everyone she'd ever loved, the concept of being searched for when she thought she had no one?

It was everything.

Bryson's hands lifted into the dark strands of his hair, playing with the ends, pushing them over his shoulders. He shivered at the contact, at the simple gesture of her playing with his hair that made a low growl rumble through his chest.

Her fingers itched to brush through it and separate the strands into braids. It was maddening, these urges. She could feel the bond like it was a living thing. Different from her bond with her familiar, more visceral, more pounding. It bled between them like a string forcing them together and wrapping around and around.

Weylyn's palm slid over her thigh. He was gentle as he pushed her leg back down, unwrapping it from his waist. He leaned up and away from her, putting distance between their bodies, taking away the heady, honey-thick air with him. She could breathe again.

But a part of her didn't want to.

She wanted to suffocate. To *drown.*

"Up, little mate." He sat back on his haunches, his body tense. "It is morning, and we must find a way out of here sooner rather than later."

Instead of sighing in frustration, Bryson curled her stomach, heaving as she sat up and met Weylyn's chest. He didn't linger a second before he was pulling away from her and tugging her with him out of the hollow of the tree.

The air was still thick with iron, yet everything around them was silent. The sunlight was bright, streaking against Bryson's eyes. She squinted against the pain of it and her temples throbbed. She groaned, shoving her crusted hair behind her ears.

"Are you well?" Weylyn asked.

She turned towards his voice and form. "I'm fine," she told him, though her voice was hoarse with the pain of iron. She felt it all around her. Down to the roots of the trees, like it had eroded and refused to leave. "My skin itches, though." She had to fight the urge to rake her nails across her body.

"It seems the iron the humans left behind in Seelie made its way here," Weylyn observed. "It was worse in Seelie. We traveled through the Iron Mountains, and it was far too embedded within the earth. It would be better if we left quickly before iron sickness sets in."

"How are we going to do that? Jump into another circle?"

Weylyn let out a noise she couldn't quite decipher. "Absolutely not. Circles are far too unreliable. We could step into one and easily end up in the Seelie Court or worse, in the middle of a monster-infested ocean. There is no guarantee where we might end up. I am not willing to risk it."

Bryson took a breath, a sudden thought gripping her. "Then how did you end up here?"

She couldn't see his expression clearly, but she could feel the way his body stilled. He didn't make a single move and she wondered if he was about to invade her mind before he answered, "I jumped in after you."

After everything that had happened, Bryson wasn't sure how she could still find it within her to be surprised. She'd known he'd ended up here somehow, but given all that had happened since she'd fallen through the circle, she hadn't questioned Weylyn's presence until now. She'd only been grateful he was there at all.

"Why would you do such a thing?"

"Because you needed me."

She dropped her mouth open, but no words came out. It seemed that Weylyn didn't want her to speak anyway because he pushed on.

"We need to get moving. The day burns brighter, and we cannot be seen by anyone within the Unseelie Court."

"Why?"

"It would be... unwise to announce our presence." There was a lingering in his words that made her wonder if maybe he wasn't being quite so truthful, but she ignored it. He was right, after all. The Unseelie Court and the Seelie Court had been at odds since long before the war with the humans had ever started. There'd been a classist divide between the two species for as long as Bryson could even remember, longer than the stories her father had told her.

Unseelie would not treat two High Fae with kindness.

"Are there even any Unseelie left, though?" Bryson had to ask aloud. "I can feel so much iron..."

"That ghoul was alive and well." Weylyn took her hand. "It is best if we don't assume anything and take necessary precautions against any and all Unseelie traps." They started forward. She could see well enough to dodge anything in their path and not trip. Despite the burning in her eyes, she could make out shapes, colors, shadows, and light. That was enough.

"What kind of precautions?" she whispered.

She shouldn't have asked, but it was better to garner any and all information she could. She'd fallen into Unseelie, a court that was foreign to her, and had nearly been devoured by a ghoul. Had it not been for Weylyn, Bryson would be dead at this very moment. And with her vision acting out of sorts, she needed all the information she could about where she was. If only to protect herself. To survive.

"What do you know about the Unseelie Court?"

"Only what I've heard in stories. That they are very different from High Fae. They can't wield magic like we can. They have glamor and magic, yes, but Mana hasn't gifted them with the same type of powers we possess. I know you aren't supposed to make deals with them."

"Never, *ever* make a deal with an Unseelie Fae," Weylyn confirmed, squeezing her hand in warning. His tone had taken a low kind of urgency. "It will only end badly for you if you do."

Unseelie Fae were tricksters. Mischievous. Bryson was smart enough to not purposefully or inadvertently make a deal with anyone no matter what. Unseelie liked to twist words to their convenience and find loopholes within their promises only to fuck you over.

Bryson had enough of that already.

"So how do you propose we get back?"

Weylyn sighed, not an irritated sound because of her questions, but it was something born of worry. She didn't think she'd ever seen him worried before. It made her gut churn before suddenly it emitted a low growl.

Heat suffused her cheeks, but she turned to him unapologetically. "I'm hungry."

"Then I shall aim to hunt and feed you."

"You don't have to do that. We can just grab a fruit or something—"

"No," he hissed. "Not everything in Unseelie is safe to eat and drink."

"Why not?" She vaguely remembered stories, but her culture was long gone, the stories dead and buried. It was hard to sift through what was myth and real.

"There are some fruits and drinks that contain magic. Eat what you should not, and it will keep you tethered to the land, or to whoever offered it to you, for years, decades, or whenever they decide to release you from their service. Eating and drinking in Unseelie is dangerous."

Her stomach churned; her appetite lost at those words. "The ghoul fed me—"

"You are safe, little mate," he assured. "It is only some things. I will help you determine what to eat and drink. Besides, the ghoul's death would have freed you from service, had that been the case."

Bryson let out a breath of relief at that. At least she hadn't fucked herself over by eating what she shouldn't have. At least there was that.

They continued trekking through the Unseelie Court in relative quiet. Bryson allowed Weylyn to guide her. She wanted desperately to ask him where he was leading her too. If they couldn't jump into mushroom circles, if they had no map, how did he know where he was going? But every step became a pain after a while. Her eyes eventually burned enough that tears slipped down her cheeks. While she could see, the brightness hurt so much that her head had already started to pound and the lack of food in her belly had her stomach twisting with every step.

Until finally, Weylyn sat her down in a shady area. The prickles of perspiration against the back of her neck cooled down with a slight breeze. She swiped her palm against it, but it only came away clammy and uncomfortable.

"I am going to hunt," Weylyn announced. "The area is safe for now. Do not move from this spot."

"Trust me, I'm not going to go wandering off in a place I have no experience traveling in. I'm not stupid."

"I never said you were. Rebellious, but never stupid."

"Yeah, well, I know when and where to rebel."

The last she heard was Weylyn's soft chuckle before he disappeared from her line of sight. She leaned back against the tree, the bark digging grooves into her hot back, and she listened for Weylyn to return. She took stock of her own inventory while she waited. A dagger at her waist and a quiver with arrows and a bow. She was sure some of them were broken because she'd fallen on them when she'd landed in Unseelie, but she had yet to remove the ones she no longer needed.

She began doing that now, pulling the pack from her back and feeling at the weapons with expert fingers. Splinters snagging onto her calloused fingertips were easy to ignore as she felt up and down on the arrows, tossing the broken ones off to the side.

Weylyn arrived once again, a dead bird in his hand of a species she wasn't familiar with. He set the bird on the ground near her feet like an offering. It was a blob of bright purple and yellow feathers. While Bryson picked the poultry into her hands and began plucking at the feathers, Weylyn got to work building a small fire.

Using the dagger at her waist, Bryson gutted and cleaned the bird, stripping and cutting it down to hold it over the fire for consumption. It was instinct to fall into that routine, even if she couldn't see it as well as she'd like.

While they waited for the meat to cook, Bryson sat back on her palms. A brief moment of peace settled over her mind. She didn't trust it. It made room for the darkness and invasive thoughts to take root.

Her nails scraped into the dirt. "We have to get out of here," she said finally, breaking through the oppressive silence. "We have to go through the circles."

"No."

"It's the only way."

Weylyn emitted a soft growl but didn't contradict her, so she pushed on.

"We would hold onto each other as we step through. Keep stepping through circles until we end up somewhere I can make contact with my familiar. Unless..." Her gaze strayed to him. He sat with his shoulders relaxed, though his lips were pressed into a shadowy line. "Can you somehow make contact with one of your people?"

"Unseelie doesn't work like that," he whispered. "It is an older, much more wicked magic that controls the Ley Lines of this Court. It does not follow the same rules of time and space as other places; therefore I am unable to reach them, and it is why Uric would not be able to open a portal. We are in different dimensions, so to speak."

"Great, that's just great then." She shook her head back and forth. "So, the circles are our only hope."

Almost reluctantly, Weylyn drawled, "Yes."

"Great. Then we need to find one immediately. I can usually sense them, but the iron in the air is making everything so much more difficult. My magic feels like it's sleeping, but I think if I try, I'll be able to get it working."

There was a pop and a sizzle of the bird over the fire.

"Of that I have no doubt, little mate."

Bryson rolled her eyes at the cool confidence he mustered. She didn't even bother telling him not to call her that. "Your faith in me is astounding."

This time, Weylyn chuckled deep and low. "I have witnessed Fae Elementals do extraordinary things. I have witnessed iron melt at our feet and rendered useless against ice. I've seen it consumed entirely with water. If anyone is able, it is *you*."

His faith in her brought a new surge of warmth that had no business nestling itself in her chest. But it also brought up so many more questions. "They can do that? Defy iron?"

"Yes."

A thrill shot through her. She'd sensed their individual power, but all of them together had been astounding. It made her wonder just how far her own abilities could extend, what she would be able to accomplish. She wanted to find out.

Discreetly, she called forth her magic. It responded far too slowly for her liking, like it was sluggish and wading through thick pools of sludge to get to her. It was the iron, but it frustrated her that it responded so slowly. Once it was there, she sent a small gust towards the fire, fanning the flickering flames.

It responded and blazed up, consuming the bird before dying down once again, leaving scorched edges behind. She smelt the charred skin and her stomach rumbled once again. With a groan she laid back down against the grass, pressing her palms against her stomach.

"You know a lot about the Unseelie Court," she murmured in the ensuing silence.

From beside her, she felt Weylyn's body stiffen a single fraction before he relaxed. "I know what everyone else knows."

"Hmm." She wanted to push, but was afraid to pry into his life. She didn't want him to think this would be anything other than what it was. They were helping each other to get out of this court. Nothing more. When they arrived back at camp, she was going to reject the mating bond, no matter what pain it brought them both. She had to make that very clear to him now. "Why did you jump into the circle after me?"

He sighed, almost as though she were annoying him. "Because."

"Because why?"

"Because you are my mate."

"That's such a shitty answer." She sat up again, turning towards him. She made him out in splotches and glared at him. "You don't even know me. I could be the world's worst mate in the history of mates. And yet you risked a lot to go in after me. Why?"

"It does not matter."

"Oh, I think it does." She scooted closer so her knees touched him. The brief bit of contact lit every nerve, and she knew he'd felt it too by the way he shivered. "You don't know me, why do you even want me so bad?"

"On the contrary, I know you rather well. I know you better than anyone in the entire world, living or dead, has ever known you."

There was a sudden thickness in her throat that made it hard to swallow. "How much does your mind magic allow you to see, anyway?"

She felt, rather than saw, the way his lips curved. She felt his stare penetrate her. She felt the phantom touch of hands glide along her back as if he were caressing her, but he hadn't moved, so it wasn't him. That she knew.

"Everything," he purred in her mind.

She swatted near her ear like one would a pesky fly. "Stop doing that. It's invasive."

He huffed and poked at the fire with a stick. "Everyone is always so quick to tell me to leave them be, but tell me, little mate, if you had magic such as mine, would you be able to control the urge, the need, the curiosity, to see what lives in another's heart?"

When she didn't reply, he shoved the stick fully into the fire.

"Exactly." There was a smile in his voice. "Everyone loves to keep secrets. Everyone wants to know everyone else's secrets–until their own are on the line or being threatened." His long fingers lifted near his face. He stared at them, flexed them, before dropping his hand to the grass. "Everyone has a use for me until they do not like what I discover."

His voice had lowered, and while she didn't detect a single hint of sadness, she felt empathy for him. She dared a few inches closer.

"Fine," she said. "I admit, I would be a bit curious. But doesn't it get tiring being in everyone else's head all the time?"

"No."

Bryson rolled her eyes. "I don't believe you."

"Why wouldn't you? I like my magic. I like picking at secrets. I like knowing things no one else does. I like to hold it over their heads and watch them squirm like fish at the end of a line. I take great joy in blackmail. Why should I be ashamed of that?"

"So, you do it for fun?"

His eyes burned as they found hers. They scorched a path down to her soul. "Yes," he hissed. "I do it for fun. Because I fucking can. Because I fucking want to. Because it makes me feel powerful. Is that so wrong, little mate?"

He asked like he truly wanted to know the answer. And Bryson's answer came immediately.

"No," she said. "It's not."

Predator or prey, her familiar had told her. She'd been prey many times and would kill not to be that again. And if using his magic to invade the minds of others made him feel the power he deserved to feel, who was she to reprimand him for it?

He flashed his canines at her. She caught the gleam of them, heard them snap together. Like he wanted to lean forward and take a bite out of her neck.

"I knew you would say that, little mate."

"Because you cheat and use your magic."

"I didn't need to that time. Don't forget that I already know everything there is to know about you. I know what vortex lies within you. I know you fight hard to keep it tamped down, but I know the truth."

She felt her breath catch. Her heart pounded. Suddenly that vortex he spoke of seemed to come alive and she had to shove it back into place. So much anger, so much feeling and nothing to turn it into, nothing for it to become, nothing but wish she could do something, anything, with it.

"What truth?" she found herself asking.

He chuckled against her mouth. She hadn't even felt him move closer yet there he was, his breath blowing warm against her lips, and she wanted to swallow his essence down like Fae wine she never imbibed in, if only to feel what she never let herself feel.

"That you want to watch the world burn just as much as I do."

In that moment, Bryson knew she hated him. She hated him so much for pulling out of her chest the words she was never brave enough to face on her own. Words that had haunted her for so long because she knew that if her mother, if her father, if they heard what ran rampant through her mind, they would be so ashamed. She had garnered darkness for years. Anger, hatred, bitterness, it grew within her and coalesced into that current that she wanted nothing more than to unleash upon the world that had wronged her.

But she couldn't bring herself to, so she hid it away. So much anger and so little to do with it.

Bryson slowly peeled herself away from Weylyn's presence, but all he did was follow.

"Don't back away from me now, little mate." There was a malicious glee in his tone. He was enjoying this. The bright, golden hue of his eyes only brightened more as he crowded into her space. Even as she tripped back against the grass and lay there, he loomed over her and smiled that dangerous smile, his hair slipping over his shoulders to curtain them. "We were having so much fun, weren't we?"

Her breathing grew labored. That anger wanted unleashed, but she kept a tight hold on it. "No," she croaked.

"You think your family was so good, don't you? You think they'd be ashamed that darkness lives inside you when only peace lived within them?"

"Weylyn," she pleaded. She wanted him to stop. She needed him to stop. She was unable to face what he was saying. It felt like he was cleaving her apart from the inside out.

"Foolish little mate," he scoffed down at her. "Darkness? Anger? Bitterness? Resentment? It lives in us all. It even lived in your precious family. You just don't want to see it. You refuse to remember it. Because those are the only memories of them you have, and you don't want them tainted."

"Don't talk about my family!"

He leaned up, his brows two slashing lines that curved with his disappointment. "Fine," he conceded. "But there is no shame in darkness. There is no shame in wanting revenge on those who have wronged you." He pushed away from her again, and this time when he spoke, his voice sounded far away as he started to leave. "Sometimes, it is the only thing any of us can hold on to."

She didn't move until she was sure he was gone. Until his footsteps had receded. Until she could no longer smell him in her nose, but he was cloying, crowded. He invaded her with his cruelty and that malicious smile and there was nothing to do to expel him from her system.

He was a menace, a cruel, terrible menace with no regard for anyone's feelings but his own.

And yet he was right.

He was *right.*

Tears burned the backs of her eyelids, and she pressed her fists against the scars, as if that could shove the emotion back down where it belonged. But it wouldn't relent. She hated it. She hated him so much it ached. Her chest burned and she clawed at it like she could reach inside and grip the bond that tethered them only to tear it out from her being.

She didn't want it; she didn't want him. She didn't want that truth haunting her because she'd tried so hard to keep it hidden. Now that it was out in the open, what did that make her?

What was Bryson if not loyal to her family and their memories?

What would she be if not what they told her what she had to be? Someone great. Someone who was meant to help. Someone who was meant to fight in the Seelie Court's war? What was she if not everything they always told her she was supposed to be?

If she stripped herself down, she'd be left with nothing but fucking bones and rage. A hollow shell of a thing.

Because what would rage do for her? What had rage ever done for anybody in the world except leave it desolate and bare?

The rage was no good.

But... Weylyn was right, too.

Sometimes, it was the only thing anyone had within them. And for so long, all she'd done was tamp it down and live within the shadow of who her parents wanted her to be. So she held on. To it. To them. But now it felt like her grip was slipping and she was falling... falling...

She sighed and opened her eyes.

And she was met with the snarling face of a creature of bone and rage.

And Bryson opened her mouth to scream.

Beast of Prey

Bryson screamed and scrambled backwards.

The creature before her may have been blurry, but she could make out enough to feel the fear. It walked on near-silent toes, heaved with odorless breath. It was a massive creature crouched on all fours with a head that resembled the skull of an animal, though it was covered in thick patches of hair. It had ears and antlers that twisted high like the branches of a tree. Three glowing eyes peered at her, and thick, sharp teeth snapped in her direction.

Splotches of green, brown, and black surrounded it like it was made of moss or grass. Its body was thick, muscular, all angry slashing lines that prowled closer no matter how much she scrambled back.

It pounced and Bryson's hands shot up. Her magic, once dormant, came alive at her command. The snarling creature yelped as the magic caught it in its deathly grip. Air shot it up into the sky and her fingers curled, letting it close around the beast with crushing force, twisting, reforming.

Her nose bled and she tasted the copper of it on her lips. Her vision hazed with the brutal force of her magic. This had never happened before, but she couldn't relent. She refused to. With a cry, her fingers curling into her palms, the magic responded...

There was the sound of bone crunching, loud, echoing throughout the forest. A single yelp of pain and her magic released its hold on the beast. It toppled to the ground in front of her, landing with a hard, wet, squelch.

Dead.

Her chest heaved and Bryson coughed, blood staining her palm.

Using magic had never taxed her quite as much as it did then. The only explanation was the iron in her system. True fear gripped her. If she couldn't use her magic, what then? Would she not be like the other Elementals, able to melt, freeze, drown when necessary?

Tears stung her eyes.

"Bryson!"

She felt strong hands grasp her arms before the haze cleared and she saw Weylyn. His eyes were blown wide with worry. His hands cupped her cheeks, twisting her face back and forth as though inspecting her for injuries.

"Bryson..." His voice softened. "Are you alright?"

Her heart was pounding up to her throat, her body ached, her eyes burned, and blood coated the inside of her mouth. She didn't know how to answer that question.

"I'm fine," she croaked.

"Forgive me." He dropped his forehead to hers. The words were a scrape of a voice, like he wasn't accustomed to apologizing often. "I did not sense it near." He pulled away then, a new sense of urgency charging the air as he looked down at the broken creature she'd killed.

Her stomach twisted.

Weylyn let out a curse and whipped back around to her. "We have to go," he hissed. "Now."

"Weylyn, what—" His hand clamped down along her wrist, and the next thing she knew, he was dragging her, their fire and meal all but forgotten as they ran.

"There's no time," Weylyn heaved, tugging her along.

She nearly tripped. "No time for what?"

"There are more of those things coming for us. A pack. We cannot let them find us. We cannot!"

A haunted howl pierced the air around them. It echoed, over and over again in a way that sounded like a haunted song drifting through the air. Over and over and over again, making Bryson realize that it wasn't an echo at all. There were several creatures. And soon those howls made way to growls and snarls and an electrifying magic charged through the air.

"Run!" Weylyn cried, his voice breaking in something she'd never heard in him before.

Fear.

"Bryson, run!"

He tugged her harder, her legs pumped faster. Her chest burned with every breath she took like iron was scraping down her throat, threatening to block her airway. Her chest seized. Her legs cramped.

"Weylyn!"

"Just a bit further," he urged. The desperation in his voice frightened her more than anything else ever could.

The snarling grew closer. A shiver slid down her spine. She could feel a presence, something swarming overhead. Close, they were so close. An almost invisible foe she couldn't scent or hear, but she felt them.

Her breath caught in her throat, and between one second and the next, everything changed.

Her hand was ripped from Weylyn's grasp by what felt like an invisible force. She cried out as she was blasted backwards, blinking furiously to find another one of those beasts suddenly above her, pinning her down with its horns.

She screamed as it opened its mouth to roar.

She grasped at her magic with trembling fingers, but it refused to respond.

Her head thrashed from side to side as she leaned away from those sharp teeth. Her eyes snagged on Weylyn as he cried out, his distress capturing her attention. She let out a scream as he was tossed through the air by one of those creatures and landed with a painful thump on the ground.

"Weylyn!"

She wanted to reach for him, but her magic wasn't obeying. And all she could taste inside of her mouth was iron and blood.

Suddenly another creature landed from the air. The very ground shook from the force. There was a clattering of jewels and the gleaming sight of gold catching the sunlight.

And Bryson held her breath, watching as all the creatures stilled when a Fae man appeared into her line of vision.

Tall, lithe, and dripping in gold was the first thing she noticed. She blinked and blinked and blinked some more to get a clearer picture. A long braid hung over his shoulder and atop his head, there was a golden crown of what looked like thorns.

The man stalked forward and pressed his boot deep against Weylyn's chest, looming over him and flashing a feral smile that looked vaguely familiar.

"Well, well, well," he purred in a voice smooth as silk and dangerous as sin. "Last I recall, you were banished from the Unseelie Court forever." He dug his boot in, and Weylyn let out a grunt. "Oh, but it is nice to see you again... little brother."

The Queen of All That Dies

Weylyn ground his teeth together as he stared up at a face he never thought he'd see again in his lifetime.

It was a face not unlike his own, though a few shades darker and uglier. His brown-gold eyes flicked with mirth, and his white smile and sharp teeth were blinding as he loomed over Weylyn, digging his booted foot into his chest.

That would leave a bruise.

"Hello, Cassimir," he greeted, smiling as though he weren't in pain. As if his heart was not pounding furiously inside his chest, threatening to rip from his rib cage. He calmed the beating, calmed the secrets his body would give away to Cassimir's hearing.

Cassimir's head tilted to the side and his smile dropped. In an instant he appeared every inch the dangerous, pompous Unseelie Fae he truly was. The golden crown that perched atop his head seemed entangled within his hair and out of place near his curving, black horns.

"That's new," Weylyn commented, trying to sit up, but Cass dug his heel in harder. "Though I have to admit, it does make you look pretentious."

Cass' lip pulled back in a sneer. "Now, now, little brother. Is that any way to greet me after all this time?"

"I could say the same to you. Sending your beasts after me? *Tsk, tsk, tsk.* Not very brotherly of you, is it?"

He let out a slight scoff and leaned back, removing his foot from Weylyn's chest. He didn't take in a breath, knowing it was no reprieve. Weylyn was smart enough and knew his brother well enough now to know that he would pounce again, and the next time he would go for the throat.

Weylyn stood slowly to his feet, trying not to sway. Unseelie was shrouded in iron, the flecks of it in the air already invading his system painfully. It was hard enough trying to stand, let alone use his magic.

He dusted his pants off and flicked his gaze around at his brother's beasts. They were flying, wingless hybrids. Creatures with the antlers of an elk, the teeth of a tiger, and thick, muscular, furry bodies. They were bigger now than when Weylyn last saw them. And there were less of them, too.

"Do you mind?" Weylyn jerked his head in the direction of the beast looming over Bryson. As much as he didn't want to draw his brother's attention in his mate's direction, he feared he had no choice.

Cass turned slowly and called out a command in the old language of the Unseelie.

"Up!"

The creature sat back on its short hind legs. As soon as it did, Bryson scrambled backwards, coughing. She struggled to her feet and Weylyn couldn't immediately run to her, even if he desperately wanted to. His brother was watching his every movement which meant that everything he did had to be calculated, cold, and purposeful.

Bryson stumbled near him, bumping into his body, and grasping him to avoid falling.

"And who is this pathetic creature?" Cass sniffed in Bryson's direction, looking at her distastefully.

Weylyn flashed his teeth, but it was Bryson who answered. "This pathetic creature killed your fucking beast and will do so again if they come anywhere near us."

Only Weylyn could feel it for the lie it was. Her magic was waning, the iron trapping her in a vicious and deadly grip. Yet still, a fierce wave of pride rose and nestled in his chest at the venom in her words and the ferocity in her glare.

He fought not to smirk, though the urge to do so died when his brother's expression tightened with anger.

"You admit to killing my pet," he said slowly. The beasts around them growled. "Had you not already been traveling with my brother, this truth would have sealed your fate regardless."

Bryson snapped her canines in Cassimir's direction, but Weylyn's brother only chuckled.

"Enough," he snapped in the Unseelie tongue. "Do not fight me, brother. It will only be worse if you do."

Weylyn set a hand against Bryson's wrist to calm her. His brother's gaze strayed to the movement, and the smile on his mouth became a knowing, dangerous thing.

Every instinct in Weylyn's body told him to flee. Not out of fear of his brother or his beasts. Not out of fear for Bryson, for he knew his mate could hold her own.

But for what he knew was to come. And his brother was right anyway. Fighting would only make it worse.

There was absolutely nothing they could do except accept their fate.

And try to make it out alive.

Chains clinked around their wrists. They'd appeared, almost as if by magic, and Weylyn hadn't fought off the Unseelie man or even tried to make an escape. Bryson had wanted to run, to fight her way out, but she figured it would be pointless. Not with her magic waning.

And this Unseelie, she wondered if he really was Weylyn's brother.

As they trailed behind him and his beasts, Bryson couldn't help shooting glances his way and Weylyn's, comparing the two. She couldn't see with complete clarity, but she could make out the same hair color and length. The Unseelie male was a few shades darker than Weylyn, but when he flashed his teeth, that smile was the same.

But if the two were brothers, then that meant...

"You're Unseelie?" she whispered.

It was Cassimir who answered, a vicious chuckle in his words. "Only half in blood."

Weylyn sighed. "Using blood quantum to make the connection between us seem like a small thing and make me feel lesser? How beneath you." He turned to Bryson. "Yes. Half in blood."

She tried to wrap her mind around that bit of information. Weylyn was half Unseelie. Honestly, it... it explained so much about his true nature. The viciousness, the mischievousness, all of it simmered down to the fact he had Unseelie blood coursing through his veins.

Unseelie were notorious for being tricksters and creating chaos where they went. It was in their nature to be cruel, a part of who they were down to their very bones.

"Why were you banished?" she asked.

Weylyn did not answer, and it prompted a chuckle from Cassimir, though he did not answer either.

Alright then, Bryson thought.

"We are nearly there," Cassimir announced from the front of the line. "Just in time for the fun to begin."

Weylyn stiffened at her side as they walked up a slope that plunged down. The roots of trees gnarled above the earth, twining through with thick rusted iron that looked like it had eroded on the ground for years. Below, there was nothing but flickers of shadow and color, and squinting only made her eyes hurt and her temples throb.

"Little mate," Weylyn dropped his voice low, urgently. "When we arrive, all I ask is you keep quiet."

"What?"

"We are going to a dangerous place. A single word will have the Fae there tearing you apart. Keep quiet. Do not speak. Let me protect you. Okay?"

Fear in its true form seized through her insides. A part of her wanted to argue, but it was only that frozen sensation that assured she didn't. She nodded and turned forward.

Each step was painful, like the iron zinged through her body. She nearly tripped several times going down, gasping when she couldn't stay upright. Weylyn didn't rush to help her, and his own steps were rocky as they made their way down, down, down...

The noise popped within seconds. Silence, and then it burst all around them. It collided into her system, everything way too overwhelming. Her shoulders pitched up to her ears as if it could drown out the sudden impact of the voices banging against her ear drums. Bodies in all shapes and sizes crowded around them.

It felt like some sort of awful procession as they were hauled in chains through the throng of people. Sneers and jeers rang high and despite herself, Bryson found herself leaning closer to Weylyn to find comfort in his body.

But as soon as that comfort came, it ended.

A dais rose from the ground. A throne made of stone stood before them. Bryson followed the path from the bottom of the dais all the way to the top, catching sight of a slender leg and higher still to the person sitting there.

"Bow before Ineciu Morgayne, Queen of the Unseelie Court and all things that die."

Something shoved into Bryson's spine, forcing her to the ground. Her knees buckled and cried out in pain as they hit. Beside her, Weylyn was also forced to his knees.

Then once again, there was silence. A single beat before a sultry purr rang out around them, the sound coming from the woman on the throne. The Queen of the Unseelie.

"Well, well, well," she drawled in a way that was surprisingly familiar. "What a surprise it is to see you again, my son."

Forged in Magic and Iron

Once upon a time, Weylyn would have bowed and fallen to his knees in fear of the power of the woman before him. He would have let his forehead kiss the ground if only to please her. But that was before. Before everything. Before pain and rage and magic swept him away in a haze of danger and a life not worth living.

Now, those old feelings, pain...rage... inadequacy... It all went rushing to the front of his mind as he was forced to the ground before the Queen of the Unseelie Court. His mother.

His forehead sizzled as it touched the iron on the ground. Beside him, Bryson hissed in pain as it did the same to her. He tried not to struggle. He kept preternaturally still and, using whatever strength he could muster, reached for Bryson's mind with trembling fingers.

The iron inhibited his magic, and so the words flickered in and out of her mind.

"Be brave, little mate."

Bryson took a breath to let him know she'd heard.

His insides hollowed out when he flicked his gaze back up again, like the queen had taken a spoon and scooped out his vital organs just for the fun of it. She glared at him like centuries had not passed since that fateful day when everything around them had irrevocably changed.

She still despised him.

And he still despised her.

He could've been swallowed up by the infernal depths of her anger in that gaze alone. He hated to get lost in it. Hated the fear that rippled through him. Hated how she reduced him to this.

The leg that was crossed over the other delicately dropped to the floor. He watched as she pushed herself to a stand, stepping down the dais and onto iron in her bare feet. There wasn't so much as a sizzle or a single wince of pain. In fact, nobody around them appeared to be as affected as he and Bryson were.

"Why have you come back?" his mother demanded. Her feet stopped shy away from his eyes. There were jeers from the crowd around them, from goblins and pixies and Unseelie of all kinds. "I told you what would happen, should you come back. Or have you forgotten?"

He hadn't.

In fact, he lived with the haunting thought day and night. He had sought his vengeance on it. Had sworn to render the world to ash because of it.

"Remind your wayward brother what the consequences of returning would be, since he seems to have forgotten." The queen stepped back up to the dais backwards and sat upon the edge of the throne. From behind the grand structure, several more bodies came out of hiding.

Owyn, Rainer, the twins Gwyn and Glyn, and Cassimir joined them at the top as well.

His gaze swept around them.

Each so similar, so different, at least from him.

The queen's head tilted up, and she smirked down at Weylyn. At her youngest and most hated son. Gold glittered on her body like a second skin painted against her form. Her long tail curled from beneath her, wrapping around her ankle as if for comfort. Long black horns towered over her long, loose hair. Hair that was spun from silk spiderwebs, as dark as the oil night was made of.

A crown of iron and gold sat atop her head.

And each one of his brothers wore smaller crowns to match. Crowns of thorns and gold perched near their horns and dark hair. Some stood in their full Unseelie forms, black claws on display, sharp teeth gnashing, golden eyes blinking, tails swaying.

Weylyn had not inherited a single thing from his mother save her appearance. They all had, but he had no Unseelie features to speak of. It was what made it easier to blend in with the High Fae. It was also what they used against him, time and time again.

Rainer stepped down. His teeth gleamed like they were made of iron and gold. He gnashed them in Weylyn's direction, brandishing his claws like a threat that Weylyn knew he had every intention of following through with. Rainer's own hair was spun from oil just like their mother's, though his curled at the ends, which were dusted in shimmering silver light like the Unseelie who spawned him.

"Let us kill him and be done with it, mother," Rainer spat. His hatred was a glimmering, poisonous thing. Weylyn did not fear it.

He did not fear any of his siblings, in fact.

No matter how sharp their teeth and claws.

"Why have you returned?" his mother asked, already sounding bored.

Weylyn could not bring himself to respond. Because she would demand truth, twist his words, attempt to pull out deals he had no business making. That was the way of the Unseelie.

It was the way of the royals.

It was the way of himself.

"Speak or I will cut out your tongue for your insolence."

And likely wear it around her neck, too.

"I stepped into a circle," he confessed. "It brought me here."

The court around him cackled at the foolery of his reply. Everyone knew to stay far away from circles because of what kind of magic they carried. But he'd be made to look a fool a thousand times over, if only it kept their attention from Bryson.

"So you came here by accident," his mother mused, though nothing in her tone was amusing. Venomous, enraged, yes. But nothing else lived in those depths.

"That is what I said, yes." He lifted his head and swept his gaze around, narrowly avoiding coughing up the blood he felt in the back of his throat. "And I see you have changed decorators. Iron makes for quite the furnishings, yes?"

The queen flicked her clawed fingers on the armrest of her throne. "Insolent as ever." Then slowly, her stare turned cold in Bryson's direction.

Weylyn fought to keep a straight face, but the queen was already standing and walking down in their direction. He didn't make a single move. Not even when the queen dropped to her knees in front of Weylyn's mate and lifted her chin with hard fingers.

"And who is this little creature?" she purred.

Weylyn wanted to jump between them. To block Bryson from his mother's sights, but it was already too late.

Bryson's scarred face was looking directly at the queen, taking in whatever her vision allowed her to see. But she did not reply. She glared defiantly.

The queen smirked at that and leaned forward, pressing her nose to Bryson's hair. She inhaled deep, a rumble echoing through the chamber of her chest. A moment later, she pulled away and exhaled.

"This Fae reeks of you," she mused. This time there was humor there as her gaze snapped back and forth between Bryson and Weylyn. "From the stench, I will take a single guess."

No, Weylyn wanted to snarl. *Don't say it. Don't say it.*

His eyes must have conveyed his wishes, because his mother stared at him and smirked. Like he was a pathetic little prey of an animal she ensnared within her claws and meant to rip apart in a single motion.

"She is your mate, is she not?"

Bryson gave nothing away, but it was too late. Already his mother had seen the truth. Their smells intermingled because of the bond, because of their proximity. And the queen knew. With a single glance, a single whiff, she *knew*.

There was a hush proceeding her words as the court processed what she'd said. Then, a ripple went through the crowd.

Mate.

Mate.

Mate.

Matematematematematematematemate—

They chanted the word like a prayer, though to Weylyn it felt more like an omen.

The queen stood to her full height and held up a hand, effectively silencing everyone within seconds. "I have decided," she said, her voice carrying.

Weylyn's heart thumped in his chest. Already he was attempting to form a plan in his head, anticipating moves and the strength of those around him. What position to take that would best protect his mate. Or at least give her a fighting chance to escape.

His muscles bunched. His canines snapped out from his gums.

"I have decided to spare Prince Weylyn's life," she announced.

His eyebrows flew up as he took in his mother and the cruel way in which she smiled down at Bryson.

"And to celebrate his return, we shall feast tonight. In his honor and in honor of his mate."

Weylyn did not breathe a sigh of relief because he knew this wasn't a peace offering. This wasn't a reprieve. He saw the farce for what it truly was.

The beginning of the fucking end.

Rules of Unseelie

The chains were removed from their wrists. Bryson and Weylyn were escorted through camp and into a large tent, where they both were promptly shoved inside.

Bryson struggled to right herself, blinking at her surroundings. With each hour that passed, her eyes only seemed to worsen. The pain made her want to peel her lids from her eyes. Her scars itched terribly, and her temples were already throbbing. Not just because the light was blinding, making it harder to see, but because of everything she'd learned within the past few hours.

Not only was Weylyn half-Unseelie, but he was also an Unseelie Prince. Son to the Queen of all that Dies. She tried to contend that to the image of him in her mind. It didn't make sense, and yet it all fell perfectly into place. She just needed answers to the thousands of questions that had already begun to plague her thoughts.

She turned, limp hair smacking her cheek. "Weylyn—"

"Sssh!"

She blinked at his form. "Did you just—"

"Quiet."

She held back her irritation as she watched him walk in a slow circle around the room. What he was inspecting it for, she couldn't be sure, but she let him do it in the quiet he'd demanded. When he finally finished, he grabbed her arm and guided her down onto a plush cushion and sat next to her.

A moment later, his fingers invaded her mind, diving in like he was a mermaid jumping home into its depths.

Blackness shrouded her and she was sucked inside with his magic. Facing him in her mind, she could see him clearly like she couldn't physically. Every worried line etched over his features was clear as day. Everything she thought that made him beautiful was torn into grave downturns. Gone was that mischief that made his eyes bright and in its place was something else.

Bryson swallowed as she took him in.

"We cannot speak aloud, little mate," he explained, taking a step closer to her. His hand reached out only to pause, almost as if he were thinking better of touching her.

She couldn't be sure why that hurt, why she'd even want him to touch her at all. But she craved it. Craved his palm against her skin and his fingers in her hair.

So she closed the space between them herself. Stupidly. Bravely.

She didn't even know if she could trust him. Not when he was disguising himself as a High Fae within the Resistance. Not when he hadn't told her the truth of who or what he was. But what truth did he even owe her, when she'd made it clear she wanted nothing to do with him or the mating bond between them?

He owed her nothing.

Yet the feeling sat there in her chest just the same.

Bryson clasped his hands in hers. They felt cold even in this mindscape. "What is happening, Weylyn?"

He swallowed, staring deeply into her eyes. His fear only served to unnerve her when it wasn't something she saw in him often.

"We are in the Unseelie Court. At my mother's court."

"Yeah, I got that bit when we were out there. You're a *prince*?!"

His lips kicked up into that smirk she was all too familiar with. "A title that is unimpressive when I am disinherited from ever taking the throne."

"Well, still. An Unseelie prince. Fuck, this is wild."

"Not as wild as things are about to get, little mate."

She eyed him curiously. "What do you mean?"

"My mother knows we are mates." His hold on her tightened.

"Yeah, I got that too." She'd sniffed it off Bryson's body. Was their bond that strong, even if they hadn't claimed each other at all?

"She did not kill us, but that does not mean she will not."

Her breath halted in her throat. "So that animosity I sensed between you—"

"She despises me." His golden eyes flared like they held fire within his depths. "Loathes me. She wants me dead. The fact that she kept us alive only means she will toy with us. She will toy with you to get to me. She will make a show of our suffering. Do *not* get comfortable, little mate. It will be the last thing you ever do."

"I wasn't really planning on it." Bryson hoped her voice portrayed more bravery than she felt inside. Inside, she was a quivering mess of fear. A part of her wanted to crawl into a puddle and drift away. Another part wanted to unleash a tornado so powerful, everyone was blown away.

Predator or prey, her familiar had said.

In the Unseelie Court, they were prey.

But they could be predators in disguise.

Weylyn's fingers grasped her chin, much like his mother's had, only his hands were far gentler, the cold of the rings contrasting the sudden warmth of his palms. He made Bryson look up at him and she found features of the cruel monarch in him. The slight curve on the bridge of the nose, the gleam in the eyes, the smile...

But Weylyn was somehow different. Maybe it was because he was half-Unseelie. Because his other half was High Fae and he hid the wildness inside better than those around them did. It was a very telling difference. The way everyone was at the edge of their seats, waiting with gleaming teeth and razor-sharp claws.

Bryson could always sense the wild in Weylyn. Never to that extent.

"She will parade us around her court," he whispered. "Let her. Do not speak, give nothing away. And whatever you do, never make a deal with an Unseelie, is that clear?"

Making deals with Unseelie was an older, more dangerous form of magic. Being trapped in a deal with an Unseelie Fae with no way to get out of one was worse than death itself.

"I understand."

"Only eat and drink what I tell you is safe."

"Okay."

"Try not to be alone with my brothers."

"I wouldn't dream of it."

Weylyn sighed and dropped his forehead against Bryson's, taking a moment to breathe her in. She did the same. It was strange that the one person she'd been avoiding for days had suddenly become her tether to life, the one she leaned to. Because they only had one another, it was easy to hold onto him. Because she was unsure if they would live to see the next day, it was easy to picture a life with Weylyn at her side. Her mate. Her Mana-chosen mate...

Something stirred low in her belly, igniting what she swore she wouldn't feel for him again.

Weylyn must have sensed it too because he groaned, but before he could press closer, Bryson's palms met his chest and gently pushed him away.

"You owe me an explanation," she whispered to break the moment, voice hoarse around them.

His eyes were glaringly beautiful in the dark. "I promise, I will give it. For now, let us go back. They are waiting for us. Remember to be cautious, temper your magic, and only communicate here."

In a shot, Bryson was jolted out of her own mind and pushed back to the present. She blinked and suddenly, creatures began pushing their way into the tent, bringing with them the smell of magic. How it was so strong among the iron, Bryson couldn't be sure. But it imbued the air. She stared down at the brownies, all in different shades and textures creaking their way through the tent.

Their fingers snapped and a tub appeared with steaming hot water. They began speaking in the Unseelie tongue, a language that was almost as old as the courts, and one Bryson did not understand. It had been spoken earlier and she hadn't been able to follow along with the entirety of the conversation. They'd switched out between the common tongue, a language spoken throughout all of Illyk, their accents thick and low.

"I will bathe my own mate," Weylyn declared to the brownies, shooing them away as they began to tug on her pants. "Find us both suitable clothing."

When he spoke like that, she could almost see how princely he really was.

"Here." Bryson's breath suddenly caught as Weylyn appeared in front of her, long adept fingers tugging at the waist of her shirt. She lifted her arms as he tugged the garment off her. Her skin pebbled with gooseflesh as soon as she was exposed. She didn't shy away as he began undressing her. Meticulously. Slowly. Like he was enjoying it rather than acting like it was a chore.

He untied the drawstring of her pants. As he leaned forward, his nose brushed against her belly, causing Bryson to suck in a breath. He looked up at her, dark lashes shadowing the gold of his eyes. He worked, as though his fingers memorized every curve of her, with his eyes firmly holding her own.

He shoved her pants down the length of her legs, his warm palms tracing her skin down to her ankles, where he helped to pull off her boots, socks, and pants.

Weylyn stood to his full height, purposefully brushing against her body as he went. Her skin felt suddenly far too sensitive, and his clothes scraped against her pebbled nipples uncomfortably. She wanted to peel the clothes from his body, feel his heat envelop her. It didn't matter that there were brownies tittering about the room, cleaning and leaving the sharp smell of their magic wherever they touched.

She wanted him so much it ached.

Weylyn's fingers began wresting at his own clothes and she dared herself to watch. Up close his details weren't so hazy, and she followed the sight of his golden-brown skin being revealed to her. His shirt came off and she was staring at his firm flesh, wanting to reach out and touch it. Before she got a chance, he was shoving his pants down, pulling them and his boots and socks off. When they stood naked before one another, Bryson dared to let her gaze travel down... down...

But then Weylyn picked her up and dunked her into the water. She came up with a sputter and a curse, but he was already hopping into the tub behind her.

Together, they made a tight fit, but it was surprisingly comfortable to have him so close.

For a moment, it made her feel less alone in the world they suddenly found themselves in. She was never good at being alone.

Weylyn was surprisingly silent behind her and kept a small bit of space between them. Her back curled and she leaned over her knees, wrapping her arms around them and sighed as he began pouring warm water down her back. He lapped it up with her hair, and each pass of his fingers felt like he was washing away the anxiety as well as the grime.

Her heart pounded an unsteady rhythm against her chest, she was sure he could feel it vibrating in the water.

Scented soap filled her nostrils and seconds later his fingers were in her hair, rubbing the foam there. He scraped his nails softly against her scalp, scrubbing against it until it bubbled. He guided her silently using only his fingers, pulling her back. Her head arched, and he dipped her hair into the bath, rinsing the suds.

When Bryson sat up again, it was to find herself pressed closer against Weylyn's chest and nearly sitting in his lap.

She gasped when she felt his length press against her backside. She tensed, waiting to see what he'd do, but he didn't press into her like she'd expected. She was surprised she almost yearned for it. She pressed down against him despite knowing she shouldn't.

Weylyn's fingers grasped her shoulders, roaming against her skin in gentle movements, kneading at the tightened muscles there.

She fell into the bliss of the sensation, moaning as he scrubbed the soap across her body. She let him guide her, lift her arms, scrub down her body, across her neck, down over the swells of her breasts. Her eyes closed of their own volition, and she lost herself in the sensation.

But Weylyn didn't go any further than just washing her. His movements were gentle, firm, and almost clinical. He didn't linger anywhere, but swiped across her skin with careful precision, slipping his hand around her front and beneath the cloudy surface.

Bryson bit her lip as he washed her curls, down her thighs.

When he finished thoroughly over her whole body he pulled her against his chest, submerging her a bit deeper into the water. She found herself relaxing against him, basking in the sensation for a few moments.

Sighing, she sat forward. "Now your turn."

Weylyn obeyed silently, switching spots in the tub with her. It was awkward, and they mostly ignored the brownies that were walking in and out with their magic fizzling through the air. When Weylyn was in front of her, between her legs and caged around her thighs, she reached for his hair.

The tresses were silky and smooth. It was quite unfair how soft it was despite their trek through the Unseelie forest. Where Bryson's curls had tangled within dirt, twigs, and leaves, knotting in several places, his was immaculate.

Bryson was equally gentle with him as he was with her, wetting the ends before tugging gently to pull him back and dunk his whole head in. Once he was dripping, she grabbed the same soap he'd used on her and rubbed it into his hair. His body relaxed into hers as she went through the motions, trying to be as clinical as possible and avoid getting lost in his body.

His addictive scent saturated her nostrils so much that she dropped her forehead to his back, bumping against the sharpness of his bones and inhaled deeply. There was something about his essence that she knew others might find too sharp, too much. She recognized it was the spice, but there was an undertone of sweetness as well. It was comforting for her.

It reminded her of the hot peppers her mother used to cook in her stews. Spicy, with just the right amount of sweet. The memory of that time was surprising. Something she hadn't thought of in years, and it brought instant tears to her eyes.

Swallowing them back, she resumed her task, rinsing his hair and running her fingers through the long strands. It was longer than hers, trailing down to his waist. The strands pooled on the surface of the water like dark snakes. Once they were untangled and rinsed, Bryson and Weylyn stood, letting the water sluice from their bodies.

Immediately, the brownies rushed to them, producing fluffy towels that appeared to be made from dandelion tuffs instead of actual cloth that magically dried them within seconds.

Trying not to be shy about her state of undress, Bryson let herself be guided by the brownies. Their bark-like hands tugged at her naked form, slipping a shimmering cloth over her shoulders. The fabric adjusted to her body like a second layer of skin. It was sheer, and when she looked down at it, it glowed silver-gold like the webbing of a spider's web. The design was all thin thread that glittered when she moved and pressed against her body, leaving nothing to the imagination.

Her eyes flicked up to Weylyn, who was being outfitted by the brownies in gold and black pants, though he stayed bare-chested. Once his boots were on, he shooed the brownies away before they reached for his hair, and he flicked the length over his shoulder, his fingers moving quickly as he twisted it into a long braid.

Bryson's own hair was tugged through with a bristled brush, though her stands were left to curl around her shoulders.

Little lights bobbed through the air, making Bryson's vision clearer. The brightly colored lights sprinkled glittering dust that shimmered down like a paste against their skin. One of the little pixies appeared, wings weighing it down as it carried a golden crown of thorns and placed it atop Weylyn's head.

"Ready?" Weylyn asked her, his voice low and grave.

Bryson wasn't. She was cold, uncomfortable. She didn't fancy wearing a dress that left a good chunk of her body exposed. She wasn't a prude by far, but she felt too exposed, too vulnerable. Especially in a court that wasn't hers, surrounded by predators and enemies at all sides, without a wider range of sight to help her navigate it.

Nerves burst at the seams within her stomach. She tried to breathe through them, steeling herself against them, but it was hard, and she felt her chest compress with discomfort.

"Breathe." Weylyn's voice was an echo in her mind. She sucked in a breath that hurt her lungs just as the tent flaps parted and a small body thumped its way inside.

Bryson blinked down, making out small features of a male goblin.

The creature turned in Weylyn's direction and bowed. Bryson couldn't see well, but she wondered if it was more mocking than reverent.

"Prince, the queen requests your presence in the relic room immediately."

Weylyn nodded at the goblin and a moment later, the air around them shifted, becoming a suffocating force. Darkness settled around Bryson's vision like a blanket. Then, everything around them dissipated before they were no longer in the tent.

Relics and Gold

Bryson shook her head as a wave of dizziness crashed over her system. She stumbled, the thin shoes digging into something hard and uncomfortable. Straightening, she looked around at her surroundings and was assaulted immediately with gold.

"Weylyn."

Bryson's entire body went on high alert as the queen's rich voice imbued the air. It was sharp like a dagger, and equally cutting and vicious, like a blade tipped with poison.

She slowly turned in the direction of that voice. The queen was merely a few feet away. Unclear to Bryson's vision, but formidable just the same. Surrounding her were several figures. Through the sharp, dangerous smell of iron, Bryson could pick up some of the scents from yesterday. Weylyn's siblings. A few goblins, crowding around her fabric-clad legs.

The queen dripped in gold as bright as what surrounded them.

The relic room, as the goblin had called it, wasn't a room at all. It appeared to be within a room, yes, but one with crumbled walls and an open ceiling where the darkening sky was visible. It looked like a tomb, from what Bryson could tell. A tomb encased in riches. It merged with iron and wildlands, with vines and plant life growing within. And just outside of the walls, she could smell the scent of smoke as it clogged through the air. Like a factory.

It reminded her of the iron prisons she'd long since escaped from.

The reminder made her chest pressurize uncomfortably. It felt like she was drowning all over again. Iron from all sides, closing in on her body, getting smaller by the second. She fought not to wheeze as the stench grew almost unbearable. She blinked the water from her vision and all it did was blur. The pain in her chest intensified to strange proportions.

It had been so long since her mind had last flashed back to the camps. Of course, it lived with her far too much, for far too long. But it was past. It was something she was moving on from. But surrounded by iron, feeling it against her skin?

It felt like she was there, and the memories drowned her, dragged her under, and she couldn't reach the surface even if she wanted to.

"I can see the iron is affecting you." The voice of the queen cut through Bryson's panic, grounding her to the present.

She blinked, feeling tears—or blood, she wasn't sure which—slide down her cheeks.

"Your eyes bleed at their proximity," the queen mused.

Bryson could feel the queen's eyes on her, but her vision kept blinking in and out of focus, blurring and darkening. Her hands lifted to swipe the blood away, though all she felt was it smearing against her cheeks.

"It's toxic," Bryson whispered, her voice hoarse.

The queen chuckled. "Toxic for you." Her hands lifted as she gestured at the space around them, as if embracing the iron. "When the humans invaded Seelie with their iron and drove the High Fae from their lands, the iron spread. It mated with magic and eventually made its way here."

"The iron should have been fatal," Weylyn said from Bryson's side.

"It was, at first. But eventually we adapted. The longer we were forced in the proximity of the iron, the more our systems embraced it. Now, we are a part of it. Our magic has melded and joined with it, and we are stronger because of it."

Bryson tried to contain her shock. She wondered, if the Seelie had stayed, would that have been the case then? Would they have adapted to iron? Would they have become stronger instead of...

Her eyes burned just thinking about it. It would do no good to hope, to dwell.

"Remarkable," Weylyn murmured. "Though I see it has also caused side effects to some."

She didn't know what he meant by that. She couldn't see what he was staring at, either. A moment after that thought hit her, her mind blackened as he shoved an image in her mind. An image of Unseelie creatures with twisted, deformed features that couldn't have been more unnatural. Twisted faces that didn't belong, even on an Unseelie.

She blinked again and the image was gone.

"Some were contaminated more than others," the queen replied, her tone dismissive. "Now, the reason I called you here."

In a swish of golden skirts, the queen turned and went deeper into the relic room. Everyone followed, so Bryson and Weylyn had no choice but to do so as well.

"You cannot see, I am sure, but my goblins have forged many relics over the years. Infusing magic and iron, magic and gold, and have created many masterpieces."

Once the pressure of iron subsided, though it was still heavy on her bones, Bryson glanced around the room. A new pressure invaded the air, this one infused with magic. It was potent, charging a static through the air that made the hairs all over her exposed body rise.

"We have an array of relics with incredible power holstered here. Rings of iron that can glamor you into anything you wish. Weapons disguised as jewelry. Swords that can shrink to the size of a quill. Mirrors that can portal you anywhere you desire."

Bryson followed down an aisle with gold and mountains of objects clustered on all sides of her. As she passed them, her skin tingled. She didn't even want to begin to know what more each of these objects did.

"My goblins will fabricate something for you as well." The queen stopped mid stride and turned to face Bryson.

"For me?"

"For your sight. All they would need is measurements. Kneel."

The command in the last word was obvious, and Bryson was still reluctant and slow to do so. She turned to Weylyn, but couldn't see his face at all clearly to gauge what he thought or what she should do. Was this an infamous Unseelie exchange? Would the queen demand something of her for this?

Bryson warred with herself as she slowly dropped to her knees. Then, bodies crowded around her. Little goblins grasping her face with their rough hands and twisting her head unkindly from side to side. Claws scraped near her eyes, over the marks of her scars, then pulled her eyelids open forcefully. A face appeared so close, she could make out the wrinkled details of rough, leathery skin.

"Iron poisoning," the goblin muttered. "Iron wounds. Scars. Sightless Fae."

Bryson huffed a breath at the clinical, rough words.

"Can she be fixed?" the queen demanded.

Bryson wanted to bristle at the callous way the queen said that. As if Bryson were broken.

"Yes," the goblin answered with confidence. "Easily, Your Majesty."

"Very good. We cannot have the prince's mate weakening our bloodline, can we?"

Weylyn huffed out a breath, the sound both exasperated and amused. "It is too late to worry about weak bloodlines now, do you not think so, mother?"

The goblin stepped away from Bryson and she immediately pushed herself to a stand. The energy in the air changed then, becoming more aggressive than the iron clogging around them.

"That tongue will be the death of you," the queen snarled.

"Really?" Weylyn mused. He injected as much humor as he possibly could into the word, and Bryson felt a sliver of fear slide down her back at the tone. She wanted to reach for him, to warn him.

Losing her sight had made Bryson perceptible to so much more than she'd ever been. To things others weren't privy to. Like threats. Perhaps the shock of landing in Unseelie had crippled her to that part of her senses at first and nearly landed her within the mouth of a ghoul. But she knew the queen was a threat. The ultimate predator.

And Weylyn was playing with fire.

She had the urge to slap him, if only so he would shut up. He had been adamant she not say a word, but it was obvious he was trying to antagonize his mother.

"I thought you would be the death of me."

"Yes," the queen crooned. "Continue to provoke me and I will be. Now that her measurements have been taken, it is time to head to the feast." Bryson felt the queen's smile like a snake ready to strike. "The court is very excited for your return."

And by Mana, those words felt more like a threat than anything else Bryson had ever heard. The fear was immediate, but the queen didn't give them a single moment to contemplate it before they were whisked away into darkness once again. A moment later, they appeared within the center of what felt like wild lands.

Welcome to the Wildlands

Music reverberated against the night sky, though it felt like it wasn't coming from instruments at all. Rather that nature was belting out song into the world, weaving it into being, mixing magic and sound to create a symphony that Bryson felt down to her bones.

The air was sharp and fizzled with a drugging magic similar to when Fae wine was created. It immediately made her dizzy and lightheaded, and she tried not to sway on her feet as everything pulsed through her in a single, forceful shove.

Weylyn reached out to grasp her hand. His firm touch steadied her, and she found a brief second of comfort in it before he was pulling away. Almost like he was afraid of who was watching. She hated that, which was strange considering she hadn't wanted him touching her at all.

But as far as Bryson was concerned, her rules went out the window when it came to being in the Unseelie Court. There were no rules here, or at least if there were, they didn't apply to this situation. She wanted Weylyn to touch her. She needed him to.

If only so she didn't feel quite so alone.

But this was a dangerous game they were playing, and she wasn't going to desperately reach for him and let everyone scent her fear. She wasn't going to be prey here.

She was going to be a predator.

"Stay by my side." Weylyn's voice flittered through her mind, beating frantically. She wanted to reach for him, but closed her nails into her palms instead and swallowed the rising lump in her throat.

Bryson focused her attention back on the party. Things had quieted down a fraction as the queen all but floated towards her throne. The same one she'd sat in when they first arrived. The difference this time was there were more bodies. There was the scent of food and drugging magic in the air, and things didn't seem as tense as they'd been before.

But they did feel equally dangerous.

There was a beat of silence. And then the queen called out, "Feast and party, my subjects. For we celebrate my son and his mate tonight."

There was a roar as sound crashed through the night once again. Bodies swarmed them, jostling Weylyn and Bryson apart. She turned, blinking blindly, letting her nose follow his scent. But it was useless. The bodies shoved at her, pulling her into the fray of the party. Music hummed and all manner of hands and arms reached for her.

She found herself clasping down on fingers as though to steady herself. But those fingers yanked her onto the grass and twirled her, over and over again until she felt like she was losing control of her own body. She looked up into the air, finding floating lights above her. Golden dust rained down over her face, trickling up her nose. Bryson sneezed to expel it, but all it did was invade her senses and cloud her vision.

"Weylyn!" She looked around, losing his scent and his form in the fray.

She caught sight of him, his long braid and dark skin and gold gleaming on his body. She reached out, grasping his hand in her own, and was shoved from behind. She landed against the solidity of his chest and gasped as a strange scent filled her nostrils.

Not of sweet and spice, but of something far, far different.

Golden-clad fingers gripped her hips, pulling her against the hard press of a tall, lithe body. She looked up, blinking, gasping, as she met a pair of eyes that glared down at her, so in contrast with the smile curving that mouth. A smile that was familiar but didn't belong to Weylyn at all.

Curved black horns adorned with gold sat on his forehead. The man, the prince, one of Weylyn's brothers, held her close. His palms closed over her hip, the other grasping at her hand.

"How very forward of you, little Fae."

This wasn't the brother who had found them and brought them to the queen in chains. This was a different one, and she tried to rack her memory for his name but came up blank.

"I thought you were Weylyn," she defended quietly.

He chuckled low and his voice enveloped her. "An innocent mistake," he purred. "One you will regret if you make it again." His fingers dug into her skin, and she bit the inside of her cheek to avoid crying out. A moment later, he was twirling her, round and round and round until her head spun with dizziness. Her feet skidded against the ground as she tried to keep up with him but failed.

More of that golden powder sprinkled from the sky and coated her skin like a layer of dust. She had the urge to swat it away, but the prince was holding her too tightly.

She could feel the hatred in his very touch. In every word that dripped from his tongue. It was venomous, this poison he felt for his brother. So obvious that they all hated Weylyn. Even if her mate hadn't told her that he was estranged from his own family, it would have been so very obvious. And that hatred, it seemed, extended to Bryson as well. Just by her association.

He held her tightly like he wanted to break her.

He would find that Bryson couldn't be so easily broken.

"I should go find your brother."

She started to pull away, but his growl stopped her, his hold on her tightening.

"My brother is occupied at the moment." He twirled her in a circle and as he did so, she caught a whiff of Weylyn's scent through her nose, and a flash of gold that could have very well been him, but she couldn't be sure.

The prince caught her in his arms again, holding her even closer than he had before.

Warning ran through her mind. Of what Weylyn had told her about his brothers. About how dangerous they were. She needed to get away from him, but his grip was fast, the bodies pressed around them, making it almost impossible for her to pull away from him.

She wondered if shoving a prince would be considered a slight. If he would punish her for the audacity of harming him and decided she would rather not risk it. Not in this court. Not with him.

"What was your name again?" she asked, She didn't want to even have a conversation with him, but she wanted him glaring at her in silence the whole time even less.

"What will you give me in exchange for my name?" he mused.

Bryson's scarred eyes rolled. "You really don't think that's going to work on me, do you?"

He chuckled low and pulled her closer by the waist. His hand slid over her hip, though the act was more clinical and unnerving than outright sexual. "A Fae can make an attempt at trickery."

Bryson scoffed.

"I am called Rainer."

"That's a mouthful." It wasn't, but she felt she needed to say something. If only because the power imbalance between them felt all too real, and she already felt entirely too small.

He chuckled and lowered his head so the tips of his hair grazed Bryson's body. It felt like spiderwebs clinging to her skin. Sticky and creepy. She fought the urge to claw at her skin. "I know of something else that is also a mouthful, if you would be so inclined to try."

Bryson flicked her gaze disinterestedly over his body then back up to his face. "I may be near blind but even I can see that you are overly compensating."

Rainer laughed, and the sound was surprisingly... pleasant. Bryson was instantly on alert as he pulled her closer. So close it felt like she'd seep into his very skin. His arms wrapped around her in a hold that she knew she wouldn't be able to break out of without a great push from her magic.

"You are very humorous, High Fae," he said against her shoulder. A second later, his tongue darted out to taste her skin and she jerked in his hold, trying to shove away from him. "It is unfortunate you are mated to him."

The vehemence in that single word made her stop struggling. She had no idea why they hated Weylyn so much, but she felt it like a palpable thing that she could reach out and choke herself with if she'd been so inclined.

"Such a shame to be tethered to him," he went on, his clawed fingers slipping over her body, tracing along her freckles. "Such a shame a stunning creature like you is now to be caught up in our familial war."

Bryson swallowed her discomfort. "What do you mean, war?"

Rainer smirked. "I suppose you will see soon enough, will you not? Since you are now a pawn in our game." His lips caressed the shell of her ear. "And you will be the first to die."

He shoved her away from him and her feet twirled in the dance, further and further from his arms. Golden dust followed where she went, bathing her in that dizzying sensation.

She nearly tripped but was caught again, this time by four arms that caged her between two bodies.

"Look at what we have caught, Gwyn," a voice said.

"A sightless High Fae, Glyn!" a second voice exclaimed.

Bryson's head darted back and forth. Her neck felt heavy, her eyelids even more so. But she managed to make out identical faces in front and over her shoulder. Twins. Princes. Weylyn's brothers.

She tried to pull out from their hold, but their arms were like iron bars wrapped around her. Suffocating and demanding.

"Our brother's precious mate," the one named Glyn said. He whipped her around so she was facing the other brother instead. She wanted to get away, but more of that sparkling dust hit her nose, causing her strength to wane.

"How unfair a life when a murderer finds his mate above all others," Gwyn lamented, sighing against her skin. "Did you know that, little Fae? Did you know your mate is a murderer?"

"She must know," Glyn volleyed back. "If she does not, then she is a fool."

"Maybe she is a fool, Glyn. Only a fool would fall in a mushroom circle."

Her head spun as it tried to keep up with the conversation. She grasped at the first thing she could with trembling fingers, one of the twin's shirtfronts, while her mind spun. "I didn't fall in," she defended. Her tongue was starting to feel heavy. "I was pushed."

"Oh, our apologies, little Fae."

Hands slid over her thighs, over the spiderweb material of the shimmering skirt. The hem lifted, exposing more of her than she wanted them to see. She jerked against them, slapping their hands as if that could shove away their wandering fingers.

"Oh, do not be so prude, little Fae." Gwyn laughed against her shoulder. "You know Gwyn and I like to share our lovers. Weylyn owes us. He should share you, too."

"He owes us a great deal, he does," Glyn confirmed. "We would only be taking what we are owed. Would you like to know what he owes us?"

"It would cost you, of course."

"A price. Everything always comes with a price."

Her head lolled a bit to the side. It was on the tip of her tongue to agree. Her entire body felt loose and agreeable, but at the last moment, something in her skidded to a halt and she remembered just where she was and who they were.

Never make a deal with an Unseelie Fae.

Those were the rules. And whatever dust they were sprinkling against her nose was giving the effect of forgetfulness. She wanted to throw caution to the wind. She wanted to tell them everything, and she wanted them to give her every secret in return.

No.

She couldn't.

It was dangerous.

She shoved at the chest of one of the twins weakly. "Let me go," she slurred.

"What if we do not want to let you go?"

"What if we want to keep you for ourselves?"

"What if we want to kill you the same way Weylyn killed her?"

"No one would stop us, you know."

"No one."

"You're all alone, little Fae."

"So alone."

"Blind and alone."

"Ours to toy with."

"Ours to torture."

"*Hehehehe.* You are ours now, little Fae. Come, let us play."

Hands grabbed her from all sides, and she tried to shove them away. Tried to drown out the taunting voices, but they only echoed inside her skull, creating a loud pounding that made her temples throb. She wanted to drop to her knees and scream. She wanted to choke. She wanted to disappear.

Weylyn.

Where was Weylyn?

Why had he left her?

A void swallowed her up and she felt truly disregarded. Like there was no one there and never would be. He'd abandoned her and they were going to swallow her alive. There was nothing she could do about it. Nothing. Nothing. Nothingnothingnothingnothingnothing—

"Leave her alone Gwyn, Glyn." A voice cut through the haze of her panic, causing the twins to stiffen around her. A moment later they released her and took a step away.

"Aw, you're no fun, Cassimir."

"Yeah, no fun."

"Go pull the wings off pixies. It is my turn to dance with our new sister."

The twins hissed and scrambled away, but not before they cursed in Bryson's direction. "She is no sister of ours," they spat in unison and then disappeared into the crowd.

With them gone, Bryson could breathe. Though her body still felt lethargic, she felt less clustered. Less suffocated. Now, she only felt dizzy and drunk.

But that wasn't right, was it? she thought. She hadn't had a drink all night. Why did she feel like she'd imbibed in way too much Fae wine?

Cassimir gripped her, pulling her back to the present. He held her close, but his touch wasn't painful like Rainer's had been, and it wasn't roaming like the twins' had been. His touch was careful. Not respectful exactly, but he didn't frighten her as much as the others did. Maybe he was better at tempering the wild nature the others so freely let loose.

Still, Bryson couldn't bring herself to relax at all.

"I would apologize for my siblings' behavior, but I fear it would not be accepted regardless." He twirled her, pressing her close. Her feet nearly stumbled, and she grasped at his hand for support.

"You're right." Bryson's words came out slightly slurred. "I wouldn't accept it."

"Hmm."

The music reverberated, drowning out everything else for a brief moment. In that moment, she lost herself in the sensation of the music of the wildlands. It was free, consuming, almost as consuming as the powder invading her system.

"Why do you all hate Weylyn so much?" Bryson found herself asking.

She shouldn't engage in conversation with him. She knew that, but she couldn't bring herself to stop. The curiosity had been killing her since they arrived, and Weylyn's answers were evasive at best. Not that she thought he would tell her the truth. Not that she thought she could trust anything he said anyway. But her tongue was thick and loose, and her head was spinning, her thoughts as cloudy as her vision.

"He has not told you?" He whirled her again, his hand warmed against her lower back.

Bryson didn't reply.

"Hmm, I suppose he would not. He would twist the truth if he did. He would make you believe that which did not happen, if only to make himself look innocent. Free of culpability from something that was entirely his fault."

Bryson's head spun. "You're speaking in riddles."

"Am I?" His palm lifted against her back and he brought her hand between them, pressing it over her chest where he likely was feeling the rapid beating of her heart. His smile kicked up. "You are nervous."

There was no point in denying the obvious. "I am. You would be too if you were in a strange court, surrounded by strange Fae who wanted nothing more than to kill you simply by association with your brother."

"You must understand it is nothing personal, little Fae." His palm splayed against her chest, trapping her hand against his. His grip was firm, but not painful. "At least not towards you. You are merely a means to an end here."

They twirled again and more powder rained down. It made Bryson feel like she was floating. Flying.

"And what end is that?" she found herself asking.

Cassimir lowered his head. Close enough that his lips pressed against her ear. Close enough that his tongue flicked against her skin. "Weylyn's demise."

Her entire body tensed at the threat that was so obvious in his tone. It left no room for second-guessing. No room for anything but the truth. They wanted Weylyn dead. And they would stop at nothing to get it, even if it meant using her to get to him.

Fear snaked through her body, wrapping around her tightly and refusing to let go.

"But why?" she whispered. Her hold tightened on him, like she could rip out the truth from his throat, from his body. "What did he do to you?"

Cassimir's eyes shuttered and the air changed with menace, danger, and she felt death merging along the horizon and it had nothing to do with the iron in the air.

And when Cass answered, that chill turned to ice and Bryson felt like she would crack and shatter into thousands of little pieces.

"He helped kill her."

Cassimir spun her out and pulled her back. This time, he left a foot of space between them. His entire body was stiff as he bowed, the perfect picture of princely manners. His crown gleamed on his head, his horns shining like obsidian. That smile of his was feral. Knowing. Threatening.

"I thank you," he purred. "For the honor of this dance. I believe my brother has need of you."

She didn't get a chance to reply before he turned and walked away.

A moment later, she was enveloped in the scent of sweetness and spice. Weylyn's arms came around her, whipping her around. She could make out the worry on his features up close, the groove in between his eyebrows as he looked her up and down as if searching for injuries that weren't there.

His gaze zeroed in on her eyes and a muttered curse left his lips.

"Are you alright?" he whispered low. His gaze darted around cautiously.

Up close, his scent made her as dizzy as the powder sifting through her nose. This close, she felt her anxieties and fears fade away. There was no longer the oppressive, cloying scent of the iron and powder. She no longer felt the creepy slide of his brothers' unwanted touch against her skin.

This close it was just Weylyn and her. Weylyn. Her mate. Her chosen. This close, she felt protected. Her arms came up to rest against his shoulders. She had to stretch because he was so tall, and she enjoyed feeling just a bit delicate next to him, though she wouldn't ever admit that out loud.

Her fingers played with the skin at his shoulders and slid down, over his chest, pressing against the thumping where his heart beat in a steady rhythm she wished she could match. Her hands went lower still to his waist only to wrap around him and pull him closer.

"Hmm," she hummed, moving her hips. Pressed this close, she felt every pane of his body against hers. The silver, shimmering material of the dress she wore was practically nothing but a layer of webbing. It did nothing to conceal his warmth. Nothing to hide his arousal as his cock rose beneath his pants and pressed against her stomach.

She felt dizzy at the proximity and felt her body sway.

Weylyn's hands came down against her own waist. His eyes flashed brightly, and she sucked in a breath.

"Bryson..." His fingers twitched against her hips. "What are you doing?"

"Hmm." She pressed her hips against him, looking for friction. The warmth of the night air caressed her every inch, twining between her legs. A gush of wetness seeped from her, near begging for his touch. "Dance with me?"

"You've been drugged," Weylyn whispered. His fingers came up to swipe at the golden powder that had been landing in gusts down against her face. "These are Unseelie drugs."

"Is that why I feel like I'm floating?" She giggled, unable to stop the sound.

So that was why she felt high... high... high.

Her body swayed again, rubbing against him. She tilted her head back and let out a groan. Her skin felt like it was on fire and the only thing that could ease the burn was his touch.

"Weylyn," she all but whimpered. "Touch me. Touch me, please." Everything faded away. The music. The bodies pressing around them, dancing with as little inhibition as she felt swirling through her own head. They all moved, powder of all colors shimmering against bodies, pressed against their skin and sticking there.

His fingers came away golden as he tried to rub the magic off.

"Bryson." His voice was firm. "No."

Tears pricked her eyes at the rejection, but she only pressed closer, standing on the tips of her toes so their noses touched. She inhaled deeply, wanting him to invade her every crevice.

She hated it before. Hated him before. But now she was alone. Now she needed him. Now she relished in him, in his scent. All the reasons she had protested their bond seemed so far away now. And if she was going to die, then she rather it be drowning in him instead of by the cruel hands of those around her.

It wasn't fair. A far part of her knew that it wasn't fair to press this close. To let her lips hover over his own. It wasn't fair when she might not want him after they left Unseelie. But there was no guarantee of survival.

And Bryson was so very tired of fighting the darkness. And Weylyn was dark. He was chaos. He was everything she tried to avoid but so desperately wanted to give in to. And why shouldn't she give in? Why shouldn't she be selfish? Why shouldn't she want what was fated to be hers?

Her lips skimmed across Weylyn's, sucking in the soft gasp he let out.

"Bryson," he groaned against her mouth, though his fingers flexed against her hips, pulling her closer. Like he was too weak to push her away, even if his eyes said he wanted to. "We can't."

She arched her neck just a bit more and kissed him. A quick press of her lips against his own. Just a taste. A small little taste of what they could have, of what they could be.

She hadn't tasted his lips before. Not like this. Not physically. Everything they'd ever done had been with the use of his magic. Mental, spiritual. It had all been a phantom, a product of desire and imagination. And it came up short to what he truly felt like. Solid. Warm.

She wanted him desperately.

"Weylyn." She pressed a kiss to his mouth once again. "Just a taste," she whispered. "Please, just a taste."

His eyes closed almost as if he were at war with himself. As if he were fighting her words, the desire she knew they both were feeling.

"Just a taste," she pleaded again.

His eyes opened and the gold burned a hole through her soul. His canines flashed and he echoed her words. "Just a taste."

And then his lips devoured her own.

Glittering Gold

Bryson groaned against the assault of Weylyn's tongue. He pillaged. He conquered. He kissed her like she was the very air he breathed and could only find survival on her lips. She kissed him back with just as much fervor, groaning and grinding against him.

The pulse of her rapid heartbeat matched the drums and songs of the night. Her moans were drowned out by the erratic calls of the wildlands and creatures of Unseelie. She knew eyes were on her, but eventually even that faded as her hands scraped against Weylyn's body, searching for purchase. Searching for more.

His hands gripped her on the backs of her bare thighs, shoving the hem of the thin material of the dress up the curve of her ass. Cold air hit her, pebbling her skin in gooseflesh. She didn't care about being exposed. She didn't care about anything except the dizzying sensation he provoked, the way he set her nerves on fire.

His arms clamped around her and he lifted her with ease into his arms. She moaned, legs wrapping around his waist in a vice. She didn't want to be pried away from him. Couldn't. It didn't matter that there was danger around; it was like it didn't exist in the first place. Her entire world tunneled into this single moment of being with him.

He gripped her ass tightly, grinding her down against his length. And then they were moving. Her world was spinning, and she had to tear her mouth from his to gasp for breath. The stars became even more of a blur above them. And when she blinked at Weylyn, it was to find golden powder from her skin transferred to his.

Her lips tingled where he'd kissed her. And still she craved more. But he was moving away from the fray of dancing bodies. Past the sounds of the party. Away from food and drink that would trap them in the court forever. Far enough away that they could still hear the music, but it dulled to a low, throbbing tempo. Far enough away they had privacy to be alone.

And once they were, he lowered her to the ground, her back touching cold earth. The trees surrounded them, and the sky loomed high above. The earth thrummed with the beat of dancing feet, making her heart pound faster and faster.

Weylyn kept her caged between his arms, hovering above her. His dark braid slipped over his shoulder to tickle her cheek.

Her hand lifted, dusting away the golden powder from the ridge of his sharp cheekbone. He caught her wrist, eyes and nostrils flaring. He brought her fingers near his mouth and licked a line of powder from the tips of her fingers.

The hot, wet flick of his tongue made Bryson moan. "Weylyn." Her hips thrust up to meet his, but he didn't take. He did nothing except stare down at her.

The desire was obvious on his face, but he didn't take. He didn't consume.

"Why won't you touch me?" she demanded. "You would have... before. Before you would have."

She didn't know where the uncertainty of her own thoughts were coming from. This self-consciousness that invaded her system. It was the drugs, she was sure of it, clouding everything from her common sense to her confidence.

"Before you would have taken me right here, fuck the consequences. So why won't you do so now?" She hated how weak her voice sounded, but hated how she felt without his weight bearing down on her even more.

"Bryson." Weylyn lowered until the tip of his nose touched her own. "You are a fool if you think I don't want you." His tongue darted out to tease the seam of her lips, but before she could open her mouth, he pulled away. "I want to fuck you. Claim you. Make you mine."

Desire pulsed, hot and heavy between her legs. "Do it," she ordered, thrusting her hips up. "Do it. Please. Please, please, please."

Slowly, Weylyn shook his head. "No. Not like this. Not here."

Tears slid against the scars around her eyes. Weylyn kissed them away, as if that could soothe the hurt he'd caused.

"Don't cry." His words were somehow both gentle and harsh simultaneously. "You've been drugged with Unseelie magic." He dusted the remaining powder from her skin. "You aren't thinking clearly. I won't do it. Not like this."

"But I need you." Her hips lifted against his, moving in an attempt to find the friction she needed. But all it did was create fire against her too-sensitive clit. She whined, feeling the tears streaming down her face. Her heart beat harder, harder, and her breaths came out shallow. Her insides felt hollow. Empty. She needed to be filled, consumed.

Her hands raked against his shoulders, tugging at his shirt, at his skin.

"Weylyn, I need you."

He dropped his forehead to hers, inhaling the scent of her. He closed his eyes, opened them again. The gold consumed like fire.

"Just a taste."

It took far too long for her to realize that he'd spoken in her mind.

"Just a taste."

"Yes," she gasped. "Please."

Weylyn's head dipped, his mouth meeting hers. She groaned. It wasn't enough. His tongue slipping and sliding, it could never be enough. Even as she met him with equal passion, she needed more. More. More.

His body splayed against hers and suddenly, they were swallowed with flames. Lost in their own world, lost in one another, unable to come up for air. Her fingers clawed and tugged, shoving the hem of his shirt up so she could feel the warmth of his skin.

Weylyn nipped and bit at her mouth. His canines elongated, snapped as he broke apart. She arched her neck in invitation, praying for a bite that didn't come. His tongue pressed against her pulse, the soft graze of his canines pressing down but not breaking the skin. He sucked, marked her, all the while his hands explored every inch.

They roved over her body, claws tearing through the material of the flimsy dress. The material parted and so did her legs as he pressed a thigh between them. Her hips lifted against his thigh, marking her scent and arousal all over him.

"Ride me, little mate." Weylyn's breath came out choppy against her neck as she did what he bade. She moved against his thigh, rubbing against the rough material.

"More," she breathed.

Weylyn's hands slid over her outer thighs, up to her hips, pressing between where their bodies connected until he met her wet center.

A mewling sound came from Bryson's throat. She didn't care who heard it. The entire world could shatter from her screams of pleasure and she wouldn't care. No. The only thing that mattered was this moment. Their bodies colliding. His fingers sliding over her folds and dipping inside.

He stretched her, scissoring two fingers through her channel while his thumb strummed a rhythm against her clit.

It didn't take long for her body to detonate. For her to be consumed. For her to explode with his name pushed against her lips. She cried out and saw the stars. The dizziness invaded and the entire world spun. The tunneled vision only darkened further. There was no light at the end. There was only darkness flickering at her from every angle, even as she tried to chase it away with the light.

It didn't work.

It closed in.

And all Bryson could do was give in.

⊱⊰

Bryson fell limp in his arms. Her pleasure had crested, shattered, and down their bond he felt the earth-quaking way everything changed between them. Like the invisible string that connected Weylyn to Bryson was pulled taut, stretched, and blanketed over them both. Not solidified, but a consumption just the same.

She fell languid against him, eyes fluttering closed. Her heart still pounded, and Weylyn stilled, waiting until her heart resumed its regular tempo. Only then did he remove his fingers from her warmth. Only then did he dare to pull away from her.

Bryson, he was finding, was as addicting as the Unseelie powder clinging to her nose. There were still remnants of that glittering gold left, and he swiped at it with his thumb until there was no trace of it on her skin.

His mother had done this on purpose.

The effects of that drug were something Weylyn knew all too well. The feeling of it coursing through the system, the languid way it made the bones liquid, loosened the tongue, and above all, tore away your inhibitions.

His family had let loose the drug, perhaps hoping it would be temptation for Weylyn, temptation enough that he would indulge in it. Lower his guard enough that he would not realize who was currently hiding in the shadows and watching while he took his mate.

He sighed and threw a glare over his shoulder, making out the form of his brother in the darkness, sitting on a branch like a predator. His shoulders were hunched, his eyes gleaming in the darkness. His claws raked across bark, and it flaked against the ground.

"Quite the show," he mused.

"I am sure it was." And if Bryson had been sober, she would have realized someone was watching them, waiting exactly for what had happened to happen. She never would have indulged in him otherwise. That was the consequence of those drugs. They made one lose their senses almost entirely, and Weylyn was sure the iron in the air wasn't helping her.

He found himself adapting to the court rather quickly. What had been painful became nothing more than a dull ache, his magic entwining with the iron.

"She is very pretty when she comes."

Weylyn did not tense, for he was sure that's what his brother wanted. He wanted to unsettle Weylyn. He wanted him feral, out of his mind like mated males usually were. While he did not relish in the thought of his slimy brother watching his mate come apart from the shadows, nudity never bothered him in the slightest. He was from Unseelie, after all, and inhibitions were low, orgies were frequent.

Bryson wouldn't appreciate the fact that he'd known they'd had an audience. But he was too weak to resist her wants and aches. He'd needed to touch her. Taste her. Let her fall apart into bliss and sleep. If only to give him this single moment of privacy with his brother.

A brother whom he very much wanted to kill.

Weylyn sat next to Bryson's sleeping form, dusting his hands against his pants. "Very," he agreed.

Cassimir chuckled low and took a leap from the tree, landing like a prowling cat on the ground. He straightened to his full height, claws gleaming and in front of him like weapons. "A shame she has been tethered to you."

A shame. Yes. A great shame, and yet Weylyn did not give an absolute single fuck. The fact was they were tethered. It didn't matter if she deserved better or not. If there were far better Fae out there for her. It did not matter that she was in love with another man. None of it did, because Bryson was *his.*

"Have you come to insult me, brother?" Weylyn asked casually, leaning back on his hands. His head dropped back, and his eyes opened to look at the stars.

The stars were far brighter in Unseelie than anywhere else. If he looked close enough, he could make out the Wild Hunt in the distance, streaking through the sky, their glorified cries rocking the clouds like thunder, their whips striking like lightning.

"No," Cass said. "I have come to issue an invitation."

Weylyn blinked slowly in his brother's direction. "An invitation," he echoed. His lips curled up into a smile. "How hospitable of you."

Cassimir rolled his eyes. Of all his brothers, Cass was the one who irritated Weylyn the least. "We are family," he said. "It is high time we put the past behind us. Considering you and your mate will be in Unseelie indefinitely..."

Weylyn did not show his alarm. He knew what his brother was saying was bullshit. If anything, his siblings would hold a grudge until the end of time, and even past the afterlife.

Not even Weylyn could forgive himself for what had happened. No one ever would. He had contended with that fact long ago.

"You think me a fool," Weylyn whispered.

"That I do."

It was Weylyn's turn to roll his eyes. "What is it you want? Truly?"

"An outing," Cass said. "It is The Hunt. You will participate come morning."

"Fine."

"Fine?" Cassimir's brows kicked up to his shoddy hairline.

"Must I repeat myself? Have you lost your hearing in your ancient age?"

"Sarcasm does not suit you, little brother." Cass turned to walk away. "Early morning," he reminded Weylyn. "Kiss your little mate goodbye and ready your spears. Our brothers are so looking forward to having you back for The Hunt."

Portals and Prayers

"This is *your* fucking fault," Malika spat in the human's direction.

The human, who still wept and had been doing so for the past hour, did and said nothing in response to that.

Uric fought not to roll his eyes and instead looked at his prince.

"Open a portal," Prince Valerio insisted.

Uric bit his tongue. He had been asking for several minutes now, and Uric had not been able to bring himself to respond. He could not open a portal, yet his prince demanded it.

The rebel leader, Arlo Blackwood, thought his man would have the answers to their problem, but they were back to where they started.

"I cannot," Uric whispered. He had wanted to say these words in private, so no one else could hear, but they suddenly brought attention in their direction. He grinded his teeth against the stares and his jaw cracked.

"Uric," Prince Valerio sighed, pinching the bridge of his nose.

"I have tried," Uric said quickly. "The moment they fell through, I tried. I cannot open portals to the Unseelie realm."

"Why?"

"Unseelie follows different rules of time and space. It is unlike the Seelie or humanlands, therefore my magic cannot access it." Uric hated that bit of weakness. Hated disappointing his prince, but there was nothing he could do when it came to this.

"So are we supposed to stand around and do nothing to help them?" Malika shouted. "We can't just abandon them to Unseelie! We have to do something!"

Uric met Valerio's gaze. They stared at one another for the longest time and in that moment, silence spoke so much more than any words ever could. Uric knew his friend too well, well enough to see the burden of guilt weighing heavily against his shoulders.

He blamed himself for this, when no one was at fault but that pathetic, sniveling human.

"What other choice do we have?" Uric whispered, low enough so only Valerio could hear.

There was nothing they could do. They could not very well travel to Unseelie themselves to find them. It would put them all at risk and they would lose far more than they had to gain if they did so.

"We cannot go after them," Uric whispered again. "It is too *dangerous.*"

Finally, Valerio sighed and pinched the bridge of his nose. "You're right," he said.

Uric tried not to feel surprised. Very rarely did his friend listen to him, if ever.

"There is nothing we can do," Valerio told everyone. "Except pray to Mana, and pray hard and fast that Weylyn and Bryson make it back to us safely." His gaze went to the mushroom circle they'd fallen through, staring at it like he could will them to come back through from the other side.

Uric had to force himself to look away from the hope in his prince's eyes, for as much as he wanted to diminish it and tell him that it was hopeless, he could not bring himself to do so. Or even want to believe it himself.

Into the Pit

Bryson awoke with an ache in her temples, her scars itching, and the sensation of her tongue being too dry to even swallow. She smacked her lips and sat up with a groan. Light pierced her eyes and she rubbed at her lids, fingers scraping across the scars on her flesh.

Magic fizzled through the air as she inhaled deep. A second smack of her lips and she nearly gagged at the coppery tang she tasted on her tongue.

"Ugh," she complained, rubbing the back of her hand against her mouth. "What *is* that?"

She blinked again, her surroundings coming into focus. She was in the same tent she'd gotten dressed in with Weylyn, sitting among a plush pile of pillows and blankets. She was naked, though Bryson didn't question it, as she vaguely remembered the thin, stringy material being yanked from her body the night before.

Her face flushed at the memory of how she'd all but pounced on Weylyn. Then another sharper memory invaded. Of powder falling against her nose and making her lose her sense of self.

Had that been the reason she'd wanted him so desperately or was there more to it than that? Bryson couldn't be sure, and she wasn't sure she had the energy to question it regardless.

Not when the morning sun was peeking through the tent, making her entire brain pound inside her skull. Not when brownies were flittering through the tent, tidying things that didn't need to be tidied, and pouring buckets of steaming warm water into the tub.

"Up, up, up," one of the brownies ordered in a squeaky voice. The creature's skin looked like it was made of red bark, with hair that resembled moss. "The queen requests an audience with you at once."

Bryson blinked away the bleariness in her vision once again, unsure if she'd heard the brownie correctly. "Me?"

"Yes, yes, yes. Up, up, up."

The brownie's rough fingers grasped at Bryson's legs, tugging on her skin, pinching her in sensitive areas. Bryson obeyed, standing on wobbling legs.

"Where's Weylyn?" she asked as the brownie guided her towards the tub.

"The Hunt is today," the brownie offered.

Bryson's eyebrows lifted as she stepped one foot into the tub and then the other. She sank low in the water. It was biting against her skin, and she let out a hiss as steam rose through her nostrils. "What's The Hunt?" she asked.

"Tradition. The princes hunt game for the feast. He left early morn."

Bryson felt a pinch in her chest. He hadn't woken her; he hadn't told her where he was going or said goodbye. He'd left her alone, and now the queen was requesting an audience with her. While he was away.

Fear was gripping, and she tried to ignore it by grabbing a bar of soap and scrubbing it across her skin until she was sensitive and aching.

"Why does the queen wish to see me?" Bryson asked as she took soap through her hair.

Instead of answering, the brownie hopped up on a stool and took the bar from Bryson to scrub it unkindly through her curls. Bryson winced as her hair was tugged and then blinked as water was poured over her and suds caught in her eyes.

"You are her youngest son's mate," the brownie tittered. "She must meet you properly."

Bryson bit her tongue and didn't bother mentioning that she had planned on rejecting the mate bond with Weylyn. Because it wasn't their business, but also because that plan was so far away that she didn't even know if she wanted that anymore. Things had changed the moment she'd gotten shoved into that Unseelie portal.

Of course, she wouldn't use Weylyn just because she was afraid of what was to come. She could rely on him, want him, desire him. She could give in to everything she repressed here. Because tomorrow wasn't guaranteed. It was a strange thing how life ruined carefully constructed plans, and Bryson just wasn't sure if it was for the better or not quite yet.

All she knew was that she needed Weylyn at this very moment. And maybe here, he was her only ally. Here she could learn to trust him.

"Just a taste." Her words from last night echoed embarrassingly through her head. She'd devoured him. She'd let him give her pleasure.

Bryson's head submerged beneath the water inch by inch. And when she rose again, she left her mouth underwater. As if that could hide her mortification.

"Shyness is unnecessary, little mate." Weylyn's voice appeared in her mind just then, causing her to jolt and slosh at the water. *"I would fuck you, even if you did not beg."*

Her face heated and she looked from side to side, almost afraid that others had heard his musings. But no one did. His words were for her alone.

"The Hunt, Weylyn?" she asked in her mind.

"A tedious tradition. And dangerous. I am sure my brothers will make a few attempts on my life on this outing."

Bryson jolted again and felt her panic rise. *"You're serious."*

"Very. But I will not die today."

Before Bryson could ask him how he was so sure of that, he responded.

"I still have yet to taste between your thighs. I will not die, because I have much to live for."

She didn't bother telling him that it wasn't going to happen. After last night, *anything* could happen, and she wasn't going to say no. Especially not when her thighs shook at the promise in his words and a gush of wetness slid from between her legs.

Bryson changed the subject. *"The queen wishes to meet me."*

Weylyn was quiet a long while. Then, *"Be careful, little mate. She is not to be trusted. I will not be able to tune in to your thoughts the entire time."*

Steely resolve sank into her bones. Bryson straightened her spine.

Predator or prey.

"I'll be fine," she told him, and she meant it. She wasn't some simpering Fae child hiding behind their mother's skirts. She was an Elemental Fae. She wielded air. She had survived loss and war and near-blindness and iron camps. She could survive the Unseelie queen on her own.

She was strong.

Predator or prey.

Predator.

"I will see you soon." And then Weylyn's voice disappeared.

"Up, up, up." The brownie ushered Bryson to a stand and held out a fluffy towel made of woven flowers and animal skin. "Time for wardrobe. And the goblin has come to see you."

Water sloshed from the sides of the rim of the tub as Bryson stepped out. She was dried over every inch by the brownies, and then she was dressed in black and gold pants and a shirt that cut off at the midriff. The high neck threatened to choke her, and she stopped herself from fidgeting at the neckline.

The brownies took a brush to her hair, pulling at all the knots, tying it in an elaborate hairstyle Bryson was sure she'd never be able to emulate on her own. Once she was dressed, the brownies opened the tent flaps and a small creature waded through.

She recognized him as the same goblin who had measured her face before.

He yanked on her pants and her knees buckled then hit the ground. His glare met her eyes.

"Here." He procured a device from his pockets and held it up to her face. Bryson flinched as he forced it onto her, setting it on the bridge of her nose. "Lenses," he grumped as they settled.

And suddenly the world became so much more...

Clear.

The blur she'd lived with for years ceased. There were no blobs of color. It wasn't as if someone had taken a brush to the canvas of the world and *blurred* it.

Her sight was restored.

A small gasp left her lips and the lenses slid down the ridge of her nose. The goblin shoved them back up with a finger.

"H-how—?"

"Magic," he answered curtly. "And science."

Bryson leaned back and looked around. The weight of the glasses on her face was strange. They were made of a heavy metallic material, though the lenses were a thick glass. The pressure they put against her nose and ears felt like they didn't belong. But it didn't matter because she could *see.*

She hadn't seen anything clearly in years.

Doing so now made her eyes mist with emotion that she held back. Every detail was clear to her now. From the threads of the tent, to the textured skin of the brownies, to the creases in the goblin's old, angry face.

He was observing her with barely concealed annoyance, but also observing the lenses to make sure they were completely adequate. He must have thought they were, because he took a step back and nodded once.

"Do not break them," the goblin said. "I won't make you another."

Before Bryson could reply, he stomped out of the tent.

"Come now." The brownie tugged at her pants. Bryson looked down, relishing in details she could now make out clearly. The way pink and purple flowers bloomed across the brownie's brown-green, tree-like skin. The young, expressive face as she smiled up at Bryson. "The queen requests your presence."

The reminder of that made Bryson's excitement diminish just a fraction. She took a breath as she pushed herself to her feet. She held her head high as she exited the tent behind the brownie. She tried not to give in, but couldn't help herself as the sunlight hit her body and colors assaulted her vision.

Her head twisted side to side, absorbing everything around her. Everything felt new, fresh. Her eyes widened as she took in the Unseelie Court in a way she hadn't been able to do before. It was rife with magic. A part of it reminded her of the Seelie Court before the humans had invaded, but a larger part of her recognized it for what it was. It was *more.*

It was pixies flying liberally through the air, creating a rainbow of floating lights and different colored powders as they rained down, softly blanketing the ground like snow. Her delicate shoes sunk into the powder, and it flew up with every step, nearly making her sneeze. She tried not to inhale it, though, and the pixies seemed to giggle at her efforts.

Other creatures milled about, a good majority of them goblins, but she caught sight of satyrs, centaurs, and an array of Unseelie Fae with animalistic features as well. Her head lifted to the sky. She caught sight of a tall iron pillar in the distance from which smoke emitted at the tip. She sneezed at that bit of iron in the air.

Her eyes still itched, and her scars still pulsed, but after days surrounded by iron she no longer felt as sick as she had before. Bryson reached for her magic, though that part of her still felt dormant and she couldn't really make out why.

She hoped it was still growing used to the iron and not because the iron itself had created lasting effects against her magic.

She weaved her way through Unseelie, following after the quick-footed brownie. They walked up a slope and then down. The layout of Unseelie was strange, and that was something she hadn't noticed before either. It felt like everything was constantly shifting, changing. As they walked down the slope, Bryson looked over her shoulder only to find it had disappeared. Trees groaned like old men complaining about rickety bones and seemed to close in on them from behind.

Bryson picked up the pace. Down the incline, there was a long table carved from tree bark and chairs topped with plush cushions. Atop the table sat a feast, the scent drifting towards Bryson's nostrils.

Her stomach threatened to growl. She felt she hadn't eaten in weeks, but she remembered Weylyn's warning about the food at Unseelie. It would not all be edible. And she couldn't even be sure what was safe to eat or not.

A part of her longed to reach out to Weylyn to ask for his help, but he was dealing with his own trials, possibly more dangerous than Unseelie food and drink. He was hunting with his siblings. Siblings who wanted him dead.

Bryson refused to be a distraction. She wouldn't be the reason her only ally—her *mate*, she thought almost awkwardly—was hurt or killed. She had to deal with this situation on her own. She had to be strong.

Head lifted, the brownie guided her towards that table, where several others already sat around and partook in the feast before them.

At the head of the table was the queen.

Bryson could finally see her clearly.

Weylyn's mother was as stunningly beautiful as she appeared deadly. All sharp angles like a blade, with a vicious line of a mouth painted red and gold, and long dark hair ornamented with dangling embellishments that looked like butterfly clips.

As Bryson drew closer, she saw they were actual butterflies, their wings flapping against her hair as they struggled to untangle themselves from the strands and failed. Golden powder sprinkled across her skin like rogue.

A great part of her body was exposed to the sunlight, making the coppery tinge of her skin almost sparkle. A sheer gold and black dress molded against her body, and several golden rings sparkled on her fingers, which she flicked carelessly beneath her chin.

"Ah, my dear." She stood and gestured to a chair at her side. "Sit. Dine with me."

Bryson neared the queen and forced herself to bow respectfully, lowering to the waist before straightening. "Your Majesty," she greeted, though the words felt weird leaving her lips.

She hated the contempt that flashed through the queen's gaze. She hated the way she spoke so hatefully to Weylyn. But this woman, this Unseelie, was still royalty. And Bryson was not. She had to be respectful, even if it churned her gut.

"Sit," the queen commanded as she herself lowered to her chair. Her fingers reached for a nearby goblet and brought the rim to her lips. Her eyes flicked over Bryson as she drank greedily, and when she pulled the glass away, red Fae wine dripped from the corners of her mouth.

It looked like blood.

Bryson sat quickly where the queen had indicated. Immediately, a plate full of food was placed before her by nearby brownies. The plate was long, extended, piled high and dripping with juicy meats, fruits, breads, and cheeses.

Bryson's stomach threatened to growl again, but among the spread, she didn't know what was safe to eat.

She didn't touch anything.

"What is your name, child?" the queen asked.

Bryson looked at her, weighing the question in her mind. Giving her name to the queen wouldn't be binding. There had always been rumors to never give an Unseelie your name unless you wanted them to hold power over you. Bryson didn't believe in that magic, but in case it were true...

"You may call me Varik."

The queen's eyes flashed with an anger that didn't mirror the way her lips twitched with amusement. Bryson held her breath for a moment, waiting to see if anything would come to cutting words or blows.

"I do not see a mating mark," the queen commented dryly.

Bryson blinked slowly, the lenses sliding down the ridge of her nose just a fraction. She pushed them back up and asked, "What?"

"A mating mark," the queen repeated. "I do not see one on your skin."

Bryson swallowed the sudden tightness in her throat.

"That must mean you have not yet accepted him as your mate." Her eyes flashed again as she steepled her fingers together and rested her chin on top of them. Her following smile was almost malicious. "I know why you have not."

Bryson's brows rose. She had to force the words from her tight throat to answer. "And why do you think?"

"He is unworthy." The queen set her hands down and leaned back in her chair. "You have found him lacking."

Bryson chewed on the inside of her mouth. She let nothing show on her face, least of all the truth that the queen would find there. Because she was right. At one point, she had found Weylyn unworthy, lacking. Perhaps she hadn't thought of it in those exact words, but she'd hated him. She hadn't wanted him. And when he lured her in his mind to spear his cock into her, she'd hated that he'd aided in her betrayal of Everette. But to hear the queen confirm what had been lodged so deeply into Bryson's heart made her feel like scum.

When Bryson didn't respond, the queen chuckled. "I will tell you a secret, little blind Fae." She reached for her goblet again and took a dainty sip. "Most, if not all, men are a disappointment." Her delicate shoulders shrugged. "I have had many lovers in my lifetime, and the only ones worthy of note were the ones who gave me my children."

To hear a queen speak so openly about lovers jolted Bryson.

"And yet, the world assumes the Unseelie Court is ruled by a male." She snorted, took another sip, and her eyes burned on Bryson. "They think a female cannot lead. Yet here I am, and on my throne I have sat for centuries. Do you want to know why that is, Varik?"

"Why?" Her palms grew sweaty as she almost dreaded the answer.

"I have power because I do not suffer men or fools. It is that simple."

Bryson nodded. "Sage advice," she said.

"Advice you would do well to take, little blind Fae. Men are useless. They will leash you. My son is no different." Her eyes flashed again. "He may be the worst of them. Like his father."

Bryson desperately wanted to ask what had happened with Weylyn's father, why she hated Weylyn so much, but it felt like prying into a story she shouldn't. No matter how curious she was, Weylyn was the only Fae she trusted around her, and she wasn't going to break that trust now. No matter how curious she was.

It didn't seem to matter what she felt though, because the queen went on anyway.

"Useless. Spineless." Her eyes flashed again and her hand holding the goblet crushed it. Red wine spilled all over her hand, dripping like blood. "Murdering Fae."

Bryson's tongue felt heavy. "Murdering?"

The queen stared at her, though for a moment it felt like she was staring through Bryson and into a past, a present, or a future. She wasn't sure. Her stare was eerie, entirely Unseelie in its countenance. "Murderer," she whispered. Then her eyes blinked, seemingly coming back to the moment. "He has not told you? I did not expect him to, I suppose. After all, how can one excuse the crime of murdering their own sister?"

Bryson blinked. "Wh-what?"

The queen's smile was malicious. Bryson knew, she knew that the words she uttered were meant to unsettle her. They were meant to turn her against Weylyn. They were meant to cause unrest between them. She could not let that happen. But even so the words floored her. Made her head spin.

"You have not touched your food," the queen said gently. "Eat. You must be ravenous."

Bryson felt her neck strain from the whiplash the topic of conversation gave her. She looked down at the platters of food. She still wasn't sure what was safe to eat or drink. Her stomach growled, but she did not wish to touch any of it.

But the queen was looking at her expectantly. Voices drifted around them, those that Bryson had nearly forgotten were there. Behind the queen, guards appeared, dressed in simple cloths around their waists in gold and black, carrying swords and draped in gold and bones.

Bryson gulped.

"Eat, drink, and we will converse," the queen urged.

Bryson wondered at her insistence, and it made her hesitant to touch anything. She did not want to be tethered to the Unseelie in any way, and choosing the wrong food would do that.

Her hands hovered over the plate, darting from food to food before her fingers finally closed around a goblet of water. She brought it to her lips, sniffed it first, and when she detected no hint of magic, took a small sip.

Setting it back down, she looked back up at the queen, urging her to continue with a delicate nod of her head.

The queen seemed to sneer but sat back. "You are entirely too clever for your own good, little blind Fae. Eat."

Bryson's fingers twitched. "I am not hungry." The lie tasted bitter on her tongue. She could almost taste the blood and rot the ghoul had given her and wanted to gag. She'd not trust an Unseelie with food again.

The queen's gaze narrowed. "Eat, I said."

"I must decline, Your Majesty. I do not have an appetite."

"Of course you do not." The queen looked her up and down. "You have been sleeping a great part of the day. I'd say you have not exercised your body enough to even feel hunger."

"Sure," Bryson agreed slowly. *That's it.*

The queen's lips curled into a smile. "Then I suppose you should get in the proper exercise. To build up that appetite."

Bryson didn't see it coming. She barely heard them as they appeared behind her. The guards grabbed her arms, jerking her out of the seat. Her feet kicked out, knocking over the platter of food as she fought back with all her might. But they were too big, too strong, and restraining her seemed to be an easy feat for them.

She tried to tap into her magic to blow them away, but her well felt empty, especially when one of the guards held an iron dagger to her throat.

She choked on the stench of it, gagging as the iron coated her tongue. She heaved and kicked out, but they wrenched her arms behind her. She howled in pain, and the lenses on her face slid down, nearly falling from position.

The scenery shifted as she was hauled back. The once green meadow changed. Darkness seemed to coil around them. Clouds grayed. Thunder bellowed. Bryson held back her scream as a pit opened beside them. The earth caved in on itself, a great tremor shaking through the ground. The guards restraining her held her still as a ravine opened and the stench of mud, rot, and decay filled her nostrils.

"Into the pit," the queen commanded.

Bryson didn't even have time to scream as the guards shoved her into the gaping hole and she fell.

And fell.

And fell.

Den of Monsters

The wind knocked out of her chest as she landed on her back. There was a crack that reverberated through her ears, and she was sure she'd broken a bone. But with the pain radiating through her whole body, she couldn't be sure which bone she'd broken.

Too stunned to even move, she lay in the wet mud, gasping for breaths that were too slow to make it to her lungs. Her vision had gone blurry once again, the lenses on her face had fallen somewhere in the muck beneath her. She wanted to reach for them, and her fingers twitched with every intention, but she couldn't.

Foul-smelling mud invaded her senses. It reminded her of when she'd first landed, but this was somehow worse. It coated her eyelashes, and she blinked it away, staring up at the darkening sky.

There was a clang, and something fell from above the ravine next to her body. The smell of overripe fruit entered her nostrils, mingling with the stench of muck.

From above, the queen peeked over the edge. Bryson could only make out a blurry form, but she could imagine the cruelty dripping from her voice.

"Eat the fruit, little blind Fae."

Bryson gasped and found strength enough to push herself to a sitting position. Every bone in her body ached, and she wondered how many she'd broken. Her wrist felt extra sensitive, and she cradled the limp part to her chest.

"Fuck," she hissed, feeling the ache in the back of her neck as she looked up at the queen. She gave her the most defiant glare she could muster. Her other hand landed beside her, squelching in the mud, as her fingers absently searched for the lenses. Her fingertips met the cold metal and glass, and she quickly brought them up to her face and adjusted them one-handed.

They were covered in muck, but they helped her see.

"Perhaps you just need a little persuasion," the queen purred from above. "A little exercise to work up your appetite." Then she stepped back, away from Bryson's line of vision.

Bryson glared up, her head whipping back and forth all along the wide, maze-like distance of the ravine. No one peeked over the edge again.

Her heart began thumping wildly in her chest and fear slid down her back. She pushed herself to a stand, purposefully stepping on the Unseelie fruit as she walked over to the edge of the ravine. The walls, while solid, were made entirely of mud. It was slimy, slipping down in clumps.

She held her breath, testing movement in her injured wrist. It screamed with its pain, but she had to ignore it if she wanted to get out of this situation alive. She had to bear it. She had borne things much more painful than this. That was what she told herself, if only to trick her mind into believing the pain didn't exist.

Gritting her teeth and suppressing her scream, she lifted both hands and gripped the edge of the ravine. White-hot pain shot from her fingers all the way up to her shoulder. Her vision turned white, and her mouth watered.

Don't black out, she told herself. *Do not fucking pass out down here.*

Once she had her breathing under control, she found a good grip and tried to haul herself up. But the mud was too slippery, and it seemed like there were layers of it to where she couldn't dig her fingers in and get a good hold. All she managed was to slide back down and fall back to the ground on her ass.

Her entire front was caked with sludge and she stood, ready to try again, but this time with a boost of magic. She reached deep into that well where her magic nestled and grasped at it with her fingers. It felt dormant, and the place where it usually was felt hollow. Still, she reached, stretched, and grasped its sleeping form, shaking it awake with all the desperation she could muster.

Before it awoke, the ground shook once again, a terrible vibration she felt straight down to her teeth. She fell backwards, putting her hands out to stop her fall. Her wrist screamed at the landing, and she felt the tears prickle behind her eyes.

The ground kept shaking, rattling her down to her skeleton. She tilted and fell, attempting to find her balance. She eventually made it to her feet, separating them hip-width apart and steadied herself. The walls of the ravine rumbled, splattering soil through the air.

Bryson's breathing grew labored and her whole body shook as she tried to hone in her senses on whatever was making the ground quake. In the distance, turning the corner, she was met with a monster of nightmares.

Her scream caught in her throat, but she kept her legs planted firmly on the ground.

The creature was a gargantuan beast like nothing she'd ever seen before. Its wide, circular, gaping mouth sported several rows of knife-like teeth. Several eyes dotted both sides of its cylindrical head, and spikes jutted out down the length of its back. It was like a snake, with stubby, clawed legs down its torso and entire scaley length.

It crawl-slid towards Bryson, and each step shook the earth. It caught sight of her with its dozens of eyes, and for a second it froze. They measured each other before the creature threw its elongated neck back and roared.

It picked up speed her way, and Bryson had no other choice but to turn and run.

Her feet slid on the ground, and she fought to right herself as she darted between the tall walls of the maze. The walls shook and she had no idea where she was going. She ran aimlessly, feeling the hot breath of the beast at her neck.

It was too close. Far too close. Her body was screaming; she knew she couldn't outrun it.

Predator or prey.

That meant she was just going to have to face it.

Bryson reached inside herself so deeply she screamed as she ripped the magic up by force. Her feet skidded as she whirled, surprising the beast.

Her hands shot out and she screamed as her magic obeyed. Wind burst from her fingers, shoving the creature back through the tight space between the walls. A riptide of a tornado spun from the bottom of its claws, sucking it into the storm.

The screech it gave was deafening. Its head thrashed side to side, hitting the walls on either side. A landslide of mud poured down from the force, and Bryson had to jump back to avoid being buried beneath the sludge. Her ankles were sucked in it, and she nearly tripped. Her magic flailed and failed. The wind whooshed down, blowing her backwards. The beast screamed as it fell to the ground and the entire world felt like it would split down the middle from the impact.

While the creature writhed on the ground in its attempt to right itself, Bryson forced herself to a stand, turned, and ran once again. It didn't matter how light she tried to make her steps, they squelched and made too much noise in the mud. She slip and slid, and it slowed her movements. But she needed to put distance between herself and the creature, just enough so she could land another blow.

Bryson felt along the walls as she ran, hoping to feel something solid. If she put in enough distance, she could fly up to the edge of the ravine and away from the monster. But what were the odds that the queen and her guards would only surround Bryson and toss her back inside?

The odds of that were very high.

There would be no winning.

Not unless she killed the beast.

She was going to need a weapon for that.

The ground quaked again as the creature righted itself and went in search of its prey. Bryson quickly covered herself in mud, rolling against it so it caked her skin and face. Then, she pressed herself quickly to the wall just as the creature thundered down the path she hid in. It rushed past her, and as soon as it did, Bryson peeled herself off the wall to face its back. She took a breath and forced her magic out. It was like taking a knife to her chest and carving out her own flesh, but she gritted through it.

A gust of air pushed her through the air where she landed on the creature's back.

It let out a roar of rage as she bent and gripped one of the spikes on its spine with her hands. Her wrists screamed and the spike cut through her flesh, but she pulled, using magic to aid her, and popped one off.

The creature cried out in pain and thrashed its tail in her direction, but Bryson was already moving away, jumping off the side of its body to land in the mud while its tail slapped down against itself, causing it to rumble angrily.

Bryson wielded its spike like a weapon. She didn't care that it grew wet and warm with her blood. Her hands shook and she fought to contain her fear and rage. She steeled herself, so when the beast turned on her and charged, she was prepared. She met it in the middle, running, ducking under its soft underbelly. With a two-handed grip, she shoved the spike upwards, piercing past hard, leathery flesh. She screamed as she sawed through it, pushing herself further and further, gutting the creature.

Guts and blood rained down over her, staining her skin and mouth. She felt her own palms split open from the force she used, but it didn't matter. She didn't let go of the spike. Even as she used her magic to help tear her away from beneath the beast, she gripped it tightly until her palms burned as badly as her eyes had once so long ago.

The monster keeled over, its great body thumping on the ground. Mud splattered everywhere, and it wasn't until Bryson was sure the beast was not breathing that she dropped the spike and raised her bloody hands to her face, wiping off the lenses. All she did was smear dirt and blood.

Her head tilted up. Several gazes stared down at her from the top of the ravine. Among them, the queen's. Bryson fought the urge to flip her the finger, only restraining herself when the queen, in all her beautiful glamor, smiled cruelly down at Bryson.

It was in that malicious, calculating look that Bryson knew she hadn't won at all.

Suddenly, the beast's body began to twitch, and Bryson's gaze snapped to it. She took a fearful step back as bones within it began snapping. Its leathery, scaley flesh started moving like something had come alive within it.

Bryson stepped back as its flesh reamed open, splitting with a terrible wet sound. Bright green blood sprayed, and rib bone pushed through carrion. One pointed bone peeked out at a time until it pushed through completely.

Bryson barely contained her scream as she was met with an enormous spider made of bone. A creature of muscle and ivory, smeared in green. It scuttled across the corpse of the beast and charged.

Bryson turned and ran on impulse. Her heart slammed up to her throat, nearly choking her. Her arms pumped at her sides, her lungs burning as she heaved. The creature slid through the mud, thundering the ground as viciously as the leathery beast.

She cursed herself for dropping the spike. She shot her hands backwards, ripping her magic out to push the thing back. She sensed it behind her, sensed the way it slid away. She could only run with all her might, but it felt useless. Her fear choked her, nearly paralyzing her. And that thing was way too fast, her magic weakening.

When a sharp bit of bone scraped against her spine, Bryson screamed. It tore through her clothes, her skin, and shoved her face-first into the mud. Her back blazed with a fire that spread down her spine. The creature dug the bone in deeper, ripping through her skin.

Bryson screamed as it dug deeper, pinning her into the muck.

Her magic exploded, but the injury made her weak. Her magic flickered like the flame of a dying candle, like the slowest breath leaving lips.

Her fingers clawed against the mud, but every jerk of her body made her back scream. The agony was unbearable, and tears slid down her eyes as she sobbed.

"Please," she cried, tasting mud, salt, and blood. The glasses slid down her face and through blurry vision, she stared skyward, finding faces leering, hearing their voices as they laughed at her.

"You can end this torment." The queen's voice echoed down the maze. "You can save yourself. All you have to do is *eat* the fruit."

Bryson sobbed. Never before had she felt so weak. She wanted to fight, but something inside her fractured the harder the creature dug into her back. She felt it push past muscle, to her own bones. She screamed, "Please, please stop!"

"Eat. The. Fruit."

"Please." Bryson tilted her head up and stared directly at the queen. "I don't want to." Something inside her broke at the sight of the queen's expression then. Half-blurry, half-clear, smeared with blood red and green and mud, but she saw clearly.

Begging was futile.

She'd either die in the mud or...

From above fruit began to fall. It landed in front of her, one fruit after another, splattering and buried in front of her face.

An invitation.

A threat.

Die in the mud or eat the fruit and remain trapped in Unseelie forever.

"Eat," the queen commanded.

Bryson stared at the half-buried red, Unseelie peach, but didn't reach for it. In retaliation, the creature dug deeper into her skin. Tears streamed down Bryson's cheeks. She screamed, she was sure of it, until her throat was hoarse, and it felt like she was spitting blood.

"Please," she moaned again.

It was useless.

Die or eat.

Die or eat.

Predator or prey.

Bryson sobbed as she reached for a peach in her shaking, broken hand. There were cheers from above as she brought the nectar to her lips. She sobbed again and tried one last time. Just one. But her magic died. It flickered and went out.

Empty. She was nothing but a broken, empty vessel.

Cheers rained again as Bryson had no choice but to open her mouth...

...and sink her teeth into the fruit.

The bone tore from her back. She swore she blacked out before she felt herself being lifted... lifted.... She was thrown unkindly to the ground. Not mud, but a harder surface. She tried to hold back her tears but failed as the pain engulfed her, pushing her in and out of consciousness.

Her eyes opened, blinking past tears and mud and blood. The queen loomed over her, smiling down.

Bryson could still taste the sweetness of the overripe fruit on her tongue, and it made her want to gag.

The queen bent and took Bryson's chin in her hand. Her grip was firm. Unkind. Unyielding.

"You are mine now," she whispered cruelly. "And I am going to take you from him just like he took my daughter from me."

The Hunt

"Is she able to see your cock at all?" Gwyn taunted.

"For her to be able to see it he would need to have one," Glyn added.

The twins chortled, bending over at the waist as laughter overcame them, shaking their tall, thin bodies.

Cass rolled his eyes and tightened his hold on his spear. Owyn, meanwhile, pointedly ignored the twins and glared in Weylyn's direction. The force of his anger was as sharp as the blade he whet with the tips of his claws, the scraping over the edge of it meant to mock and intimidate. Weylyn only wanted to roll his eyes in his brother's direction.

Owyn was out for Weylyn's blood, and he knew it meant he was to take greater care with him than the others. Gwyn and Glyn were dangerous, but they were only dangerous together. While the two were rarely separated, Owyn was the one who would very obviously strike for Weylyn's throat. He was violent, ruthless, but he was also dumb. If anyone were a true threat, that was Cassimir.

But Cassimir seemed intent on keeping the peace for the Hunt.

"Control yourselves," he admonished the twins. "Do not speak about our brother's mate this way." He slid off the side of one of his beast's, placating it with a hand to its snout. "We have much more important things to focus our attention on."

"Like killing this traitor?" Owyn snapped in Weylyn's direction. His sharp teeth gnashed and his tail swished side to side in obvious agitation.

Weylyn let nothing of his true thoughts show on his face. He merely regarded his brothers coolly, one after another.

They all shared the most beautiful aspects of their mother and the most terrible ones as well. Each brother was a distorted, reflective pool of another. The same, yet different. And Weylyn? He differed from all of them. As half-High Fae, he had not inherited horns or other Unseelie features. He'd inherited nothing but his mother's coloring. He doubted he'd inherited anything from his father either. In truth, he had never even met the Fae.

His mother had drove him to madness and murdered him before Weylyn could even speak.

"Owyn," Cass snapped with impatience. "The Hunt will begin soon."

They had roused Weylyn before the sun even rose, forcing him to leave his resting mate. He had hated to leave Bryson when she had ingested that addictive, golden drug that he was too familiar with. He had hated to leave her alone in Unseelie at all, but he had to force himself not to show his worry.

Worry was a weakness.

Having a mate was a weakness.

Yet he was feral for her. It did not matter to him. He would behead everyone here if it meant protecting what was his.

"Your anger grows boring," Weylyn mused. He dug his own spear deep into the iron-ridden dirt and leaned against the handle, smiling over at Owyn, flashing his teeth in a way he knew would drive his brother mad. He then turned to the twins. "And your insults are old. If you wish to harm me, you will have to try just a little harder."

Owyn emitted a low growl that did not faze Weylyn at all. He dismissed him, turning towards Cassimir.

"Lead the way, older brother," Weylyn purred. "The light will soon rise, and my spear has a taste for blood."

Cass' eyes flashed, but he did not say any more. He turned towards his beast and slapped its rump. The beast spread its wings and took off in flight, pushing gusts of wind against them.

"Spread out," Cass ordered. "You remember the rules, little brother?"

Weylyn smiled. He could not forget if he tried. Unseelie was ingrained down into his very pores. It lived in his bones; the wildness sang through his blood and pumped through to his heart. He would die before he forgot his origins.

And no one here would ever let him forget.

That seemed to be answer enough because Cassimir smiled back, the gesture equally malicious. "The first to find the golden stag and bring it wins."

"Mana be in your favor," Weylyn said.

Just as the light began to peek over the trees, they all ran.

Weylyn's feet banged against the earth like a drum. His heart pounded like a symphony. The hoots and laughter of his brothers was a wild song he would never admit he missed. This was life. This was freedom. For a second, he let himself forget everything. His past, the betrayals, his own sadness he'd fallen into after everything. The only release he could find had been glittering powder in his nose and then the sweet taste of revenge at the tips of his fingers.

For a moment, he was lost in the haze of The Hunt. He did not track or scout, simply let himself be. He peeled away from the others, putting enough distance between them so he could no longer hear them, and they could no longer hear him.

Killing the golden stag was a tradition that went back generations in Unseelie. Every year when the Hunt approached, those who participated would scout, track, and hunt the creature. Killing it brought magic down upon the land along with good luck and prosperity.

It was a matter of pride to find it before anyone else, and it had grown into a brutal competition between them.

One Weylyn had left behind, but now... Now he was back and his heart beat in time to his pounding feet.

The golden stag was one of the hardest creatures to catch because it did not often show its face. It did not dwell in a single spot. It was nearly a phantom. A ghost. Almost untraceable. Which meant that finding it was the ultimate achievement.

Weylyn slowed to a slight jog. As the sun rose, the pixies that danced through the air diminished their light, becoming mere glowing specks that he swatted away when they came too close. His head swiveled around the clearing he found himself in. A light, open space that glowed with magic. It seeped into the very pores of the ground and leaked from the bark of the trees, sprinkled down from the leaves, and drifted with the wind.

Golden specks that flickered in and out of being.

Flowers grew beneath the impression of hoof marks on the ground. Trails of gold shone brighter beneath the thin beams of light that pierced past the canopy.

Weylyn stepped deeper into the clearing, tightening his grip around his spear as he bent to observe the track marks. Bright silver and gold flowers grew where the stag had stepped. He ran his fingers across the petals and his skin came away stained silver.

The hairs on the back of his neck stood on end, and he let out a sigh.

"So, you've come to kill me."

He felt his brother step out from the shadows behind him. "Did you expect anything else?"

Weylyn sighed and stood before turning around. Owyn stood across the clearing from him, arrow pointed at Weylyn's chest.

"You are very predictable." Weylyn appeared unbothered. His heart did not beat faster, his pulse did not jump. But his body did tense, readying for what he knew was to come. "I heard you breathing from miles away as you followed after me like a dog."

Owyn let out a warning growl. From the distance, Weylyn could make out the tears in his brother's eyes. Maybe before, his chest would have felt an ache for he knew that the grief he'd harbored was shared within his family. Yet what they blamed him for was a greater suffering indeed, and he no longer felt for the plights of others when his were far worse.

He'd grown cold over the years. Vengeance had a way of freezing one from the inside out. And it was in the promise of violence in which he would thaw.

"Well?" Weylyn adjusted his grip on his spear. "The morning grows brighter, and The Hunt will soon end. We haven't all day, brother."

"*You* haven't all day," he corrected. "Because *you* will not live to see the rest of it."

He let an arrow fly. It sped between them at a near blinding pace. Weylyn lifted his spear, parting the arrow in half before it could strike. The wood didn't even hit the ground before his brother was in front of him. A knife swung towards his face and Weylyn ducked low, sweeping his legs out. Owyn fell back, grunting as he lashed out.

They became a blur of violence and tangled limbs. Of slashing blades and flying fists. Weylyn pushed himself far away from his brother when he untangled himself from the fight, picking up his fallen spear as he went.

"You're a coward," Owyn spat. Blood stained his sharp teeth. "You run away instead of facing the fate you deserve."

"I have never deserved your ire."

"You killed her."

Weylyn closed his eyes against those words, as if blocking out the sight of Owyn could make the words hurt any less. He hardened himself against them, opened his eyes, and threw his spear.

Owyn's eyes widened in surprise as the weapon barreled towards him. He ducked at the last moment, rolling along the ground. When he straightened on his knee, an arrow was notched on his bow. It went flying, but Weylyn was already moving. He tackled his brother to the ground, yanking the weapons from his body and tossing them.

But his brother had an advantage that came in the form of Unseelie claws. They shredded through Welyn's skin and he growled, snapping his teeth near his brother's face, even as he sunk his claws deeper into him.

"Your life is mine," Owyn spat. His claws pierced muscle and bone. Weylyn refused to cry out in pain, but it was a near-blinding sensation, spitting over him.

"What are the two of you up to *now*?"

Weylyn and Owyn parted in surprise. They scrambled to a stand, Weylyn breathing heavy, the warmth of his blood staining his entire front. His life force spilled out of him and his trembling hand clutched to his wounds as though he could push the blood back inside his body.

Cassimir stepped into the clearing astride one of his beast's. He stared at the two of them with the exasperation only an older brother could wear.

"Cassimir, he—"

"I think I have heard quite enough out of you, little brother."

One moment, Owyn was blinking, breathing.

Then, he was on his knees, an arrow lodged deep into his throat.

Weylyn's eyes widened as Owyn fell face first onto the ground, his own blood pooling beneath him. As that blood touched the grass, flowers sprouted from the ground.

Weylyn turned back to Cass in time to see his brother slide down from his beast, a new arrow notched and pointed in his direction.

He knew he would let it loose. He knew his brother would kill him. He'd known all along. But seeing Owyn dead on the ground came as a surprise.

"What did you do?" Weylyn's heart beat faster and faster. Seeing the way Owyn's blood pooled beneath him awoke something inside his mind. Memories he'd wanted buried but were always at the forefront. The reason for his being, the cold glimmer of revenge that fueled his every waking moment.

He would have killed him himself, but seeing the ground part and swallow his brother into the depths, was shocking.

"I expected your thanks. Seeing a dead sibling isn't new to you, is it?" His eyes flicked to where the earth had taken their brother. A price for his life spilled. He would feed the world they lived on. Create a forest, a fruit tree, a field of flowers. Something to make Unseelie thrive. "He was a nuisance. Detrimental to this family. As are you."

"They'll know what you've done," Weylyn warned. "The queen will know what you've done."

"Will she?" His brows kicked up and a smirk appeared on his lips. "Do you think she will suspect her second favorite child murdered Owyn, or will she believe it the fault of the one who took her favorite from her? It is my word against yours, Weylyn."

"You are right." Weylyn pressed his palm deeper against his wound and straightened. He would not show fear, and he knew the odds were stacked against him, but unlike Cass, Weylyn had something—someone—to live for. He would not leave his mate alone in a strange world without him. He would fight.

He would kill if he had to.

He would tear apart his brother's mind from the inside out until—

Magic fizzled through the air. The clearing became bathed in a golden-silver light that nearly blinded them both. Weylyn winced. Every single hair on his body stood on end. The magic was so heavy, it coated his tongue and made it swell. It was like nothing he'd ever felt before. His entire body felt heavy as he slowly turned away from his brother to face the splendor of the stag.

The stag's horns were like thick branches that sprouted shimmering flowers. Magic oozed from the stag's thick, dense fur like sap from the bark of trees. Eyes as black as the sky that the Wild Hunt rode, with an infinite amount of secrets and knowledge, regarded Cassimir and Weylyn both.

Staring into that gaze was equivalent to being hit straight in the chest with magic at full blast. The impact nearly had Weylyn staggering backwards. He almost fell over. Behind him, he could hear Cass fumble with his weapons.

Golden stags were rumored to be creatures of infinite wisdom. They were all knowing and rivaled seers in what they could see. They were powerful, ancient creatures.

And they were meant to strike it down in The Hunt. A barbaric age-old tradition that Weylyn did not understand, even as he revered and celebrated with the rest. Stags brought luck for generations. Even staring at one felt sacred. Weylyn wanted to drop to his knees in reverence.

For a moment, Weylyn and the stag stared at one another. His vision tunneled and he felt what others must have felt when *he* used his magic on them. He was freefalling into a mind that wasn't his own. A voice echoed in his head, whispering in an ancient voice that held far too much power. It echoed through what felt like an empty chamber, a symphony so powerful, his entire body quaked.

Then it was gone. The world became clearer, and Weylyn turned to his brother, his every breath heavy.

"Let me live, brother," he whispered. He would not beg. Weylyn was too proud for that. But he would do what Unseelie were best at.

He would strike a deal.

His brother managed to tear his gaze from the stag. "Why would I do that?" He did not sound surprised, though it was his expression that gave it away.

"Because if you do this for me, then the stag will give you your greatest desire."

Cassimir blinked. "You lie."

Weylyn flashed his teeth and let his consciousness drift towards the stag. Their minds linked and he pulled Cassimir's in as well, showing him the terrible greatness the stag had showed him. A future of Unseelie that was none too kind, and a destiny they would be forced to follow.

Cassimir staggered backwards, clutching a hand to his chest. He breathed heavily, staring between Weylyn and the stag.

"Choose, brother," Weylyn ordered. "And choose now."

A deal or death.

Those were his options.

A moment of silence.

And then Weylyn's brother lifted his arrow...

...and fired.

Gilded Cage

Unseelie was rife with festive energy. They were already celebrating The Hunt, even if they had no confirmation that the stag had been caught at all. It wasn't until Cassimir and Weylyn came forward and hauled the carcass of the beast behind them that their cheers became deafening.

Gwyn and Glyn trailed behind the stag, looking forlorn because they hadn't been the ones to catch it. Rainer followed, but Owyn was nowhere to be found, not that anyone questioned his absence. His moods were volatile. It would be long before anyone knew him to be dead.

As they approached the throne, jeers and cries grew louder. A crowd had formed near the queen on her throne. Her court surrounded a tall gilded cage, poking spears and swords through the gaps.

And from within, whimpers and cries that Weylyn recognized immediately.

He dropped the legs of the stag and rushed forward, shoving aside bodies that blocked his way until he pushed himself to the front. His fingers clasped around the cold, gilded bars, and he pressed his cheeks between the gaps, staring at his mate on the inside.

She was covered in mud and blood, crouched low on the ground as she shivered. She lay there naked, wounds open and gaping on her back.

When he'd gone that morning with his brothers, he had the utmost faith that his mate could care for herself. She was strong, capable. But he'd underestimated the cruelty his mother possessed.

An instinctive rage gripped him in a bloodthirsty fist. He wanted to lash out, but he only managed to tighten his hold on the bars.

His mate looked at him, her string of curls plastered to her pale skin. Her scarred eyes found him, squinting as though she could barely make him out through her hazy vision.

"Weylyn." Her voice cracked and her shaking hand moved towards the bars.

That's when he saw it.

A golden band tattooed around the flesh of her arm, pulsing and burning with a terrible magic he never wanted for her.

Slowly, he turned to find his mother and her entire court smiling malevolently at him. They awaited his reaction, and as much as he wanted to give them one, he couldn't. He could not show his weakness, even if it was evident in the furious pounding of his heart, in the whites of his knuckles as he grasped the bars of his mate's prison.

"She is mine now," the queen said cruelly. "And she can *never* leave Unseelie."

"Release her," Weylyn gritted out. "Now."

His mother's brow kicked up. She was enjoying his pain far too much. He'd never wanted to take a dagger to her chest more than he did at this moment. To feel her blood slip from between his fingers. Feel the warmth of her life go cold.

"You give me orders now?" she questioned.

"Release my mate." His eyes flashed with the threat of a warning. "Or I will kill you all."

There was a collective gasp from the court. Weylyn had always been the most hated child. He had never hidden the violence he felt deeply rooted within him, but he had never openly threatened anyone. Least of all his mother. Least of all the Queen of Unseelie.

There must have been something in his eyes. She might have had teeth and claw, but he had something powerful of his own. High Fae magic. And he could render her mind useless within a second if he dared.

And she knew that.

A dagger would be in his heart the moment he tried, but he'd do it before he died. He would die for this. For Bryson Varik, he would die. For his mate, he would kill the queen.

His mother sat back on her throne with a dignified huff. "A fool in love," she said lightly. The court chuckled, though stared with uncertainty. "Take her from her cage, then." Her fingers flicked and the cage disassembled itself, falling apart around Bryson, who flinched. "But your mate is still my property."

Fighting back the snarl that came to his lips, Weylyn went forward and moved as quickly and as gently as he possibly could, cradling Bryson to his chest. Before he pulled her close, her hands trembled over the ground, searching for something. When she found what she was looking for, she pressed a pair of goblin-made lenses to her chest and held them tightly.

Weylyn lifted her into his arms and stood. When he turned to face his mother, Bryson buried her face into his chest, silently sobbing.

"Happy Hunt," Weylyn said. "Cassimir took down the stag. Long may he bring luck to Unseelie."

"Long may he bring luck to Unseelie," everyone echoed.

His mother narrowed her eyes at him, but she echoed his words before she turned to the stag and ordered it be cut up for the feast.

As Weylyn walked away, he caught Cassimir's gaze. His brother's eyes were hard and unyielding, but knowing, secretive.

Weylyn looked away and marched away as swiftly as his feet could carry him. His mate cried in his arms, each sob an arrow that pierced his already aching chest wounds. He didn't stop until they reached their tent.

Brownies were already inside, flittering around and setting out clothes and pouring scented, medicinal soaps into the steaming tub. They scrambled out of the way when Weylyn made a dismissive noise. It wasn't until they were gone that Weylyn finally put Bryson to her feet.

Her knees shook and nearly buckled, but he held her tightly by the elbows. Once she was steady, he pried the lenses from her grip and set them aside before grabbing a warmth cloth. When he faced her again, there was a broken, vacant look in her eyes as she took him in. When he first swiped the cloth against her body, clearing away the mud, a fractured sob tore out of her.

"Weylyn—"

"Ssh," he interrupted, giving another pass of the cloth.

"I didn't—"

"No," he said firmly. Then, in her mind he added, *"Not here, love. Do not speak. Just let me care for you."*

Bryson took in a shuddering breath but nodded to let him know she understood. Then he began the meticulous process of cleaning the mud from her body. He took his time, making sure to get every crevice. As he did so, he took stock of her wounds. Every scrape against her precious skin, every gaping, bleeding part of her he memorized. Every whimper, every flinch, he put deep into his mind so that he would remember forever.

And he vowed he would kill whoever had done this to her.

Starting with his mother.

The wounds on her back were what gave him pause. A single circle like a spear had pierced through her flesh. It was already healing, but still angry and red and fresh.

He took a deep breath to avoid raging and when he made it back to her front, he took her hand, the one with the golden, irritated band, and led her towards the tub. Once she was inside and resting comfortably, he shucked his own clothes and climbed in with her.

Weylyn pulled his mate to his chest and rested his forehead against hers. Then, he sprung into her mind.

"What happened?" he asked.

Bryson began to sob. She clung to him, her mind open and vulnerable. Images flashed through her mind, pushed onto his. She couldn't recount what had happened to her in words, but she gave him her memories. Bright, full of fear, angry, vicious. The fear that clung to her bones like the mud she'd been stuck in. The way the creature had pinned her to the ground. The way her trembling hand reached for the fruit. The rotten taste as she sank her teeth into it.

The memories pulled away, but the feeling they left behind still clung to him. Sticky, filled with terror.

Bryson shook, her cries and sobs terrible. "I didn't want to, Weylyn." She grasped him, hands sliding against his bare skin. "I swear. I'm sorry. I'm so—"

"Ssh." Weylyn held the back of her head, burying it into his chest. Her nails scraped at his skin, and the hand that held the mark burned. "It will be alright, little mate."

Bryson shook her head back and forth and pushed away from him. "Stop." Her voice was hard. Even with her scarred eyes streaked with tears, she looked regal. "Weylyn, this ends *now*, do you understand? Stop keeping me in the dark about what's going on here. Your family hates you." She took a breath. "And I have a right to know why."

To Murder a King

Embarrassment washed over Bryson. Humiliation. Rage.

Prey.

Prey.

Prey.

Her mind whirled with far too many things and her body contained far too many feelings. Failure was a prominent one alongside the irrefutable sense of humiliation. She'd been degraded. She'd failed to do the one thing she was supposed to. *Don't eat anything,* Weylyn had told her. The sensation nibbled away at her insides as her mind flashed back to the other Elementals. All the great things they'd done. Melting iron. Freezing and shattering it. Drowning entire cities with the force of their magic.

What had Bryson done other than get caught? Than be thrown into a pit, hurt and humiliated, forced to strip herself bare before a court that jeered at her from behind golden bars. She'd been reduced to little more than an animal in a zoo.

Humiliated all because she was Weylyn's mate. But there was a deeper reason for their hatred. A death that lay between them all. It was the root of their ire, and they'd pulled her into it.

Bryson had a right to know why.

"Tell me," she ordered viciously, her anger burning away the humiliation. Her palms slapped against his chest, nails raking across his skin like she could pull the truth out of him with violence.

His expression shuttered and he pulled away. Like he meant to hide. Wear that mask. Only, it wasn't a mask. It was an innate part of him that he'd adapted to his very being. Unseelie. High Fae. He was both. And it was that Unseelie mask that fell into place right then between them. The intentionally cruel expression that she'd despised and craved in equal measure.

"Don't," Bryson warned, grasping for him. "Do not pull away from me. I deserve the truth. Look at what they did to me."

Weylyn's eyes closed.

"Look at me!"

His eyes opened to face the tears. The blood. The scars. The pain she wore like a raw wound.

And his own eyes reflected the same thing.

They were in his mindscape, surrounded by the privacy of his mind walls. They could speak freely here without the worry of someone dropping in or overhearing. Yet Weylyn almost looked... afraid.

"Weylyn." Bryson grabbed his hands. "Please. Just tell me."

He took a breath and when he opened his eyes next, the mask was gone and there were decades worth of pain haunting his every feature.

"It is a long and painful story. If I tell you, perhaps you will despise me as much as they do by the end of it."

Bryson wouldn't make him empty promises. The truth was, she didn't even know what she would feel after she heard his story. But she needed to hear it regardless.

"Tell me," she said.

Weylyn swallowed and took a deep breath.

"Do you know why there is no King of Unseelie?"

"Because your mother doesn't suffer fools or men?"

His lips twitched. "Because she does not keep men alive long enough to overthrow her."

"I can see that." She seemed a rather paranoid Fae, but Bryson supposed all those in power were.

"When she fancies a male, she will either woo them to her side or take them without their consent and trap them here. She uses them to create heirs, and when she has no further use for them, she discards them like trash."

"That's awful."

"That is life in the Unseelie." Weylyn shrugged. "And my father... he was a High Fae man. My mother took him from Seelie and entrapped him here with fruit. She seduced him. Kept him for years. And after I was born, she killed him for being a nuisance. I never knew him..." His voice grew wistful, filled with pain. "But she spoke of him often. Of the High Lord she managed to snatch from Seelie."

Bryson's eyes widened. "*A High Lord*? Your father was a High Lord?"

"The High Lord of the Gold Court."

Bryson sucked in a breath, blinking as her mind whirled in a whirlwind. "Corvina is—"

"Corvina." His voice softened as he said her name. "I knew who she was the moment I reached for her with my magic. A bond that tethered us, different from that of a mate, of a familiar. A bond of Mana just as sacred. Of blood. Of family."

"So Corvina is..."

"She is my cousin. My mother kidnapped her uncle from Seelie, bred him, disposed of him. Corvina's father assumed the position when his brother never returned home. She is my flesh and blood. She is the only connection I have to the father I never knew. She and Basil are the family I always desired. One, at least, that did not try to kill me every few minutes."

She recalled it then. The soft way he spoke to her as opposed to everyone else. The gentle way he handled Basil, how fierce he had protected them both, especially when Basil had gotten lost.

Because they were family. His blood. Corvina was his cousin.

Bryson leaned forward and grasped his hand in hers, offering him support. "Why haven't you told her?"

His jaw tightened at that, almost as if he were too afraid to answer, but Bryson could read his silences well enough.

"You're afraid she will reject you like your other siblings do."

He didn't give her confirmation of her words. He just continued his story. "I was the youngest until... until my mother met a male she actually loved and Cossima was born. My sister." His golden eyes lit up. "We all loved her. As much as an Unseelie can love, we *loved* her. And when her father died, the queen was devastated. Devastated enough to protect the princess with all she could and all she was. We all protected her from the cruelties of our own court."

"What was your sister like?" Bryson asked.

She couldn't recall the last time anyone had asked that of her when it came to the memories of her family. She didn't speak of them often, if ever. She should have. She should have kept them alive by speaking about what they were like instead of burying them beneath layers of hurt and pain. Beneath her own bitterness. She'd tried to keep their memories alive by being what they'd always wanted her to be, but instead she'd become a bitter, angry creature and had lost their memories as well as their lives.

Weylyn looked at her as though he felt the same. As though no one had ever asked him, and she supposed they hadn't, because he'd kept her a secret. He'd kept his whole identity a secret from everyone. She wondered if he'd ever lost himself in the process of keeping all those secrets.

"She was sunshine," he whispered. "And starlight and magic. She illuminated our darkness and evil. She was mischievous, but she was good. Better than anyone I've ever known." His eyes shone with what Bryson suspected were tears. "I loved her. And she loved me, more than anyone else. She was my greatest friend." He took a breath. "Until I killed her." His expression hardened and he pulled away from Bryson, distancing himself from her touch.

"*You* killed her?" She didn't want to believe that, but there was pain in his voice, so bad it fractured her. "*How*?"

"One thing you have to know about Cossima is that she was too adventurous and far too manipulative. A trait she got from our mother, no doubt. I am unsure how, but she wanted to leave Unseelie. To explore beyond the borders of what she knew."

"And you took her," Bryson guessed.

Weylyn gave a mirthless smirk. "She was very convincing. In and out, I told her. Before our mother could catch on to what we were doing."

"Why did she ask you?"

"Because of my ties to Seelie." He shrugged. "I'd gone before, in secret. She knew and she exploited that. So I took her, not just to prevent the queen from discovering my exploits, but to indulge my sister's curiosity. So I took her to the border where Unseelie meets Seelie." He choked and that burning anger flamed higher in his eyes. "I should not have taken her there."

"Weylyn... what *happened*?"

"We were doing nothing wrong when they showed up on their horses. Majestic beasts covered in jewels. Arrows pointed at us. I will never forget the leader of the group, astride a black stallion, crown atop his fucking head as he stared down at us... I will never forget the way he smiled down at us or the thoughts that flicked through his mind as he looked at us. Unseelie scum, tainting his precious court. His thoughts were vile, and when they saw my sister..." He shook his head. "He wanted her dead. He wanted us dead. For nothing more than merely existing, for stepping onto his lands. I should have eliminated him then. Gone into his mind and rendered him nothing but a shell, but I was young. Too young and inexperienced with my own magic. I was too slow, too fucking slow to stop it. I tried to fight, but they got me. They got her. And they made me watch as they killed her. Slowly. Painfully. And they left her body there on the ground to bleed out. Flowers grew around her. Even in death her blood had created something beautiful. But me... they thought they'd killed me. Mana spared my life. I thought it was so I could take my sister's body back to Unseelie, but when I did, it was in shame.

"My mother was... *furious* is too kind a word. She broke. They all did. I did. And when she had me beaten, whipped with iron, I deserved it. It was my fault. I killed her. I killed my own blood by taking her into Seelie. It was my fault and I deserve their scorn. I always have. And I tried to drown my sorrows in Unseelie drugs. In powders in my nose that would help me forget, but there was no forgetting what I'd done, and there was no forgiving either.

"They'd all come to hate me far more than they'd ever had before. But they never hated me more than I hated myself. My mother could no longer stand to look at me, and I was banished to Seelie. She had hoped, prayed I am sure, that the one who murdered my sister would find me and murder me, too.

"But when I arrived at Seelie, he was no longer there. Her blood was no longer there. And I had nothing but my own pathetic sorrow, a pocketful of powder that slowly began to kill me, and wounds that never truly healed.

"So, I wandered through a court I'd always longed for but never truly belonged to. A place I knew of no one but my sister's murderer. For days I survived on powder alone. It kept me tethered to my anger and my rage. It helped feed it until I was a starving Fae aching for only one thing that could sate me: revenge on the Fae man who had done it.

"Eventually it was those thoughts that weaned me off the drug. It was that anger that pushed me towards the Seelie Court to study and spy and find the perfect opportunity. But then the war with the humans came and the world rendered into chaos. I thought I'd lost my chance. I thought I would no longer bring his head back to my mother as a gift, an apology.

"But then he came to me with his horde. They found me, turned their weapons my way. I stared the Fae in the eyes, and I wondered if he'd recognized me. Years had already passed. So many years. But for me it was like it had happened a day before, hours before, minutes, even. It was so ingrained into my being that it felt too close. But when he looked at me, when my thoughts reached for his, I knew he did not remember me. He did not remember my sister.

"The rage I felt. The way I wanted to reach out and rip his heart from his chest. We'd been just another moment to him. Something unworthy of note. We warranted no remembrance. The death of the most beloved person in my family's world had been nothing of consequence to him. I knew then that I would not just kill him, I would kill everything he loved and held dear. But I would take no gratification from doing it slowly.

"He did not deserve such an easy death. So, I infiltrated his mind. I gave him a hint of my magic and magic like mine is far too rare. I pledged myself to him. I got down on my knees before my sister's killer, and I fucking *bowed* even if everything within me revolted at the action. I pretended to revere him. I feigned my loyalty if only to get close to him. To read his thoughts. To learn his court. To find the perfect opportunity to let the world around him fucking *burn*. Because killing him was not enough. No. I wanted to completely and utterly destroy his house. His court. His crown."

Weylyn took a breath and looked up at Bryson then. There were tears. Of sorrow, loss, rage. They made his golden eyes shine that much brighter and made her heart pound that much harder and her feelings for him grow that much larger.

"I have been at his side for years, waiting. Because when I murder him, I want it to be slow. I want to watch his soul bleed out of his body, and I want to laugh the way he laughed when it was the blood of my sister trickling onto the ground. And when I have his head, I will hang it above my mother's throne so the entire court can see that I, Weylyn Xanth, *murdered* the Seelie King."

Tears had slipped down Bryson's eyes, but she didn't wipe them away. The salt was strong against her lips, and when she sucked in a breath, it tasted of the sea.

Weylyn took a breath and his own tears slid down his cheeks. He straightened, expression hardening once again. "So you see, my little mate? You see what a monster I truly am. I caused my sister's death. I killed her. I have been pretending to be loyal to the monarchy that tore my family apart. I am planning on murdering your king. I am unworthy of you, of *anyone*, because of what I have done and what I will do. That is why they despise me. That is why they will take it out on *you* every opportunity."

Silence pulsed between them and when Bryson finally found the courage to speak, she shook her head and reached for his hands. "I don't believe that." He tried to pull away, but she held firm. "You're not a monster."

"Were you not listening?" He huffed a frustrated breath.

"I was, and you know what I learned of you?" She pushed on before he could respond. "I learned that you're a man who dreams of a family who loves him. A man who loved his sister more than anyone in the world, so much that you'd do anything to make her dreams and curiosities come true, even at the expense of your own well-being. I learned that you suffered misplaced hatred from your entire family for years. You have suffered violence and drugs, and yet your love was so strong it became an anger acute to revenge. You know what I learned about you, Weylyn Xanth?" She sobbed. "I learned today that you and I are the same, and if there is one thing that you are, it is worthy. And if there is one thing I know, it is that if Mana gives me the choice, I will choose you, my mate, every single time. And if you choose me, too, then I will be happy to watch the world burn alongside you."

Tethered to a Mate

"You are not a monster. If anyone is a monster, it is the Seelie King."

Her hatred for him burned. Someone she'd once wanted to meet. Someone her mother had fought and died for, and he was a terrible being. One who killed innocents for pleasure. One who had made Weylyn's entire life a nightmare for selfish, cruel reasons.

She understood Weylyn just a bit more now. She knew him. She felt him. Did his trauma forgive the cruel things he'd done since she met him, like invading her thoughts, breaking past her boundaries to take what she said she wouldn't give? No. It didn't. He was not good. But he was not a monster, either. He was something in between, a shade of gray in between darkness and light.

It was who he was. And it was something she knew she could not and would not change. She realized that now. Hadn't he been the one to tell her that darkness lived in them all? For so long she'd been trying to follow a path of light and righteousness. The one her parents would have wanted her to follow.

But Bryson wasn't her parents. She was a product of despair and war and loss. She had become anger and revenge. Predator and prey. She'd become a killer. Not light. Not darkness. But somewhere in between just like Weylyn had.

And after all, weren't they all doing what they could in order to survive? Adapting to what their environment forced them into? Hadn't they just become the creatures that the monsters made them into?

"Darkness lives in us all," she reminded him. "And when faced with tragedy, you had to decide if you'd become predator or prey." She leaned closer to him. "You did what you had to do to survive."

Weylyn regarded her with an unreadable expression. "You... do not think I am a monster?"

Bryson shook her head. "No."

He closed his eyes and leaned close, close enough that his forehead pressed to hers. Close enough that she was enveloped in the dizzying scent that had always made her lose her own inhibitions.

"How wrong you are, my perfect, beautiful little mate." The tips of their noses touched. "So, so wrong."

"Then if you're a monster, I'm one too."

Their eyes opened and held. Close enough she could see every fleck, every emotion. "No, my perfect little mate. You are no monster. You know what you are?"

Predator or prey.

"What am I?" she whispered.

"You are *everything*."

Tears flowed from her eyes once again. All at once the earlier humiliation faded and made way for a sensation she was far too familiar with. An anger with all the force of a tornado, ready to sweep away anything if she only commanded it.

She wondered if Weylyn could sense it inside her or maybe he understood it as profoundly as he understood his own.

"Yes, little mate," he praised. "Let that feeling consume you and hold onto it. Because together, we will bring our revenge to life, and we will let all those who wronged us perish beneath its force."

She knew a part of her knew she should tame that wildness within him. She should temper his anger with her own calm. But she couldn't bring herself to do it. She didn't even want to. She wanted to unleash it. She wanted the both of them to do that and make everyone regret the day they crossed the two of them.

"Our revenge will happen," he said the words like a vow of a mating bond. Like it was a promise, a deal he meant to keep.

Bryson opened her eyes. "I belong to *her* now," she reminded him.

Between them, Weylyn grabbed the hand with the golden, burning brand. Like a leaf, it was stamped into her skin. Around the gold, her skin was red, itchy, and irritated. She had the urge to scratch at it, like she could claw the brand off herself, but she could not. It was there forever.

"No," he said firmly. "You do not. I promise you, I will free you from this." He held her hand up. "That is my vow to you. On my own life, I will free you from this, my little mate."

She couldn't bring herself to say anything, but she was sure the doubt was in her eyes. Her future was uncertain. Their future was uncertain. She belonged to his mother now. She could never go back to the human lands because she'd tethered herself to Unseelie the moment her teeth sunk into rotten fruit. And there was nothing anyone could do about it.

And she could read Weylyn easily enough. He would throw himself into danger and violence and promises to his own detriment if only to keep his promise to her. He would not lose another person he cared about. And Weylyn did care about her. In his own twisted way, he'd always had. And maybe Bryson had cared about him too. Even if on a surface level, she'd hated what he'd done, she'd always been drawn to the darker parts of him, because they mirrored her own. And she would not change that. She'd not ask him to not be violent. It was already so ingrained into him, that he could not stop.

And she didn't want to stop him.

She wanted to embrace him. In all his vicious shades of gray, she wanted to embrace him. Because if this was the moment they both fought and died, she wanted it to be on her own terms. The Unseelie Queen might own her and keep her there, but she wouldn't. Not truly. And Bryson was still the owner of her heart, her soul.

And she would do with those what she pleased.

"Weylyn..." Her breath picked up as she looked at him. at this terrible, vicious Fae. At her mate. "I want you," she whispered. "Here, now, I want to bind myself to you. I want us to be mated. In every possible way."

Weylyn's eyes widened and even in his mindscape, she could hear the rapid, nervous beating of his heart in a way he'd never displayed before.

He took a breath. "You are sure..."

"I've never been more sure of anything. I want to be tethered to you. I want us to control our own fate. I want—"

Weylyn did not let her finish her thought.

Because he was already consuming her.

Toxic Love

Weylyn pulled them out of his mindscape and back to reality. Bryson blinked away her brief moment of confusion. They were submerged together in the bath and as soon as they were back in the present, he pulled her towards him, water sloshing over the rim of the tub.

She fell onto his naked lap with a gasp, but the sound never fully formed as he completely devoured her. Like he was starving and only she could sate him. and maybe he was starving for her. For she'd made him wait for far too long. And in denying him, she'd denied herself this pleasure she knew only he could give.

Falling into his arms was a consuming force. It ignited her all over. Her body came alive. Pain didn't exist, and only pleasure took its place. Her body tingled. Every nerve came alive as she curved herself against him, as their lips consumed one another. Their canines bit, tongues tasted, mouths devoured.

It was with great reluctance that Weylyn pulled away. And it was only to grab a cloth and scrub it with soap before he swiped it along her body. His movements were quick and anxious, a mirror to the way Bryson felt inside. She held her breath and helped him hurry along, eager to get to where they both needed to be. Her own hands slipped through the tresses of his dark hair, soaping and rinsing. Her hands glided across his smooth body just as quickly until they were both shining clean.

Only then did Weylyn grasp her by the hips and lifted her, pushing himself to a stand. She cried out as she scrambled to grab his shoulders, to wrap her legs around his waist. He held her tightly as he stepped one leg over the tub and then another. Water sluiced from their bodies and onto the floor. It didn't matter as he went and laid her over a blanket of furs. His mouth found hers again. He kissed her like he was dying of thirst.

Like he'd waited his entire life for this moment.

She supposed he had. Because Fae could spend an entire lifetime looking for their mate and never find them. It was a work of Mana to find a mate. Bryson hadn't dreamt of Weylyn, but she wanted him now. She wanted his unapologetic violence. She wanted him in all his broken pieces. The most toxic parts of him brought to life the most toxic parts of her.

And she let her mouth and her body speak for her. She kissed him back with equal fervor. Their tongues tangled together, and she would have died happily without air then, but Weylyn pulled away to press his mouth against her neck. His eagerness to have her only made slick wetness drip from between her legs. She groaned as he devoured her, as he nipped and marked her neck.

Her hips lifted to meet his, his hard length slick against her inner thigh. She wanted him closer to her heat. She wanted his cock inside her with an ache.

She muttered her pleas, her nails raked down his back. The spicy, sweet scent of his body made her head spin with want and need. "Weylyn," she gasped. "Please."

His canines sunk into her throat, breaking past the skin. She got no warning, and the invasion brought a fresh wave of pain that had her crying out. She gasped as he dug them deeper with that mating mark, nearly tearing at her throat.

She didn't fucking care.

She wanted more.

White hot pleasure zapped through her body, blinding her, sending lightning through every crevice of her soul, flashing behind her eyelids. The pleasure was immediate, and a release went through her, made her body shudder. And when he pulled away, tongue sliding against her skin, she leaned up and clasped his own throat with as much violence and pain as he'd inflicted on her.

Blood coated her mouth. Rich and tinny, it filled her mouth. The moment their mating bond snapped into place like a rope pulled taut, his cock pressed inside her. No warning and with as much eager violence as his teeth.

She screamed around the mouthful of his blood as his hips snapped violently against hers. They slid across the furs, the desire between them and their bond incrementing. Weylyn held himself up, his arms caged around her. For a moment they stopped. Staring at one another. His blood coated her lips, and she was sure it stained the sides of her mouth. He looked down at her with so much tenderness, so much wonder that it hurt. And maybe she could never see clearly before, but in this there was no doubt. Something a lot like love pulsed between them, but neither dared whisper those words aloud.

They stayed connected, staring. His eyes flickered white, and words rang through her mind.

"Little mate," they whispered. *"You're mine now and for always."*

And then he moved. She cried out. His hips slammed against her waist, and with every deep thrust against her, he stroked her clit harder, deeper. He had every sensation rising higher. She met him with thrusts of her own.

Their eager passion became a quick joining. Nothing but rough and fast strokes as they desperately climbed for that release they both craved. She cried out, muffling her sounds against his skin as she bit and bit down again. Each bite only seemed to pull the bond tauter between them. So she kept doing it, like she could keep him, pull him down to her very soul. And every time her teeth pierced past his flesh to mark him as hers, he grunted his own pleasure into her ear like a symphony.

Weylyn stopped thrusting and leaned up, yanking her newly tattooed hand to his chest. She whimpered as he touched the sensitive skin and shivered when he brought her wrist to his nose and sniffed. He trailed his tongue against her pulse right before his teeth clamped down against her skin there, lightly piercing her flesh.

The bond yanked and she screamed as another orgasm crested through her body. She trembled in his hold as his tongue slid against the newly branded mark. The one that covered the queen's like he was countering her hold on Bryson with his own.

Something in her chest warmed and tears spilled from her eyes anew.

Weylyn stared down at her with such a tenderness it brought an ache pulsing between her breasts. And when he pulled out of her, she felt empty. But he lowered himself, languid as he kissed his way over her bare chest, sucking her nipples into his mouth until they were sharp, sensitive points. He licked down her belly, lower still. His hands massaged across her outer thighs just as the stubble on his chin reached the sensitive area around her inner thighs. He scraped along there before licking and nipping at her skin. Bryson shuddered beneath his ministrations, and she arched her back and screamed when his teeth clamped down against her, piercing past the sensitive flesh of her inner thigh.

He marked her hard there, lapping up the wound until it healed. Then he blew warm breath against it. Bryson was already shaking. Pain and pleasure blossomed inside her like wildflowers. It wouldn't take much for her to ignite. Already she felt herself balanced on that delicate edge. So close to it that when he pressed his mouth against her center, she detonated like a bomb. He pulled her clit into his mouth, suckling until she couldn't take anymore.

Thrashing against his hold, her fingers dug into his long hair and yanked him upwards. He went willingly, and she shoved, switching and rolling him onto his back so she lay above him.

The action mirrored one they'd done before. Back then it'd only been in his mindscape and she'd been on top of someone else. Now there were no dreams surrounding them. Just this reality consuming them both entirely.

Her palms slapped down against his chest, nails carving into his skin until she drew blood. There was a healing wound over his chest, the question in her eyes obvious, but he shook his head as if to say 'Later' before he gripped her hips and thrust into her hard.

Her back bowed, her moan echoing through her tent. She was sure the entire Unseelie Court could hear what they were doing, and she didn't care. She was tired, so tired of worrying about what everyone thought and wanted. Arlo. Everette. Malika. Her dead family.

It was time to take what she wanted.

No holding back. No restraints. No inhibitions.

Her pleasure echoed through the tent. Their bodies slapping together crudely in the most delicious way. She held on as she rode him, chasing her own desire with every undulation of her hips. The faster they moved, the deeper she carved her nails into his skin, drawing thin lines of blood against him. She leaned down, smearing it against her own body as she pressed close to him and claimed his mouth.

She poured all her emotions into that single kiss. Their hearts pounded in tandem, threatening to burst and intertwine as close as the threads of their souls. Weylyn's hand buried into her hair at the nape of her neck. He gripped tight enough to cause pain, but she found happiness in the gesture, so much it threatened to explode.

Their mouths came apart and Weylyn whispered against her mouth. "Come, my little mate. Follow me into the darkness."

And she did.

They came together with quick pumps of their hips. Jets of his release shot within her, a flood of warmth claiming her entire body as she fell apart. She shuddered and cried and moaned until she had nothing left within her to give.

Until she collapsed against Weylyn's chest, the new bonds burning fresh against her body. The necklace of teeth around her throat. The mark against her wrist. The bite on her inner thigh. It pulsed and burned and hurt in the best possible way, and for the first time in a long time she felt sated. Content.

And soon after, she fell asleep and dreamt of the stars.

Unseelie Deals

"*Why haven't you killed him yet?*" Bryson whispered into Weylyn's mind.

As much as he wanted to lay languidly against the words and whisper to one another all night, he knew how dangerous such a thing was. Anyone could overhear. Here, at least, no one could infiltrate his mind or his thoughts. No one could listen and they could be as intimate with one another as they wanted.

"What?" His fingers paused against her hip, where he'd traced figures of stars and Unseelie animals of old.

"The king. Why haven't you killed him yet?"

Weylyn's entire body tensed like it always did whenever talk of the king came up. For years, he had held his hatred in so deeply, he'd choked on it. For years he had kept his plans so tightly leashed. Now that someone else knew them, he was almost afraid his mate would judge him. But she only ever asked with curiosity.

"You have had plenty of chances to kill him, haven't you?"

"Not as many as you would think," he confessed. "He is constantly surrounded by his courtiers. Getting him alone has not been such an easy task."

"But what about Prince Valerio?"

"What do you mean?"

"You've been alone with him before, haven't you? You've had time to kill him. The crown prince. You vowed to destroy the crown. Valerio is part of that crown. Why haven't you killed *him*?"

Weylyn resumed sliding his fingers against her hip. "Do you want the truth?"

"Always."

"I do not know what the truth is."

He had had plenty of opportunities to kill the sniveling Seelie heir. But anytime he wanted to, something always held him back. He told himself it was because of the dissatisfaction of the act. He would not enjoy it because the king would not bear witness to his line ending. Therefore, he could not strike. No matter how badly he wanted to.

"You know what I think?" Bryson turned so she was on her back and he leaned over her, his hair curtaining around her face.

She looked at him with a tenderness he'd never experienced before in his life. He never thought she would look at him that way. If he thought he'd loved her with all that hatred and anger she garnered inside and aimed his way, he found he loved this so much more.

"What do you think, my little mate?" He flashed his canines in a smile.

"I think you like the Seelie Prince."

Those words had the smile dropping from his face in an instant.

"No." Denial came easily. "Absolutely not."

Bryson smiled wider. "You do. You like him which is why you haven't killed him. It's what's been holding you back. Because he isn't like his father."

"The Seelie Prince is a fucking fool."

"A fucking fool he may be, but you like him. Admit it."

"No."

Bryson poked his bare chest. "You do. I know it."

"I have vowed to destroy the Seelie line. Feelings are irrelevant. That is not a confession," he added hastily.

Like the Seelie Prince? He snorted and shook his head in his mate's direction. The only thing he felt for the Ashera line was absolute contempt. The king was a cruel, remorseless bastard that deserved to die. The prince was an idiot who knew nothing of what it was to rule. His heart was far too soft, and it made him stupid.

The way Weylyn saw it, they both deserved to die.

"You'd still kill the king, even if you respect Prince Valerio?"

"Would you stop me?" This question seemed crucial. Like something that would determine how their future as mates would go. If she would try to temper the only thing that had brought him so much life. If she would try to stop him from fulfilling the one goal he'd strived for his entire life.

He held his breath as he waited for her answer.

Finally, she looked at him. "No," she whispered. "I would not stop you." Her hand reached for his shoulder, sliding over his skin. Her discolored eyes seemed to burn with conviction and rage. "I would help you push the knife into the king's back. And I'd take joy in it."

A smile pulled at Weylyn's lips. Some would have called it cruel, but it was the most joyous thing Weylyn wore. He leaned down, unable to resist the pull of his mate's bloodlust. He captured her mouth and her body curved against his almost immediately. His cock grew hard between them, weeping and eager for another taste of his beautiful mate.

His mate.

Mate. Mate. Mate.

He knew she would give in to him eventually. Not like this. Not in Unseelie. But it didn't matter. She was his now. He had tethered them together. Forever.

Or for as long as they were alive, at least.

As soon as that thought took hold, he pulled away. Ideas had already begun taking motion in his mind, all of them wild and desperate. But he knew without a single bit of doubt that he would do all that was within his power and beyond to get them out of Unseelie.

He pulled away from his mate, and his magic reached out for her mind.

"I swear I will get us out of this court, little mate."

"How?"

"Do you trust me?"

"Yes."

The immediate answer brought warmth to his chest.

"Then this is what I need you to do..."

It was with the taste of his mate on his mouth and his body that Weylyn slipped from their tent to go in search of the Unseelie Queen.

His mother was blessedly alone. She sat on her throne, chin resting against her hand, as she contemplated whatever evils lived within her dark, twisted mind.

When he approached, her eyes flicked with boredom.

"What is it?" she grumbled. "Have you come to beg for your mate's freedom from Unseelie's hold? Why waste my time with foolery that cannot be when we can spend it with far greater pleasures."

"Like what?" He stopped shy of reaching her throne.

"A game of truth, perhaps." She straightened to her regal posture. "You can tell me where Owyn has gone. I have not seen him since you took off for The Hunt."

"I do not know."

It wasn't a lie. Though Owyn had died and Weylyn knew the exact spot, he did not know where the earth of Unseelie had sucked him to. He did not know what awaited his brother in the afterlife. He did not know where Mana had taken him. Perhaps his soul had been reaped by the Wild Hunt. Or perhaps he was in the human concept of hell.

He did not particularly care.

He could be food for the maggots.

His mother regarded him with suspicion, but he gave nothing away. It was not as if he'd killed the fool anyway. Though it didn't matter if he told that truth. She would not believe him.

"Hmm," she hummed. "What do you want?"

"I want you to free my mate from Unseelie and your hold."

"How boring and predictable." Her fingers flicked against the armrest of her throne. "I thought you would at least come to me with a deal to counter her binding."

"Free her and I will bring you the head of the Seelie King."

His mother scoffed with disinterest. "You have promised me his head for years and I have yet to see it above my throne. I have grown tired of the empty promises you keep."

"I have infiltrated his court. I have a direct line to him. I can promise you his head now."

"You are a liar and I tire of these games, Weylyn. You have been in his court for years and have done nothing. How will you do now what you have not done before? Is it because of your mate? Because now you have the motivation?" The queen scoffed. "Your sister's death should have been motivation enough for you and yet it was not."

Weylyn tried not to let his own desperation show. "What if we made a deal?" he asked.

This gave his mother pause.

Everyone knew Unseelie did not enter deals lightly. Only the foolish found themselves trapped in one and Weylyn, in all his life, had never, ever made a deal with his family. He knew the concept of one was intriguing to his mother, and she would dissect his words from the inside out to make sure it was beneficial to her. And damning for him.

Which was what he was counting on.

"That depends." She leaned forward. "What would this deal entail?"

"Free my mate from Unseelie completely. I will bring you the head of the Unseelie King, and my mate will help me deliver it."

His mother shook her head. "No. Should a deal be struck, she would remain here while you fulfill it."

"Absolutely not."

"There will be no deal." She leaned back and turned her head away as though she were dismissing him.

"What if I promised you my mate's life in exchange?" he asked.

The queen's head snapped towards him. Her shock was evident over her features. "*What?*"

He didn't think he'd ever seen his mother so speechless.

The deal was one no sane Fae would make. Then again, Weylyn had never been known for being sane.

"Temporary freedom to come with me where I require. No tricks, or her life is forfeit. We bring you the king's head and the deal dissolves. She leaves with me. Our debt is fulfilled."

A Song of Air

Feeling fresh in a new pair of pants and tunic, a light jacket to shield her from the cold wind, her hair pleated thanks to Weylyn, Bryson made her way towards the goblin forgery. With the lenses on her face, it made navigating Unseelie far easier. Her eyes still burned, and seeing the world in such bright colors was new in a way that made her temples throb. The iron was still thick as it coated the air, and she felt the tang of it on her tongue.

Her back ached from where it was slowly healing. Far too slowly for her liking. Back in the humanlands, she would have healed far easier, for the iron in Ielwyn was not as thick as it was in Unseelie. Here it eroded so much into the land, it was a part of everything. Even in the air.

So it made healing slow. It made her magic flicker in and out. She tried grasping for it, but it was far too tired to come forth. The lack of her magic made her nervous. She tried not to think of all the great accomplishments of the other Elementals. All that they'd done and all that she felt she was failing to do. Thinking that way would not help her. She could accomplish just as much as they had.

With or without her magic.

She would make sure of it.

She was Fae. And even if her magic was waning, she would be a predator they would all fear.

Their survival was dependent on that.

No one tried to stop her as she walked towards the goblin forgery. The tall spires of the smoking, iron forge nearly touched the sky. The smog that spit out of the tips made the sky a dreary gray that reminded her of the iron camps of the humanlands.

It made bad memories surface, and she shoved them down as she passed by goblins hard at work, hammering away across their tainted land. They regarded her curiously but didn't stop her. Not even as she made her way to the relic room.

Immediately she was slammed with a wave of magic.

She'd forever be in awe of how they trapped magic within objects. It felt like its own type of magic to be able to create something that way. And what they'd created in here would help her and Weylyn aid them.

Bryson passed by mountains of glittering gold and jewels. Her fingers grazed against them but she pulled them away just as quickly. She didn't need riches or jewels. She'd come in for one thing only.

The words of the queen on their guided tour came back to her as her head swiveled back and forth.

"We have an array of relics with incredible power holstered here. Rings of iron that can glamor you into anything you wish. Weapons disguised as jewelry. Swords that can shrink to the size of a quill. Mirrors that can portal you anywhere you desire."

Bryson could sense the raw power of that magic around her. It was a pulsing force that closed in around her from all sides. She reached out with her own flickering, faulty magic, searching, pressing. Her gaze swiveled around. She could see everything far better this time around than she had at first.

So when she found what she was looking for, she rushed towards the object in sight. Her fingers closed around it, and she observed it before shoving it deep into the recesses of her pocket. She turned to leave as quickly as she'd come in, but nearly tripped over the small body of a goblin she'd never even heard approach.

She jolted backwards, nearly sliding on a pile of golden coins.

"You frightened me!" She pressed a hand to her chest and regretted the words as soon as they left her lips. It was no good to confess her fears within the land of Unseelie. Not even to the goblin before her.

She recognized him immediately as the one who had given her the lenses. The funny little goblin was staring up at her with glaring, hateful eyes.

Bryson immediately took a step back and her legs bumped into a mountain of gold.

"Is there something you needed?" she asked. Her gaze flicked briefly over his body and scanned the room to make sure no one else had come with him. There was no one. She cast wary glances back at him.

The goblin bared his fangs at her. "Thiiiieeeeffff," he hissed.

Bryson blinked.

"You're a filthy thiiiiefff. Trying to steal what I created for yourself. You thiiiiefffff." He whipped out a dagger and lunged.

Bryson cried out and jumped backwards, landing hard against a mountain of hard gold. The breath left her lungs and she scrambled away from him as he advanced on her with a vicious, cruel gleam in his eye.

"I am the protector and creator of the relics, and you are a thieefffff." He raised his arm, and it came slashing down in an arc. It caught against her jacket, ripping at the material. Narrowly missing her body. She rolled backwards, landing on the ground with a huff. She scrambled to her feet, jumping up just as he lunged. He pounced like an animal, a feral sound scraping from his throat.

He was little more than a beast right then. Bryson grasped for her magic, but the closeness to the iron made it far too difficult to grasp it. She managed to send a gust of wind in his direction, pushing him backwards. He let out a yelp as he fell but stood almost immediately after. He was fast on his little feet and cut her off as she ran towards the exit.

They were a parry of fast-moving bodies. And the next time he lunged for her, his blade cut across body. She cried out, cradling her bleeding arm to her chest.

"Thieefff," he hissed once again. The silver of the blade gleamed amongst the gold, the red of her blood dripping from the tip.

Bryson's breath hitched and the lenses slid down the ridge of her nose with the action.

"I created for you, and you steal!" He lunged again, his body nothing more than a blur as he jumped at her. She screamed as she tried to reach for her magic. But it didn't respond and by the time she realized it wouldn't, it was already too late.

The goblin tackled her. Her back screamed as she fell, hitting hard rubies and coins and iron. She tried to move, but the blade was already tight against her throat, and when she swallowed, the sharp edge cut into her skin. His vicious little body pinned her to the gold. The lenses he'd created slid from her face and his heavy, thick breaths fogged against the glass.

The blade pushed deeper into her neck. The scar on her back burned like it was crying out. Like it knew her death was imminent. Like it was waiting for it, ready to create a fierce and deadly force of nature, if only to tell the world that the air Elemental was no more.

And she laid there and waited for it. She waited for the blade to dig into her throat. To rip her apart. She waited for life to escape her grasp.

She waited for an imminent death, realizing she'd been playing at being predator this whole time.

But, that wasn't quite right, she thought. She wasn't prey. She wasn't even the other Elementals. She'd not melt iron like Shula because she didn't possess fire. She'd not freeze it or become ice, because she was not Iona. She'd not drown whole cities like Corvina had, because she was not them.

She was not light and goodness.

She was an angry shade in between, where the dark met the light. She realized in that moment, with her life hanging on the precipice, that she would never be like them. And she did not want to be. She did not want to be the other Elementals, and she did not want to be prey.

She wanted to take the anger that she kept so tightly bottled and finally let it sing.

Something inside her stirred, responding to her revelation. Like it had known that's what she'd needed all along. Her well of power deepened. Her rage shot forth. All she knew was the magic of the wind nestled inside her. Bryson grasped for it, cried out as she yanked it forward. The wind howled, it sang like a cry of lament and rage both until it became a physical thing she could make out as it whirled and whirled between her body and the goblin's. It shoved between them, pushing him backwards so hard, he hit a spear hanging on the far wall of the relic room.

It pierced through his chest, holding him up. His legs dangled beneath him, and he hissed, his eyes wide and bloody. And Bryson stood, shoving those lenses back up the ridge of her nose as she took him in. Her magic was a force around her, and she could no longer contain it as it fought against the hold the iron tried to have on her.

"Thiiiiefff," the goblin whispered right before she rent the relic room apart. Her air magic ripped from the seams. It burst outwards, a tornado with absolutely no control. It ripped the iron apart. It tore the relic room, gold by gold, brick by brick, iron wall by iron wall, and reached outwards even further. The buildings and forgeries around her came crumbling down. The entire ground shook from the force of her magic. She tore everything apart from its foundations, her own magic protecting her from the crumbling debris.

Bryson ran out and air followed, lifting her as she rose from the crumbling, decimated structures of the forgery. Where science and magic met, but where iron had tainted the ground. Her elemental magic recognized it for the blight that it was.

It ripped it apart. Fire blazed, buildings crumbled to the ground. Dirt created a cloud of chaos through the air. Goblins shrieked and cried as they ran away from the chaos. Bryson ran away from it too, right before she sent the strongest gust of wind she could muster and watched the building completely fall.

She stood off to the side as the dark night lowered and the buildings were destroyed. Her breathing grew harsh, and she felt blood trickle along her neckline.

"My, what a mess you've created," a voice whispered near her ear.

Bryson yelped in fear and whirled, her magic shooting out and pushing against Prince Cassimir.

The prince kept his legs firmly planted on the ground, though he shielded his eyes from the debris that flew his way. Her magic died and he smirked.

"My mother will be furious at you," he said with amusement.

The brand on her arm burned almost as if it was reminding her who she belonged to now.

"Have you come to torture me like the rest of your court did?"

"Of course not. I am not without compassion. I've come to take you to my brother."

She regarded him with suspicion. "Which one?"

Cassimir's lips twitched. "Smart Fae. I will take you to Weylyn, for he is waiting for you."

Bryson wanted to take that step forward, but she didn't trust him. She didn't trust anyone in Unseelie. She'd already made the mistake of eating a fruit and getting herself shackled here. She did not want any more surprises. And Weylyn had never mentioned Cassimir when he left their tent that morning.

"I vow I will take you straight to Weylyn. No detours, no trickery."

Bryson couldn't relax, even after the vow left his lips and a gold band appeared from magic, snaking around his neck like a collar.

"Is that good enough for you, sister?" he asked, eyes shining sarcastically.

"For now."

He smirked again and let out a low whistle. Immediately one of his beasts flew from the sky and landed behind him.

"Hop on, little sister." He patted his beast on its flank. "It is time to fly."

A Debt Repaid

Bryson was glad her hair was pleated because the rushing wind of the sky as she sat atop a beast was brutal. When they circled and then landed in the forest, her entire body was on alert until she caught sight of Weylyn.

He was waiting for her, and she let out a breath of relief as she jumped from the creature's back and rushed to her mate.

Her neck throbbed from the marks of his canines. So did the inside of her wrist and thigh, but it was a burn in the most delicious of ways. She hadn't known what mating would be like. What it would feel like. It was like a part of her was tied within his soul. She could feel his absence and closeness in equal measure.

And she ached for his tongue to trail against those burning, healing marks. She needed that reassurance. She needed to be close to him.

It took nothing for her to wrap her arms around his neck and pull him close. Their hearts beat in tandem. When they pulled away, he pressed his forehead to hers in a quiet intimate moment before Cassimir interrupted.

"Your mate made a mess for me to clean up."

Weylyn's mischievous smile warmed her from the inside. "Did she now?" Though he asked the question, his eyes shone as though he already knew what she'd done. She would not apologize for it. And he looked as though he didn't expect it of her either.

"Mother will be furious." Cassimir slid a hand down his beast's neck.

Weylyn reached for Bryson's hand. "Fortunately, the two of us will be gone before she reaches us."

Bryson's heart thundered and her gaze snapped up to her mate, questioning with no words. "You did it?"

"Did you doubt me, little mate?" his voice purred in her head, causing her cheeks to flush.

"Remember your vows to me, little brother," Cassimir interrupted.

"As if I could ever forget them."

Weylyn turned to Bryson then and nodded. She took a breath and reached into the pocket of her pants for the mirror she'd stolen. She held it up before them and Weylyn squeezed her hand in encouragement.

"Home," Bryson whispered.

The black reflection changed. The surface of the mirror rippled and changed, distorted. They couldn't see anything on the other side, but a bright light shone through the relic and enveloped them in its embrace. Bryson looked up one last time at the eldest Prince of Unseelie and found him smiling. Not angrily, mischievously. But genuinely. And she smiled back at him, right before the light sucked both her and Weylyn inside.

Out of Unseelie.

And back to the humanlands.

Time to Live

Their feet touched the ground on the humanlands. Daylight shone brightly. Birds chirped. And Bryson, after weeks of what felt like being trapped beneath a drowning surface, was finally able to breathe.

Above her, a hawk screeched, and she reached out for that connection to her familiar. Her familiar's mind was tumultuous like a storm, but the moment Bryson touched it with her own, the hawk settled.

"You're back."

"I will always come back to you," Bryson whispered.

The hawk cried out and Bryson cast her gaze around. They'd landed in the middle of the rebel camp. Their sudden appearance garnered attention, and one by one, people came out of their tents, gasping, calling out to her.

Tears pricked her eyes. She thought she'd never see them again. Even now, the steady burn of the brand on her hand pulsed with a threatening reminder of a promise unfulfilled.

She hid that hand beneath Weylyn's so they couldn't see the mark, and he held her tightly.

Arlo and Everette appeared. And so did the Resistance. Her magic immediately reached out for the Elementals as they approached, eyes wide as they took her in. With the lenses on her face, she could see them clearly and make out details that had been lost to her before.

Like the scars on the water elemental's hands and bent fingers. The golden hair and bright eyes.

There were absolutely no familial features she shared with Weylyn at all, as he favored his mother, but now that she knew the truth, something in her warmed towards the other female. Bryson resisted the urge to run to her and wrap her arms around her.

"Bryce." Malika pushed her way forward. Her gaze went down to the hand Weylyn clasped against hers and then back up to the lenses on her face. "You're here. You're back. How?"

"It's a bit of a long story..."

"Bryce!"

Bryson turned and watched as Everette pushed his way through the crowd to reach her.

"Bryce!"

She jolted as he all but tackled her, wrapping his arms around her waist and pulling her close.

Before, she would have relished in his touch. She would have wanted that closeness from him if only to feel a connection to someone after so long. But now that he touched her, she felt a small trace of bitter anger right next to absolutely nothing.

"Bryson, I was so worried about you." He pulled away, and she could just make out the truth in his words. The torture in his gaze. The heavy bags beneath his blood shot eyes like he'd been buried beneath his own tears.

She did not feel sorry for him in that.

"I'm so sorry, Bryson." His tears fell once again. "I didn't mean to push you. I swear it. I never would have, had I known. I—" He cut off, shaking his head back and forth. "I swear to you, I will spend the rest of our lives making it up to you. I promise. I swear it." He leaned forward then, to capture her lips in his, but Bryson leaned away before he could do it.

Beside her, Weylyn growled.

The instant and obvious rejection had Everette jolting backwards. His arms dropped from her waist, and he took a step back, then another, staring between the two of them. And Bryson couldn't stop the not-so-subtle movement of her neck. She extended it so they could just make out the collar of healing teeth marks around her throat.

Her mating bond with Weylyn.

Everette staggered back in shock as his eyes took them in. Several emotions passed over his face at once. Shock. Disbelief. Sadness. Anger. It was the most prominent among them all, and it transformed his features. He shoved his dark hair away from his face.

"I see." His voice was clipped and his tone said, *"I told you so."* Like he'd known this would happen all along.

Maybe he was right. Maybe Bryson had been a fool to deny what Mana had set out before them. After all, Mana fated mates together for a reason. Mana had known Weylyn and Bryson were meant to be. That their darkness inside was a perfect match.

Bryson had been the fool for fighting it the entire time. For denying what was right in front of her. But now she knew him for what and who he truly was. The pain he carried inside, the terrible things he had to do and would do. She would not stop him from completing his goals. She didn't believe in changing someone. He was who he was, and if she loved him, which she suspected she did, she would be beside him. She wouldn't temper him.

She would let his rage sing.

"Well, you didn't wait long at all, did you?" His bitter tone threatened to cut through Bryson. While she was angry with him for how he'd acted, she hadn't wanted to hurt him. They'd shared a lot together in all their years and she had cared deeply for him. She did not have to like him now, though she did not like his tone. It was unfair to blame her for what she'd done to survive. Weylyn had been the only one standing beside her in Unseelie. And it had been Everette's fault they'd been there in the first place.

"Time passes differently in Unseelie," Weylyn said coolly as he leveled his gaze with Everette's, the threat in his eyes obvious. "It has been a day here, hasn't it? It was weeks in Unseelie for us."

Bryson blinked. It had felt longer. An eternity of torture and fear. Of waning magic and shattered lungs without air.

"I see." Everette glared at Weylyn then at her. He opened his mouth like he wanted to say more, but Bryson couldn't bear it.

"Don't," she warned. "You don't get to judge how I chose to survive when you were the reason we were there in the first place."

Guilt slammed over his features, but Bryson refused to feel the same.

"He is my mate," she said, loudly for everyone around them to hear. They'd already been listening intently, watching the events unfold and eating it up like a pastry. "And I will not apologize for that."

"No one would ask you to." Corvina stepped forward. The shy elemental's voice had grown hard with determination, solidarity. Her gaze was unwavering, and Bryson's chest warmed. "We are just glad you are okay."

"Yeah," Iona agreed. "We would have been lost without you."

Bryson's eyes brimmed with tears she didn't dare let fall. Instead, she took a deep breath. Her future had always felt so uncertain. She'd always felt like she didn't quite belong, like she should have been doing more. After everything she'd been through in Unseelie, she was finally ready to embrace the side of her she'd never wanted to acknowledge. The darkness. The bitter anger. It was hers to accept and she was done living for others.

It was time Bryson lived for herself.

Her eyes met Arlo's. The hard work of his jaw let her know he was not happy with what she'd done, but she was far past caring. She knew what he was. Knew the manipulation tactics he used to keep Fae and humans tethered to him. She would forever be grateful to him for saving her life. For pulling her from that wagon all those years ago. But she would not lower herself to becoming his slave for eternity because of it.

She had already paid back her debt tenfold.

So it was looking at him that she said, “I’m ready to go with you. Long live the Resistance.”

Iron Rings

"Are you sure you want to do this?" Malika asked quietly.

Bryson took a breath. "My time here has come to an end."

"Mine too. I've already lost so much of it, I don't want to waste anymore. My sister needs me. Besides," she nudged Bryson in the arm, "I can't leave you alone. You're my best friend."

The affirming words warmed Bryson's heart. For a while, she'd feared Malika would forget about her now that she had her sister back. She'd been a fool to feel so bitter towards the ice Elemental. People didn't have to be shackled by one thing or one person. They had many facets to them. They could have several people in their lives that meant so much to them. It didn't make anyone else any less special just because someone new—or old—came back into their lives.

Her love for her friend was not so fragile that it would break over something like that.

"I'm ready for this new chapter," Bryson confessed. "But I'm not looking forward to this." She nodded at Arlo's tent, which they were currently standing in front of.

Malika sighed. "Yeah," she said. "Me neither."

"But it has to be done."

"He'll be upset."

Bryson nodded. "I know." She squared her shoulders. "But he'll get over it." And then she walked towards the tent.

Arlo was bent over his desk when she went inside. He was staring at his map, his knuckles digging deep into the surface of the wood. He didn't look up when Bryson stepped inside. But his shoulders did tense.

There was a pregnant moment of silence. He didn't say anything, and at one point that silence would have unnerved her. It would have made Bryson want to rush to please him. To make it right if only so he'd look up at her. Speak to her.

She was no longer the same Fae who felt indebted to him, so his silence was no longer a weapon he could wield against her.

"I've come to say goodbye," Bryson finally said. Short, to the point.

"You will regret it," he said without looking up.

"I won't."

"You will."

Frustrating man.

Bryson sighed. "You saved my life, Arlo, and for that I will be forever grateful. But you cannot keep acting like what you do is a service that should be repaid when those you saved never asked you for your help in the first place."

He still didn't look up.

"I won't spend the rest of my life trapped in these woods as your slave."

Arlo scoffed and looked up then. There was anger and hatred oozing from his pores. "No," he spat. "You'll be a slave to the Resistance, though."

Bryson shook her head sadly at him. "That's where you're wrong. See, I've been locked within the iron camps. I've watched my family die. I've been chained and forced to do the humans' bidding for years. I know what the difference between slavery and free will is, Arlo. But I didn't come to argue with you. I came to say thank you. And goodbye."

He grunted and looked back down. "Farewell then, Bryson Varik."

Bryson started to turn around but hesitated. "Will you tell Everette goodbye for me? And that I'm sorry."

"Sorry for what? For breaking his heart? For being unfaithful?"

"For letting us go on for far longer than I should have."

She didn't wait for Arlo's response then. She merely turned and walked right back out, nodding to Malika as she passed. Her friend would say her goodbyes, and then they'd leave with the Resistance. The Resistance was packing their things now, getting their party ready.

Bryson had a bag already on her shoulder and she was eager to get going. She'd said every goodbye she needed to say and now she was ready to get back to Weylyn's side and—

She stopped in her tracks as she stepped beside Kerrigan's tent. A pulse of power and magic came from within.

His tent had always felt rife with magic, but this was different. This was something that felt far too familiar. Something she recognized, had come to know only recently.

She stepped inside the tent without announcing herself and found Kerrigan there.

"Bryson," he greeted, his long tendril-like hair flowing over his shoulders.

A pulse of familiar power came from him as he waved her inside, and her eyes zeroed in on his hands and the rings adorning his fingers.

The Unseelie Queen's words came back to her when a single, iron ring caught her eyes.

"We have an array of relics with incredible power holstered here. Rings of iron that can glamor you into anything you wish. Weapons disguised as jewelry. Swords that can shrink to the size of a quill. Mirrors that can portal you anywhere you desire."

"Kerrigan." Bryson's heart beat faster and she prayed he couldn't hear it. "I—I've come to say goodbye."

His eyebrows rose. "How kind of you, but very unnecessary."

"You know I have a fondness for your masks."

He smiled. "No one has appreciated those quite like you."

Bryson held out her hands for him to reach. They met in the middle and she grasped his fingers with her own, squeezing tightly and passing her fingers over the iron ring. Power flowed through her the moment she came into contact with it.

"It was nice knowing you, Bryson Varik," he smiled.

"And it was nice to know you, Kerrigan."

She slid her hands away and stepped backwards. She nodded once and turned away, exiting his tent as she clenched her fists tightly at her sides. She took a breath, and it wasn't until she was far enough away from him that she brought her hand up to her face.

Kerrigan's iron ring sat on the palm of her hand. It thrummed, the Unseelie magic flowing through it strong enough to make a shiver glide down her back.

A relic of the Unseelie Court, sitting in the palm of her hand.

"We have an array of relics with incredible power holstered here. Rings of iron that can glamor you into anything you wish. Weapons disguised as jewelry. Swords that can shrink to the size of a quill. Mirrors that can portal you anywhere you desire."

She closed her fingers around it, and when she looked up, Bryson smiled.

Strings of Destiny

His finger slid against the empty space where the iron ring had been and Kerrigan–or George, as he'd previously been known–smiled. With the heavy weight of it gone, the glamor it afforded him fell apart only to reveal his truest form.

It had been far too long since he'd last been himself, but he supposed it was for the best. He knew if you wore a mask for too long, you became the facade which you painted upon yourself. And, much as he enjoyed weaving a fabulous vision for others to gawk at, his true form was far more magnificent than anything Unseelie magic could conjure up.

He turned, catching sight of himself against a reflective pane of glass that housed a plant that swallowed pixies whole. His teeth flashed a vibrant white, a shade that was too bright to be anything but magical. His dark eyes were the real mystery. Nothing but black voids and if he looked at himself enough, he could just make out the entire cosmos lying within the center of the darkness.

He turned away before he got lost within himself and swiped a hand in front of his chest. It activated that which tethered him to others. Bright filaments glowed from his chest, the thick strings spreading across the universe, severed into different parts like a spiderweb that marked destinies.

Kerrigan found himself staring at the strings a lot more lately. They'd started thrumming like an instrument, growing brighter and hotter. It was almost as if they were trying to speak to him, but he didn't need to sing their song to know that things had been set in motion. The tides were shifting and destinies were firmly in place, each piece exactly where it needed to be.

And perhaps the Fae did not know it yet, but soon they would. Soon, Bryson Varik would know that it wasn't just magic. All actions came with a price.

At Reign's End

The Seelie King stared out to the ocean that surrounded the kingdom of Dana. His hands were clasped firmly behind his back. The wind rustled against his long, dark hair as he glared at the horizon. There were several tense moments of silence before the king finally turned to Weylyn.

His smile was a cruel, vicious thing. It did not inspire fear in Weylyn, but he wanted to rip his lips from his face. He wanted to lunge across the space that separated them and kill.

Whenever he looked at the Seelie King, all he could see was the blood of his sister, tainting the ground. That cruel smirk. The vicious laugh as he left them for dead.

For years, Weylyn had dragged himself on his knees behind the king. For years, he had become the king's fucking *dog*, if only for this single moment in time to occur.

For the king to trust him enough for them to be alone together.

"Two more Elementals," the king said. "Two more and we will have an advantage over the emperor. Two more and we will be free."

Weylyn nodded, though remained silent.

"What is this Elemental capable of?" the king asked. "Is she as worthless as the rest of them?"

Weylyn gritted his teeth. "No."

He'd have his tongue for that comment. This he vowed.

"Good. We need stronger Fae to help us win this fight. The slaves here are building up their strength, but they still make a pathetic display." He walked his way towards the throne he had claimed as his own and sat down. Tall. Regal. Arrogant. "Now tell me what happened. Spare no detail." He leaned back and waited impatiently for Weylyn to recount the events.

"Would you prefer I show you, Your Majesty?" he asked, stepping closer.

The king's brows rose. "Yes."

"A brief pinch of pain, Your Majesty." Weylyn lifted his finger as he approached. "And you will see the truth as I have." And then Weylyn pressed his finger to the king's forehead.

The Seelie King seized as his mind was assaulted with memory after memory. They invaded every part of him, a consuming force, and Weylyn did not relent. He let the past invade. Every single painful recollection. Slashes of swords. Cruel laughter. The flow of blood.

Death.

Weylyn pulled away and the king slumped on the throne. He looked up almost weakly, staring at Weylyn no longer with confidence, but with fear and anger, as if he were seeing him for the first time.

"Y-you—"

Weylyn smiled. "Yes," he whispered. "*Me.*"

And finally, he lunged for the Seelie King.

All the anger and pain he'd harbored for years pushed him faster. The king had no time to blink. To react. To lash out that mysterious magic of his. He opened his mouth in a silent scream right before Weylyn's nails dug into his thick neck.

He fought back, ancient years of strength evident in the blows he dealt Weylyn's body. Those years of life and experience were nothing compared to the anguish Weylyn had swallowed whole and let consume him. But when the king's mysterious magic lashed out, crashing against him, he was unprepared for how much it would hurt. The impact made his teeth chatter together and his vision blur. The metallic taste of blood coated the inside of his cheeks and he grunted, digging his nails in deeper and refusing to let go.

"Treacherous bastard," the king managed to spit out. "I will end you."

His magic fractured something inside of Weylyn. His bones, his vital organs. Weylyn was not so sure, but the pain was a crippling force that brought him slamming down to his knees. His fingers slipped from the king's neck a fraction and what little advantage he had seemed to have slipped through his fingers...

No! This could not be it. This could not be the end. He vowed over and over he would avenge his sister.

And so he would.

With a growl of savage rage, Weylyn lifted on his knees, lunging with both hands for the Seelie King. They wrapped around his thickly corded throat and the rapid pulse that beat there. He fought through the hold of that dark magic, something akin to death itself, and held on tightly.

Weylyn let loose his own magic just then. His mind reached out, tearing through the barriers of the king's, and injected him with images far more potent than any venom or violence could ever be. His weapon of choice had always been secrets. His greatest strength was watching from the shadows and collecting images into the darkest pockets of his mind for a time he'd need them most.

That time had come.

A shroud swept over the king's vision and he screamed, thrashing like a wild man as the same scene took flight over and over again within his cruel mind. He'd been unsure it would truly work on the king. But even the bravest trembled when their nightmares were given form. Even the bravest trembled when they were forced to watch themselves die time and time again.

The vision he'd implanted gripped the king like a vice until he succumbed to his tears. That bit of weakness seemed to make him thrash harder, stronger. Strong enough that Weylyn's hold on the cretin slipped. Magic blast him backwards and he landed hard against his back, the blood of the king dripping from his fingertips.

The king fought against the images of death. He was strong, and tore through it momentarily. A crazed look pushed past the usually perfect picture of composure he made. He snarled, his lip peeled back, canines flashing like a threat. And he lunged–

But froze as a gust of wind held him in a tight and deadly grip.

Weylyn smiled as he pushed himself up on bloody fingertips and turned to meet his mate and the absolutely lethal expression she wore.

"Do not," she gritted out, "touch my mate."

The king's eyes widened as Bryson stepped deeper into the room. Her hand splayed out in front of her, pointed in the king's direction, her brown-white eyes wearing an expression of absolute hatred.

"Do it, Weylyn," she whispered. "The king isn't going *anywhere.*" As if to prove her point, her magic wiggled him about in a way that was mostly comical.

Weylyn smirked and prowled close to the king. He floated, his feet dangling close to the floor. From that position, the king overlooked him, but Weylyn felt far taller.

Decades of pent-up rage unleashed. The years Weylyn spent allowing himself to be humiliated by this Fae and his ilk. Years of degrading himself in the most vile of ways, of bending the knee to his sister's murderer. It had all led to this.

And suddenly, Weylyn could not contain the feral part of him that wanted revenge any longer. He'd wanted him to suffer but now, all he wanted was him dead.

His fingers raked out, slashing across the king's chest. Over and over again, he screamed his rage and his pain and drew blood from the monarch who had ruined his life so long ago. He scraped past robes and tunic and down to the flesh underneath and even then it wasn't enough.

Weylyn lifted his bleeding fingers to the king's neck, finding the grooves he'd left in the king's skin before, inserting his nails in like pieces of puzzles that had found their way home. The king tried to move. To flinch. Bryson held him tight enough that the air seemed to seep from his lungs.

"I'm going to kill you now," Weylyn whispered. "And your reign will finally end."

Weylyn inhaled the fear and relished it. His smile came slowly right before he let out a cry and began hacking viciously through the king's neck with his bare hands. The squelch of blood and the crack of bone were melodious enough to make him laugh. Once he began, he could not stop the sound from pouring out of his mouth. He laughed and howled as the first layer of flesh slowly peeled from his body.

It was not pleasant.

It was painful.

It was not a quick death.

Every layer Weylyn peeled seemed to heal as quickly as it was shed, only for Weylyn started the process all over again. And the king screamed behind a gag of wind, eyes filled with tears as the pain consumed him, until his energy seemed to wane and his flesh parted open for Weylyn to tear through.

Yet with one last surge of strength, the king unleashed his magic. It reached further than where Weylyn stood.

The king's shadow magic shook the entire castle of Dana. It groaned and shrieked and threatened to crumble down. But Weylyn was already yanking past flesh and vein and bone, tasting the blood of the king who had killed his younger sister. It sprayed a geyser across his face and he tasted the vengeance on his tongue like a nectar. Weylyn's smile widened as he wrenched the king's head from his shoulders. Blood spattered. Bones cracked. It came off with a satisfying pop.

And Weylyn stepped away from the floating body, clutching the Seelie King's head tightly in his hand. He held it up to his face, relishing in the open-mouthed expression the king wore in death.

And still it was nothing compared to what he and his court had done to his sister.

The castle gave one final groan, like the bones of it were shuddering against the king's death. Rejoicing, even.

And Weylyn smiled and tasted the blood on his teeth.

He whirled, the king's head swinging in his hand, and faced his beautiful, terrifying dreadful mate.

Bryson stood there, staring at the gore and the blood dripping down the throne as it pooled at Weylyn's feet. He waited for the disgust, the horror, but she just moved her shoulders as she took the breath of relief he felt inside. Her Elemental magic released and behind him, the king's body dropped like a sack of stones with a wet plop.

The tension he'd been holding in for years eased as he stared at his mate. She seemed to say, *'It's okay, I'm here.'*

"It is done," Weylyn whispered. "The Seelie King is dead."

Valerio sat at a large table with a feast before him. Servers filled his plate, piling it high with vegetables and meats and fish. He didn't reach for his meal. He stared across the table at his friends. He couldn't explain why there was an uncomfortable churning in his belly. Why something felt looming, a sense of impending doom that overcame him like a premonition.

He swept another glance around the table. Weylyn was predictably missing as the moment they'd arrived, his father had cornered him and demanded his presence in the throne room, while completely ignoring Valerio's existence.

The fourth Elemental was nowhere to be seen.

He only wanted to assume that perhaps she'd gone to lay in wait for Weylyn, however he could not help but feel a thorn in his chest in regard to her. There was something about her that Valerio didn't wholly trust. Not only because she was Weylyn's mate, but that she'd so readily accepted him. And Valerio did not trust Weylyn, therefore he was sure he could not trust her either.

Sure, she had agreed to help them. She seemed to get along well enough with the other Elementals, but there was still something off about her. Like she did not quite fit into the fold, or at least held herself back from them partly.

It's not like he expected pure, blind loyalty from everyone who joined them. None of the others had given it to him. But he still had the sense that something was wrong.

"My prince?"

Valerio's attention drew towards Uric beside him. His friend was staring at him with furrowed brows. "Are you alright?"

Valerio opened his mouth to answer, but suddenly the entire castle began to shake. Like the very bones let out a roar and shattered through the halls. The ground trembled, and Valerio gripped tightly to the edge of the table to hold himself steady as the chair beneath him began wobbling back and forth.

It trembled for a few minutes before it just... stopped.

Once the world was steady again, Valerio pushed himself to his feet, his heart thundering in his chest. He recognized the signature of the magic that had rumbled through the castle.

"Father," he whispered before he broke out into a run. He was vaguely aware of the others rushing behind him, calling out, wondering what was wrong. But his vision tunneled to a single moment, that feeling of wrongness growing far more prominent by the moment the faster his feet carried him. He ran to the throne room and found the air Elemental at the entrance, staring inside.

Valerio pushed past her unkindly, and the scent of blood assaulted his nostrils.

At first, the scene before him didn't register. Not right away. It didn't seem real. It felt more fantasy than reality. His mind did not want to believe what was before him. Not the blood, pooling on the floor, not the body of the king, and most certainly not his father's head, gripped tightly in Weylyn's hand or the blood tainting Weylyn's feral grin.

Valerio stood in shock, staring at the scene before him. His heart thundered faster and faster. Behind him, the others had caught up. The moment they registered the scene, shocked gasps drummed a beat in his ears.

His father. The king.

Dead.

Dead.

Dead.

"Y-you killed him..." Valerio's shock expression found Weylyn's. And the Fae had the audacity to smile. There was no remorse, no sadness. He just... looked at Valerio as though daring him to do something to stop him, though the deed was already done.

"What have you done?!" Valerio's magic gathered around him like an accumulating storm ready to be unleashed. "You killed my father. You—you killed the king!"

His magic started to lash out for Weylyn. Ready to kill. To extract revenge.

But within one blink and the next, the air Elemental was in front of Weylyn, shoving a gust of air at Valerio and shoving him back. His magic fractured and broke apart.

He blinked away the confusion, staring at the Elemental and her fierce, protective stance.

"Don't," she warned, her hands held out like she was holding her magic at the ready.

"You will stand beside this murderer?" Valerio threatened. His blood boiled. He had known there was something about her, but he'd never expected *this*.

Bryson tilted her chin up. "I will stand beside my mate."

"Then you will die beside him."

And Valerio's magic shot out.

And havoc wreaked through the room.

Unseelie Truths

Valerio's magic lashed out. Bryson didn't know what it was, not until the tight grasp of mania gripped her mind and threatened to choke it. She screamed and her own magic pushed out, causing a whirlwind through the throne room.

Darkness invaded her mind, and it caused her to drop to her knees. It pushed through her senses, threatening, ready... and then it just... vanished.

The fog on her brain cleared and she looked up through hazy vision. Valerio was no longer before her. Instead, it was the Elementals in her line of sight. Standing between them, holding their magic in the palms of their hands. Fire. Ice. Water. They held it out like shields and barriers between two opposing sides brimming with the promise of war.

"Wait!" Iona ordered. "Everyone just wait a fucking minute!"

There was a single moment of pause. Valerio let out a growl.

"I am the prince..." His voice broke. "And I order you to move aside so I may bring these traitors to justice."

"I understand," Iona told him gently. "But there has to be an explanation for this. Give them a chance to explain."

"What excuse could they possibly have for what they've done here?" he spat.

"I promise you there is a very good excuse for what Weylyn did to that monster," Bryson said. Her every breath was heavy and her heart was pounding a crazy beat against her ribcage.

This wasn't something she'd ever thought she'd face. Staring down the prince of her people, caught between Elementals in a battle they were sure to lose. But she would stand by Weylyn like no one else had before.

The king deserved what he got and more.

"I am telling you to stand aside, Elemental." Valerio unsheathed his sword and pointed it in their direction.

"No," she said firmly. "I won't."

Valerio growled and the room grew dark with the use of his magic.

"Valerio, wait." Clay stepped up beside Valerio and pressed a hand to his shoulder. "Wait one second, cousin."

"No!" Valerio shouted. "I want his head!"

"You will not have it," Weylyn said slowly from behind Bryson. "And I will not apologize for what I've done. Your father deserved this and more for all the crimes he's committed."

"Crimes?" Valerio spat. "Crimes?! You have committed the greatest crime of all. Regicide is punishable by torture and death."

A fierce wave of protectiveness rose in Bryson. A growl rumbled from her chest, the instinctive urge to protect her mate. To protect Weylyn.

"You can try," she whispered darkly. "But I won't let you."

"Then you will fall too!"

"You would really condemn him for killing the man who murdered his sister in cold blood?"

The entire room fell silent at that. Behind her, Weylyn tensed. They'd never agreed to share this story. It was not even hers to tell, but they deserved to know. It deserved to be heard. Valerio deserved to know what kind of a monster his father truly was.

It was Clay who broke the silence. "What do you mean?"

Bryson threw a small glance over her shoulder, searching Weylyn's eyes for permission to speak. To tell the story he'd kept locked away for so long.

He took a breath and his mind touched hers. "It's alright, little mate."

Bryson turned back to the group. "Weylyn is the son of the Unseelie Queen."

More pronounced silence. And then...

"What?!" Clay shouted. He was staring at Weylyn with open shock.

Weylyn chuckled. "I am only half-Unseelie, half-High Fae."

"His father was Alfric Rhian of the Gold Court."

This time it was Corvina's gaze who whipped up, shock coloring her features. "Wh—what?"

"Your uncle was kidnapped by the Unseelie Queen," Bryson said gently. "He was held in their court. They had a child. Weylyn is your cousin, Corvina."

Corvina stared at Weylyn unflinchingly. The shock melted into what Bryson could almost swear was genuine affection. Her voice dropped to a lower whisper. "I'd wondered," she said softly, "why I felt so drawn to you. Like Mana was telling me something I couldn't quite interpret." She stared hard at him, like she was trying to find parts of her uncle in Weylyn. "Is my uncle—"

"Dead? Yes," Weylyn said. "The queen killed him."

Corvina swallowed and tears brimmed her eyes, but she didn't let them fall. "Cousins," she echoed. "We are cousins."

"He's lying," Valerio spat.

"He's not," Bryson defended. "Your father killed his sister and left Weylyn for dead."

Valerio raised his sword. "I do not believe you, trickster. If that is true, why has he been my father's faithful lapdog this entire time?"

"Even you cannot be so dimwitted as to question why I would keep my enemy so close," Weylyn purred. "Foolish Seelie Prince."

"You know..." Shula interrupted thoughtfully. "This makes sense. Why you're so mischievous. You're Unseelie. It's in your blood to weave chaos."

"I have waited years for my revenge," Weylyn declared, ignoring Shula completely. "It would have come eventually. Yesterday, weeks from now, years from now, I would have extracted it regardless. But now?" Weylyn held up the Seelie King's head, taunting Valerio with it. "He had to die quicker. And a quick death was not what he deserved."

Valerio growled again. He stared at the head of his father, and Bryson wondered if Weylyn was digging into his mind to gauge his feelings, to understand him just a bit more. She thought he looked confused, torn.

"Waste no tears on your cruel father," Weylyn said. "Had he not died, Bryson would have."

"What do you mean?" Corvina asked softly.

Bryson held up her arm, pulling down her sleeve and displaying the golden band that still burned around her skin. "The Unseelie Queen has me tethered to her lands," Bryson explained. "She would have killed me."

"She asked for the head of the one that killed her daughter in exchange for my mate's life," Weylyn continued. "I swore on my mate's life that I would give her what she wanted in exchange for Bryson's freedom. And if it ever comes time to choose between my mate and the world, you can bet I will burn down the entire fucking world to save my mate's life."

There was another tense moment of silence. Everyone stared at the head in Weylyn's hand, at the band around Bryson's arm.

And then Clay stepped closer towards them. "Maybe... maybe they can be forgiven?" he suggested, turning back to Valerio.

The prince looked at him with barely concealed disgust.

Clay shrugged. "I am sorry, cousin. What can we do? If you kill Weylyn, you kill Bryson. We need Bryson, and I very much doubt she will help us if you kill her mate. She will die alongside him. You cannot win this battle."

"The king killed your sister?" Corvina asked.

"Show them," Bryson whispered.

Weylyn tensed, but eventually she felt his mind touch hers. And she knew his mind was touching everyone else's too, sending the memory directly into their brains. The same images he'd shared with her. His sister. His love for her. The pain as he was struck down. An even greater pain as he watched his sister die before his eyes.

And then he was pulling back, leaving everybody stunned.

"I am sorry for your loss," Clay said, and the words were genuine. He was staring at Weylyn as though everything had finally fallen into place. As though he finally understood his reasoning. And then slowly, he went and stood beside Weylyn and Bryson both. Corvina followed with slower but surer steps.

They turned and faced Valerio, but he still held his sword up and still pointed it in their very direction. He did not drop it. He looked torn. Angry. And revenge brimmed around him like a tangible toxin.

"Valerio," Iona said. "I think... I think you should put down your sword." She stepped backwards in their direction, siding with them.

"Iona," Julius snapped. He glared at his mate as she took Weylyn's side and stood firmly on Valerio's end, his big arms crossed against his massive chest. "He killed the king. Whatever his reasons, he still broke the law. He should be punished."

Iona glared at her mate. "I know, but... I can't condemn him for it."

They stared at one another, and Bryson could almost visibly make out the rift that splintered between them.

And then Shula broke that tension by slowly making her way towards Weylyn's side.

Ryker followed, though stopped in the middle, as though he wasn't sure who to stand with. There he stayed.

It was Valerio, Uric, and Julius who stayed firmly on one side.

And just like that, The Resistance was divided into two.

"Valerio," Clay whispered. "Cousin, put your sword down. We need the Elementals."

And they couldn't afford to alienate a single one of them.

Bryson saw that war on Valerio's face as he took them all in. He needed them to win his war, and if he killed Weylyn, he'd have to kill Bryson too. And if he killed Bryson, they didn't have a chance at returning to their former glory.

There was no winning in this situation.

And Valerio seemed to realize it too, because he slowly, reluctantly, lowered his sword. And then the tears slid down his face, almost unbidden. Angry, full of sorrow.

And Bryson's chest ached for him. Because even if the king was a monster, he was, after all, Valerio's father.

"Do not cry, Valerio," Weylyn said as he reached into Bryson's pocket and pulled out the mirror they'd taken from Unseelie. It activated at his touch, glowing brightly within the throne room. He held up the Seelie King's head to the surface and that light swallowed the bleeding head, taking it back to Unseelie, where it would hang above his mother's throne. "After all, you are king again. And is that not what you wanted?"

Valerio made a choked sound and looked away.

The light disappeared along with the mirror.

And the band circling Bryson's arm vanished to mark a debt paid.

And finally, they were both free.

Fractured Resistance

"He will never forgive me," Weylyn whispered.

They'd washed the blood of the Unseelie King from their fingers. The servants had removed his body from the throne room in preparation for burial. The blood had been cleansed from the floors, but Bryson knew the memory of it would haunt the stones forever. It would haunt Valerio forever.

Bryson knew who Weylyn was talking about. She lifted her head to stare into his eyes. He had not displayed remorse in the throne room. Everything had been tense after Valerio's begrudging acceptance. Something within the Resistance had seemed to fracture. They'd all firmly been on one side, but with the death of the king, Weylyn and Bryson had created a terrible unrest between them all.

Bryson smoothed her hand down Weylyn's long hair. "I knew you liked him," she whispered, if only to lighten the moment.

His pained expression turned to her. "Perhaps I do, and I did not realize it until that moment when he was staring at me from over his sword. I touched his mind and he wanted to kill me. He would have, if given the chance. He still might."

Bryson's chest ached to think of Weylyn dying. They were free from the chains of the Unseelie Queen. She did not come this far with him just to lose him now.

"Don't think of it," Bryson whispered, though her voice cracked. "We are free now, and isn't that what matters?"

Weylyn's frown was replaced with a soft smile as he gazed at his mate. He didn't say the words aloud or in her mind, but she didn't need to hear them just like she didn't need his mind reading magic to know what it was he was thinking.

They were free.

And nothing was ever going to tear them apart.

Long Live the King

The entire kingdom had gathered around the castle of Dana. Fae and humans alike clustered together to look up at Prince Valerio as he stood before them all in his best robes. His cutting features glared furiously across the crowd. They looked up at him, some stoically, some smiling. He could feel the eagerness vibrating through them as he slowly knelt to the ground and bowed his head low.

He had lived through this once before. Back when he had assumed his father had died. Back when he'd taken up the mantle of King Regent, hoping against all odds that his father was alive. He'd thought his father dead once. It had cleaved him from the inside out, but that was absolutely nothing compared to what he was feeling right then.

He'd lost his father twice, and the second time was no easier than the first.

It was harder, because this time he could not even hold onto the feeling of hope that he really was alive. Not when he had seen his father's head dangling from Weylyn's fingertips. Not when he had seen the way his body slumped against the throne. Not when he'd seen his own reflection in the pool of blood at his feet.

His father was truly dead.

And he could not help but wonder that maybe he'd been the one to bring it into existence. He had grown angry at his father for taking Valerio's conquests as his own and shunning Valerio at every turn. There were moments when he wished he was king still, so he could rule their subjects. So he could no longer face the scrutiny of the Fae who had done nothing but hate him since his birth.

But now that he'd gotten his wish, he did not know how to contend with that fact. He could not rejoice, for rejoicing in his coronation would mean being glad at his father's death.

And if he felt that, then what type of monster would that make him? Was he as much a monster as his father? For he had seen Weylyn's memories. He had felt the other Fae's pain as though it were his own. He had seen his father laugh cruelly as they struck down a young Unseelie woman. He had witnessed the cruelty for himself.

He had always known something monstrous lived and breathed within his father. He had witnessed it himself. In the snap of whips against his back, against Uric's. It had lived in those cutting words, in the hatred that had oozed from every pore.

He had been a hateful, cruel Fae. He'd killed without remorse. An evil had lived and breathed within his body. Valerio had known of its existence, but sometimes he tried to remain ignorant to its extent. Until he was faced with the cruel reality of what he'd done. Of who he'd hurt. And the lengths Weylyn had gone through to get his revenge.

Swallowing that truth was not easy.

He barely heard the traditional words that echoed through the kingdom of Dana, but he did feel when the crown was placed upon his head. It seemed to weigh him down, the expectations of it, but how he'd come to earn it was an even greater burden that he did not want to contemplate.

He held his breath as they told him to stand.

He did as he was told, staring down at the subjects with tears burning behind his eyelids and hatred overflowing in his heart.

"Long live King Valerio Ashera!"

"Long live King Valerio Ashera!"

There were claps and cheers and there was celebration, but Valerio's own mood was a somber, dead thing.

He was king now, and his crown could not be taken from him by anyone.

So why did Valerio feel so dead inside?

To the Valley of the Dead

Valerio stood near a pillar. His shoulder leaned heavily against it, and his distracted gaze looked out into the ocean waves as they crashed up the side of the castle. The crown perched above his brow lay at a crooked angle, as though it were about to topple off and fall to the ground, and he would let it.

His melancholy mood was understandable, and Bryson's chest almost ached for him. She could feel sorry for the prince's loss without actually being sorry about who had died.

Because staring at him hurt, she turned her attention to the rest of the Resistance instead. There was a brewing tension between all of them that she was sure would bubble over at one point. But right now, they were all gathered together in the throne room in tense silence. The Elementals all sat on the ground in a circle, a map placed on the floor in the center of them.

Shula held a pile of six stones in her hand. She played with them, turning them over in her palms in a distracted movement as she stared down at the map.

"So," Bryson broke the terse silence. "What do we have to do?"

"We all hold the stones together," Shula explained. "We concentrate on the Elemental and we drop the stones. They'll all land on a location and we'll know which one we have to find next."

Bryson hummed and stared down at the map of Illyk. It was crumpled along the edges, torn at the corners.

"How will we know which is next?"

"We just know," Iona said softly. She looked up at Bryson. Her eyes were red-rimmed, as if she hadn't slept or had been weeping.

Bryson swallowed and wondered how badly she had fought with her mate over what Weylyn had done. A part of Bryson felt the urge to apologize for the unrest they'd caused, but she shook it off.

The king had earned his fate. Nobody else had to agree with what Weylyn had done. Nobody else even had to like her for it. Yes, they'd chosen their side, but still Bryson could feel their turmoil as they sat near her. And still, she felt like maybe she didn't quite belong with them.

She tried to shake that off.

"Okay," she whispered. "Let's do this, then." She held out her hands, palms up and waited for the others. They all did the same, cupping the undersides of Bryson's hands. Shula put the stones on Bryson's palms and closed her hands around them. They shook the stones together, and Bryson concentrated on the Elementals. The ones around her as well as the ones they were destined to find.

They stayed like that, before some instinct that seemed to grip them all had them turning their palms over and letting the stones fall onto the map.

Bryson watched them bounce one by one.

Four stones landed onto the part of the map that marked Dana.

Another further north, landing on the Valley of the Dead.

The sixth seemed to bounce around the map, never settling on a single place for too long.

And then something strange happened.

A light glowed on the map, sending a string from Dana towards the north like it was marking the path they needed to take.

"Where to next?" Julius asked gruffly from above them.

"You can't see that?" Bryson whispered, staring at it with awe.

"Only we can," Corvina supplied.

"Where to?" Julius asked again.

"Please tell me it's not the Valley of the Dead," Clay whispered as he leaned over Corvina. There was horror in his voice. "Please not the Valley of the fucking Dead."

"What's wrong with the Valley of the Dead?" Corvina asked.

"It's rumored to be the home of all manner of monsters," Clay said. His gaze swept over them all. "Please tell me we aren't going there."

Bryson was not afraid of rumors. She'd lived through monsters in the Unseelie Court, she'd lived through the monster that was the Unseelie Queen herself. She'd lived through iron camps, the death of her family, and the threat of death herself.

She was not afraid.

She looked up at Clay. "We're going to the Valley of the Dead."

He let out a curse and stepped back, shoving his hands deep into his pockets. "I am not looking forward to this," he whispered. "Anyone want to take bets on who the next Elemental is? Earth? Spirit? And maybe who gets their mate next?" He said the words as if he wanted to diffuse the tension that permeated the room.

But nobody laughed.

Nobody responded.

Nobody said a single thing at all.

They just stared at the map and the glowing line that led from Dana towards the Valley of the Dead.

And though there was the feeling of discomfort in her chest, of a premonition that something was going to go terribly wrong, Bryson tilted her chin up.

Predator or prey.

And she vowed that she would never be anyone's prey ever again.

"Time to go." She looked up at her mate. "We have another Elemental to find."

The War Begins

Deep within the Empire of Illyk, in a castle shrouded in shadows and darkness and the memories of horrors no one dared whisper, there was a throne. Embedded deep into the iron there were ivory bones of dead Fae. It rose up on a tall dais, upon which sat a man, cloaked in sheer, gossamer cloth that shrouded his view of the world.

The throne seemed to burn through his skin and his fingers curled upon the armrest as he looked down at his court as they bowed deeply before him, foreheads touching the floor.

And then, the earth around them began to rattle. The courtiers gasped and cried out, struggling to right themselves. But the man lifted his head. He watched the heads and skulls mounted above his throne begin to rattle.

The skull and bones of a healer. The ribcage of a traitor. And more recently, the head of an infuriating seer glared at him as it wobbled.

He gripped the throne and pushed himself to a stand just as the rattling died down. Half of his body itched, and he resisted the urge to tear at it with his nails. A flash of intuition crippled through him and as soon as the world settled and his courtiers righted themselves, he took a breath.

And then the Emperor of Illyk smiled and said, "The Seelie King is dead. And now our war can truly begin."

To be continued in book 5...
For A Song of Air Bonus Content and freebies, join my Newsletter.

Acknowledgements

And that's a wrap… and what a wild ride it was. This book has been one of the most challenging of the entire series so far, and I'm not sure I can exactly pinpoint why. I think because book 3 (A Shield of Water) was so dark, and shortly after I finished editing and publishing I had my second child, it was just hard for me to get back into the groove of this world. There was so much I was criticizing in my work and it made me very unhappy to the point where I didn't feel I could work on it because I never feel like I'm good enough. My editor and best friend is always telling me that I'm my own worst critic and that if it was bad, she would tell me. As we've been friends since we were fifteen years old and she's never been anything but honest in all this time, I should believe her. But it's so hard to tell my brain to do that sometimes. Every time I finish a book, I wonder if it's boring. If maybe that's the reason I don't feel like I'm where I should be. Like maybe there's a reason I don't feel 'popular enough' or 'good enough'. I'm not sure if that feeling will ever go away, to be honest. But if there's one thing I want to do, it's thank all the people who make me feel like I am good enough. So, thank you Lisa for going above and beyond editor duties to help me finally get this written and polished. Thank you to my cover designers and formatter of course for giving me motivation with such pretty books. Thank you to my faithful readers. You are the Resistance. Your support for this series and dedication to it is truly humbling. I appreciate you. Thank you to my husband for being the best and most supportive spouse when it comes to my writing. Thank you to my family for babysitting some days when I needed to work or edit. Thank you to Jess, Tati, and Kai, for helping beta this book and giving me honest and helpful feedback. And, because I feel it needs to be said twice, thank you, readers. For always coming back to this world.

Aleera Anaya Ceres is the USA Today Bestselling author of several series including the Origins of the Six series and the Daughter of Triton series. Like most introverts, Aleera prefers to curl up with a good book, listen to music, paint, read tarot cards, and snack on the tears and heartbreak of her readers. A proud Mexican-American from the state of Kansas, Aleera currently resides in Tlaxcala, Mexico with her husband and children.

You can find/contact her here:
aleeraanayaceres.com
aleeraceres@aacbooks.com

Adult Fantasy series

Fae Elementals
A Dance with Fire
A Sword of Ice
A Shield of Water
A Song of Air

The Dark Waters series
Riptide

Why Choose Series

Royal Secrets
Secrets Among the Tides
Whispers Beneath the Deep
Caresses Between the Sand
Death Beyond the Waves
Royal Secrets Box Set

Royal Lies
Slave to Ice & Shadows
Princess in Frost Castles
Queen of Frozen War
Royal Lies Box Set

Origins of the Six series
Academy of Six
Control of Five
Destruction of Two
Wrath of One

A Daughter of Triton series
Triton's Academy
Triton's Prophecy
Triton's Legacy
A Daughter of Triton Box Set

Why Choose Standalones
Queenie & the Krakens
Lourdes & the Mafia

Paranormal Romance Series

Deep Sea Chronicles
Fall in Deep
Siren Queen

The Blood Novels
Love Bites
Blood Drug
My Master
Last Hope

Young Adult standalone
The Last Mermaid

www.ingramcontent.com/pod-product-compliance
Lightning Source LLC
Chambersburg PA
CBHW021957040826
48979CB00046B/2616/J
* 9 7 9 8 9 8 6 9 5 4 6 7 7 *